WISDOM'S DAUGHTER

ALSO BY INDIA EDGHILL

Queenmaker: A Novel of King David's Queen

WISDOM'S DAUGHTER

---•◆•---

A Novel of
*S*olomon *and*
*S*heba

---•◆•---

INDIA EDGHILLED

St. Martin's Press ⚏ New York

ROT

www.stmartins.com

Map and family trees by David Cain.

Quotation from "The Teak Forest" by Laurence Hope used by kind permission of Fredonia Books.

Library of Congress Cataloging-in-Publication Data
Edghill, India.
    Wisdom's daughter / India Edghill.—1st U. S. ed.
      p. cm.
    ISBN 0-312-28937-5
    EAN 978-0312-28937-9
    1. Sheba, Queen of—Fiction. 2. Solomon, King of Israel—Fiction. 3. Bible. O. T. —History of biblical events—Fiction. 4. Israel—Kings and rulers—Fiction. 5. Queens—Sheba (Kingdom)—Fiction. 6. Women in the Bible—Fiction. I. Title.

PS3555.D474W57 2004
813'.54—dc22

2004050714

First Edition: October 2004

10   9   8   7   6   5   4   3   2   1

Dedicated to Bonnie S. Wilford
May 19, 1949–March 10, 2003

*"She worketh willingly with her hands . . .
let her own works praise her in the gates."*

Acknowledgments

My grateful thanks to those who read this book in its first and second drafts and provided their comments and opinions: Dawn Cox, Joanna Daneman, Rebecca East, Melissa Galyon, Haley Elizabeth Garwood, Roberta Gellis, Nicole Jordan, Michael Kourtoulou, Alida Liberman, Annie Liberman, Cass Liberman, James Macdonald, Tamara Myers, Andre Norton, Laura Pilkington, Niloufer Reifler, Virginia Saunders, Dora Schisler, Bonnie Wenk Stallone, Ron and Jenny Stone.

Special thanks go to Nichole Argyres, for hand-holding and desserts above and beyond the call of duty; Matthew Balducci, for great marketing; Danny Baror, for making my books truly international; Susan M. S. Brown, for knowing what to do about semicolons and too many cloaks; Ellen Bushyhead, for truly insightful questions; David Cain, for the gorgeous family trees and map; Tanya Farrell, for great PR; Anna Ghosh, for being the absolutely perfect agent; Diane Higgins, for helping me see what my book was really about; Nicole Jordan, who lit hope and inspiration for me to use as a candle against a great darkness; Cheryl Kamm, for insightful comments; Shari Manfredi of Merriweather's, for blending the Queen of Sheba's perfume; Brenda Martell, for Lady Leeorenda's support of the Dutchess County SPCA; Karen O. Miller of H&R Block, for handling a taxing task for me every year; Myra Morales, for the title; Debbie Osterhoudt and Lisa Wallace at Copy-A-Second on Main Street; Susan Polikoff, for "timely" assistance; Cheryl Mamaril, for coordinating production, flawlessly; Susan Walsh, for superb interior design; Henry Yee, for his artistic touch.

Thanks are also due those who don't know me but who provided much needed inspiration: Sean Bean, Cate Blanchett, Brian Blessed, Susan Hampshire, Cherie Lunghi, Keith Michell, Sam Neill, and Kate Winslet. My thanks as well to Kayhan Kalhor and Shujaat Husain Khan for *Moon Rise over the Silk Road*. And then there are those who have gone before us and will never know how much they inspired me: Anthony Hope, Margaret Irwin, Ava Gardner, and Stewart Granger.

My eternal gratitude belongs to my grandmother Mary Kravetz Wenk and to her son James Henry Wenk, my father, who taught me their own love of reading and of history, and whose beloved books keep me company now that they are no longer here; to my mother, Gloria Edghill Wenk, who gave her favorite books into my hands and has never demanded them back; and above all, to my sister Rosemary, without whose endless support, patience, and ability to make me think things through—not to mention her vital comment about the original Woodstock, her ability to tune out endless repeats of *Moon Rise over the Silk Road*, and her sapient observation about rubies—I could not have told Bilqis and Baalit's story.

Anything you liked in *Wisdom's Daughter* is due to them. Anything you didn't like is entirely my fault.

Players in the Queen's Game
(Names in italics are of people who died before the tale of Wisdom's Daughter *begins.)*

In Sheba

Allit, Queen Bilqis's daughter

Baalit, Allit's daughter

Bilqis, Queen of Sheba

Boaz, an emissary from King Solomon's court

Hawlyat, head of the Sheban Cloth Traders' Guild

Hodaiah, captain of King Solomon's merchant fleet

Irsiya, Queen Bilqis's handmaiden

Jotham, King Solomon's brother and his emissary to Sheba

Khurrami, Queen Bilqis's handmaiden

Mubalilat, Queen Bilqis's vizier

Nikaulis, Amazon captain of the queen's guard

Rahbarin, *Sahjahira's* son

Sahjahira, Queen Bilqis's younger half-sister

Shakarib, master of the court, Queen Bilqis's chief steward

Tamrin, the chief eunuch, Irsiya's brother

Uhhayat, the royal chamberlain

In Jerusalem

Abiathar, high priest during *King David's* reign

Abishag, King Solomon's first wife and first love, Princess Baalit's mother

Absalom, Solomon's older half-brother

Adonijah, Solomon's older half-brother

Ahijah, the new great prophet

Ahishar, the palace steward

Amnon, Solomon's older half-brother

Amyntor, a visitor from Caphtor

Athaniel, Ishvaalit's brother

Baalit, daughter of King Solomon and *Queen Abishag*

Bathsheba, King Solomon's mother

Benaiah, the king's general, commander of the army

Chadara, overseer of the women's palace

Citrajoyti, King Solomon's wife from India

Dacxuri, King Solomon's wife from Colchis

Dathan, servant of Elihoreph, the scribe

David, King of Israel and Judah, King Solomon's father

David, King Solomon and Queen Makeda's son

Dvorah, one of King Solomon's Hebrew wives

Elihoreph, the chief scribe

Gamaliel, head groom of King Solomon's horse farm

Gilade, one of King Solomon's concubines

Helike, King Solomon's wife from Troy

Ishvaalit, Princess Baalit's friend

Jeroboam, superintendent of the Forced Levy

Joab, King David's war-chief

Keshet, Princess Baalit's handmaiden

Lahad, Prince Rehoboam's friend

Leeorenda, one of King Solomon's concubines

Makeda, King Solomon's wife from Cush

Melasadne, King Solomon's wife from Melite

Michal, King David's queen, King Solomon's foster-mother

Miri, a palace slave

Naamah, King Solomon's wife from Ammon, Prince Rehoboam's mother

Nefret-meryt-hotep, King Solomon's wife from Egypt

Nimrah, Princess Baalit's handmaiden

Oreb, Prince Rehoboam's friend

Pelaliah, Prince Rehoboam's friend

Rehoboam, King Solomon and Queen Naamah's son, the crown prince

Reuben, a stable boy

Rivkah, Princess Baalit's maid, once *Queen Abishag's* servant

Ruth, one of King Solomon's minor wives, once known as Surraphel

Tamar, King Solomon's older half-sister

Tobiah, King Solomon's servant

Yahalom, gem carver and seal ring merchant

Zadok, the high priest of the Temple

Zhurleen, *Queen Michal's* friend, *Queen Abishag's* mother, Princess Baalit's
grandmother

SOME OF PRINCESS BAALIT'S OTHER HALF-BROTHERS (KING SOLOMON'S SONS BY VARIOUS WIVES AND CONCUBINES)

Abner

Caleb

Eliakim

Eliazar

Ishbaal

Jerioth

Joab

Jonathan

Mesach

Samuel

Saul

SOME OF KING SOLOMON'S OTHER WIVES AND CONCUBINES

Aiysha

Arinike

Arishat

Halit

Jecoliah

Marah

Naomi

Nilufer

Paziah

Rahab

Ulbanu

Xenodice

Yeshara

The Royal House of Sheba

Female names in Italic
Male names in Roman

Baalit
(died with her mother)

Allit
(died bearing Baalit)

Girl
(died)   *Girl*
(died)

Rahbarin

Oldest Girl
(died)   *Middle Girl*
(died)   Bilqis

Sahjahira
(died bearing Rahbarin)

Bilqis's mother
(died bearing Sahjahira)

The Royal House of David

Female names in Italic
Male names in Roman

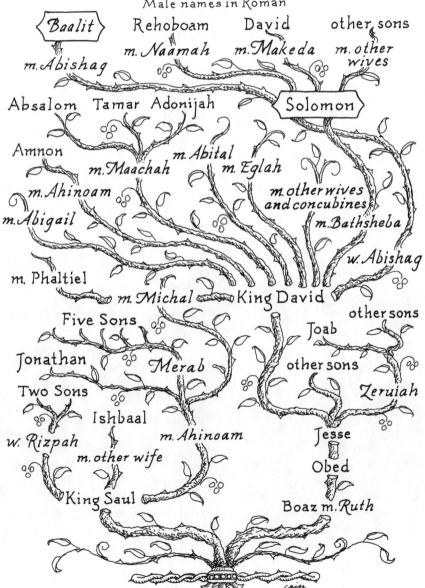

⟨Baalit⟩   Rehoboam   David   other sons

m. Abishag   m. Naamah   m. Makeda   m. other wives

Absalom   Tamar   Adonijah   ⟨Solomon⟩

Amnon

m. Maachah   m. Abital   m. Eglah

m. Ahinoam   m. other wives and concubines

m. Abigail   m. Bathsheba

w. Abishag

m. Phaltiel

m. Michal   King David

Five Sons   other sons

Joab

Jonathan   Merab   other sons

Two Sons   Zeruiah

Ishbaal   m. Ahinoam

w. Rizpah   Jesse

m. other wife

Obed

King Saul

Boaz m. Ruth

cain

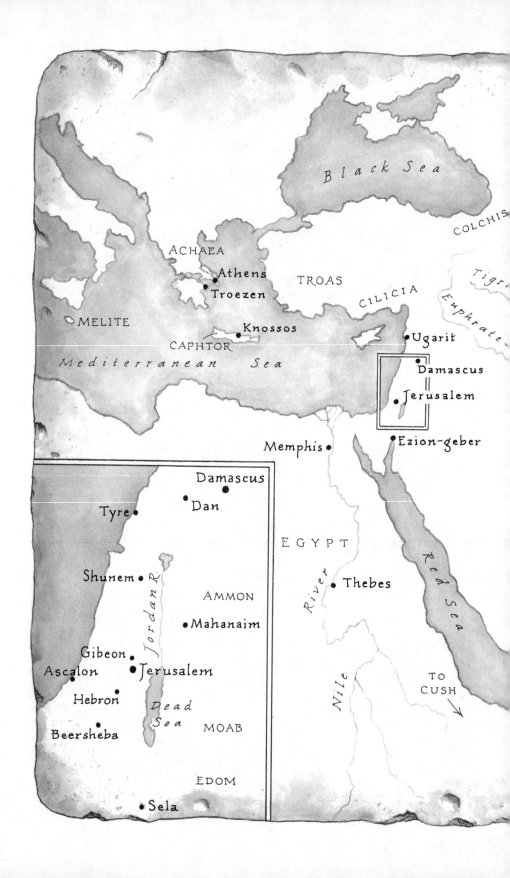

Black Sea

COLCHIS

ACHAEA

Athens

TROAS

Troezen

CILICIA

MELITE

Knossos

Ugarit

CAPHTOR

Damascus

Mediterranean Sea

Jerusalem

Memphis

Ezion-geber

Tigris

Euphrates

Damascus

Dan

Tyre

EGYPT

Shunem

Jordan R.

River

Thebes

AMMON

Red Sea

Mahanaim

Gibeon

Ascalon

Jerusalem

Hebron

Dead Sea

TO CUSH

Beersheba

MOAB

Nile

EDOM

Sela

The Lands of
SOLOMON and SHEBA

Map by David Cain

0   Miles   500

Caspian Sea

R.

R. Baghdad
Babylon
CHALDEA
Ur

Indus River

SHEBA

Ma'rib

OPHIR

Preface

Once there was and once there was not a great and wise king...

The story of King Solomon and the Queen of Sheba is found in I Kings
10: I–13:

[I] And when the queen of Sheba heard of the fame of Solomon concerning the name of the LORD, she came to prove him with hard questions.

[2] And she came to Jerusalem with a very great train, with camels that bare
spices, and very much gold, and precious stones: and when she was come to
Solomon, she communed with him of all that was in her heart.

[3] And Solomon told her all her questions: there was not any thing hid
from the king, which he told her not.

[4] And when the queen of Sheba had seen all Solomon's wisdom, and the
house that he had built,

[5] And the meat of his table, and the sitting of his servants, and the atten-
dance of his ministers, and their apparel, and his cupbearers, and his ascent
by which he went up unto the house of the LORD; there was no more
spirit in her.

[6] And she said to the king, It was a true report that I heard in mine own
land of thy acts and of thy wisdom.

[7] Howbeit I believed not the words, until I came, and mine eyes had seen

it: and, behold, the half was not told me: thy wisdom and prosperity exceedeth the fame which I heard.

[8] Happy are thy men, happy are these thy servants, which stand continually before thee, and that hear thy wisdom.

[9] Blessed be the LORD thy God, which delighted in thee, to set thee on the throne of Israel: because the LORD loved Israel for ever, therefore made he thee king, to do judgment and justice.

[10] And she gave the king an hundred and twenty talents of gold, and of spices very great store, and precious stones: there came no more such abundance of spices as these which the queen of Sheba gave to king Solomon.

[11] And the navy also of Hiram, that brought gold from Ophir, brought in from Ophir great plenty of almug trees, and precious stones.

[12] And the king made of the almug trees pillars for the house of the LORD, and for the king's house, harps also and psalteries for singers: there came no such almug trees, nor were seen unto this day.

[13] And king Solomon gave unto the queen of Sheba all her desire, whatsoever she asked, beside that which Solomon gave her of his royal bounty. So she turned and went to her own country, she and her servants.

This is repeated almost word for word in II Chronicles 9: 1–12. That's it; that is the entire tale as it's told in the Bible. The great love story of Solomon and Sheba comes not from the Bible, but from three thousand years of romantic folklore—for who can resist the story that should be there and isn't? The wisest king in all the world and the richest queen under the sky meet and then . . .

. . . and then we invent our own stories for them. Here is yet another. So I will start this one as Mark Twain started another story long ago . . .

"I will set down a tale . . . It may be history, it may be only a legend, a tradition. It may have happened, it may not have happened: but it could have happened. . . ."

For this is wisdom; to love, to live
To take what fate, or the gods, may give.
To ask no question, to make no prayer,
To kiss the lips and caress the hair.
Speed passion's ebb as you greet its flow
To have—to hold—and—in time—let go!
                              —Laurence Hope

WISDOM'S
DAUGHTER

Prologue: Baalit Sings

SOLOMON WAS A GREAT KING, A MAN OF WISDOM AND POWER; *Bilqis was a djinn's daughter, a creature of sand and fire.* So a harper would begin this tale; it is tradition, after all. And so shall I begin my own song to tell the tale of my father and the woman who became more to me than my own mother—for when one has broken every rule and violated every commandment, only tradition can redeem that tale, make it sweet to swallow.

Sing it so, if you choose: a golden king and a queen from the land beyond morning, well met in a contest of wits and wills. She tried him with hard questions; he answered each with ease. Whereupon the lady bowed before his wisdom, praised his greatness, and then retreated to her faraway kingdom, laden down with priceless gifts freely given by the all-knowing king.

Whatsoever she desired, sing the harpers now. *King Solomon granted all the great queen's heart desired—*

But not freely. No, what Solomon the Wise granted unto the foreign queen from the south, her heart's desire, was given unwilling, forfeit to a king's honor. The harpers do not sing of that; hard Truth is no man's daughter.

So I shall sing their song in my own words, and in theirs, trusting their tale to the winds of time. I, who in my turn shall be Queen of the Spice Lands, Queen of the South—I will sing for you the tale of Solomon the Wise, and Bilqis, Queen of the Morning.

PART ONE

———— •◆• ————

The Queen of the South

Abishag

I am no more than memory's echo, but my name is still spoken and so my voice whispers to the living, carried upon the winds of time. For many tales still are told of Abishag the Shunammite, and not all of them to my credit. But this much I can call my heart's truth: I never schemed to become queen. The plots I aided, the intrigues I carried out, all were done to one end only: that Prince Solomon should wear the crown when King David died. That goal I worked towards always, after I was brought to King David's court.

For that—and to win Solomon for myself, to turn his heart to me and to me alone. What was a king, or a crown, compared to that prize?

And I was granted my heart's twin desires, for all the good either did me. For I was denied the one thing that would have paid for all the rest, have redeemed all the deeds that put Solomon on the throne and a queen's crown upon my head: Solomon's son, a prince to be king hereafter. That prize, I was not to win.

But in the end, it did not matter.

Bilqis

Her land of dreams and spices lay beyond the morning; its very name meant "sunrise." Spices and dreams, twin jewels in Sheba's crown—a crown that had smoothly passed from mother to daughter, from aunt to niece, from sister to sister, in a chain of life unbroken for a thousand years.

Until now.

The ancient treasure rested in a casket created for the circle of gold and gems so long ago that the images carved into the ebon wood had all but vanished, worn smooth by generations of reverent hands. The court's high clerk could recite the details of the design as clearly as if it were new-carved. Upon the ancient wood, Ilat, goddess-mother of Sheba, bestowed the gift of spices upon Almaiyat-Ququus, Sheba's first queen, herself born of sun and fire.

The goddess's gift had been wealth and peace; Sheba's queens had guarded both, loving mothers to Ilat's land and people.

From sister to sister, from aunt to niece, from mother to daughter. Bilqis lifted the crown from the casket; a circle of flames burned in hammered gold. *From queen to queen.*

Until now.

Now she was the only woman living who could claim pure descent from Sheba's royal lineage. *I am the last queen.* She stared at the crown weighing down her reverent hands. *Why? I have been dutiful, devout, dedicated. Sheba's good has been dearer to me than my own life.* Always, always, she had cherished her kingdom like a child. She had given it her life. She had given it a daughter, only to see her child die before her.

Now she alone remained. And Sheba's crown waited. . . .

Sighing, Bilqis gently set the crown back within its ancient casket, smoothing her fingers over the cool metal flames. *I will not betray you,* she vowed. The line of Sheban queens would not end with her; it *could* not.

She closed the crown's casket and lifted the silver mirror from her dressing table. Without vanity or illusion, she studied her face in the creamy light that streamed through the tall windows.

Sunlight through alabaster; softly flattering.

Gently lying. Just as her mirror lied, its burnished silver surface reflecting only her kohl-darkened eyes, her carmined lips. In mirrors, her painted face still claimed youth and beauty.

But someday, someday soon, alabaster windows would no longer soften light enough to deceive, nor would silver lie. She set down the mirror, gently, and turned away.

I must face this truth; I begin to grow old.

That in itself was no tragedy; all that lived aged. But for this Queen of Sheba, it signaled disaster.

If Allit had only lived——! But her only daughter, raised and trained to rule

Sheba, to step easily into her mother's place as queen in her turn, now lay entombed with the infant girl Allit had died bringing into the world. Daughter and granddaughter both gone between moonset and sunrise, taking with them to the grave the last precious blood of Sheba's rulers. . . .

And I too old to bear another daughter. Though her smooth face and shapely body still denied her true age, she was too old to conceive another child. She had tried, dutifully, after her daughter died, spending many nights in temple pleasure-gardens—all save those of Ilat's Temple—lying with men who never saw her face, seeking a hero strong enough to father another heir so the royal line might continue.

But her efforts failed; her reluctant body bore no new fruit. Now each moon-circle of days made her more certain in her bones that she could no longer create new life.

Yet an heir she must have. An heir *Sheba* must have. Somehow she must provide Sheba's new queen, the queen who would lift the heavy crown from her own proud head, the queen who would rule after her, caring for Ilat's land and people. *And how am I to give them this blessing?* The problem could no longer be ignored; it haunted her like a questioning ghost. *For I am too old, and there is no other woman of my blood to share this burden. How?*

That fatal question haunted her constantly, allowed her no true rest. To what good would all her years of queenship lead if she could not provide a ruler to follow after her?

Even her nights were unquiet now. Sleeping, she wandered through a land barren of hope, of dreams, of life. She woke each dawn drained and weary, unready for her days. By day, she concealed her constant worry as she would any weakness. It was her trouble, and she must not spread her own unrest to others.

But she knew she must provide for Sheba's tomorrows, and soon. Life, even a queen's, was uncertain; the future could not wait.

And after a long night in which she lay and watched the stars rise and set again, she knew she, too, could wait no longer. Rising with the sun, she climbed the stairs to the palace rooftop. There she gazed across the still-drowsing city. Ma'rib, Jewel of the Desert; Ma'rib, Queen of Spices; Ma'rib, beloved of Ilat, Sun of their Days.

The burning sun climbed the arc of heaven; she stared into the brightening day and prayed, dutifully. *Grant me an answer, Sun of our Days. Grant me an answer, and I will pay whatsoever price You ask of me.* She waited, her arms outstretched to the fiery goddess soaring into the clear sky. But there was no answer, only a land stretching golden and quiet beneath the rising sun. At last she lowered her arms, and sighed, and already weary, turned away to face the day's duties.

I am so weary I shall die of it. Ah, well, perhaps tonight I shall sleep after all. She had walked through the day's hours like a jeweled doll, long habit bringing the proper words to her lips. Now, although she wished only to fling herself down upon her bed, she stood patiently as her maidservants stripped her gown from her body, washed the day's heat and sweat from her skin, spread a cloth over a stool for her to sit upon. And when she sat, Khurrami moved behind her to take down her tight-braided hair, while Irsiya gathered up her discarded finery and began to place the rings and bracelets, the necklaces and earrings and anklets, the gem-studded pins that had fastened her gown, within the sectioned silver box that awaited them.

Ritual, each night the same. Irsiya and Khurrami had tended her since they were maidens new-initiated into womanhood; had been raised to serve her as she had been raised to serve Sheba. And however much she might wish to be alone, it was their duty and their right to tend her. Dismissing them would only hurt their feelings— *And not ease mine. If only—*

"My queen is troubled?" Khurrami began unpinning the elaborate braids coiled about her mistress's head.

About to deny it, Bilqis suddenly changed her mind. "Why do you say that to me?"

"You seem—changed" was all Khurrami said, her fingers moving deftly over the queen's hair.

"How changed?"

Khurrami set aside the twelve crystal-headed pins that had confined the queen's braided hair. "My queen, I have tended you for many years; your secrets are mine. How should I not know when you dream unquiet dreams?" Khurrami began unweaving the close-woven plaits, shaking the queen's hair to lie heavy over her shoulders. "Your mind seeks ease it does not find."

I should not be surprised; no woman holds secrets from her maidservants.

"And those who love you grow troubled," Irsiya added. "We would see you happy."

"That is kind." She weighed the virtues of silence against those of confession, and compromised. "You are right, Khurrami; I am troubled. And, Irsiya, I, too, would rather see me happy!"

Irsiya smiled obediently at the queen's small jest and continued to lay the day's jewelry into its resting place within the silver casket.

Khurrami took up a carved ivory comb and began the long task of grooming the queen's heavy hair. "What would make you happy, my queen?" she asked quietly.

A daughter, Bilqis thought. But that she could not say. Need not say, for Khurrami was no fool. *Nor is Irsiya, nor all the rest of my women. Nor are my nobles and my merchants.* The succession concerned her people deeply; her spies reported that the question of who would follow Queen Bilqis upon Sheba's throne was growing more common among her subjects. *What would make me happy? A queen for Sheba.*

Behind her Khurrami stood calm, coaxing the queen's unbound hair to sleekness; the ivory comb swept through the night-dark waves in steady strokes. Bilqis sighed. "It is good of you to ask, my dear, but what I need cannot be granted by any woman."

"By a man, then? Someone who spurns the most beautiful queen in all the world? Shall I chastise him for you, Lady?" Laughter rippled through Khurrami's voice. "Shall I have him dragged before you in golden chains?"

The queen laughed, as she knew Khurrami had intended she should; Khurrami saw life through laughter. "How kind—but no, no man either. Only the gods can bring me peace."

A pause, then Khurrami asked, "And they will not?"

"They have not yet." Although she had prayed and offered at the temples endlessly over the past year— The memories kindled a thought, but it flared too briefly; she could not form its image as it died, emberlike. . . .

"God-time is not man-time." A sober, steady girl, Irsiya repeated the platitude with appropriate gravity; the queen knew that, behind her, Khurrami smiled at Irsiya's solemn piety.

"Gods have endless years; queens have not." Queens grew old, and died, eternal only in their daughters' memories.

"Then perhaps," Khurrami said, drawing the comb hard through a tangle of hair, "the queen should remind the gods of that fact."

"Perhaps I should—" Suddenly the smoldering ember burst into flame. She sat silent, barely noticing the comb's pull through her knotted hair, fearing to quench the brilliance flooding her.

Ask the gods—yes, I shall ask again. For a heartbeat her blood slowed, chilled. *They have never answered you before; why should they now?* This was the great secret she held, the shame that poisoned her blood. She had done all a queen must to please the gods; bowed, devout, before Ilat's image. But never had she received the signs by which the gods made themselves manifest in the hearts of those who served them. Sometimes, when she stood in empty silence before Sheba's great goddess, she wondered if the gods even existed.

No. This is no time for doubt. I shall go to the great Temple, I shall seek Ilat's guidance. And She shall tell me where I shall find the next Queen of Sheba. And if She remains silent—

Sudden confidence flowed warm beneath her skin, burned like hot wine. If Ilat remained silent, Bilqis would know that the gods trusted her to act as she must. *Yes.* A sense of rightness, of affirmation, warmed her.

"Yes, perhaps I should." She smiled, and patted Khurrami's slim hand. "That is excellent advice, my dear. And this time when I ask, I know that my prayer will be answered."

And I must give thanks for what I have already been granted. Perhaps there were gods after all. For who but Ilat Herself could have put this audacious plan into her head?

Ma'rib was a city of temples; the Shebans were a godly people, their temples jewels in their crown of good fortune. Ilat's Temple was chief among those gems. A precious setting for a most precious goddess, the house of the Queen of Heaven lay at the city's heart.

All were welcome into the Temple's outer courts, whose doors stood open both by day and by night. Anyone might enter the outer courts— woman or man, Sheban or outlander, crone or child. All were welcome there to worship, or to offer gifts, or to bask for a time in Ilat's peace. The outer courts offered the goddess's gifts freely.

But beyond the welcoming outer courts with their smiling priestesses, their cool fountains, their bounty of food and drink and rest, lay another realm. Past the rose trees and the gentle fountains, past the walls painted bright with leopards and lilies, past the shrines and statues given by grateful petitioners, past the glitter and laughter—past all the sweet soft joys bestowed by a loving goddess—lay the Temple's Inner Court.

No one entered the Inner Court lightly. Most never entered that court at all, content all their lives to go no farther than the clear, simple pleasures the goddess offered to all. The Inner Court demanded more than innocent devotion, more than unquestioning worship. It demanded wisdom and courage, and an iron refusal to surrender to illusion.

But for those who were dedicated, or desperate, the Temple's secret heart offered a path to their true desire.

Bilqis had walked that hard true path only twice in her life. The first time had been the day the Morning Crown had been placed upon her head and the clawed scepter in her hand, the day the girl Bilqis became the Queen of the South. That day she had feared her own weakness, and dared the Inner Court to learn her own strength.

The second had been the day her daughter died. That day she had sought peace, and submission to fate's knotted thread. That day she had failed, her own grief and fear overwhelming her until she fell into darkness. She had lain weak in bed for seven days after, slowly mending her shattered self. She had not dared return even to the Temple's outer courts since that disastrous day.

But now I must. She held out her hands before her. They were steady. *See, I am calm.* She rose from her dressing table and turned slowly before Khurrami and Irsiya. "Is it well?" she asked. No idle question, today; her gems and garb must be faultless.

"You are the goddess Herself," Irsiya said.

"Not yet," Bilqis said, and looked to Khurrami, who studied her carefully.

"Yes." Khurrami knelt and brushed her hand over the gown's skirt. "Yes, it is well, my queen."

"Good. Now the veil."

Khurrami and Irsiya lifted the shimmering mass of cloth from its gilded basket and shook it out before tossing the sacred veil over her head. The world turned to golden shadow; the goddess's veil was woven of silk as sheer and pale as sunlight. Threads of gold glinted as the veil rippled into place, flowing over her from the crown of her head to her ankles.

Her handmaidens settled the veil with delicate touches of their hands. When they were satisfied, Khurrami nodded. "You are ready, my queen." Khurrami hesitated, then added softly, "Good fortune, Bilqis."

Having overruled the wishes of her chamberlain, her honor-maids, and her guards, Bilqis walked alone through Ma'rib's streets. The occasion was too important to turn into a queen's processional. "In this I am suppliant, not queen. I will not succumb to false pride and vain show."

And she was wise enough to know that the sight of the queen herself walking veiled and alone to the great Temple to plead for Ilat's favor would be remembered longer than any procession, however rich or royal.

There were other reasons for such blatant piety, such humble pride. It was expected, although not demanded, that a petitioner seeking the Inner Court walk, meek and submissive, to the Temple gate. Today such humility was not only pious, but politic as well. All Ma'rib would see the queen sought truth from Ilat Herself, and since none sought such truth lightly or wantonly—

—*whatsoever I say our goddess revealed to me, I shall be believed.* The thought of such deceit turned her mouth sour. But she must have an answer; she *must.* And if the Sun of their Days would not unveil Sheba's future—once again Bilqis silently repeated the words she clung to in hope, intangible talismans against a cold future.

If Ilat will not reveal what is to come, then I will know She trusts me to summon what future I will.

The thought was reasoned, logical. It might even be true. If only it were consoling as well. . . .

She tried to set all thought aside; it would not do to approach the Queen of Heaven uneasy in her mind. Once past the palace gate, she found it less difficult to control her willful thoughts; long practice granted her forgetfulness as she concentrated on walking smoothly and with grace.

The journey from palace to Temple seemed timeless, endless. But at last she walked across the wide hot square to the outer doors of the great Temple.

A priestess greeted her there, as all who came to the goddess's Temple were greeted.

"Welcome to our Mother's House, child. What do you come for?"

This was her last chance to change her mind, to refuse to walk the path she had chosen for herself. But already she was speaking the words that would begin the ritual.

"I come for wisdom."

"Many come for wisdom," the priestess said. "Nothing more?"

"I come for the future."

"The future will come for you. Nothing more?"

"I come for myself," she said, and the priestess bowed and backed away. Bilqis walked forward, stepping over the doorsill into the Temple's first lure.

Ilat's great Temple was formed in seven rings circling about its heart. The outer ring housed the courts of love and comfort. Roses scented the air; fruit trees lined paths which wound in aimless coils through the pleasure garden. Those who followed those pretty paths would, in time, return to their beginning, never having ventured farther into the Temple mysteries than that soft, sheltered garden.

For many, that was enough.

I wish it were enough for me. But she had set her feet upon a different path, and she would follow where it led her.

She walked smoothly through the garden, into the second outer court; passed its comforts, too, without a pause. Then the third, and then she was past all comfort, all common human joys. Praying her spirit would not fail her, she looked upon the first of the barriers between the outer Temple and the mystery that lay at the Temple's heart.

All are equal before Her. She looked through the golden shadow of her veil at the gatekeeper, and the gate behind him—the first of seven she must pass through to reach the goddess. The gate was gilded and jeweled, the bar that held it closed carved from a single elephant tusk.

"What do you seek?" the priest guarding the gate asked.

"To go within." She knew all the responses by heart, had learned them long ago. She had never thought to speak them more than once, upon the day she had set the crown of Sheba upon her head.

"Those who go within must walk meek and humble. Will you leave pride and folly at this gate?"

"I will," she said.

"Then leave them here, and enter."

She bent and untied her gilded sandals, slipped them from her feet. Rising, she offered them to the priest, who accepted them with a slight bow before he lifted the ivory bar and swung the gate open. "Enter meekly and humbly, then, and may you find what you seek within."

Heart pounding, she walked through the gate. This marked the true beginning of her journey; from this gate, there was no turning back. The jeweled gate swung closed behind her, leaving her alone to face what lay within.

I have passed the first gate. Surely that is the hardest. The first gate, the first of the seven through which she must pass. Each gate led deeper into the goddess's heart; each stripped one layer of the mortal world away.

Seven gates those who would enter the Inner Court must pass, and at each, a garment or a jewel must be surrendered. Sandals at the first gate, so the petitioner walked barefoot to reach the ultimate sanctuary.

Girdle unclasped at the second gate. She handed the band of woven gold and silver to the priest waiting silently before the gate's smooth panels of polished jade.

Necklace at the third gate; bracelets at the fourth. At the fifth gate, the elaborate gold earrings fashioned to look like flaming suns. At the sixth, she unpinned her gown; the heavy silk slid down her body, hissed softly to the floor. She stepped carefully over the mass of fabric and walked onward.

One thing only remained to her: the goddess's veil. Until the seventh gate, the veil protected her. There, even that illusion must be surrendered.

Silence lay thick about her, the air itself heavy and soft, like warm honey. Emptying her mind of fear and desire was her task now, a goal she knew she failed to attain. *I did better the first time I dared this, and the second. What is wrong with me, that I fail now?*

You know why. Now the stakes are too high. If you fail, Sheba falls.

The seventh gate was made of wood from the frankincense tree, polished smooth and sheathed in horn. Here there was no priest to ask for and to receive the symbols of her womanhood. This gate she must pass alone.

Beneath the veil she lifted her arms and raised the jeweled circlet from her head. As if pleased to be released, the goddess-veil slithered over her upraised arms and down her back to lie in a glinting heap upon the floor at her feet. She stared down at the abandoned veil, opened her hands and let the circlet fall onto the crumpled cloth. Now there was nothing between her and the Inner Court but the gate of wood and horn before her.

Now she was ready to stand before the goddess, a supplicant like any other. She set her hand to the bar and opened the seventh gate.

Light flooded over her; she walked forward, into the goddess's Inner Court. There was no idol here, no statue to confine the Sun Herself within its golden skin. There was only a roofless courtyard, gilded walls encircling her, amber floor warm as blood beneath her feet. Sunlight poured into the courtyard, pale and harsh; the walls blazed bright as noon sun. Within that circle of burning light, only goddess and worshipper remained, what passed between them sacred to them alone.

Golden light blazed so hot she closed her eyes against its force. She neither knelt nor petitioned; the Bright Lady required no words to know what was in Her human daughter's heart. Bilqis had come not to speak, but to listen.

So hard, to stand and wait, to be nothing but a cup for the goddess to fill or not, as She chose. In this place of pure white light, nothing was hidden, nothing shadowed. Naked to her goddess. No concealment possible.

Naked to herself.

That, even more than her openness to Ilat's sun-eyes, frightened her. Although she had stood here in this circle of gold and light twice before, today she feared more deeply, as if she looked farther into eternity now.

I must not fear. I must not despair. And I must not hurry. I must wait.

Wait and empty herself of all thought, all passion, all desire. Even the worthiest longing must be smoothed into patient acceptance.

Wait. And trust Ilat. Why had she come, if she did not trust the goddess to answer? *Look within yourself, to see how you fail, and why. Look within, Bilqis.*

The voice was her own, reminding her of what she must do here. Obedient, she looked, her mind spiraling inward, seeking. *You know what must be done; why do you fear to do it?*

Because the cost of failure was too high to be borne. A cost that would be paid not by her, but by all those to come after. *If I fail, Sheba is punished, not I.*

There it was, the lump of terror frozen at her heart's core. Her Sheba, her land, her people—all rested easy, certain of her power. Certain of their future.

A future only you can give them, child. The words came from nowhere, written in white fire before her dazzled eyes. *Only you.*

"What must I do?" she whispered into the blinding light.

You know. Seek and you will find what you seek. How else?

Seek and find—

The answer came, clear as sunlight, so simple she laughed in surprise and relief. If she could not bear a daughter, she must find one.

You must seek a true queen to rule over the sunlight land, the incense land, the land gods love. The words sang clear, revealing a truth she had refused until now to admit. *How could I not have understood what I must do?*

She had known all along that she must choose a successor. But that was not easy to do, not and leave peace as her legacy. For she could not choose a girl from one of Sheba's noble families to raise up; any choice she made among them would breed quarrels. Quarrels bred war. But now, at last, she had an answer, saw a way to escape the maze of family ties and tangled loyalties.

So our Mother will grant me a daughter—but I myself must seek the child out, and must travel far to find her. She must seek elsewhere, undertake a quest to some far land from which she could return with the next Queen of Sheba. *With a girl whose right to rule none can dispute, for she will be my true daughter, a daughter chosen by our Mother Ilat, by the Bright Lady Herself.*

Now she knelt, pressing her lips to the blood-hot floor in gratitude for the goddess's aid, for the comforting certainty that flowed through her, easing all pain.

Sheba's crown would pass gently to its next queen; the goddess promised this boon. Now it remained only to learn where, among all the world's kingdoms, the Queen of Sheba must search for the girl the goddess would choose—

Even if that goddess is I.

That night she slept deep and dreamless, awakening to find herself rested in body and easy in mind. And for all her secret doubts of Ilat's true concern for Sheba's future, it was upon that day, the day following her visit to the Temple's Inner Court, that emissaries of a foreign king came to Ma'rib, came to petition the Queen of the South on behalf of a king of whom she had never heard.

The king of a land far to the north of Sheba and its treasures of gold and spices: Solomon, King of Wisdom.

It was not the queen's day to sit in judgment, and so she had claimed the day's hours for her own. Clad only in a skirt of fine linen, she sat quiet in her garden upon a bench carved of rose-red stone; savored the scents of lilies and lilac, the warmth of the sun upon her unbound hair. Such interludes were rare in Queen Bilqis's life, so when Khurrami came soft-footed along the garden path with a message, it was with hand outstretched in apology.

"I crave the queen's pardon for disturbing her peace."

Bilqis sighed. "You would not do so without reason. Speak."

"The chief steward asked me to bring word that a king's emissaries have arrived in Ma'rib and crave audience with the queen."

And this news could not wait? She folded the thought away, struggled to show Khurrami a placid face. "Emissaries? They must be important or importunate indeed—"

"To trouble the queen without delay," Khurrami finished for her, and lifted one smooth shoulder in annoyance. "But we all know what the chief steward is; he swore the matter urgent."

"Ah, well—" Bilqis smiled in rueful agreement; Shakarib was an excellent master of the court—but he did seem to treat all matters as equally weighty. "Tell me of these urgent envoys."

"I will tell what I know, which is that they come from a land far to the north—"

A land far to the north. . . . Something in those words kindled the queen's blood, caused her breath to thicken in her throat. A vagrant breeze stroked her, and suddenly she knew it was the Bright Queen's answer to her ardent prayer. These men from beyond the burning sands somehow held the answer she had sought for so long.

"—so far away that their kingdom lies beyond the great desert itself. Although they did not travel over the sands but voyaged down the Red Sea, in a merchant's ship—"

As Khurrami spoke, Bilqis fought the temptation to demand the travelers be summoned at once before her; that would be neither kind nor wise. She held up her hand, and Khurrami fell silent.

"I do not care how they came; they are here now. A far land, you say? A long journey, then; give these strangers all they desire, and then, when they are rested, bring them before me and I will question them, and learn why they have come."

Courtesies satisfied, Khurrami bowed, and Bilqis turned away. Both knew why the men from the north had come so far, and what they would ask. Merchants who dared the journey paid well for Sheban spice—and reaped a hundredfold reward for their daring in their own marketplaces.

Spice lured all the world to Sheba.

A land far to the north—in that far land a queen for Sheba waits. Seek, and find—

Although her very blood craved haste, Bilqis refused to surrender to that pounding urgency. *These men have traveled far and long to reach me and petition for the treasures I hold in my gift. They will not flee for an hour's wait—or a week's.* Or even a month's, come to that. No, those who came to bargain for Sheba's spices waited patiently upon Sheba's pleasure.

So she made herself wait a day before she told Shakarib that the emissaries from the land to the north might come before the Queen of Sheba's ivory throne.

Abishag

My mother reared me to be a queen, although I never knew it until long after the crown was set upon my brow—just as I never knew her patience ran deep as a well, her faith strong as stone. I knew nothing of my mother's true worth until I was a woman grown, and married to the man of my heart's desiring.

I first saw him when I was a small child and my family dwelt in Mahanaim, a city east of the Jordan. All I remember of my life in that place is that once King David himself lodged there, during the days of Prince Absalom's rebellion. I remember that when the soldiers marched in, the street was so crowded I looked down from our rooftop and saw bronze helmets moving like a metal stream. And I saw a royal prince, a boy who looked up at me with eyes bright as the sun. I remember that. And I remember that, upon our windowsill, my mother kept a hyacinth in a painted pot.

Boaz

"A strange thing, to find a land ruled by a woman." Jotham frowned. "I don't like it."

"You never like anything new, Cousin. Why petition to come at all?"

Boaz stared around the rooms they had been given—rooms rich enough even for King Solomon himself. *A generous people, these Shebans—but they are so wealthy gold means little to them, and silver nothing.*

"I am the king's brother; it is my right and my duty to serve him. Solomon asked me to deal with the Shebans. He forgot to mention I would have to deal with a woman as if she were equal to the king of kings."

"I forgot you never listen to travelers' tales." Boaz lifted a cup and turned it over in his hands. Ibex leapt about the curves of a goblet formed of silver; the beasts' horns gleamed gold. In most palaces such a costly item would be reserved for the banquet table. "These Shebans must be rich beyond dreams. Look upon this." He tossed the goblet to Jotham, who caught it easily in one hand.

"Fine work" was all Jotham said, after studying the silver cup for a moment. He set the goblet back upon the table. "I don't see why your eyes stretch so wide; if Sheba did not possess what all the world desires, we wouldn't be here."

All the world desired Sheba's fabled spices. Cinnamon, spikenard, pepper; those and others equally precious passed through Sheban hands on their journey from the lands beyond the morning to lusting markets in the kingdoms of the west. But most vital of all was Sheba's frankincense. Incense to summon gods, incense to pleasure goddesses. Even Israel's austere god favored incense. The incense trees grew only in the land of Sheba; smoke of Sheban incense drifted across the wide world, more precious than gold, more coveted than rubies.

"Incense beyond price and a queen guarding Sheba's treasure—is she beautiful, do you think?" Boaz asked.

"I think all men will call her so, whether or not she is fair to look upon. What do I care? I have a good wife waiting for me at home."

"I've heard the queen is a djinn; that no man can resist her. That she chooses men as she does jewels—for a night only. If she beckons to you, do you think you could resist her wiles?"

"I think you should stop guzzling Sheban wine and listening to Sheban gossip. The queen is not important—the spice trade is."

Boaz regarded Prince Jotham with rueful amusement. "Of all the men King Solomon could have chosen, he sends one unmoved by beauty, unintrigued by mystery, unimpressed by riches."

"We are not here to lust after beauty, unveil mystery, or covet riches. We are here to seal the spice trade for King Solomon." Jotham walked across the soft-woven carpet that covered cool marble tiles until he reached the moon-round window. He pushed aside the drift of silver cloth that curtained the opening. "Come and look, Boaz. Feast your eyes upon Sheba now, for when we go before the Spice Queen, we must go clear-eyed and clear-headed."

Boaz stood beside his cousin and gazed upon a city more dazzling than pearls. Jerusalem, City of David, crowned a rocky hill, an armored guardian of the land around it. But Ma'rib stretched out freely, its houses circled by gardens, its streets lined with trees. Fields green as emeralds surrounded the city, tangible proof of Ma'rib's ability to summon water from the desert.

"The Shebans must be great sorcerers, to force the sand to yield crops," Boaz said, and Jotham laughed.

"The Shebans must be great engineers, to create a dam to channel the only river for a thousand leagues. I may not listen to travelers' tales of gems and djinns, but I do take heed of our agents' reports. Now go ask that sly chamberlain just how much longer King Solomon's envoy must wait before the Queen of Sheba deigns to admit him to her presence."

Bilqis

Despite the wealth of Sheba, the queen's throne was a simple thing, formed so long ago that the ivory itself had grown old. Once pale as bone, the chair from which a thousand queens had ruled shone golden as honey; time-burnished. Before the ivory throne hung curtains sewn of leopard skins and embroidered Cathay silk, hiding the queen from those who waited in the great court. When she lifted her hand, the eunuchs whose task it was to shield her would pull upon golden cords, drawing the curtains back to re-veal the Queen of Sheba seated like a goddess upon her ancient throne.

An effective image; created to imbue awe in the beholder—and render newcomers to Sheba's marketplace vulnerable to her merchants. Bilqis had no reason to suppose the waiting men from King Solomon's court would prove less malleable than any others—

One of the eunuchs cleared his throat, pretended to cough; the small noise drew her attention, and Bilqis realized they had been awaiting her signal to pull back the curtains—a signal she should have given long since. But the wild urgency that had driven her since Khurrami brought her word of the men from the north had deserted her. Passion had chilled to fear.

For if I look upon these men and listen to their words, and still find no answer—what then?

She lifted her hand, and it seemed to her that never had her own flesh weighed so heavy. The curtains that had concealed her swept back, and she looked at last upon the men who had sailed down the Red Sea from the court of a king called Solomon the Wise.

The men from the north neither knelt nor bowed. They stared upon her as openly as if she were not a queen whom they must petition, a priestess whom they must propitiate. She had seen such men before, men from lands of men who looked upon a woman and saw only weakness.

Oh, yes, I have seen you all before. You with your scornful eyes and your rough manners, who think that because I am a woman my word is less than law. Without taking her eyes from the men standing before her throne, she lifted her left hand; as smoothly as sand flowing over a dune, Uhhayat, the royal chamberlain, paced forward and knelt.

"Who seeks the Queen of the South?" Bilqis spoke in the Traders' Tongue, courtesy to her foreign visitors. Ritual must be observed, however rough-hewn a guest's conduct.

"I am—" the group's leader began; ignoring his words, the royal chamberlain answered, her voice ringing clear over his.

"O Queen, Light of our Days, Lady of the Morning, those who seek wisdom and favor of the Daughter of the Sun would approach." Uhhayat's face remained as bland as her voice, but her glance at the foreigners cut like a blade. The leader's face darkened; whether with shame at his ill-conduct or with anger at Uhhayat's contempt the queen could not tell.

In the silence that followed Uhhayat's words, Bilqis sat quiet and counted heartbeats. At last, when the men behind the leader shifted, restless, she spoke the time-honed response.

"Those who seek the queen's wisdom and the queen's favor may approach."

Without waiting for Lady Uhhayat to summon them forward, the men strode forward. *No grace, and no manners.* And their garments were well-woven but lacked style.

Just before the first step to the throne, the group's leader stopped, standing proud and gazing straight into her face. She recognized the gleam of curiosity mirrored in his dark eyes—and the glint of contempt ill-hidden. Well, Sheba would teach him better manners, at least. *If you wish my spices, you must bend before my will.* So thinking, she smiled, and saw the leader's face change; caution replaced curiosity.

"The Queen of the South greets you, men from the north." She gestured to the three broad steps that led up to Sheba's ivory throne. "Sit, and speak. Tell us all that is in your hearts."

A graceful gesture; a signal honor not to be refused. But once accepted, that honor ensured that the man sat awkwardly at her feet, as if he were a babe playing before his nurse. *Now make your speech, little man. Spread your king's demands before us and see us laugh.*

But however scornful, the man at least was no fool; seated, he looked up, past her jeweled feet and silk-clad thighs, past the girdle of pearls circling her waist, the ropes of amber falling over her breasts, until he stared once more at her face. "I, Prince Jotham of Judah, thank you, O Queen, for this sign of your favor. May it herald a prosperous outcome to our journey."

Very good, Prince Jotham of Judah. Many men had sat where he sat now, and some could not tear their eyes away from the sheer cloth clinging to her legs, the shadows hinting at the secret garden hidden between her thighs. She smiled again.

"May it herald prosperity indeed. Now tell us where your land may be found, Prince Jotham of Judah, and what men call it, and who rules over it—and you."

"My land lies north, past the great empty desert. My king is Solomon the Wise, son of Great David, who rules all the land from Dan to Beer-sheba, and more besides."

Much more, apparently; building upon his father's conquests, King Solomon now ruled an empire—or so his envoy claimed. "No man travels between the Great Sea and the Great Desert, between Egypt and Damascus, without paying toll to King Solomon the Wise."

King Solomon the Wise; a noble title. Is he wise in truth, or only in men's flattery? One never could be sure; did not men still call her Bilqis the Beautiful? *The true question is whether this King Solomon owns the wisdom to know he is flattered—or whether he is deluded by gilded words.*

"A great realm indeed. And what does King Solomon the Wise wish of Bilqis, Queen of the lands of Sheba?"

"Her goodwill and her friendship." Prince Jotham's gaze never wavered. "And her spices."

Unable to resist, she permitted herself to laugh. "Your king has sent an able advocate indeed! It has taken some men a month of audiences before they dared utter those words!"

For a breath, dismay flooded his face, then he shrugged. "What else does a man come to the land of Sheba to gain but her spices? Why not say so?"

"Why not indeed?" Her amusement encouraged her courtiers to smiles and low laughter at this brazen truth. "Tell me, Prince Jotham, does King Solomon the Wise desire nothing more of Sheba?"

This time he hesitated before speaking, but still his words were as blunt as before. "My brother King Solomon would enter into agreements with Sheba. Trade must continue, spices flow safe along the Incense Road. A pact between our kingdoms is what King Solomon desires."

"And what does the king your brother offer that Sheba does not already possess? What does King Solomon own that Sheba lacks?" Something seemed to arouse her as she uttered the words; an intangible caress slid like perfumed smoke across her skin.

"I do not know," Prince Jotham said, "but I have brought scrolls from the king, and a scribe who has memorized all the scrolls say. Doubtless my brother has thought of something."

Does King Solomon know what manner of men carry his words? Still, such crude speech has saved us all endless hours of deference and debate before even beginning our bargaining. In exchange, I will turn a blind eye and a deaf ear to their blunt manner. For did she not also wish something of them—although they did not yet know it?

"Rise, Prince Jotham of Judah, and know you are Sheba's guest. And know also that the Queen of Sheba will speak with King Solomon's scribe, but the queen alone can promise nothing."

As King Solomon's envoy rose ungracefully to his feet, plainly baffled, she raised her hand. "The queen will consult our Mother Ilat in this matter; the queen will act as the goddess advises." With that, she nodded, and the court eunuchs released the heavy golden cords; the curtains of leopard and embroidered silk fell before the ivory throne, hiding her from the court. A good ending, she thought, rising from the throne, and a decision no one could quarrel with. A decision that committed her to nothing.

Once more veiled from all but her intimates, she beckoned to the chief eunuch. And when he drew near, and bowed low, she smiled. "I have a task for you, Tamrin. Bring Prince Jotham of Judah to my garden."

"At once, Sun of our Days." But however humble Tamrin's words, however deep his bow, Bilqis clearly understood his deep disapproval.

If the gods would grant me one wish—other than a queen for Sheba—I would ask for handmaidens and servants and eunuchs who had not tended me since before I grew breasts! Sometimes their care nearly stifled her—and their meticulous solicitude curbed most wild impulses almost before she uttered them.

"Oh, it need not be at once," she said, restraining her desire to remind Tamrin that she, not he, ruled as Queen of Sheba—even if he *had* served her mother. "But I must speak with him—I wish to learn more of this King Solomon than I shall hear in a public audience. And whatever you can learn . . ."

"Of course, my queen. You may trust me for that."

Smiling, she laid her hand softly upon his bowed head. "I do. I trust you to bring me words that tell what sort of man King Solomon is—or at least, the sort of man his subjects think him."

Pleased still to be of such import, Tamrin bowed even lower, lifting the tassel of her girdle to his lips. "Light of our Eyes, you shall have what you desire. My slaves will glean knowledge from those uncouth barbarians until even King Solomon's own mother shall know him less well than you."

In some acts, haste never prospered; if a Queen of Sheba mastered nothing else as she trained for the day the sun-crown would rest upon her hair, she learned to command patience.

Fools battled life's hungers, and in the end lost all.

So Bilqis had been taught; so she ruled her own life. She had waited three full days, and now she would learn what sort of man King Solomon had sent to plead for him. *And I will learn what sort of man King Solomon is—or seems to be to his trusted servant.* She smiled, and spread the peacock feathers of her fan across the bench beside her. For this meeting, she had chosen to seem what men of other nations called womanly, and displayed her body like a prize. A gown rich with gold fringe wrapped her; sheer cloth molded the curves of breast and hip and thigh. A dozen bracelets adorned each wrist, chimed with each movement of her hands. Carmine painted her mouth, so that her lips flamed hot and red.

Unless this man from the north is dead, or a eunuch, he will succumb. A man dazzled by a woman's charms was a man easier to bargain with.

Prince Jotham of Judah seethed with impatience; his mouth was set in a thin line and his body moved stiffly, like a clay doll's. Bilqis smiled as he approached, and extended her hand, palm up, so that her hennaed skin glowed rose in the sun.

"The Queen of Sheba greets King Solomon's emissary. She is eager to speak with him again." Swiftly gauging his temper, she added, "No, do not kneel; you may sit before me."

Plainly Prince Jotham had not even thought of bending his knee to her; her careless dismissal of that protocol seemed to startle him into noticing he should pay her more homage than a scowl. "Thank you, Highness," he said. "But I will stand."

Bilqis laughed softly. "Stand then, but I fear you will grow weary, for I long to hear all you have to tell me of your land and your king. So when you tire of standing, I give you leave to sit at your ease so that we may talk as friends."

King Solomon's emissary regarded her cautiously, as if she were a venomous serpent he had found drowsing before him. Again Bilqis smiled; faced with a woman of power, this man of action found himself at a loss. "Now," said the Queen of Sheba, "speak to me of King Solomon."

"What do you wish to know?"

"Why, whatever you wish to tell me, of course. That he is a great king, wise and powerful—that I will grant. Are not all kings so described?" She lifted the peacock fan and began slowly waving the brilliant feathers, creating the smallest of breezes across her skin. "And that he wishes to gain my spices—that too is common to all kings."

"Then what can I tell you that you do not already know?" Jotham demanded. "Your ministers have read the king's scrolls by now. Have they not told you what they say?"

Gently, Bilqis lowered the peacock fan, rested it across her thighs. Plainly

Jotham of Judah prided himself on blunt speaking and held women in light regard. Time, Bilqis thought, to invoke the Mother to rule him, bring him to heel.

"I have read the scrolls, young man, and yes, I know what they say. Now I shall give you some advice, Jotham. It would be wise of you to remember that you are here not for yourself but for your king. And it would be even wiser of you to remember one thing more."

"And what is that?" he asked after a moment, filling the silence, as she had known he would.

She noted with satisfaction that his face had flushed with chagrin and rising anger. *Ah, and now he expects me to fling my power in his face, to threaten.* She smiled, and once again lifted her peacock fan.

"That not only am I a queen, I am old enough to be your mother—or at least your aunt," she added, laughter rippling beneath her words. "Now come and sit before me, Jotham of Judah—there, upon that cushion—and tell me what I wish to know."

So easy. Bilqis continued to smile as King Solomon's brother capitulated, sitting upon a cushion at her feet as if he were her son, or her harper. Obtaining obedience from men was a skill; like any other craft, it must be not only learned but honed with constant practice.

"Never utter an order you know will be disobeyed, Bilqis. Never give a man a chance to disobey, to show less than respect. Grant him what he does not yet think of taking." Her mother's voice whispered down the years to her, imparting women's wisdom. *Yes, Mother,* Bilqis replied silently, *I remember. See how this proud hard man now bends before me, and does not even know he has surrendered.*

As she had anticipated, once he had begun to speak, Prince Jotham gradually revealed far more than he thought; certainly far more than he had intended when he strode into her presence. The chance to boast of the virtues of his monarch and the greatness of his kingdom inspired him to longwinded praise.

And if I believed even half of what he says of his wise king, I would have to fall down and worship Solomon! To hear Jotham of Judah tell it, King Solomon was more god than man.

"Handsome, generous, and wise in everything; your king is a true paragon of all the virtues." Smiling, Bilqis plied her peacock fan, sending a warm breeze over Jotham's sweat-damp face. The movement of the heavy air carried the scent of her perfume to him, a tantalizing fragrance of frankincense and roses. She noted that, without realizing it, Jotham leaned towards her, instinctively seeking to draw nearer.

"Solomon is a great king indeed—almost as great as his father, King David. Do you know how exalted our king is, in what regard he is held by the kings of all the world?"

"In most high regard?" Bilqis asked the question lightly, as if she jested; Jotham sprang to his ruler's defense.

"So high his wives are kings' daughters—yes, and his concubines too. Even Pharaoh gave a daughter to King Solomon, and sent her to him with the city of Gezer as dowry." Jotham spoke as intently as a suitor seeking to impress his beloved's mother.

And although she revealed no emotion other than amused interest, Bilqis was impressed. Royal Egypt did not grant its daughters lightly. To send a Daughter of the Two Lands to an alien kingdom to wed an outlander king had been unheard of—until now. That King Solomon could be granted such a wife spoke more clearly of his influence than an hour's effusive praise by his loyal brother.

"King Solomon is favored by the Lord as well, for all his wives bear him only sons."

The poor man! Bilqis lowered the peacock fan and ran her fingers over the iridescent feathers as if to smooth them. "Nothing but sons? How unfortunate."

King Solomon's emissary stared at her, plainly baffled; she laughed softly.

So, Prince Jotham, you have forgotten that, in Sheba, it is the mother who weighs heaviest in the scales. It is good to know I can still bedazzle an outlander. I am not yet useless.

"So great, so favored a king—with so loyal a servant, so faithful a brother. And so astute a king; did you not speak of him as Solomon the Wise?"

"So he has been called since he became king. On his first night as king, Solomon prayed to the Lord our god for wisdom to rule well and justly. And the Lord was pleased with Solomon, for he had not asked for riches or power for himself. And so the Lord granted the king the wisdom he had desired. Solomon has ruled wisely as king ever since that day."

How pious—and what a clever tale to plant; what sweet fruit it produces! Perhaps this Solomon is truly wise.

"So now I know something of the king who desires Sheba's spice." Bilqis regarded Solomon's advocate with a tolerant smile. "A wise man born under fortunate stars. It must be hard to refuse such a king anything he might desire."

"Why refuse? Grant King Solomon what he desires, and he will repay you with friendship."

"I have not said Sheba will refuse—but Solomon will need to give more than friendship for Sheba's spices. Does he offer nothing more, this god-favored king?"

Before Prince Jotham could summon an answer, Bilqis laughed softly to assure him that she had taken no offense at his words. "No, do not answer; this is not the time or place to discuss trade and treaties. Come walk with me in the gardens and I shall display our finest flowers to you—and you, Prince Jotham, shall tell me how our blooms compare to those of Solomon's kingdom."

But by the time the sun rose towards midmorning, Bilqis abandoned the attempt to stroll the garden paths with the visitor. The man plainly cared nothing for gardens and even less for spending an hour discussing flowers. Alone, she bent and cupped a small fragrant rose between her hands and closed her eyes to inhale the blossom's dark perfume.

What manner of men does King Solomon rule? Harsh men, rough and much burned by sun. *What sort of land breeds such men? What sort of king rules such fierce subjects?*

A king owning all a man's virtues and all the world's wisdom. Has he no weakness, then?

No man lived free of fault; the trick was to divine that defect, to turn that weakness into a weapon. A weapon held in reserve, perhaps a weapon never wielded. But a weapon nonetheless.

Opening her eyes, Bilqis stared into the rose's crimson heart. *Can any man be so great, so wise? Perhaps,* a voice seemed to hiss, the word echoing silently in her ears, *perhaps you should go and see for yourself. . . .*

A command. An answer. A promise.

Bilqis straightened; her fingers slid over the velvet petals of the rose. At last she saw a path, a bridge to Sheba's future. A road that led north.

North to the court of King Solomon.

Rahbarin

"I do not like these men from the north. They—" Rahbarin hesitated, seeking the right word to describe the unease troubling his mind. He stared into Ilat's eyes, hoping to find inspiration in their jeweled depths. "They are—rude," he said at last. "They lack respect. I do not like the way they look upon my mother's sister. I do not like the way they look upon Your Mirror on Earth. Can she trust them, and their king?"

The alabaster image never altered; the goddess's lapis eyes glowed serene in the lamplight, gold flecks glinting in the deep blue like stars at midnight. Rahbarin did not know whether that meant Ilat did not listen, or that She did not care. An idol was but an image; a form the goddess could inhabit, if She chose. This evening, She did not choose to reveal Herself. The statue remained merely a mirror in which to reflect upon the goddess it portrayed.

Rahbarin set another nugget of incense into the crystal bowl at the idol's feet, bowed, and backed away. Tonight he would receive no answer. *I must ask again later.* Another time, he might elicit an answer from Ilat—or he might not. If She and the queen already wove a net of their own devising, neither would reveal as much to him.

That thought forced him to admit what he had been denying, that his aunt plotted something—*something she knows I will not approve.* And if that were true, he had a better chance of coaxing an answer from his goddess than he did from his aunt.

Bilqis

I must go north. That much was clear enough, goddess-granted. How she was to achieve this journey, and explain it to her councilors and her subjects—that apparently was to be left up to her own ingenuity.

But like any good ruler, Bilqis possessed a bountiful store of cunning. The answer came swiftly; she would announce that Ilat Herself had spoken, had commanded the queen's obedience. That she must submit to Ilat's wishes concerning the northerners and their king's desire to trade with Sheba. *All know I have consulted our Mother in Her Inner Court. Now I need only proclaim Her commands.*

She kept King Solomon's men waiting for a week before summoning them again to her presence. During those days she spent many hours praying before the public altar within the great Temple, for she had no intention of there being the least doubt that what she would do was the will of Ilat Herself. So when the leopard skins were drawn back, revealing her upon Sheba's throne, she smiled upon Solomon's emissaries and told them she had carefully weighed their words, and those of their king.

"I have laid your words before our goddess Ilat. You are fortunate men; our Mother smiles upon you and your king." Bilqis noted that Prince Jotham's expression reflected distaste; she shrugged inwardly and continued. "Sheba will grant King Solomon's request—and the queen herself shall carry this word of our Mother's favor to him."

A low susurrus of whispers began among her courtiers; Bilqis raised her hand for silence. "You all know I have dared the Inner Court to receive Ilat's wisdom. You know that I have spent the last seven days in prayer and fasting. I have been granted knowledge of Her wishes; I will not dispute them."

She glanced around the court, noting who looked shocked, who disapproving, who pleased. Then she turned her attention back to King Solomon's embassy. "You have told us much of your king, and of his wisdom, and of his golden city. Now I will travel north with you, that your king and I may come to agreement together."

The court was silent; Bilqis heard the soft insistent buzz of a bee against one of the alabaster windows as the insect vainly tried to fly free. Gauging the moment, she went on before any of her ministers could speak.

She smiled at Prince Jotham. "At Ilat's command, I shall accompany you to see this golden city for myself—and to test the wisdom of King Solomon."

She had too much experience ruling men and women to permit her audience a chance to consider her words, or to question them. A nod to her attentive eunuchs, and the leopard-skin curtain fell, concealing her from those in the courtyard. Bilqis rose, and stretched, and stopped as she saw her nephew waiting for her beside her throne.

"Is that truly our Mother's answer? That you journey north with these

uncouth men?" Rahbarin frowned even as he held out his hand to steady
her as she descended the steps from the ivory throne.

"Did I not say so?" Bilqis set her hand upon Rahbarin's, and sighed inwardly. He was going to be difficult. For her nephew was nothing if not
single-minded in defense of Sheba's crown and queen, willing to protect her
even from herself if necessary. Prince Rahbarin was strong, loyal, intelligent—
if only he had been born a girl!

Yet even as Bilqis sighed over that useless wish, she knew Ilat had not
erred in creating Rahbarin male instead of female. For Rahbarin also was
gentle-natured and amiable, as good as a desert spring—and as transparent
as that spring-water. Guile and subtlety he lacked. And guile and subtlety a
ruler must have, to rule well and wisely. Rahbarin owned all the virtues of a
good man; those very virtues would be disastrous in a ruler.

For a queen must be able to speak false as well as true, with no one the wiser. To rule—
to nurture a country and its people—a queen must veil her true nature, her
true self. Only one thing must count with her: her people's welfare.

Not her own wishes, or her own happiness—or her own good. Theirs.

And the pause to speak with Rahbarin had permitted others to gather.
Now the court chamberlain, the chief steward, the vizier, and the chief eunuch stood before her, all demanding to know whether the Queen of the
South had gone mad. Only the captain of the queen's guard, Nikaulis,
remained silent.

"O Queen, your vizier has heard not a word of this journey." Mubalilat's
tone plainly indicated that he wished he had not heard a word of it now. "It
is impossible—absolutely impossible—"

The chief eunuch interrupted him, only to continue the protest. "Of
course the Lady of the Morning may do as pleases her, but to undertake
such an endeavor—"

"It is too risky," Uhhayat finished; the court chamberlain could be
counted on to counsel prudence above all. "We know nothing of this king
or his land; his emissaries are barbarians who never smile."

Bilqis held up her hand, and her courtiers fell silent. "And the captain of
my guard? Has my Amazon nothing to say?"

Nikaulis regarded her queen, eyes gray and hard as iron. "Only what others have said; that such a journey is folly. But I am the queen's captain. What
she commands, I will perform."

This is the outcome of training officials to speak their thoughts freely, unafraid of reprisals if their ruler dislikes their words! So thinking, Bilqis laughed softly, watching the puzzlement on her officials' faces at her amusement.

"The queen has heard your words, and thanks you for your concern for her safety and the kingdom's. But you must know that I go at Ilat's bidding and at Her promise. From our land, I shall bring King Solomon gold and spices. And from his land I shall return bringing the queen who will wear Sheba's crown of fire when I am gone."

For a heartbeat they stared at her in silence. Then Mubalilat asked, "This is what the Sun of our Days revealed?" The vizier's voice held an odd mixture of awe and doubt.

"Yes," said Bilqis, "it is what She revealed to me. There will be a queen to follow after me; a queen granted us by Ilat Herself."

"A queen from the north?" The chief eunuch, Tamrin, shook his head so hard a jeweled pin fell from his tight-curled hair. "How is that possible?"

Her most trusted and most loyal ministers stared at her, awaiting her answer. Only truth would serve; they deserved nothing less.

"I do not know." Bilqis held out her hands, as if in supplication. "I only know that I humbled myself before our Mother and this is how She has answered my prayers. I ask that you trust Her, as I do. Now you have the queen's permission to leave her presence."

They obeyed, bowing themselves off with reluctance. Uhhayat and Tamrin walked together; already Bilqis knew they were forging an alliance whose intent would be to keep her here in Sheba. The chief officers of her court and the lesser dignitaries doubtless would spend the next hours grumbling to each other, unable to comprehend such an unheard-of journey.

Nikaulis remained, her iron eyes blade-keen, questioning. "My queen?"

"Speak, Queen's Captain."

"Cannot another journey north in your stead?"

Bilqis shook her head. "No. I must go myself. Who else can choose Sheba's next queen?"

For a moment Nikaulis seemed to hesitate, as if about to speak again. The moment passed, and the Amazon merely bowed her head, as if accepting the queen's words as final. Then Nikaulis, too, retreated, leaving Bilqis alone with her nephew.

"You, too, may leave me, Rahbarin." But Bilqis was not surprised when he regarded her steadily and said, "I wish to talk to you, my mother's sister, if you will permit it."

Bilqis sighed inwardly; she had hoped to avoid an immediate confrontation with Rahbarin and his principles. *Still, as well now as later, I suppose.* Bowing to the inevitable, she permitted him to accompany her to her own chamber. There she sat before her dressing table, and Irsiya began to unpin her hair.

Rahbarin waited; knowing he would silently wait until next moonrise, if necessary, Bilqis sighed, and said, "Speak, Nephew."

Rahbarin looked at Irsiya. "Send your maidservant away."

"No; there is nothing either of us can say that is secret." And a witness might prove useful; who better than the queen's most intimate servant? "Now, what have you to say to your aunt and queen?"

Given permission to speak, Rahbarin hesitated, then said, "I know you have spoken with Ilat Herself, but—but to leave Sheba and journey north, to a far land none has ever seen—is this wise, Bright One?"

"Not wise, perhaps—but necessary." She stared into the polished silver mirror; her face was still a fortune in men's eyes. "Our Lady Ilat has promised me a daughter from the north; I cannot expect the winds to blow the girl across the desert into my arms!"

Rahbarin regarded her with that steadfast, stubborn devotion that made him such a good follower, and would make him an equally poor ruler. "It is too far, and too dangerous. Send me in your stead."

"What, will you bear a child for me?"

"You are too old for that. Whatever the goddess means, She cannot mean you are to bear a child yourself! You would die birthing the babe."

No one could ever accuse Rahbarin of empty flattery—always he would say plain truth, whatever the cost. "Who can say what She means? A daughter, She promised—and one of my own body and blood would be best. If I die bearing an heir to Sheba—why, I die. I trust you to raise my daughter up to be a great queen; she could have no better counselor or truer friend."

"I don't like it," Rahbarin said.

"You don't need to like it, Rahbarin; you need only obey. Her will is clear: I must go. And you must stay, and guard Sheba while I am gone."

"And if you do not return, Aunt? Then what?"

Trust Rahbarin to spot each weak point and take careful aim. "Then,

Sister's Son, you must consult Ilat for yourself, and act as She directs—and as seems best to you."

Knowing that order could not be improved upon, Bilqis dismissed her nephew and braced herself to face her handmaiden; Irsiya was sure to be as disapproving as Rahbarin.

"You have heard what I told the prince. So you may begin packing, my Irsiya—we leave when the Israelite merchants sail north."

Irsiya stared at her round-eyed. "The queen is serious?"

"Irsiya, do I sound as if I jest? Ilat has spoken, remember; I must obey, however far I must journey in Her service."

"But to King Solomon's court? That lies at the other end of the world— the merchants travel months and months only to reach the Silk Road, and Jerusalem is farther still!"

Bilqis laughed, deliberately making light of Irsiya's protest. "Oh, Jerusalem is not so far as that. Damascus lies beyond Jerusalem, and yet our merchants trade often in the City of Roses. And the Silk Road, like the Spice Road, crosses many lands, including King Solomon's. Be easy; I shall not waste half a year in travel."

Not when the sea lay beside the desert, its waters a swift road to the north. By sea, the journey would last weeks rather than months. Bilqis smiled and patted Irsiya's hand. "I shall journey north to King Solomon because our Mother Ilat bids me do so. I may trust Her to smooth my path."

"Of course," Irsiya said, but Sheba sensed her handmaiden's pious agreement was less than wholehearted. But then Irsiya was a true daughter of her bloodline: cautious and conservative as a cat. Irsiya's world was bounded by the golden sands ringing Ma'rib; her desires centered upon home and temple. So long as she trod a path laid out precisely for her careful steps, there was no better servant than Irsiya. But ask her to contemplate change, even in so little a thing as the colors of the flowers to be placed within a vase, and she became worried; worried, Irsiya became stubborn, clinging to the pattern she knew.

She will loathe journeying to unknown lands, but she is one of the queen's ladies. I cannot leave her behind, for she would hate that quite as much. There will be no pleasing Irsiya in this quest.

But so long as she returned from King Solomon's lands bearing Sheba's next queen with her, Bilqis did not care who objected now.

Abishag

When my father died, my mother packed all we owned and took me to dwell in Shunem. In those days Shunem was a prosperous town, a decent place for a widow to raise her daughter. Shunem stood at a crossroads; the King's High Road ran past the town's walls. So as well as a good marketplace, there was also a temple to comfort foreign travelers, and a Grove.

My mother need not have remained alone after my father died, for she was beautiful still, and my father had left her enough to dower her well. But she turned away all men who came seeking her favor.

"You do me too much honor," she told those who sought her as a wife. And to me, when we were alone, "Never again; I have had enough of men. Now I may live my own life and ready you for yours."

"But I thought you happy with my father," I said, and my mother smiled and wiped tears from my cheek with her slender fingers.

"That is because I was happy with him, Abishag. He was a good man, and kind, and he fathered you, for which I would forgive him much. But no more men for me—at least, not here, where they all smell of grapes and of sheep!"

Then she laughed, and when my mother laughed, it was impossible not to laugh with her.

Rahbarin

After he left the queen, Prince Rahbarin headed straight for the great Temple, seeking solace and guidance. Easy enough for his aunt to say *"Stay, and guard Sheba—"* As if he had the knowledge or the cunning to do so, need only lift his hand to accomplish wonders, to replace the Queen of the Morning at a word.

Sometimes he thought his aunt was too confident of others' abilities. She herself was fearless and wise, and believed others as skilled as she herself. Witness her placid instructions to him!

"Act as the goddess directs"; that was simple enough. But for the rest of it—

How am I to know what is best to do? Not for the first time, Rahbarin wished that his aunt would not place such faith in him. Someday he knew he must disappoint her, and that would be hard to bear. But if the queen wished him to guard Sheba in her absence, he would obey.

And he would try to have faith in her mission—hard though it was to believe that such a journey was the goddess's wish, and not the woman's. But if the queen did not hear the goddess truly, then what hope was there for her, or for Sheba?

Goddess-sent or no, I pray she finds a new queen on this quest. For if she does not— Without an undoubted heir, Sheba would succumb to the same disease that ravaged so many surrounding lands. *War.* War setting family against family, brother against sister. In such conflicts, there were no victors.

To avoid that fate, the queen would fight any battle she must. And if he could do nothing more to aid her, he could at least follow her orders to the best of his ability.

As he stood before the image of the goddess, Rahbarin opened his heart to Ilat and prayed that he would rule well in his aunt's absence—and that the queen's prayers would be granted.

And failing that, Rahbarin prayed for peace, and for his aunt's safe return.

The men from the north stalked grimly through Ma'rib's streets, hard and cold. Rahbarin could not imagine them ever smiling, laughing, enjoying life's soft pleasures. Nor could he envision a land full of such men welcoming the Queen of Sheba warmly and with pleasure.

Let her go and return safely, he begged the silent image of Ilat. *Let her return unharmed to Sheba—with or without an heir.*

Hodaiah

"Another chest? Stow it aft, with the others—no, not there, fool! Do you want to unbalance the ship?" Swearing in half-a-dozen languages, Hodaiah, captain of King Solomon's merchant fleet, grabbed the confused porter's tunic and thrust him towards the right section of the deck.

I don't like this. I don't like it at all. Sailing was unchancy enough without adding a foreign queen and all her finery, her slaves and her servants and her endless treasure chests, to the cargo. But no one had consulted him; no, he was simply expected to provide accommodation for the woman and all her chattels and goods. No matter that the Tarshish ships were designed for slow, steady transport of bulky cargo, not the swift conveyance of royalty. The Queen of Sheba commanded, and even foreign captains must obey. Hodaiah spat, clearing his throat, and continued his vigilant supervision as the loading continued.

Chests of gold and cages of apes; bolts of fine cloth and jars of spices; if pirates spot us, we'll be slaughtered like wingless ducks. And then there are the women—

And such women! Flaunting themselves like harlots, striding about like men—Hodaiah had sailed from Tyre to Troezen, Knossos to Massilia, and never had he seen such women as dwelt in the land of Sheba.

"You there—take those bales of cloth to the other ship! No more on this one!" *Idiots, fit only to feed to the sharks.* Hodaiah turned to the flagship, *Jael*. Upon *Jael*'s deck, slaves were erecting a pavilion, a sanctuary for the Queen of Sheba and her handmaidens during the voyage north.

As if the sea cares she's a queen! If anything, the sea, always a harsh mistress, would be twice as jealous of a queen as of a common woman. It would be a chancy voyage, with women aboard, with the sea lying always ready to claim her rivals.

But master of ships or no, his opinion didn't count, not laid in the balance against a queen's whim. And what did it all boil down to but another woman for King Solomon—*as well send a honeycomb to a beehive!*

And here was the queen herself, riding down to the dock on a horse—a woman sitting upon a horse, whoever heard of such a thing? Beside her rode a warrior; an Amazon—*long years since I've seen one of them. She'll not like sailing; her kind doesn't favor water.* A gaggle of women followed, all aflutter in bright garments of cloth so fine the wind from the water pressed the fabric against their bodies close as a second skin.

There were some men as well—eunuchs, guards, grooms—but mostly there were women. Too many women.

At the foot of the gangplank, the Queen of Sheba dismounted, handing her horse's reins to the nearest sailor, who was so startled he took them. Followed by a slim pale hound, she walked up the planks to *Jael*'s deck.

"The Queen of the South greets you, Captain, and thanks you for your care and kindness." She caressed her hound's long silky ears. "The journey will go well."

"With luck," Hodaiah added hastily; it didn't do to let the sea think you scorned her power. "And with Yahweh's aid." Sailors lived and died on the lift of fortune's waves; Hodaiah clung to the old way of calling upon his god by name, that there might be no question whom he petitioned.

"Always with the favor of the gods." When the queen smiled, lines creased the skin at the corners of her eyes; in the bright sunlight, you could see she was not young.

But it didn't matter. Young or not, the Queen of Sheba's smile kindled a slow fire in a man's blood. Hodaiah hoped the queen's own blood ran cool, or the voyage up the Red Sea would be endless trouble.

"Almost everything's aboard," he said. "The pavilion's nearly ready for you and your women."

"I—and my women—thank you. Now we have only to load my servants and my courtiers, and my horses, and then we may begin our journey as soon as wind and tide are propitious."

Even as he agreed, Hodaiah's heart sank. *Asherah's eyes, I forgot about the damned horses!*

"Do not look so dismayed, Captain." Laughter rippled through the queen's voice as sunlight danced over waves. "All will go well, and our voyage will prosper. Can you doubt that the gods look with favor upon this enterprise?"

"I can doubt anything," Hodaiah said and strode down the gangplank to the dock, to find his quartermaster and begin the process of loading the queen's horses upon the ship that had been prepared for them.

Horses and hounds and harlots. When I turn this voyage into a tavern tale, no one will believe me. He only hoped that when the Tarshish fleet at last docked at the port of Ezion-geber, the city governor there would be put to even half the effort and expense Hodaiah himself had been.

And that King Solomon found the Queen of Sheba's visit worth its cost.

Nikaulis

So much water. Until now, the greatest expanse of water Nikaulis had ever seen had been the Goddess's Mirror, the lake that lay at the feet of the Shining Mountains. The Mirror was pure and cold as ice, a daughter of mountain streams. Nikaulis had grown to womanhood beside the Mirror, played games of the hunt and the quest upon its shores.

But the Mirror was a small thing; even a child standing upon the Mirror's edge could see the far shore across its smooth water. The sea was different.

The ship floated upon water as changeable and restless as clouds. Water rippled about the hull, flashed phoenix-bright as wavelets shifted and danced in the sun. To the east, Nikaulis could watch the land as the ship slid past, but to the west, water covered all the world, shimmered and glinted to the far horizon. She knew there was land beyond this sea; the kingdoms of Cush and Egypt. But staring out across the expanse of restless water, it was hard to believe.

"A pomegranate seed for your thoughts."

Almost startled—the water's constant slap against the wooden hull, the creaking of boards and rustle of canvas hid lesser sounds; she had not heard Khurrami approach—Nikaulis swiftly turned, her fingertips just touching her knife's hilt.

"Peace, Nikaulis," Khurrami said, "it is only I."

Nikaulis inhaled slowly. "I did not hear you, that is all." *I am too tight-drawn. I must ease myself, or I shall snap as hard as a dry bowstring.*

Khurrami moved closer, smiling, and put her hands upon the rail. "What do you think of the sea? Is not so vast a quantity of water a miracle? And salt too—I tried a mouthful, and the water truly is salt enough to poison one. I wonder how the fish survive it?"

"Doubtless they are accustomed to the salt."

"Perhaps they find it pleasant." Khurrami stared down into the lucid water. "So many fish, and so pretty; do you think the queen would like some for the palace fountains?"

"They would die there." Nikaulis watched a school of fish swirl past. Blue and red and yellow—an invisible signal sent the fish flying back the way they had come, dashing beneath the ship. Forward and back, side to side, a pattern as explicit as dance. . . .

"Perhaps." Khurrami leaned forward; a bead slipped from her braids and fell into the sea below. A dozen fish broke ranks, converging on the sinking bead. An instant's flurry, then the fish merged into the larger group once more. "Do you suppose they ate it?" Khurrami asked.

"Perhaps." Nikaulis glanced sidelong at Khurrami. The queen's hand-maiden was teasing another bead from her elaborate braids, plainly willing to lose a second bauble for the pleasure of teasing the hopeful fish. Khurrami freed the bright bead and tossed it overboard; again a small group of fish flashed toward it, tested the offering, abandoned it as inedible, vanished among their brethren. Then Khurrami said in a low, steady voice, "What think you of our queen's quest, Nikaulis?"

Is this a test? Everyone knew Khurrami was the queen's eyes and ears— *So even she must know her idle queries carry much weight.* And test or no, courtesy demanded an answer.

"It is not my place to think anything. It is my place—"

"To guard and to obey. Yes." Khurrami's fingers twined in the end of her long plait of beaded braids, fretting the prisoned hair free. She glanced sidelong at Nikaulis. "Nothing more than that, Queen's Guard?"

Something in Khurrami's tone—a subtle undertone of mockery, barely sensed—rasped harsh as salt on skin. "What more should there be? The Queen of the Morning commands we journey to a far land so she may face the King of Wisdom. We journey."

"Our Mother commands."

Khurrami's correction pricked light but sharp; Nikaulis countered with a query of her own. "And you, Queen's Lady? What do you think of this venture?"

"I?" Khurrami's painted eyelids swept down like glittering green wings, hiding her cat-pale eyes. "Oh, I think nothing—save the journey is long and the sea wide—and the men from the north coarse and strange. I wonder what their king is truly like; his servants are uncouth, unsubtle. Can their king be better?"

"Even if he is not, Ilat Herself has commanded our queen to seek him out."

"Yes."

"To ask his aid?" Nikaulis heard the question underlying her words, betraying the fears that troubled her dreams. *It is time to ask plainly.* Odd how speaking out could be the greatest fear of all. "My lady Khurrami—do you think this journey wise?"

To question her queen's command, her goddess's oracle— *Truly I am uneasy in my heart. Danger lies ahead. Am I the only one who foresees evil at journey's end?*

Apparently enchanted by the water dancing below, Khurrami did not move. At last she said, "Do you think it folly, that our queen should obey Ilat's will and court the King of Wisdom?"

"And when we enter the realm of this wise king? What then?"

Without looking up, Khurrami shrugged; sunlight rippled over her skin, supple as the water below her. "Why, then the queen will do as she must, and so will we." Then she glanced slantwise at Nikaulis. "Do you think I know the goddess's mind, or the queen's?"

"I think you know." Nikaulis stared into the crystal water. Fish flashed bright, fleeing a larger shape; danger lurking in the shadow of the ship. "And I think you will not tell."

Bilqis

Until she stood upon the ship's wooden deck and looked out upon the sea's glass-smooth surface, Bilqis had remained the queen, had refused to listen to her own longing heart. Always, always since she was ten years old, always she had obeyed the dictates of duty. Duty to blood, duty to land, duty to temple. Never had she wavered from that narrow pathway; never had she hesitated over a choice.

Duty, always duty. Such devotion had not come easily to her; she had been the youngest of three royal daughters, late-born, a true love-child, born to the man her mother had taken only for pleasure. Born when her two sisters were already women grown.

She had been the favored child, the indulged and pampered child. *The daughter my mother could claim as all her own.* The daughter who could choose her own way in life. The eldest for the throne and the second for the temple, and the youngest—the youngest for freedom.

Such indulgence had seemed safe enough; her mother's duty to land and to heaven had been done. Both her sisters had already chosen consorts, already begotten children for Sheba. Indeed, her eldest sister had already bestowed two girls upon the royal family. The ancient line of queen's blood assured, her mother had taken pure joy in her last-born daughter, rearing her with all the liberty any Sheban child might know. Chains bound her sisters, invisible bonds of tradition and honor—

"But you, my Bilqis—you will fly where the winds blow wild, swim where the sea swirls high. The Sun of our Days has promised you a bright life, a life that shines forever, shines like the Morning Star—"

But her mother had been wrong. Plague had swept over Sheba, death on silent wings. And when those dark wings lifted, her sisters and their children lay dead, and all that remained of the bloodline of the ancient queens was a ten-year-old girl. Between sunset and sunrise, death bequeathed Bilqis an unsought crown.

"You are my heir now." Her mother's words fell flat against her ears, like blows. *"You must learn new skills and put away old. And I—I must—"* Her mother

had not finished; her words faltered and she fell silent. But Bilqis knew life had forever altered. Wild winds could not carry one bound to earth by a crown's weight.

From that moment, she no longer ran free; duty lay before her, and she had accepted the burden. As had her mother; a queen with only one heir to offer the land placed the future at risk. So, despite her age, Bilqis's mother had devoted herself to conceiving another daughter—a hard task and one that, in the end, cost her life.

But she succeeded in providing a sister to Bilqis. Sahjahira. In duty and love, Bilqis had raised Sahjahira to womanhood, only to see her younger sister, in her turn, die in the attempt to grant Sheba a daughter.

My poor 'hira. She did her best—as did I. For as soon as permitted, Bilqis had chosen a consort and striven to create security for Sheba, daughters for the crown. Daughters she had conceived and borne—only to watch them die before they cut their first teeth. Only Ilat Herself knew what it had cost Bilqis to persevere, what deep unhealed scars marred her heart. But she endured and persisted, and at last she had borne a daughter who cut her teeth, and walked, and learned to say "Mother."

Allit. Oh, my dear child—

Allit, born of a full moon spent at the Temple, of a father never known. Goddess-child, golden and perfect; reared to follow proudly in the footsteps of all the queens before her. She, too, had enslaved herself willingly to her duty—

More willingly than I wished to let her. Fearful, Bilqis had been reluctant to permit her only daughter to take a consort, to risk herself in childbirth. But she had consented at last, forced to bow to necessity. *"For how will you ever have a granddaughter, Mother, if I never bear a daughter? You worry too much over me; trust Ilat, as I do."*

Allit had lived and died in that trust; Bilqis had sat beside her, holding her hand, as Allit's life bled away, and lied to ensure her daughter's faith never wavered.

"Don't cry, Mother. I've given Sheba a girl. I told you to trust our Lady Ilat." Allit's fingers squeezed hers, a pressure soft as a butterfly landing upon a flower. "Is she all right?"

Bilqis smiled at her daughter. "Yes." She bent and kissed Allit's cold forehead. "Your daughter is perfect, Allit. Perfect."

"I knew she would be. Baalit . . . my goddess-child. Sheba's queen, Mother. . . ."

Allit died never knowing her newborn daughter had gone before her into the night beyond the sunset. Bilqis prayed that Allit's shade would forgive her for the lie.

With Allit dead, only two remained who carried the royal blood of Sheba in their veins: Sahjahira's son, Rahbarin—and Bilqis herself.

We hold the future in trust, Rahbarin and I. We will not fail those who will come after. So Bilqis had vowed.

But now, as she stared out over the slow rise and swell of the pale green water, a weight seemed to lift from her heart. *As if the waves wash away my years, the sea-wind blows away my burdens.* For the first time in many years, she permitted herself to remember her dream as a girl: *To wander the wide world, seeking wisdom—*

But duty had bound her; she had set such girlish hopes aside, locked them deep within her heart as she had laid her toys within a wooden chest and closed the lid upon them. And now, at last, she had been bidden to unlock her heart and follow her long-buried desire.

So much water. So much sky. Stare at either—sea or sky—for long and the eyes dazzled, the mind shattered into a myriad jeweled infinities.

So much sky. So much water. So much temptation. But always she dragged herself back from the edge of the abyss; sea or sky enticed, promised sweet unending rest, in vain. *I cannot.* Whatever temptation lay before her, she must cleave to her covenant with her land and her people. *I am their mother, their queen. I cannot abandon them. I must give them their next queen; their future. Without a queen to come after me, what is Sheba? Nothing! Another kingdom of the weak, prey to those who watch with greedy eyes.*

For the Land Beyond the Morning, the Kingdom of Spices, was a prize beyond the riches of kings. Only strength kept that prize safe. Let but a single crack show in the wall that kept out the world, and Sheba's treasures would be ravaged by the fierce, the savage.

A hundred generations of queens have not held Sheba safe only to lose all through my weakness. No matter what I must do—

No matter what she must do to bring the next queen to Sheba's throne, she would do it.

I do not care what I must do; if I must walk barefoot to the world's end; if I must humble myself before King Solomon and all his court; if I must lie to my people and my gods. Whatever the test, that I will do.

She would pay the price for Sheba's future without flinching. She would live without love, without joy, without hope. She would pay with her life, if that were the sacrifice she must make. Only one thing was unthinkable, only one fate unendurable.

Failure.

PART TWO

• ◆ •

The World's Wisdom

Abishag

In Shunem, I grew from child to girl to woman. True to her laughing vow, my mother refused all men's offers, remained a modest widow. All her efforts centered upon raising me—raising me, although I did not know it then, to tread safely along a jeweled path.

She taught me what every girl learns, to spin and to weave, to sew and to bake. "How well your Abishag sets her stitches! You teach her well, Zilpah. She will make a good wife." My mother smiled modestly at such praises, murmured that I was a clever, biddable girl, and pretended not to understand hints that a son, a nephew, a cousin sought such a clever, biddable bride—and one so well-dowered, with no sisters to diminish my inheritance.

"You will not marry here in Shunem," my mother told me.

"How do you know that?" I never doubted her words, for everything my mother wished seemed to come to pass.

"Because I know my past, and so I see your future. And it does not lie here."

"Where, then?" I asked, and my mother only smiled, and said that I would learn that in the world's own time.

"Never seek to hasten the stars in their courses, Daughter. What is the chiefest virtue for a woman?"

"Patience," I said, mindful of her teaching.

"Be patient then. Now let us see what the cloth merchant has to show today."

Baalit Sings

When I was a child, nothing in my father's court seemed strange to me. For my father was Solomon the Wise, king of Israel and Judah, and kings are not bound by the laws that rule lesser men—or so my grandmothers taught me, each of the three in her own way.

I did not think it strange I had three grandmothers when other children owned only two, just as I did not think it strange I had so many stepmothers—for kings must marry widely and wisely. I saw the world through the shining veil of a much-indulged childhood until the day my father wed the Colchian princess. That marriage did more than seal another treaty; it set one too many weights in the scales my father fought to balance.

And it unbound the veil of childhood from my eyes. After that day I could no longer see and not understand. And after that day, I was no longer content to be only my father's pampered daughter. But what else I wished to be, even I did not yet know.

The Colchian princess was late; the royal women had waited half the morning in the gallery that overlooked the great throne room, and still King Solomon's newest bride had not arrived. Restless, I drew out a ball of linen thread and began to play at cat's-cradle with my handmaiden Nimrah. King David's City truly held the wide world within its walls, for Nimrah's family came from some land so far to the north that snow covered the land half the year. Her northern blood shone in her straight pale hair and her wide pale eyes; winter sunlight, winter ice.

All about me, my stepmothers waited, the queens in the front of the gallery and the concubines behind them. Each passed the slow time in her own fashion: some gossiped, some fidgeted with their hair or gems or gown. One or two played games, as did Nimrah and I. The Egyptian queen, Nefret, listened as her maidservant read softly to her from a scroll. Queen Naamah sat smooth-faced, refusing to disturb the flawless drape of her veil or the elegant coils of her hair. Queen Melasadne caressed one of her tiny white dogs, ignoring the affronted glares from those of my father's wives who followed the laws of our own god, for whom dogs were unclean beasts. Queen Makeda sat dark and still as deep night, her thoughts shielded behind her gilded lids. Lady Leeorenda sat serene, motionless save for her fingers, which gently stroked the blossoms she held; from time to time she moved one flower, trying its color against another. Lady Dvorah spun, making me wish I had brought my own spindle to occupy my restless hands.

Nimrah lifted the tangle of red silk from my fingers again; I looked down from the queens' gallery to where my father sat upon the Lion Throne. The court was full of men richly clad, but my father outshone them all. As befit a royal bridegroom, he wore scarlet and purple fringed with gold. The wide crown of Israel, gold set with flawless emeralds, circled his head. In his hands he held a lion-headed scepter, a gift from the Scythian king.

The high priest Zadok sat upon a stool beside my father's throne. Zadok had been high priest long before I was born; he was an old man now, and standing long was a hardship to him. It was a measure of my father's generous heart that he thought of Zadok's comfort, and permitted him to sit when he held court. All the rest must stand—the king's general and the king's guard, the ambassadors, the other priests, the courtiers and the princes. Even my brother Rehoboam, who was my father's heir, must stand before him. And even at this distance, I saw the scowl marring Rehoboam's face; the crown prince was bored and didn't care who knew it.

My eyes did not rest long on my brother; gazing down like a hunting falcon, I sought more enticing prey. Ah, there he was, leaning against one of the polished cedar pillars, half-shadowed by the sham forest my father had created to ring the great court. His hair twined down his back in long curls; a ringlet coiled over one shoulder, spiraled down his half-bare chest, ebony against honey. He wore a kilt of soft blue leather sewn with golden bees, and a gilded leather belt two handspans wide clasped his waist. Upon Amyntor of Caphtor, such old-fashioned garments seemed oddly dashing. In contrast, the nobles of my father's court appeared overburdened in their layers of rich cloth. And where they held scrolls, or tablets, or goblets of gold and silver, Amyntor held in his hand only a Damascus rose, red as blood.

I admired Amyntor, who came and went as pleased him. Who gave, always, the impression that life itself amused him. As other men waited, frowning, for the king's newest bride to arrive, Amyntor watched as if the king and all the court had been summoned only so that he might observe them. Yes, I admired his fearless laughter more than his handsome face— and I envied his freedom with an ache that sometimes made me wonder if I craved more from Amyntor than I wished to admit even to my mirror.

As I studied Amyntor, he looked up across the court at the queens' gallery, seemed to stare through the shielding latticework straight into my eyes. From so far away, I could not be sure, but it seemed that he winked at me. I know he smiled, and lifted the small crimson rose to his lips.

Although I knew Amyntor could not see me, heat pricked my cheeks; I turned my eyes away from him, back to my father's throne. I saw my father's fingers absently stroking the lion's head upon the scepter; my father, like my brother, grew impatient. For a moment, I wondered what he thought, as he awaited yet another wife. Then Nimrah slipped the web of red silk back upon my fingers, and in trying to keep the net smooth and taut, I forgot lesser matters.

What was one more queen to King Solomon—or to me—after all?

Solomon

All women begin to look alike to me. Solomon knew this was unjust, but by now he had greeted so many royal brides, accepted so many bejeweled concubines, that one pretty painted face blurred into the next. Trade and politics bred alliances both of words and of flesh. What surer sign of submission to King Solomon's power than the surrender to him of a woman of royal blood?

And so here I sit, waiting for yet another woman, when forty more important matters await the king's attention. But Solomon had sat waiting upon the Lion Throne to welcome each of the women given into his care; he could not cease the custom now without giving great offense. *Although this princess will look just like all the others, say the same words—* No. I must not think this way. I have many women, after all, and they have only one husband. This new wife, too, must be greeted with respect.

Though not with love. Love had belonged only to his first wife, the bride of his heart. He could not grant that love to another.

But respect—yes, each woman was entitled to respect.

And so King Solomon must wait in all his glory upon the Lion Throne, although the sun neared its zenith and there was no sign yet of the king's latest bride. The caravan from Colchis should have reached the city gates by now, that the procession might wind through Jerusalem's streets while the late autumn sun still shone bright. Now the new queen's arrival at King Solomon's court would be less than perfect—

"But it is not our fault, my lord king! Forty times did we warn them that they must break their camp early, to arrive at the appointed hour. But nothing would do for the Colchians but they take their own omens, and delay until the princess sacrificed to her outlandish gods. Now the flowers will be wilted and the onlookers impatient, and—"

Solomon held up his hand. "Enough, Ahishar; no one blames you. I least of all." The king smiled. "Now calm yourself. Patience is a virtue."

The palace steward bowed his head. "Yes, my lord king. Shall I go and tell the king's wives that there is no sign of the new queen as yet?"

Surely they have guessed that by now. Solomon glanced up at the queens' gallery that overlooked the great court. Shadowed gems flashed, gold shimmered; his wives, too, must have grown restless from the long delay. Solomon sighed, and nodded. "Go and tell them, but I charge you not to turn a delay into a disaster."

"As the king says." Ahishar bowed again and hastened off, stiff with indignation.

The steward Ahishar loathes disorder as the prophet Ahijah loathes sin. With the palace steward safely out of sight, Solomon permitted himself a rueful smile. Each time he took another royal bride, the same rituals were observed—yet poor Ahishar fretted over the ceremony of each of the king's marriages as if it were the first, as if no precedent existed to aid him in his task. *And as if one misstep would bring the sky down around us.*

Still smiling, Solomon rose to his feet and laid the lion scepter upon the throne. "As the bridal procession has not yet reached the city, I will return when I hear that it has passed through the Horse Gate."

Having escaped the throne room, Solomon chose to retreat to the rooftop above, hoping to find a moment's peace. He laid his hands upon the stones of the wall, stones smooth-fitted and sun-warmed beneath his skin. From the city below rose an ebb and flow of noise, a sound steady as ocean waves. *The sound of peace, of prosperity.* Jerusalem boasted two marketplaces, a modest one in the Old City and a bazaar larger than many villages by the Sheep Gate. Anything in the world could be procured in the King's Marketplace, from iron arrowheads to silvered rose petals.

Solomon gazed down at the bazaar, watched colors shift as men moved bales of cloth and baskets of fruit through the market, noted bright flashes as women walked through the crowds, seeking bargains. Then he lifted his eyes beyond the bazaar to the Street of Gods. Foreigners who lived and worked in Jerusalem desired to worship their own gods in their own fashion. Solomon had granted their petitions to build shrines and temples of their own—and had pulled the fangs from any opposition by requiring those shrines and temples to pay a tithe to Lord Yahweh's Temple and priests.

And so everyone prospers and is pleased enough to keep the peace. Solomon smiled wryly. Almost everyone. Alas, nothing pleased the prophet Ahijah.

Not even the Lord's great Temple pleases him. Certainly I do not, nor any of my laws.

He stared across the city to the Temple. The holy building crowned the new city; so much gold had gone into its making that the Lord's House burned like a second sun in the noon light. *So great a Temple*— Yet sometimes Solomon wondered if the Temple truly had been worth its endless cost.

But it was too late now to draw back. In truth, it had been too late long before the first stone had been laid in the Temple's deep walls. For the Temple was more than a building raised to the glory of Israel's god.

The Temple was a trap; a trap so subtle and so burnished with gold and perfumed with spices that Solomon only now realized just how strong were its chains, how heavy its yoke.

A trap my father eluded. And yet they call me *Solomon the Wise!*

Still, he had earned that epithet honestly enough. *I asked the Lord for wisdom to rule well, to judge justly and fairly. I never thought to ask for freedom as well.*

But despite his efforts to bring peace and justice to the kingdom, men grumbled. Too many taxes, too many building projects, too large an army . . .

Although how they think the roads may be kept safe and the marketplace profitable without taxes and soldiers, I do not know. Solomon stared again over the palace rooftops to the great Temple. The building crowned Jerusalem, its glory a shining beacon to the Lord's people. The Temple had taken seven years to complete, and the treasury still paid Hiram of Tyre for the cedar and purple and gold-work that had created a fit house for the Ark of the Covenant, symbol of their god's presence among them.

But all most men see is that the Temple was finished long since, they do not understand that it must be paid for still. That it must be paid for forever. Just as the king's court, and the king's guard, and the king's army must be paid for. And the Temple must be supplied with incense and spices and oil; the priesthood tending the Temple must be fed and clothed and housed. And—

"Here now, it is not fit the great King Solomon look so troubled—and on such a day, too!"

Solomon smiled and turned. "And what is so special about this day that I should be mindful of it, Amyntor?"

The Caphtoran's fanciful garb glittered in the sunlight; the crimson rose tucked behind his ear glowed like dark fire. Amyntor flourished the silver bowl he carried; golden fruit gleamed against the pale metal. "Why, it's the king's wedding day."

"Again," Solomon pointed out.

"Again. How many wives is it now? The last harpers' tale I heard credited you with a hundred, each more beautiful than the last!"

"Too much credit. Why do men invent such wild tales?"

"Oh, they are bored, or envious, or simply born liars." Amyntor laughed, an easy, unfettered sound that rang through the cool air. "Do you even recall how many women you possess, King Solomon?"

"King Solomon numbers forty wives. And can name not only his wives, but his sons." Solomon paused, added, "I possess none of them."

"King Solomon is notoriously wise." Amyntor leaned easily against the parapet, balancing the silver bowl upon the smooth stones. "Which is doubtless why he secludes himself upon his rooftop—watching for his latest queen—and eluding the ubiquitous Ahishar. That man does fuss so!"

Solomon smiled. "Yes, I came up for that, and for peace in which to think."

"Oho, the king is thinking again. What wisdom have you caught in your nets this time?"

Solomon looked at the farther hilltop, at the great Temple glowing under the sun's hot light. "That peace and justice are not free. I wish I could make my people understand that."

"Well, you can't. I doubt even *your* god—fierce as he is—could make men understand anything so unpleasant as the truth. Don't waste time wishing for what can never be." Smiling, Amyntor offered Solomon a gilded fig. "Oh, take it, my lord. Kings should know what gold tastes like."

"As they should know what gold costs." Solomon bit into the gleaming fruit; the thin coating of gold melted away like mist upon his tongue. It left no taste at all in his mouth.

"And what does gold cost? A marriage with Colchis?" Amyntor tossed one of the gilded figs into the air, caught it neatly. "Colchis for gold, Troy for horses, Egypt for barley and beer. All the world's wealth weds Israel now."

Solomon did not answer; instead he pointed towards a slow river of bright color flowing up the Kidron Valley road to the Horse Gate. "My new bride approaches. Amyntor, will you carry word to the palace steward? Great king that I am, I cannot endure his fretting."

"With pleasure—and then I shall obtain the first look at your new queen." With a graceful flourish, Amyntor presented Solomon with the silver bowl and strode off to the stairway, leaving Solomon staring down at half-a-dozen gilded figs, and a puzzled bee that had landed upon the sweet shining fruit.

Gently, Solomon set the bowl down, leaving the bee to discover for itself that the fruit was no more than a bright snare. "I thank you, Amyntor, for your good wishes," he said softly. Another marriage, another wife. *I do not need another wife; I have too many already. But the kingdom needs another alliance, and so—*

And so he would marry to seal yet another treaty, to provide another market, to gain another treasure. For as king, he must care for his people, and think for them, too— *So they need not!* Solomon smiled ruefully, knowing a fleeting desire to share the tart jest. But despite a palace full of people, a harem full of wives, there was no longer anyone with whom he could speak with total freedom. Even Amyntor could not truly understand what bound a king.

No one lives with whom I may share my mind and my heart.

That was true loneliness. Solomon sorely missed the bond that had linked him and his foster mother, Queen Michal, the woman who had nurtured his mind, just as his own mother, Bathsheba, had nurtured his heart. He had been able to speak of anything to Queen Michal and be understood.

And even more keenly, he longed for Abishag. *Abishag, my dove; my heart, my bright jewel among women. . . .* Although twice seven years had passed since her death, the pain of her loss still bit sharp. Sweet Abishag, clever Abishag, dearest comfort who knew always what to say or do, aiding him in his quest for the right path to tread. . . .

But Abishag had died bringing their only child into the world. Their daughter, Baalit. Baalit, who was all a father could desire: affectionate, dutiful, obedient.

And fast growing into a woman, a woman for whom he must find a husband. *But not yet! She is a child still. Her marriage can wait.*

Even as the thought comforted him, Solomon knew he deceived himself. His daughter neared her fourteenth summer; it was time to settle her future. Past time, were he honest. Baalit should have been betrothed two years ago. *But I cannot bear to lose her.* She was all that was left to him of Abishag, beloved wife of his youth.

Nevertheless, the sacrifice must be made, for the girl's own good. *She is entitled to rule in her own house, to have a husband and children. Yes. I will find her a good man here in Jerusalem.* Solomon refused to think of marrying her to a king in a far country. *Baalit will not be used as a playing-piece in the game of politics.* His daughter would wed here, live here, under his eye.

Yes. I will seek a husband for her. Soon.

But not today. Tomorrow waited, endlessly patient; Solomon knew it would win, in the end. But for today, Abishag's daughter remained his most precious treasure.

Among so many contentious sons, so many scheming wives, his daughter's pure affection shone like a jewel in the mud. Baalit was clever, intrepid, and perceptive.

If only she had been born a boy! What a king she would have made.

But no good would come of such thoughts; the world did not mold itself to suit men—even kings. *Rehoboam is my eldest son, and he will be king after me. And Baalit—*

King's daughter or no, Baalit was still only a girl. Few futures lay open to her. In the end, Baalit would live the life her father chose for her.

It was a father's duty to choose wisely. And a daughter's to obey.

And truly, there is peace in my household; have I not labored mightily to ensure that? Having watched as his father played one son, one wife, one priest, against another; as he kept each uncertain of the king's true intent, Solomon gave to each son with an even hand, treated each wife with equal favor. And he honored the priests without preference.

Yes, I treat all men and women justly and with due honor. Peace will reign under my roof, peace within the walls of David's City, just as there is peace wherever my word commands. So Solomon reassured himself.

Justice, and peace; the king's truth, acknowledged by all men. Why, then, did his blood flow as cold as if he lied?

Ahishar

Despite the king's calm words, Ahishar had walked swiftly along the corridor until he could cross through the gateway to the women's passageways to throne room and court. Once past that gateway, he had nearly run to bring the king's wives the king's message. All very well for King Solomon to say, "No need for haste"—

"For he is king, after all, and need not confront a gaggle of women as proud as peacocks and fierce as geese," as Ahishar pointed out to Elihoreph, when he had returned to the great court to find that the king had tired of waiting and vanished. "And now the king has gone, and when the Colchian princess *does* arrive—whenever that may be—I will have to find *him*."

The chief scribe shook his head and sighed. "King or no, I should have been informed where he goes; how am I to record the wedding properly if I am told nothing?"

"I will tell you as soon as I myself know, Elihoreph." Almost Ahishar wished he had not allowed himself to confide in Elihoreph, for the chief scribe collected slights as other men did silver. *Still, Elihoreph means well, and he is one of the few who truly understands how difficult my tasks can be.*

"Well, I hope the new princess won't be troublesome. Do you know the last one brought not one scrap of a record of her possessions? My scribes were expected to tally all her dowry goods, and her slaves gazed at them during the entire task as if they were robbers. I tell you, Ahishar, sometimes I wonder if it's worth being a king's man at all. Don't you?"

"Of course not; I only wish King Solomon would take greater care, sometimes. He is too heedless of his rank."

"Yes, and of ours." Elihoreph fingered the ivory tablet that hung upon a scarlet cord about his neck, token of his royal office. "Well, he was the youngest son, after all. It's not as if he were born to be king."

"True, true. Still, King Solomon is wise and just."

"Oh, yes, yes, he is just—no one knows that better than I, who record his deeds," Elihoreph added, and Ahishar nodded agreement, for under King Solomon's tolerant, prudent reign, the kingdom basked in a golden calm. A man might tend his vineyard, herd his flocks, without fear. A merchant need not worry as he traveled, for the king's roads were safe from robbers.

In the span of three lifetimes, the land of Israel and Judah had been altered beyond imagining, grown from an alliance of brawling tribes to a kingdom—and an empire. Within the lifetime of three kings.

Saul. David. And now Solomon.

Few mentioned King Saul now, for his achievements were shadowed by madness, and overshadowed by his successor's blazing glory. King David's legacy was empire, an empire King Solomon strengthened with alliance and trade, with a strong army and with judicious marriages. All roads led to Jerusalem the Golden, crossroads of the world.

"Yes, I say King Solomon is just and wise," Elihoreph announced, as if any might doubt either the king's virtues or Elihoreph's loyalty.

"Wise and just." Ahishar stared across the sunlit court at the Lion Throne and the scepter that lay upon the seat, waiting for the king's return. *Peace, and justice, and prosperity—*

"Still," Elihoreph began, "sometimes I wonder—"

"Sometimes I wonder what it was like to serve Great David," Ahishar said. "It must have been glorious."

Ahijah

Another royal harlot. From his post before the Horse Gate, the prophet Ahijah watched the slow approach of King Solomon's newest bride. The procession advanced in a clamor of brass timbrels shaken by black-robed attendants— priests of whatever foreign abomination the Colchian princess groveled before. False gods, false women, defiling Yahweh's city—

And the king does nothing. No, worse; the king greeted these abominations with smiles, with open arms.

Now the Colchian's escort passed through the great gate, set unclean feet upon the stones of Jerusalem. Men clad in flowing fringed gowns, their soft faces painted like a harlot's; women garbed in crimson leather trousers laced tight about their thighs—those creatures alone were enough to set fiery teeth gnawing below Ahijah's heart, clear sign of Yahweh's anger. But there was more, and worse. There was the Colchian herself, sitting brazen in an ebony cart inlaid with silver moons and serpents. A cart drawn by dogs.

Abomination upon abomination. Ahijah pressed his fist against the fire searing his chest. Dogs—no wonder fangs seemed to gnaw him from within. Black beasts as large as donkeys, harnessed in scarlet leather and led by small boys clad in collars hung with silver bells—*unclean, unfit to set foot within Yahweh's city.*

Goaded by the fire within, Ahijah stepped from the shadow of the Horse Gate into the path of the black dogs. He held up his staff before them; the children leading the animals halted and looked back to their mistress. Ahijah raised his gaze to the royal bride. Above a silver veil, eyes dark as sloes and flat as a serpent's stared back.

"Come no farther, for you offend Yahweh, affront the living god with your harlotries and unclean beasts." Ahijah gained strength as he spoke and knew he had read the signs rightly. "Go, our king does not need your vile wealth."

The Colchian princess said nothing, and Ahijah knew she did not understand. *Of course she does not; a foreign witch speaking no known tongue! Folly upon folly, King Solomon!* Ahijah turned to the onlookers, those men and women who had gathered beside the road to watch King Solomon's newest bride arrive.

"Are you lost to shame? Will you let such a creature enter King David's City?" Ahijah demanded. No one moved, or spoke; many slid their eyes away, as if hoping the prophet would not notice them. And before Ahijah could berate them further, a man clad in the purple and gold of King Solomon's high officials strode past the dogs to stand before Ahijah.

"Greetings, Prophet. The Great Lady Dacxuri thanks you for your welcome." The interpreter smiled broadly and bowed, continuing, "Now I beg you, in the king's name, to stand aside."

"And I order you, in Yahweh's name, to turn back. Turn back before it is too late."

"We are already late," said the interpreter. "King Solomon is waiting."

As Ahijah gazed into the Colchian's night-cold eyes, a new pain speared hot behind his eyes. The princess seemed to shimmer before him, her face ringed with pulsing light, light that burned and pierced—

Hands pressed to his face, Ahijah stumbled back, shielding his blinded eyes. By the time he could see again, the foreign witch and her corrupt attendants had entered into Jerusalem, continued on their way to King Solomon's palace. Behind them, small clay figures littered the street, luck-idols tossed by the Colchian's servants. As Ahijah watched, men and women scooped up the idols, laughing.

Suddenly weary, as if he had grown old between one breath and the next, Ahijah leaned upon his staff. *If no one else has eyes to see, I have.* He bent and caught up one of the little idols, stared at a clay dog's head, its pointed snout painted black and red. Slowly, Ahijah closed his fingers over the blasphemous thing.

I see, and I will make others see as well. Somehow, I will stop these abominations. I swear it upon the Law. So vowing, Ahijah stood upright and began to walk slowly, as if he were an old man, along the broad high road that led up the hill to the king's palace.

King or no, he is only a man in the eyes of Yahweh. So Ahijah reminded himself for the fortieth time as he waited in the great courtyard for King Solomon to pass by. What, after all, was a king but a man whom others chose to obey? *And when men weary of obedience to one who is no better than they, then they see the error of their ways and return to obedience to Yahweh's Laws.*

And to Yahweh's prophet, a small voice hissed. *No. No, I will not listen. I, too, am only a man.*

But a man who heard Yahweh's voice, who carried Yahweh's word. That, too, was truth—which was why the silent lure possessed such power. But Ahijah refused to yield to that seductive trap. *I am no better than any other. I am Yahweh's messenger, that is all.*

He clung to that thought as to a lifeline, a chain strong enough to bind him to his endless task. For Ahijah had that day stared into Abomination's black eyes, stood firm against alien seductions. *Now I will stand firm against King Solomon. I must show him how gravely he has offended, tell him that Yahweh orders me to chastise him.*

Just as the prophet Samuel had chastised King Saul, and the prophet Nathan rebuked King David. *So will the prophet Ahijah reproach King Solomon, turn him back to the path set before our feet by our own god. If he will listen, and heed. If he will not—*

If King Solomon would not heed, then what? Surely if Yahweh's favor were withdrawn, King Solomon's proud dreams would fade like mist upon sunrise. *For I am right and the king and the priests wrong. Why will they not see? O Yahweh, how have I failed that I cannot make them see the pit they dig before their own feet?* Pain lanced behind his left eye, a hot spear of burning light. A warning, a sign that Yahweh's patience was not limitless. *I will make this king see your will, Lord. I must—*

His silent struggle so absorbed him that, when the king strolled through the rows of cedar columns that edged the public courtyard, Ahijah did not notice until the easy laughter of the king's companion beat upon his ears. Amyntor of Caphtor, one of the many foreigners infesting the palace like locusts devouring standing grain. Forcing himself to ignore the fire behind his eye, the keen fangs gnawing within his stomach, Ahijah drew a deep breath and slammed the tip of his staff against the smooth stone beneath his feet.

"Solomon! Listen and heed!"

The king stopped, and turned; his face revealed nothing save smooth courtesy. "Welcome, Ahijah. You look weary, come and rest easy as we talk."

Ah, the king himself had granted an opening; Ahijah seized upon it. "How can Yahweh's prophet rest easy when abominations defile Yahweh's land? When vice profanes His people?"

Solomon's expression did not alter, but even a dozen strides away, Ahijah could sense the king's withdrawal, his unwillingness to heed the truth. And beside the king, the Caphtoran regarded Ahijah with amused contempt, as a man looks upon the antics of a foolish child.

The king came forward, hand outstretched. "This is neither the time nor the place for such words. Come and we will speak quietly together."

"What better time? What better place? I speak as Yahweh commands, and Yahweh's words are not to be whispered in corners but shouted from the housetops."

Solomon smiled; neither smile nor welcome reached the king's eyes. "Very well, Ahijah; speak as you will. What have you to tell me?"

Perhaps today the king would listen—truly listen. *I must try.* The prophet stood straight as his wooden staff. One hand clutched the smooth wood, the other clenched into a fist. "I have come to warn you that you go too far, O King. Do not mock, but heed Yahweh's words before it is too late."

"I do not mock," Solomon said. "I try to heed the Lord's words, Ahijah."

"Yet you wed strange women, consort with them and with their gods. You court Yahweh's wrath—and your crown will not shield you." Ahijah opened his fist and flung what he had held at Solomon's feet. A dog's head gazed up at the king with sightless clay eyes.

"That is what your latest bride brings as dowry, O King! Idols and abominations. Remember Yahweh's first and greatest commandment!"

"I do," the king said. "That commandment is that we shall have no other gods before Him. That commandment I keep, Ahijah; these others all take lesser precedence than the Lord. I myself worship only our own god."

"Can you still say that truly, King Solomon, who dare not even speak Yahweh's name? Does not your heart turn to your foreign women? And do they not turn your eyes to their foreign gods, their idols of wood and stone?"

"Answer me a question, Ahijah." King Solomon spoke in the soft voice the king used to soothe, to disarm. To deceive. "Do the idols in my wives' temples possess any power? Are they truly gods?"

"Of course they are not! Can wood and stone possess power?"

"And if such idols are mere images, with no more power than my daughter's doll, then what harm can it do merely to look upon them?"

"It is a sin against Yahweh! They must be smashed, smashed and burned to ash, their temples destroyed. All must be banned from this land, or Yahweh's anger will destroy you. The king's house—this so-called palace—must be cleansed of idolatry and abominations! Unclean beasts walk its halls, its walls reek of wickedness and unholy practice! Beware, O King, lest your feet be set upon the road to disaster!"

"I thank you for your warning, Ahijah. Truly I shall endeavor to do what is right."

"Then send the Colchian witch away, and her corruption with her. Put away all the idolaters you have taken to wife. Cleanse your palace of foreigners, cleanse King David's City of abominations. Purge our land of temples and groves to false gods and falser goddesses. Only then will Yahweh's will be done."

"I hear your words, Ahijah, and I thank you for your care of our people. But—"

"But you will not yield to Yahweh's will." Scorn edged Ahijah's words; anger burned beneath his heart. "You flout our god's commandments. You consort with strange women and evil men. Today all Israel and Judah watched false gods and their wanton priests enter the gates of King David's City. You have turned Yahweh's people into idolaters and harlots."

The prophet paused to draw breath; the king seized the moment's grace. "Is that all, Ahijah? For I have many calls upon my time today—including worshipping at our Lord's great Temple. The Temple that *I* built for our god and His glory."

"His glory? Or your own?" Ahijah stared into the king's cool eyes and found only rejection there. "I see the king will not listen." Ahijah's words fell into the silence like cold stones. "Remember, Solomon, son of David—what Yahweh has chosen, He can repudiate. You are but a man. Heed and obey before it is too late."

"I will consider your words, Prophet. And I will pray for guidance, as you have asked I do."

"And you will not put away even one of your sins."

"I will do as I have sworn, Ahijah."

"And so will I." The prophet's eyes gleamed bright with scorn. "Go, then—go to your foreign bride, submit to yet another strange woman. But remember that even a king is not above Yahweh's Law."

Ahijah did not give Solomon a chance to answer; he turned his back on the king and walked away. Behind him, he heard Amyntor of Caphtor ask, "Why do you endure that unkempt fellow, my lord king? Only say the word and half-a-dozen of us would happily—"

"No! He is a prophet, not to be touched in anger."

"—bathe him for you," Amyntor finished smoothly.

And as Ahijah strode away, he heard King Solomon laugh.

Anger burned righteous through Ahijah's bones, carried him through shadows and light until he reached the great gate of Solomon's palace. There strength abandoned him; suddenly weak, Ahijah sat upon the ground beneath an olive tree and pressed a fist to the searing pain that flared below his heart. That King Solomon refused to heed him was bad enough—but that he should laugh—

He laughed at me. Laughed at me, the voice of Yahweh. Once he would not have dared. Once prophets were great men in the land; once prophets were heeded. Feared. But now—

Now my words go unheeded and sinful men mock Yahweh's will. Not for the first time, Ahijah wished he had been born in the long-ago days when the great prophet Samuel had reigned as the undisputed voice of the Lord of Hosts. Samuel had made kings, and broken them, too.

But somehow, in the years that stretched between Samuel's day and Ahijah's, such power had slipped from the grasp of prophets. Today it was kings and high priests who counted, rich, slothful men who followed their own wishes and called that path straight and godly.

Ahijah knew better. *The path of riches is the path of fools and of sinners.* Abruptly he rose and strode out of the palace gate, down the hill to the great market street. His face was stern; his eyes darted from side to side, weighing each corruption, each iniquity he passed.

Men consorting with idolaters, bargaining away their honor and flouting Yahweh's Laws. Women whose painted faces proclaimed their wickedness.

And as if that were not bad enough, there were the temples. *Houses of abomination.* Jerusalem was infested with temples to dozens of foreign gods; alien idols worshipped by the strangers who came in their hordes now that the city Yahweh had given into King David's hand cared more for trade than for the god they now called Lord, claiming his name too sacred to utter.

Hypocrites. They will not utter His name because they fear to call upon Him and draw down His wrath. Yahweh's people must see the pit yawning before them, must draw back before they fall to utter ruin.

That was Ahijah's deepest fear, an endless ache in his bones. *They look on desolation of spirit and call it good fortune. They embrace evil and call it virtue. And Yahweh will smite them for it.* And if he could not lead Yahweh's people back to their harsh covenant with their god, their destruction would be on his head, as well as on theirs.

If he failed, the kingdom would shatter; Yahweh would not endure a rebellious people. *If I fail, my people destroy themselves. If I fail—*

He halted before the porch of a building whose crimson pillars proclaimed it the House of Atargatis. A woman stood between the pillars; her mouth was stained red and her eyelids green. A three-pronged trident was painted in blue upon her forehead. She smiled and beckoned to Ahijah. "You seem troubled, friend. Come within and let Laughing Atargatis ease your distress."

Cold revulsion slashed him; although every instinct urged him to shrink away from the priestess, vessel of sin, Ahijah forced himself to stand his ground. *I am Yahweh's prophet,* he reminded himself. *I fear no one.* Letting outrage speak for him, Ahijah glared at the painted woman. *I am strong. You will not beguile me away from the path of righteousness, though your lips drip honey and wine!*

After a moment, his temptress shrugged and abandoned her attempt to entice him. But what Ahijah had refused another man eagerly accepted as the prophet strode on. Ahijah sighed inwardly. Only when Jerusalem was burned clean of such abominations would Yahweh's people be safe.

Only then— He strove not to wince as the pain he carried on behalf of

Israel bit deep. He permitted himself to press his hand below his heart, where the burning fangs of his own guilt gnawed hottest. *Yes, Lord. I understand. I must try harder. I must not fail.*

He dared not. Unseeing, Ahijah walked through the crowded streets of Jerusalem. *If the king will not act, then the Temple must. Yes. I will speak with Zadok.*

And if the high priest refused to listen, as was all too likely—

Then I must find another weapon to serve Yahweh's will. Once a prophet had played kingmaker—and kingbreaker. If necessary—if Yahweh willed—perhaps a prophet could once again bring an ungodly king down, his wickedness dust blown on the wind.

A wicked king and his strange idolatrous women—yes, I will bring them down. Down into dust. Solomon and his women both.

Solomon

"Poor Ahijah." Solomon watched the prophet stride off; noted the stiff fury of Ahijah's movements. "He does not see that times change, customs change. That our kingdom and its people must allow the wind to blow new customs through our land. I feel sorry for him."

"O King, you feel sorry for everyone," Amyntor said. "A piece of advice, my lord: don't. Most of them aren't worth it, and the rest revel in misery."

"Surely you are too harsh."

"Surely I am not. Do you not know women who are never happier than when complaining?"

Solomon stared at Amyntor, kindness quarreling with truth; as always, Solomon tried to blend the two. "I try to ensure that my wives have nothing to complain of. That they are happy." But they weren't, and in his heart Solomon acknowledged this without understanding how he might mend matters. *Ah, Abishag, if only you were here to guide them—* Surely his women had been happy once? *Or did I close my eyes to all but my own joys?*

"You brood again, O King."

"Upon my faults."

Amyntor laid his hand on Solomon's shoulder. "My friend, you have the fewest faults of any man I know. You paint shadows where there is only sunlight."

"You are too kind."

"I am too selfish," Amyntor said. "I prefer my companions smiling and my pleasures unmixed—and my women pleased. And so do you—and that's part of your trouble, my lord king."

"What is?"

"You have too many wives and not enough women."

"I marry as I must. Now come and marvel at the gold and the horses Colchis has sent—in them you will see reason enough for this marriage."

"It's to be hoped they haven't sent dogs instead. What an entrance!"

"Yes," Solomon said. "I admit I had not expected that. I suppose I must smooth over the matter with the prophet—"

"Why? You are king, not he. Forget him," said Amyntor. "And if he troubles you—why, there are remedies for that."

"No." The word fell flat and heavy between them. "No," Solomon repeated, his tone lighter, "that is not how I rule."

"It's how all kings rule, in the end," Amyntor said, laughing. "What's an army for, after all?"

Smiling, Solomon shook his head. Amyntor's lighthearted comments amused him—but in the end, Amyntor could not understand the burden under which a ruler labored. *And that is as it should be. But it would be pleasant once again to talk with someone who truly understands.*

As Amyntor laughed, Solomon gazed at the little idol that lay broken at his feet where Ahijah had thrown it. At last he bent down and grasped the pieces; the edges rasped his skin, rough as a cat's tongue. Yet another foreign bride, yet another alien god.

Both necessary, vital to the smooth running of the kingdom, to the wealth of the lands and peoples ruled from King David's City. Solomon weighed the shattered idol in his hand. A small thing; little enough to grant to keep his wives happy, to keep alliances strong.

My people are prosperous. My priests are honored. My wives are content. What more can they ask of me than that?

"Behold, O King—your devoted steward Ahishar approaches, doubtless with news of your eager bride." Amyntor's lighthearted speech forced Solomon to banish shadowed thought—and the palace steward's announcement that the Great Lady Dacxuri at this very moment was being borne by her slaves through the palace gate forced him to return to the throne room, to begin a ritual he knew so well that he need pay no attention to it at all.

Zadok

Yet another wife—ah, well, kings are not as other men. With this comforting thought, the high priest Zadok smiled as the king greeted the Colchian princess. As always, King Solomon welcomed a new bride with ease and grace; never, by word or gesture, did the king betray any emotion save pleasure at her arrival. The Colchian was no exception. King Solomon even managed to smile upon her escort, never blinking at the outlandish appearance of the men, the blatant display of the women. Zadok admired the king's composure; Zadok found pleasing one wife onerous enough. To please forty—*and with new wives arriving with each new treaty*—yes, King Solomon must be wiser than all other men, to keep that peace!

Zadok had witnessed King Solomon's weddings to a dozen brides; like the king, the high priest knew the ritual that followed the formal greetings so well he could chant the words by rote. The king had already wed the foreign princess by proxy before she had left the protection of her father's walls, and it now was necessary only that King Solomon's court witness the confirmation of those vows.

Once the last words of the wedding ceremony had been spoken, the king gave his new bride into the charge of the chief steward of the harem. When the Colchian princess had been taken away to the women's palace, Solomon came over to Zadok.

"That was well done," Zadok said, and Solomon smiled and shook his head.

"That was hard done; the lady speaks not one word of any language I know. And I must warn you now, High Priest—she arrived in a cart drawn by black dogs." Solomon always knew everything that transpired in Jerusalem long before it was common knowledge; Zadok supposed he himself would hear about the Colchian dogs when he went home for dinner.

"Where are the dogs now?" the high priest asked.

"I ordered them locked in the stables until I discover whether they are the Lady Dacxuri's dearest pets or merely beasts of burden."

Zadok frowned. Dogs were unclean beasts, and— "Black dogs are unlucky."

"Twice unlucky; they are sacred to the Dark Goddess."

"Give them to the Dark Goddess, then." That seemed an easy enough way to dispose of the creatures.

"An excellent idea, Zadok." Solomon smiled again. "I am sure that will please everyone."

"As the king says." Zadok had never yet had reason to doubt any of Solomon's statements; truly the king was both wise and just, a very restful combination. And now that he was old and full of years, Zadok valued peace and comfort. "My blessings upon you both."

"Upon us all," King Solomon said, and glanced up at the queens' gallery. All the king's richly clad and brightly jeweled women had vanished when the Colchian was led away, hastened off to the women's palace to welcome the latest arrival.

"My blessings upon you all." Zadok smiled and raised his hands in benediction. "Upon Solomon the Wise and upon all his household, peace."

Of course there would be peace under the king's roof. Solomon was wise and just, fair and fond equally. To Zadok's uncritical eyes, this king's household ran smoothly as rain down a wall. *Not as things went in King David's day!* King Solomon's reign might be duller than his father's had been—but it was infinitely more comfortable.

Abishag

Everything my mother said or did served as a lesson to me; by the time I was twelve I could with equal skill choose a good pomegranate or a good pearl, bake soft bread and braid my hair into a triple loop without a maid's assistance, sew a smooth seam and paint my eyelids with sleek lines of malachite and kohl. Some of these skills I was permitted to display: the shawl I wove myself, the cakes I baked, the border I embroidered.

Other crafts I learned to keep veiled. How to move my body as soft and supple as water, to perfume my skin with roses and with spices, to laugh low and sweetly, to love my own body and to cherish it as a precious jewel—these lessons were secrets my mother shared with me. I was proud to own her love and trust, and swore never to betray them, to which fervid vow my mother responded.

"Never say never, Abishag. You are strong, Daughter, but life is stronger, and no woman knows what awaits her on its road." Then she smiled, and kissed me upon the forehead.

My mother was right; I never guessed that her secret lessons held any purpose save creating beauty. Certainly I never dreamed that her teachings would provide me with weapons— weapons in a battle I never dreamed I must fight.

For what awaited me upon my road was a dying king, and a rising one, and a queen who held both within her cool hands.

Baalit Sings

I will not pretend I was better than any other woman in my father's palace; I, too, stared wide-eyed at the Colchian's outlandish attendants. Men garbed as women and women garbed as men—

"And dogs; huge black dogs!" That news had been carried to the queens' gallery by at least a dozen maidservants before the Colchian princess set foot within the upper city. Queens without spies are queens without power. "They say she feeds them upon newborn babes!"

Nor will I claim I scoffed at this—although I can swear I wondered how enough babes could be born daily to make this possible. To my shame, I admit I suggested to Nimrah, who also doubted Colchis could supply enough newborn infants to sate the black dogs' appetites, that perhaps the Colchian fed them upon other meats as well.

"And feeds them babies when they can get them." I thought this a possibility. Nimrah looked doubtful and pointed out that the Lady Melasadne's dogs ate nothing but minced quail and crumbled honey-cakes.

"The Lady Melasadne's dogs are smaller than the Lady Nefret's Egyptian cats! These Colchian dogs are the size of horses."

"Then perhaps they eat grass and grain," Nimrah said, and we both giggled and ran after the queens and concubines and maidservants, back to the women's palace. Like all the others, we wished to see the Colchian bride—and her enormous dogs.

With a new royal wife to welcome, the queens' palace had seemed to hum like a beehive; each queen, each concubine, labored over her appearance as if she were herself the bride. Now they gathered in the Court of Queens to greet the princess from Colchis. And for once, each woman there was glad of my presence.

For my father had no favorite among his women; not since my mother died had a woman owned his heart. Quarrels over precedence were common. The two most important among my father's women were Naamah and Nefret. Queen Naamah was mother of the king's eldest son—but Queen Nefret was Pharaoh's Daughter.

So my status as my father's only daughter smoothed sweet oil over wounded feelings and awkward protocol. And at last I was old enough to act as chief lady of the palace, a position none of my father's wives wished to question. Now I stood before all the rest to greet the Colchian bride and welcome her to her new home.

My stepmothers had labored mightily over my appearance for this ceremony, vying to adorn me in the hopes I would speak well of them to my father. Naamah garbed me in a gown soft and pale as sunlight; Nefret smoothed malachite over my lids and painted long lines about my eyes; Melasadne braided my hair, and Arinike adorned Melasadne's work with golden pins shaped as butterflies. A dozen women had toiled half the morning that I might do honor to my father's palace—and look kindly upon them.

Now I stood at the forefront of the assembled women, the work of their hands as much as if I were a veil they had woven to their own taste. And as I stood there, clad in gold and in scarlet, with a band of pearls set about my brow, I felt like a true princess. I will not lie; I took great pleasure in being the petted darling of the palace. Now I see how much of me was child still. The woman I thought myself that day had not yet been born.

My two handmaidens, who were also my chief playfellows, stood behind me, clad as moons to my sun. As the great cedar gate opened to admit the Colchian princess, I heard Nimrah whisper, "Have the black dogs eaten the prophet, do you think?" and Keshet's soft giggle and, behind them, murmurs from the waiting women.

"Be silent," I said, thinking myself very regal, and sensed rather than heard both girls' muffled laughter. Then the Colchian walked through the Queens' Gate and all laughter ceased.

No black dogs followed her, which was a disappointment to me. Only a dozen black-robed handmaidens attended her—or so I thought at first. When I looked closer, I saw that half her escort were men garbed and painted as women. Eunuchs; others of my father's wives owned such half-men among their servants. But the eunuchs I knew did not pretend to be what they were not. It would shame them to dress as women.

Without a single glance about her, the princess walked forward until she stood just so far from me that if we both had stretched out our arms, our fingertips might have touched. Her eyes glinted, opaque as black glass. I summoned my royal manners and bowed, uttering the formal words of greeting I had learned.

"To the palace of King Solomon, be welcome. Enter and dwell among us as a sister." I smiled and held out my hands, but she did not move. I repeated my greeting in the Traders' Tongue spoken along all the great trade roads, but she did not respond to that, either. Unsure, I sought aid. "Is there any here who speaks a tongue the Lady Dacxuri can understand?"

After a moment's uneasy silence, there was a rustle as women moved aside, letting the Lady Helike come forward. "I, perhaps. I will try."

I was surprised, for the Lady Helike spoke but seldom and rarely came among the other women, who liked her as little as she liked them. Overproud, and coldhearted; that was what was said of the princess from horse-proud Troy. Hastily, I thanked her and watched as Helike bowed before the Colchian and then spoke, slow careful words that the other listened to without a shadow of response.

When Helike fell silent, the Colchian regarded her with flat unyielding eyes; Helike flushed and lowered her gaze. I saw Helike's fingers curl into the palms of her hands, hard, so that her knuckles stood out white as bone.

At last the Colchian slid her dark gaze to me; she nodded, once, and then held out her hand. Hiding my reluctance to touch her, I grasped her fingers only so long as custom demanded. Her skin was pale and cool as marble.

"She will go with you, Princess," Helike said, and I smiled and thanked her. "We are fortunate that you know some of her own speech."

"A little only," Helike said. "I learned it—long ago, and have forgotten much." Her hands still remained clenched, half-hidden in the folds of her heavy skirts.

I thanked her again and looked beseechingly at Naamah and Nefret. "We must have someone who can speak with her; send to my father for her interpreter." I thought it strange that Lady Dacxuri knew not one word in our language; in her place, I would have studied the language of my new homeland swiftly, lest I be left at the mercy of strangers. Nor had she troubled herself to learn the Traders' Tongue, as I had; double folly, for one who traveled far.

But at least Helike's aid let me perform my duty to my father's new wife. I guided Lady Dacxuri and her attendants through the labyrinth the women's palace had become as it had grown to satisfy the demands of each new queen. I remained with her only long enough to ensure she had no immediate fault to find with her rooms before I hastened back to the queens' garden courtyard. There I found my father's women clustered like flowers, heads together as they tore at the newest wife with words keen as iron blades.

The chatter ceased a moment as I returned, then resumed when the women saw that it was only I.

"Night crows," Adath said, "and she the queen of the crows. The king likes bright colors, bright words—she has no chance."

From the group of the Hebrew wives came Yeshara's voice, words sour as vinegar. "None of us has a chance, let alone an idolater from the world's end."

"At least our god isn't ashamed to show his face," Adath snapped back. Incited by the sharp voices, Melasadne's little dogs began to bark, shrill, demanding sounds that cut through the next spiteful remarks and reminded the women of the true victim of their malice.

"I hope she has another gown; black is ill luck for a wedding." "This bride is ill luck for anyone. Did you see how she looked upon our princess? I wouldn't be surprised if she had cursed her with that look." "I don't envy her maidservants—or are they man-maids?" "Men in women's clothes— even if they aren't true men—only the priests of Dagon dress so, and we all know about *them.*" "I don't envy our lord king when that new prophet hears about *this*. Black dogs and—"

"I don't envy our lord king his wedding night," Queen Naamah said, and those close enough to hear her laughed.

"But then," Melasadne said softly, "you have never cared for dogs, Naamah."

Silently, I summoned Nimrah and Keshet. My father's wives and concubines had become so engrossed in their gossip that no one noticed when we left the queens' garden court, walking calm and soft-footed until we were past the painted pillars. Safely beyond recall, the three of us looked at each other; we grasped each other's hands and ran as fast as we could down the long corridor towards the kitchen wing. At the kitchen gate we stopped and laughed until we ran out of breath.

"Black dogs and black hearts," Nimrah said, just as we had ceased, and set us off again. We were young enough still to find the small battles our elders waged no more than fuel for our laughter.

Later, after the wedding ceremony was long over, I sat quiet while my maid-servant Rivkah carefully unpinned and unbraided all my stepmothers' painstaking work—grumbling all the while that *she* could have dressed my hair better—"Am I, who was good enough for Queen Abishag, now not fit to tend Princess Baalit? Queens' folly!" she added, and I tried not to laugh, for Rivkah had belonged to my mother long years before I had been born, and Rivkah had tended me since the day I came into the world and my mother left it. It was from Rivkah that I learned what I knew of my mother. So I soothed Rivkah's hurt feelings, and let her ready me for bed. But that night, I could not sleep.

Although Nimrah and Keshet lay asleep in their bed and the night was quiet, my mind was not. I thought of all my father's women had said in the sunlit garden—and when I tried to summon up my heedless laughter at their folly once more, I could not. Coiling my unbound hair about my fingers, I considered that day's events, searching each for the shadow I sensed, the flaw that forbade laughter.

All I saw, when I told over what had happened, was my father's women. Fair women and dark women; women from lands near world's end and from villages in Judah's golden hills. All of them beautiful, all of them polished as fine gems. . . .

Something flickered in my mind, but I could not yet seize upon the thought. Frowning, I began to tell over all my father's women, wives and concubines, gifts and alliances. But I had only ten fingers and quickly lost count. So, by the light of the small oil lamp Rivkah kept burning against night's darkness, I used my store of unset gemstones as counting markers.

Nefret, of course. And Naamah, mother to the next king and too proud of it. Gilade, and Helike; Melasadne and Makeda. Women from faraway lands; women whose ways were foreign to our people. I laid six gems upon the shining cloth that covered my bed. Against the brilliant crimson, jewels seemed almost dull; an odd trick of color upon color, light upon light. Too splendid a background, and even gold shone less bright.

I continued to count my father's wives, setting the gems in straight rows across my bed. Arishat, the Sidonian princess who had brought King Solomon two port cities as dowry. Aiysha, whose dowry had been truce with the Bedouin who harried our kingdom's eastern borders. Nilufer, the Persian girl, with eyes cool and aloof as those of the long-haired cats she cherished. . . .

I paused, then swept my hand across the shimmering cloth, gathering up the diverse stones. For a moment I stared at the gems; I let them drop through my fingers and poured the rest from the ivory casket. I divided the jewels, placing all of a kind together in smaller heaps. When I had finished, I saw that I had more turquoise and pearls than I did any other stones; those would serve as my new markers. I began again—and this time I used turquoise for those women who belonged by blood to Israel and Judah. Pearls tokened foreign queens.

When I had done, I stared at the design formed by numbering King Solomon's wives in turquoises and in pearls. So few turquoise markers; so many pearls. Against the crimson cloth, the pearls glowed like scattered moons. The turquoise stones lay dull beside the pearls, sky-blue beauty obscured by the rich silk beneath.

So many pearls. I studied the pattern I had unwittingly laid out. Now, in the neat rows of turquoise and of pearl, I gazed clear-eyed on what my father's marriages had created: a court of strangers. Behind the gateway to the queens' palace dwelt, not daughters of Israel and Judah, but foreign women who had carried as their dowries not only gold and cities and peace, but strange gods and distant customs.

No wonder Ahijah rages like a madman against the king's court. The prophet was new-come to Jerusalem, seeking to fill a place long vacant. Not since Nathan died had a prophet held the king's favor—and Nathan had died before I was born. Ahijah loathed my father's court and all foreigners dwelling in it. He ranted in the marketplace against the temples to strange gods that had sprung up as more and more merchants came to Jerusalem from other lands. No one in the city seemed to pay much heed to him, which did not stop Ahijah's furious diatribes.

I looked at my turquoise markers, and at my pearls. And then I took another pearl and set it within the circle of its sisters. Another foreign wife; another alien pearl, this one from a land beyond the north wind. The Lady Dacxuri, Princess of Colchis.

I remembered the black-clad attendants who followed her; saw again the flat glint of her eyes as she studied the women with whom she would now dwell. Whatever foreign customs the Colchian brought as her gift to King Solomon's court, I did not think I would find them pleasing.

I stared at the gemstones laid out before me. Pearls glowed in the lamplight; turquoise vanished in shadow. Pearls and turquoise.

And for the first time I wondered how many pearls my father's court could hold before the turquoise became altogether lost among them.

Naamah

She had been destined from birth for a king's bed. When it came time to show her to the goddess Astarte and receive the name that would define her being, the flames dancing upon the oil confirmed her fate. *Naamah*, she was named. *Beautiful.*

Her father, the King of Ammon, owned a dozen daughters, but she outshone her sisters as a full moon outshines stars. Always, her beauty had been all that was required of her. No one cared that she was clever with numbers, that she was skilled with cloth and color, that she liked to dance.

They cared only that her hair flowed lustrous as shining water down her back, that her skin glowed like heavy cream in an alabaster bowl, that her hips and breasts curved as perfectly as the full moon. Those who watched the princess, weighing her worth, cared only that she was beautiful.

So when the new ruler of the kingdom David the Harper had shaped from the lands between Ammon and the Sea-Cities wished to treat with her father, she was part of the treasure sent to the court of King Solomon.

"Your beauty will be a jewel in his crown," her mother told her, and her father said, "Your beauty will make you his favorite."

No one asked her if she wished to be a jewel in King Solomon's crown, or his favorite. She was beautiful; to be a king's wife and a king's mother was her destiny, and marriage sealed treaties.

No one told her beauty was a snare, a trap for fools. That truth Naamah had learned painfully, and for herself.

"Hold the mirror still, or I cannot see myself clearly." Naamah posed before an oval of bronze as large as a warrior's shield, its surface burnished to sun-bright clarity. An idea of her own; while her bronze mirror did not provide so fine an image as did silver, its size permitted her to see herself as a whole, to judge her total worth.

As two of her maidservants supported the bronze mirror, Naamah studied her reflection in the polished metal. Yes, she looked well. Despite having borne a child, her body remained supple, rounded and womanly, fit vessel for any king. *Even the great Solomon of Israel.* The thought was sour; Naamah watched herself frown and swiftly smoothed away the lines of dissatisfaction. Too often indulged in, temper marred the face. Naamah could not afford that luxury. *Solomon has so many women!*

The Israelite king's harem was as full of women as a Damascus bazaar of rich trade goods. Naamah shared her royal husband with women from every people she had ever heard of, and some she had not. Now dark Colchis, Kingdom of Gold, had bowed at last to Israel's greatness and sent the Colchian king's eldest daughter as gift to King Solomon.

So many queens. So many beautiful women. But the last woman to bask in the king's favor had been Abishag. Now Naamah realized how restful her life had been during those early years of Solomon's reign—for it had been useless to try supplanting Abishag in Solomon's heart, and every woman in the harem had known it. No matter how beautiful, how skilled, what woman could triumph over the girl who had been the king's first love?

But Abishag had lain dead more than a dozen years, and the child that had killed her was only a daughter. Praise to Milcom for that blessing, for surely the son of Abishag would have been proclaimed crown prince, no matter when he was born! As it was, Naamah's son was heir to the throne; King Solomon had sworn again to that upon Rehoboam's last birthday, when the boy had turned fifteen. Sworn to it publicly, too, so there could be no doubt in men's minds.

But a doubt lingered in hers. *This kingdom is built on sand, its kings are crowned by whim. I must ensure that Solomon keeps his promise; that my son sits next upon the Lion Throne.*

Naamah turned before the mirror, gauging the effect of the spangled shawl draped over her smooth shoulders. Thin crescents of silver glittered against fine cotton cloth dyed deepest blue—as she had hoped, it seemed as if the midnight sky shrouded her body. The extravagant shawl was her own design. Wearing it alone, with her ripe body gleaming beneath the sheer cloth, she would rival Astarte, would seem the Rising Moon herself. Surely Solomon could not resist her then.

But that is not the problem! Naamah found herself frowning again. For the king found her pleasing, he had told her so. He enjoyed her well-tended body, complimented her upon her taste and her cleverness, admired her original designs.

Just as he enjoys and praises all the others!

That was the heart of Naamah's trouble. Solomon did no more for her than he did for every other woman taken into the royal harem. No woman received special treatment from the king, from Pharaoh's Daughter down to the newest, rawest concubine from the Cilician hills.

How could she trust that dispassionate fairness? For it would last only until a new woman captured his heart—*and if such a one gives Solomon a son, I would not wager a moldy fig on my son's future crown, king's word or no!*

So, to ensure her son's inheritance, she herself must somehow become the woman Solomon preferred over all others. It must be possible; there must be some net that would ensnare him!

"What do you think?" Naamah asked her attendants. "Tell me truly."

She knew they would; Naamah was clever enough to value honesty from her maidservants.

"Queen Naamah is beautiful as the night sky," her maid Tallai said promptly.

Naamah regarded her sternly. "I ask not of my beauty but of my garment's. Does it please the eye?"

"Oh, yes." Tallai's admiration shone from her dark eyes. "It is beautiful. I wish *I* owned such a shawl."

"And all the other women in the palace *will* own one by the next new moon!" Ora promptly responded, and Naamah laughed.

"So they will—but the king will have seen mine first!"

Seen her clad in starry night, her skin glowing like the full moon and her hair flowing like dark clouds. . . . Naamah smiled.

"And by next new moon, Queen Naamah will have thought of yet another new fashion," Ora added, pride in her mistress's cleverness warming her voice—and though Naamah's smile remained fixed upon her painted lips, her heart sank.

Yes, by then I must design something else new, something enticing. Something to catch the king's eye—and keep it upon me. Suddenly weary, Naamah stared at her reflection in the bronze mirror, knowing she could not afford dismay. Her son's future was at stake, and her own as well. When she was the queen mother it would not matter whether her body were fat or lean, her face smooth or lined, her hair glossy or gray. The king's mother would be honored and protected.

Next moon is many days from now. By then—by then I shall think of something! I must.

Melasadne

When she had been called before her mother's chief eunuch and informed that the new-made treaty between the island kingdom of Melite and the swiftly growing empire of Israel was to be sealed by marriage, and that she had been chosen as the treaty-bride, Melasadne had bowed her head and most properly feigned modest reluctance.

"As my mother and my queen orders," Princess Melasadne had murmured, "but I am not worthy of such an honor." To her secret relief, no one had paid the least attention to this pious objection. She had been packed off to her new home in great state, and in even greater haste— *Lest the King of Israel change his mind!* had been her scornful thought.

Melasadne knew King Solomon could not change his mind, any more than her mother could. For the island kingdom needed this alliance as desperately as a rich beautiful widow needed a strong husband.

Once Melite had been invulnerable, guarded by the sea around it and the ships that ruled that sea. But that halcyon age had ended a dozen lifetimes ago in a night of fire and death that swept the Dolphin Fleet from the Great Sea. Now all that remained of the Sea Kings and their empire were defenseless island kingdoms and memories of vanished glory. Without the protection of the Sea Kings, little kingdoms such as Melite endured only at the random mercies of the gods—and of the pirates who ruled the Great Sea.

Now a new king had risen in faraway Canaan, powerful enough to force peace upon the restless sea. Tales of King Solomon were sung by every traveler who made landfall upon Melite; Melasadne hardly dared believe half of them. But if even half of all she had heard were true, King Solomon was a second Minos!

Rich and powerful and wise—and handsome too. What more could I desire? What luck that her eldest sister had fallen prey to the Mouse God's plague and pox scars now marred her cheeks, and what luck that her prettiest sister had already been given to the Lady's Temple! Melasadne had been the bride chosen to wed the new power in their world, and sent to King Solomon with the most lavish dowry Melite had ever granted an outlander. In addition to Melite's goodwill, King Solomon would receive a safe port free of all customs levies, and a free market for Israel's wool and oil.

Melasadne herself had smuggled out her own gift for the husband who had unknowingly delivered her from life as handmaiden to her mother: a pair of the small white dogs that only the royal family might own. She still smiled as she remembered King Solomon's startled laugh when she had knelt and presented him with a covered basket that uttered high-pitched barks.

"What gift is this, that sounds so distressed?" Solomon had asked, and lifted the basket's lid to stare into two pairs of bright black eyes. The tiny white dogs had stared back at the great king and then began scrambling out of their basket; Solomon had caught them up before they could fall, their long fur flowing over his hands.

Only later did Melasadne come to understand how truly generous this gesture had been, for never had it occurred to her that the people among whom she now must make her home considered dogs unclean.

"They are the luck of our House," she had said. "Only those of royal blood may own such dogs. They are my own gift to you, my husband." She had smiled, wishing him to understand that she was pleased with this marriage.

"That is kind." King Solomon regarded the little animals quizzically; the dogs wriggled and licked his hands with quick pink tongues. After a moment's hesitation, the king smiled and held the dogs out to Melasadne. "I ask that you tend them; I know nothing of such animals, and clearly they must have the best of care."

And so, to her great delight, the dogs had remained hers, although Solomon always remembered to ask after their welfare when he visited her. The royal dogs prospered and proved fruitful, and now Melasadne walked amidst a pack of tiny white dogs whose long fur flowed about them like water.

She, too, had prospered. Two merchant ships had been part of her dowry, and she dealt cleverly in trade goods, sending fine cloth and elegant pottery north and bringing furs and amber south. She had borne King Solomon two sons, handsome boys who had inherited their father's cleverness and kind nature.

Life is good. She was a queen in King Solomon's palace; she was the mother of two fine boys who one day would oversee her own ships. All her prayers had been answered.

Melasadne had never ceased to remember that, and to be grateful.

Ruth

Tomorrow was the Feast of First Fruits—and this year, she, too, would carry a sheaf of wheat and a pomegranate up the hill from the king's palace to the Lord's Temple. *This festival I, too, will worship joyfully. This year, I am Ruth.* She had cast aside her old name and her old gods; the Lady Ruth bowed only before the god of Abraham, the god of Great David.

This year I am no longer blind. This year I go rejoicing in the Lord's light. Ruth smiled and continued lifting her gowns from the sandalwood chest, weighing and judging. Only the best would do for her first offering at the Lord's Great Temple.

How different this year was for her than the last. Then she was Princess Surraphel, the King of Chaldea's daughter, a treaty-bride too stiff and shy to say more to her new husband than "As my lord the king pleases."

But King Solomon had been so kind there was little she would not do to please him—save for one thing. She would not relinquish her own gods.

So she had held aloof, scornful of King Solomon's god, who seemed a poor deity indeed compared with her own protectors. How could one surrender oneself to a god with no face, no form? How could one respect a god whose own people refused Him an image to adorn with gold and with jewels? So for many months she had silently jeered at the Hebrew queens, had clung to her own gods.

How stubborn I was; how foolish. But that folly vanished one morning as she looked upon the Temple crowning the hill. She had often looked upon the Lord's Temple and silently mocked. But that morning—ah, that morning had been different. That day, the rising sun poured light over the god's house, and between one breath and the next the Temple seemed to catch fire, a beacon summoning those with eyes to see.

As she had seen at last.

That golden fire kindled answering flame within her, and the blaze of that sacred flame revealed the truth to her: the Lord ruled her small world as He ruled the great worlds of gods and men. The Lord promised nothing, demanded everything. Who could refuse worship to so great a god? And as the god-light faded, she had fallen upon her knees and uttered her first prayer to the Lord of Hosts. *O god of Solomon, make me worthy of you!*

That day she cast aside her own gods and turned to her husband's, only to endure mockery and suspicion from those women who had been born under the Lord's sheltering covenant. But upheld by the promise the Lord had written in fire, she persevered. At last she had asked King Solomon, upon the night that was hers, to aid her.

"O King, your handmaiden craves a boon of you." She knelt before him as a supplicant; Solomon smiled and bid her rise and sit beside him on the bed.

"There is no need to humble yourself, wife; ask, and I will judge your request fairly."

"My king and husband, I wish to worship your god. I would learn to do Him honor, as you do."

King Solomon looked intently into her face. "You need not, Surraphel. I have sworn my wives may keep their own gods; you need not fear yours shall be taken from you."

"I fear only that I shall not honor the Lord as He would wish." She raised her head and prayed that the king would see the new passion burning within her. "My soul longs for your god to be mine as well; my heart yearns for Him. Do not deny me this, I beg of you."

King Solomon had granted what she asked, sending the high priest Zadok to instruct her in those rites sacred to the Lord. And the king had done more; he had called those of his wives who were daughters of his god's Law before him and placed her in their keeping.

"Here is the Lady Surraphel, who wishes to become a good Daughter of the Law." King Solomon held her hand in his and held out his other hand to Paziah, who was well-known as the most pious of the king's Hebrew wives. "Will you take her as your sister and teach her?"

What could the Lady Paziah say but "If the king wishes it," and let Solomon set her hand in Surraphel's? "Welcome, Surraphel. Be thou my sister now." Paziah's voice held no welcome, but Surraphel smiled as if she had been embraced warmly, and bowed her head.

"Call me not Surraphel, for that woman is dead. Give me a new name, I beg of you, a name fit for a daughter of the Lord."

Paziah hesitated, and then clasped both Surraphel's hands. "Then welcome—Ruth." And she kissed her new sister's cheek.

The new name suited Ruth, as did the worship of her new god. She learned the Lord's Laws, and strictly obeyed them—and in exchange for her homage received a peaceful mind and a cheerful heart.

What more could a woman ask from any god?

Abishag

When I turned fourteen, my mother gave me a new veil, a woman's veil, as light as blue smoke and sewn with thin silver disks that shone like bright moons. That year, the news from Jerusalem told of King David lying old and frail—some claimed he would not last out the summer. These tales shocked me as much as anyone—indeed, I think they dismayed the young more than they did the old, for the old could remember a time before David. I could not. How could King David be dying? He had been king more years than I had lived.

When my mother heard this news, a veil seemed to slide over her face, and I could not tell her thoughts. At last she said, "So it begins. Go comb your hair, Abishag, and do not let me see you beyond our doorstep without your new veil again." That was all. But after that, my mother refused to permit me to take one step outside our house without smoothing my hair and rubbing carmine on my lips. Nor was I permitted any longer to walk out alone. My maidservant Rivkah was with me always.

Zadok

"The prophet Ahijah wishes to speak with you, High Priest." The acolyte's face remained bland as he imparted this information, his voice remained steady and deferential. Never would one guess that young Jeremiah, like most of the Temple priests, thought the prophet Ahijah mad.

Oh, no, Zadok thought with miserable guilt. Not again. Ahijah never appeared at the Temple except to rant over the sins of the people.

But to Zadok's mind, there was no harm in a woman baking a few cakes for the Queen of Heaven, or in a man granting a lamb to Baal, so long as he offered up a bull to the Lord. After all, their Lord only demanded to be first among the gods—and surely if the Lord's people angered Him, the Lord would make His displeasure plainly known, as He so often had in times past.

"Will you receive the prophet, High Priest?" Jeremiah asked, and for a moment Zadok longed to deny himself to Ahijah. The king's wedding witnessed, the Temple sacrifices made, Zadok had thought his duties done and looked forward to an evening's peace.

But refusing to see Ahijah now would only anger the prophet further, making their eventual meeting even more unpleasant. Zadok sighed, and capitulated. "Bid him enter."

Ahijah strode in and stopped, erect and proud— As if he were about to address the king's army, rather than one tired old man. Bracing himself, Zadok nodded in greeting. "Be welcome, Ahijah. Come, sit, have wine. This is last year's best, sweet and—"

"I did not come to guzzle wine, High Priest, but to speak of Yahweh's will."

I am not "guzzling," Zadok thought querulously, wincing inwardly at the prophet's insistence upon saying the Lord's true name—as if to point out that Zadok no longer spoke that Holy Name aloud. *Well, it is no longer fit that every man should hold the Lord's name in his mouth! And surely as high priest, I, too, am privy to our Lord's will as much as Ahijah!* Trying not to sigh again, he said, "Speak, then."

For a moment Ahijah remained silent, glaring at Zadok like an angry eagle. "Yahweh is not to be mocked," Ahijah at last declared.

"Of course not." Zadok hoped to placate Ahijah with pious agreement, a hope that vanished with the prophet's next words.

"Yahweh is not to be mocked, nor is His prophet to be mocked. Though a crown circle a man's head, he can be raised up or struck down at Yahweh's pleasure." Ahijah's voice began as a low, intense near-whisper; Zadok found himself thinking of vipers. Ahijah's words carried venom, potent and deadly.

"Yes, struck down. Down into dust. He and his foreign women! He forgets he is set upon his throne to do Yahweh's will—not to raise pillars to wanton Asherah, to plant groves for every false god whose worshippers he wishes to placate. Such a man does evil in the sight of Yahweh—whose name he dares not even speak!"

Ahijah's tirade continued, but Zadok ceased to listen to the prophet's words. *Woe unto my hope that for once Ahijah's diatribe will be brief. Have mercy, Lord, I beg of You; remember I am an old man and the day has been long already.* Zadok tried to listen in serene patience; even Ahijah must eventually cease to talk.

"Woe betide such a land! Woe betide such a people! Woe betide such a king!" Ahijah paused dramatically—or for breath—and Zadok hastily filled the momentary silence.

"Of course, of course. But surely if the Lord is angered, the Lord will make His anger plain?"

Ahijah stared at him iron-eyed. "He has made it plain to *me*."

"But not to me," Zadok said firmly. "The Urim and Thummim give only pleasing answers; the sacrifices burn bright." He held Ahijah's gaze a moment—not an easy task—and added, "In any case, I do not understand what you wish of *me.* I abide faithfully by all our Lord's Laws."

"King Solomon does not." From the vicious triumph in Ahijah's voice, this was the heart his verbal blade sought.

"King Solomon also abides faithfully by our Lord's Laws, Ahijah."

"He consorts with strange women and indulges their vicious whims." Ahijah drew a deep breath, and Zadok knew the prophet had barely begun. Zadok also knew precisely what Ahijah would say at such great length; while custom granted a prophet unlimited freedom to speak, no law required Zadok do more than appear to listen respectfully. So while Ahijah ranted on, Zadok contemplated the savory new dish his good wife had promised for their evening meal, and nodded from time to time.

But gradually his attention was drawn back to Ahijah's diatribe, for this attack upon the king seemed more intense, more personal than usual. And the repeated mentions of strange women, coupled with the accusations of idolatry in the king's own household, made Zadok oddly uneasy. Did Ahijah think to play Samuel, to make and break kings?

But King Solomon was no Saul, tormented and unsure. And times had changed; king now held more power than prophet.

When at last Ahijah ceased, Zadok spoke swiftly, lest the prophet begin again. "There is much in what you say, Ahijah. Much. I will think on it."

"Solomon is only king, he is not Yahweh Himself. Solomon treads a dangerous path."

"Yes, yes." Zadok nodded. "I will speak with him." That, Zadok could safely promise.

When the prophet had gone, Zadok tried to recapture the contentment he had enjoyed before Ahijah's visit. He failed; the day's peace had been shattered beyond repair. Ahijah's diatribe had ruined his pleasure in the drowsy evening and the good Samarian wine.

Was I ever that young, that sure of myself—and of Yahweh—of the Lord? Yes, Zadok supposed he had been. Once he had been a lion, bold and proud. As a youth he had marched to Hebron and joined David's cause when that great hero was only king of Judah. He had served King David faithfully through good times and through bad. *When that young fool Prince Absalom revolted against his father and his god, who was it led the priests from Jerusalem? Who was it carried away the Ark so that Absalom could not claim its blessing? I.*

That had been no easy task; no one at the time had understood why Great David should flee his own city because a spoiled boy marched against it. The priests had argued hard against risking the Ark of the Covenant beyond Jerusalem's walls. It had taken all Zadok's skill to persuade the other priests to follow him into exile with King David.

"David is Yahweh's king, the Ark is Yahweh's dwelling place upon earth," he had said. "I follow David, and the Ark, and Yahweh. If you will not come, then I shall take the Ark if I must yoke myself to it and draw it like an ox."

I led, and they followed. And I was right, for our Lord put victory into King David's hands. And Joab, commander of King David's armies, had slain Prince Absalom. *A deed well-done; that boy had no respect for the Temple.*

Zadok frowned, correcting himself mentally. Of course there had been no Temple then. Still, Prince Absalom had been a shallow, feckless youth, contemptuous of priests and princes both. And too proud, far too proud— *as was his brother Adonijah.*

Another prince who would be king, Adonijah had at least had the sense to offer sweet words and promises to those who would espouse his cause. Many had, among them the high priest Abiathar.

But I saw Adonijah clearly for what he was. Like Absalom his brother, Prince Adonijah lacked true respect for the Lord and His priesthood. Neither prince would have supported the priests as King David did all his days. *King David gave us honor and glory. King David knew what was due the Lord's priests.*

So Zadok had turned away from Adonijah's outstretched hand, cleaving to King David. And once again, Zadok's instincts had proven right; Adonijah and those who had sworn fealty to him went down to dust. The office of high priest had been stripped from Abiathar. From that day forward, Zadok had reigned as sole high priest of the Lord Yahweh in the lands of Israel and Judah.

I was wise then. Poor Abiathar; he was too quick to scorn and to judge. Abiathar had always despised King David's many women, believing they turned the king's mind from Yahweh, absorbing wealth that should have gone to build the Lord's Temple. In vain had Zadok explained that the prophet Nathan had foreseen that King David would but prepare the ground for the Temple, that a king to come after would build their god's House on Earth. But Abiathar would not be soothed.

"The prophet Nathan is tied to Queen Michal's girdle, and she seeks all glory for Prince Solomon." Abiathar had spat upon the ground to show how cheap he held Nathan's prophecies. "We shall see that slut Bathsheba's son upon the throne next—and *that* is a better prophecy than any of Nathan's!"

"Prince Solomon is a good, wise boy." Zadok had tried to placate Abiathar—uselessly, of course. Abiathar would not be appeased.

"Prince Solomon is the child of sin, the son of an oath-breaker and a mindless harlot. He is not fit to be king."

"Yahweh decides who is fit to be king," Zadok had corrected. "And Yahweh does not judge as men do."

Abiathar had looked long at Zadok then; Zadok had shifted uneasily beneath that steady gaze. "No," Abiathar had said at last, "but perhaps He judges as women do."

"I do not understand," Zadok said.

"No," said Abiathar, "I don't suppose you do."

That had been the last true conversation Zadok had ever had with Abiathar. After Prince Adonijah's ill-advised coronation feast—a festivity ended when King David learned of it and promptly crowned Prince Solomon as king—Abiathar had been sent into exile.

He should have known better than to go against Queen Michal's son—no, King Solomon was the Lady Bathsheba's son; odd how hard it is to remember that! I grow old; my mind jests with me. Still, all the world had known Prince Solomon was as dear to Queen Michal as if he were the child of her own body. *And truly, the boy resembles her far more than he does the Lady Bathsheba.* So it had been twice folly for Abiathar to defy not only his king's wishes, but the queen's.

And that is why I sit here today in comfort and honor, and Abiathar died far from the king's court. Poor Abiathar.

Yes, and if I cannot summon wisdom, soon it shall be "Poor Zadok." The warmth of self-satisfaction faded as Zadok considered the dilemma before him. Prophet or no, Ahijah was becoming troublesome. *Who knows what such a man may do?*

He would, Zadok decided, have to warn the king. Carefully, and tactfully; the high priest had no wish to upset the even tenor of King Solomon's life.

Or of his own.

Solomon

The king's day had started poorly—he had been begged to adjudicate between one of his wives and another; both claimed the same slave girl as handmaiden, and Solomon had been hard put to devise a solution that would satisfy any of the parties to the dispute—and continued to worsen. The steward had begged audience to complain about the suppliers of foodstuffs for the palace, and the superintendent of the regional governors had gotten wind of that audience and come along to beg the king's indulgence for those same suppliers.

Solomon had assumed the capstone in this procession of complainants was Jeroboam, the superintendent of the highly unpopular Forced Levy. Once the king had managed to sympathize with the steward and soothe the superintendent of governors' sore feelings, he had hoped for a respite, only to hear that Jeroboam had most humbly begged a few moments with the king's grace. Solomon had no choice but to acquiesce, although talking with Jeroboam never left a sweet taste in the mouth.

"O King, the Danites refused to surrender the thousand men I ordered them to supply for the roadworks. I beg leave to pass the king's harsh judgment upon them."

Solomon raised his eyebrows in questioning surprise. "Truly? I have heard no rumor of such a revolt."

"The Danites gave up the men at last, but not before defying the king's decree."

"Either they defied the decree or they did not. If the thousand men are now working upon the roads, the Danites have obeyed, have they not?"

"Yes—but they protested, refused to comply with the order until I myself confronted them. They must be punished for such willful folly." Jeroboam stood spear-straight, affronted by the mere thought that men dared question his orders. If the man were not so good at his job, a job that brought opprobrium down upon his head almost daily, Solomon would long ago have replaced him.

For he is not only effective but ambitious. Ambition was not a bad thing, in a man— *But like fire, it makes a fine servant and a poor master.* Solomon repressed a sigh and began the laborious task of forbidding Jeroboam to summarily execute judgments upon the unruly Danites without wounding Jeroboam's touchy pride. To Jeroboam's complaint that leniency would be perceived as weakness, Solomon said only "I am not weak, nor are you, and if the Danites press on to outright mutiny, they will discover that to their cost. But punish men only for speaking their minds? No."

And now, just as he had a few moments to study the new maps of the Silk Road his spies had painfully acquired for him, the chamberlain interrupted him once more.

"O King, the high priest craves audience."

O Lord, what is it now? To Solomon, it sometimes seemed that the old man always wanted *something*—to be fair, much of what Zadok asked was for others, and not for himself. But the high priest seemed to regard the treasury as inexhaustible, the king's resources as infinite. Solomon sighed faintly, and nodded to his chamberlain.

"Very well; the high priest may approach." Setting aside the maps he wished to peruse, Solomon summoned up a smile as Zadok entered. "Come in, Zadok, and be welcome. And tell me how the king may be of service to the high priest today."

Zadok bowed his head, acknowledging the king's greeting. "Peace unto you, King Solomon. This time it is I who may be of service to you."

That will make a splendid change. Not by the slightest shift of muscle or glint of eye did Solomon betray this unworthy thought. *Unworthy, unjust. But if I cannot complain even to myself*—Who else was there? Even those a king trusted could not bear the burden of his human weaknesses.

So Solomon smiled again, and gestured to the padded bench beneath the window. "Sit, Zadok. Shall I send for wine?" Not waiting for answer, he glanced to the servant standing vigilant beside the door; the man nodded and strode off to do the king's unspoken bidding.

"That is kind, but I did not come here for wine—even for such wine as yours." Slowly, Zadok sat and regarded Solomon gravely. "O King, yester eve I endured a visit from the prophet Ahijah—"

"Then it is well I sent for wine." Solomon kept his tone light, careless. "I am sorry you were troubled. What is it this time? Women's vanity again?"

Zadok held up a minatory hand. "You jest, but truly, I am troubled by Ahijah's words to me. He spoke of the king's household and the king's women. There were accusations of idolatry in the king's household."

Solomon sighed. "We have spoken of this before, Zadok. I will not force my wives to abandon their own gods."

"It would be better if the king's wives did not worship idols," Zadok said, with the indifference of a boy repeating a dull lesson.

"It would be better if the prophet Ahijah tended his own affairs." Solomon did not blame Zadok; the fault lay elsewhere. "Does Ahijah have any idea how vulnerable the kingdom is? How fragile its alliances?"

A whisper of sound at the doorway; a slave entered bearing a wine jug; a second followed carrying two wine cups. Solomon waited until the boys had set down silver jug and golden cups, until he himself had poured a full measure of wine into one cup and a scant measure into the other, until he had handed the full wine cup to Zadok and the high priest drank.

Then Solomon said, "Now tell me, why trouble yourself to come and recite Ahijah's ravings? He can have said nothing you have not heard him say forty times before. What is it that so disquiets you this time?"

Frowning, Zadok stared into his wine cup as if seeking his answer there. "Truly, O King, I do not know. Ahijah has spoken such words many times before, but this time—this time it was different. He spewed venom as does a viper." Zadok sighed, and drank again.

Smiling, Solomon lifted the silver jug and poured more wine into Zadok's empty cup. "I thank you for your warning, Zadok. A thousand pities that Ahijah loves discord better than peace."

"Prophets are nothing but trouble. Oh, I know prophets speak for the Lord—but so do I. I am High Priest, after all."

"And I am king, and Ahijah chastises us both as if we were erring boys." Solomon cradled his own wine cup in his hands; the gold vessel warmed to his flesh. He gazed into the dark red liquid; crimson shadows swirled. "King, and high priest, and prophet—do you know, Zadok, sometimes I wish old Samuel had not bowed so easily to the people's will and anointed a king over Israel all those years ago."

"But that would mean you would not be king now."

Solomon smiled. "In truth, it would mean I would never have been born, for if Samuel had not anointed Saul king, David would never have been king after him. And had my father not been king, he would not have stood upon a palace balcony and seen my mother bathing."

"My king!"

"Don't sound so shocked, Zadok—even you cannot think I grew up in David's palace without hearing all David's scandals."

"King David was a great man, and beloved of the Lord our god."

"You recite that as a schoolboy does a well-learned lesson. But perhaps you are right; for all his faults and flaws, my father died peacefully in his bed, full of years." *Full of years, and of wickedness, yet hailed as a great king. What will the world say of King Solomon? Will the future call me a great king as well?*

Queen Michal had reared him to be a wise and just king, but he was no longer so certain that her teaching was enough. *You raised me to be a good man— but can a good man be a good king as well?*

Kingship was a complex game, its rules shifting as constantly as desert sands. A king required skills foreign to good men toiling in the fields or bargaining in the market. It was not enough to be kind and merciful and just—for those virtues ruined kingdoms unless balanced by a calculating ruthlessness that weighed the true cost of any action. A king's vision must see beyond hate, and greed, and ambition—and even beyond wisdom and love.

To be king is not so easy a task as rebels think, when they grumble and boast around their fires.

Queen Michal had sought to mate fire with ice, a heartbreakingly impossible task. Sometimes Solomon wished that she had never tried; that one of his elder brothers had grasped the crown instead. But innate honesty, even with himself, forced him to admit that he had been the best choice, the only one of King David's sons not dazzled by the prize . . .

"Zadok, do you ever wonder what the kingdom would be like had my brother Adonijah become king rather than I?"

"No," said the high priest, "for I dislike thinking of unpleasant things."

"You think King Adonijah would have been unpleasant?"

"If the Lord had meant Adonijah to be king, then he would be. But you are king, so you must be meant to be king."

"You are hard to refute, Zadok; there is no profit in arguing with you."

The high priest looked relieved, and Solomon felt a pang of guilt at mocking the old man, even though he knew Zadok had not understood the gibe. Zadok did not regard the world cynically, nor did he endlessly question his own beliefs and values.

"You are a fortunate man, High Priest," Solomon said.

"Yes, I know, O King, and I give daily thanks for our Lord's bounty—and for the king's benevolence," Zadok added hastily.

On the other hand, the old man knows which cup his wine is poured in!

Although the day had already stretched long, Solomon sent messengers seeking Ahijah throughout the city. By sundown, Solomon knew they had failed to find the prophet; a failure he accepted with mingled relief and dismay, for delaying a confrontation with Ahijah only increased the prophet's wrath against the world and its sinful flesh. And if Ahijah had heard Amyntor and his mocking laughter on the day of the Colchian wedding . . .

If Ahijah heard, then I can expect a scolding to make the Lord Himself weep. Solomon sighed inwardly. *I wonder if my father endured this hectoring from old Nathan?* King David would have known how to cozen the prophet to sweetness, sing him to silence; King Solomon's only weapon was reason, and reason failed against Ahijah's furious faith.

In a way, Solomon felt sorry for Ahijah, a man of stern morality and harsh pride railing against the changing world. *As well command the west wind to cease blowing.* But Ahijah could not be permitted to destroy what Solomon had spent so long creating.

And if I send away all my wives and tear down all foreign temples, who will thank me? Not the merchants who can no longer trade with all the world. Not the farmers who can no longer sell their harvest. Not the soldiers, or the priests— For the empire Solomon now ruled had been built by trade and by marriage—and by tolerance.

But that truth Ahijah would never see.

Duty commanded a king's days; a king's time was not his own to squander. Upon days that stretched long, Solomon sometimes wondered why any man would wish to rule. The question seemed particularly insistent when he held open court, judged between one man's truth and another's. Upon such days, it was with relief that he retreated to the calm of the Lady Nefret's chambers.

Although Nefret was Pharaoh's Daughter, she held no higher title than queen—ruthlessly fair, Solomon granted all his wives that royal title, just as he allotted each an equal set of rooms, an equal wealth in fine array and in precious gems. And as he allotted each a night to be spent with her royal husband; he kept no favorite. Once he had thought this meticulous equity would keep peace in his vast household—a vain hope, he now knew. Oddly enough, the harem had run more peaceably when Abishag lived, and reigned as undisputed queen of his heart.

But Nefret was the nearest Solomon now permitted himself to a favorite among his wives, perhaps because she cared least for his heart. Pharaoh's Daughter had been reared in the rigidly sophisticated court of the oldest kingdom upon the earth; what the Lady Nefret did not know about civilized behavior was not worth knowing. Solomon found her cool manner restful. Now she smiled at him over the playing-pieces.

"My king is troubled tonight?"

"My lady Nefret has keen eyes, for it is a small trouble only." Conversation with his Egyptian wife was a delicate sparring with words; tonight Solomon enjoyed the minor challenge.

She moved a hound. "No matter that troubles my lord is small to me."

"My lady is kind as well." Solomon moved his fox two holes, out of danger.

"Not so kind she will grant her lord the game, does he not deserve the victory." Nefret reached over the board and lifted another hound, sent it after his fox. "Will my lord permit his wife to banish his small trouble?"

"It is nothing; only that— Nefret, do you never tire of being a queen?"

Nefret gazed at him steadily, her long-painted eyes calm and inscrutable as her cat's. "No, my lord. But then, I was most carefully bred and raised."

The insult was so beautifully phrased it forced admiration rather than anger. Solomon laughed, softly, and Nefret smiled.

"My lord suffers a common illness. He is bored."

Startled, Solomon accidentally dropped his fox into the wrong hole. *Bored? With all I must do, all I must accomplish, all I must supervise, my wife can call me bored?*

"The hounds have won the game," Nefret said, flicking Solomon's misplaced fox with one gilded fingernail.

"Do you really think me bored?" Solomon abandoned formality, addressing her as he would any other woman.

"My lord shows every symptom of that disease."

"Nefret, I am never idle."

"Your wife did not say that her lord husband was idle, but that he was bored." Nefret stroked the sleek-furred cat curled upon her lap; the small beast purred, long whiskers quivering. Solomon found its intense sun-gold stare disconcerting.

"True, my lord is never idle—but my lord never takes time for unalloyed pleasure, either. Even a king requires rest."

"Perhaps, but even a king cannot add hours to the day."

"But he can carve years from his life." Nefret's hand continued to caress the golden-eyed cat. "My lord must not deny himself pleasure and rest, lest his health suffer."

"My lady must not trouble herself." Solomon smiled. "Here I find both rest and pleasure."

"Then my lord stays this night?" Nefret's voice carried no hint of her emotions. For all Solomon could tell from her smooth face and quiet voice, she felt nothing.

"Alas, he does not." Solomon watched her closely, but Nefret's face revealed nothing. She said only "Does my lord wish to play another game before he leaves?"

Never once has she protested at anything I have chosen to do. Never once has she complained. She deserves more than I can give her. Solomon smiled.

"Yes. Let us play one more game." It was not much to offer, but it was all the king had to give. He wondered, as he watched Nefret's long fingers set the playing-pieces back into the board, if Pharaoh's Daughter were truly as content as she seemed.

Perhaps she is. Truly, she seems as easy to please as her cats. Yes, I think Nefret is happy. Solomon smiled, and waited for his Egyptian queen to make the first move in the new game.

Nefret

After Solomon had gone, Nefret sat motionless, staring at the ivory and lapis gameboard. Her lord the king tried so hard, and there was so little she could do to comfort him. She understood him, but King Solomon could never understand Pharaoh's Daughter, not even if he lived a thousand years.

How could he? True, he had been born a prince, just as she had been born a princess. But she had been raised to be a king's wife. Solomon had been King David's youngest son, far from the throne, unschooled in power and protocol. He had achieved kingship by means that shocked Nefret.

But then, this entire gods-forsaken country had abandoned *ma'at*. Truth and balance.

Instead, the empire Solomon ruled commanded such wealth and power that even Pharaoh sought alliance, had for the first time in Egypt's memory offered up a Daughter of the Two Lands in exchange for trade concessions. *As if I were a bale of linen, or a tusk of ivory. As if Pharaoh's Daughter were trade goods to barter.*

Marriage to King Solomon had banished her to a crude, rough land. A land without elegance or art, literature or grace. Its dances lacked symmetry, its music lacked charm.

Worse, they had no manners.

Only Solomon himself made her exile bearable. "Neither one of us is a fool," he had said to her upon their wedding night, "and so we both know that I am greatly favored—and also that Pharaoh needs Israel's goodwill now, or you would not be here." Then he had smiled and said, "But I will try to make you happy."

He had kept his word; her courtyard and her rooms had been built in the Egyptian style. She kept her own servants, and her own fashions, and her own gods. In exchange, Solomon owned her perfect fealty, and all her talents. He did not have her love, but then, he did not desire it. She offered him quiet comfort, and respect, and friendship.

And King Solomon offered Pharaoh's Daughter the same courtesies in return.

Slowly, Nefret gathered up the slender ebony and ivory playing-pieces. Slowly, she began setting them back in their holes upon the gameboard: fox, hound, fox again, until each piece stood neatly in place once more.

Respect, and friendship. She was not even the mother of a child. Considering the fratricidal nature bred into the House of David, Nefret counted herself blessed that she lacked children, rather than cursed.

I have my lord the king's regard, and his affection. I have my own occupations. Nefret painted, an alien skill in this backward culture. For her own amusement, she kept a record of life in Solomon's Court, painting daily life in bright colors, storing the papyrus rolls in precisely labeled jars. And she gardened, another skill only half-known here. To design a courtyard garden, to experiment with its flowers and fruits, provided civilized pleasure. Nefret cultivated lilies.

Yes, all in all, my life must be regarded as satisfactory.

Nefret placed the last fox into its hole. The board now stood as it had before the latest game.

Then she rose to her feet and walked calmly to her bedchamber. The

room was ornamented in the Egyptian style, its walls decorated with images
of a lush riverbank, its reeds teeming with birds: ducks, ibis, geese. She
stopped before her favorite among the painted memories: a family of swallows soaring high above the reeds. There she stood, serene as a painted statue,
while her handmaiden Teti gently unpinned and undraped her pale linen
gown, unclasped her wide necklace of lapis and carnelian, lifted the heavy
beaded wig from her head.

At last Teti took a soft clean cloth, dipped it into water scented with
lemon, and gently wiped Nefret's face clean of its saffron, malachite, and
carmine. Teti, as well-schooled and as tactful as her royal mistress, did not
comment on the dark smears of kohl spreading beneath the Lady Nefret-
meryt-hotep's tear-damp eyes.

Benaiah

This is no life for a warrior. No life for a war-chief. But he was no longer a war-
chief; he was the king's general, head of all King Solomon's armies.

And so he had spent most of the morning listening to his scribe read
lists of provisions and equipment; the afternoon discussing the logistics of
regarrisoning half-a-dozen border towns, an activity interrupted for an
hour by the urgent necessity of soothing the wounded vanity of a royal captain of a thousand who had lost precedence when a cousin was promoted to
a sinecure coveted by both men. Now the shadows stretched long, and still
Benaiah had not been able to claim one moment in which to set foot beyond the confines of his office.

Sometimes this place seems more a prison than a palace. For what was a prison but
a place one could not leave at will? *It was not like this in the old days, in King
David's time. Then a war-chief's sword found work. Now—*

Now the king's general sat and listened to the deeds of other men. Sat
and listened to the recitation of lists by men with soft voices and softer
hands. Sat and rotted.

Listen to yourself. You sound like an old man. Benaiah sighed, and rubbed his
eyes; the lamp oil smoked—*another detail I must put right.* Benaiah made a men-
tal note to tell his manservant Eben to see to the matter.

He knew what Eben would say: that Benaiah needed a wife. But Benaiah
had been wedded to his sword too long; it was too late for him to succumb
to softer lures. *And I am no prize for a young woman.* Marriageable girls dreamed

of young heroes. Heroes such as King David had once been, beautiful in body and eloquent in wooing.

Girls do not dream of hard old men with scarred hands and graying hair. Benaiah shook his head and smiled, rueful. No one would believe that the king's general brooded on such matters. Not Benaiah the clever, the strong, the endlessly-loyal sword arm of kings. But time served men as a whetstone served blades—sharpened them, honed them to keen use. And in the end, wore them away to nothingness.

"Truly, Benaiah, you sound like an old man—one as morose as a lion with toothache." Voicing the words lightened them, turned his glum thoughts to grim jest. Benaiah knew he was not old—not yet. But life in a king's court pressed men into strange, uncomfortable patterns. Luxury and indolence—no life for a fighting man.

Ah, yes, that is the stone in my sandal. I am not a fighting man. Not anymore. Now all I am is the king's general. A man who orders other men into battle and danger.

Now he was a man who led a life too easy, too lavish. A man who had lost his keen fighting edge.

But it did not matter, for the king Benaiah now served had no need of such a man. King David, now—King David had required men of stone and iron to serve him. King Solomon prized peace; wished to wield his army not as a whip forcing compliance, but as a shepherd's staff urging cooperation.

Yes, things have changed since King David's day. In King David's reign, Benaiah had commanded only the palace guard, the king's new-formed corps of foreigners, mercenaries. Benaiah had accepted the post reluctantly; it put him at odds with Joab, the king's general, commander of the army. And those who opposed Joab did not prosper long.

Nor had Benaiah liked the sight of foreign warriors pacing the halls of the king's palace. But King David had smiled at him, and spoken soft words. "You are a good man, Benaiah, I need good men about me, men I can trust with the safety of my wives and my children." When King David had spoken, Benaiah had felt the intensity of the king's need. How flattering to a young soldier, to be raised high and told that the king trusted him. That the king needed him. Benaiah had bowed and taken up the charge King David had laid upon him.

Commander of the king's guard—never before had there been such an office in Israel. But after Prince Absalom's rebellion, and the revolt of the northern tribes, Benaiah had understood King David's fears for his family's safety.

Or thought he had. Gradually he came to see the guard he commanded for what it truly was: a weapon, a counterweight to the unruly army.

An army commanded by the king's nephew Joab—and while Joab's loyalty was beyond question, his methods were harsh and brutal. Joab would do anything that he thought good for King David. Anything, including murder.

Abner, Absalom, Adonijah. Those were only three of the deaths laid at Joab's door. Abner, who had been King Saul's war-chief. Absalom, who had been King David's treacherous, rebellious son. Adonijah, who had been King Solomon's too-ambitious brother. All had sought power from David; all had received death from Joab's hand.

But Prince Adonijah was the last of Joab's kills. For Adonijah grasped at the crown as King David lay dying—only to be thwarted by his father's sudden proclamation of Prince Solomon as successor. Adonijah had not been wise enough to accept defeat with grace; instead, he had stood before his brother and demanded possession of the king's maiden, Abishag, to console him for the loss of the crown he had so coveted.

Abishag had been chosen by King David's chief wife, Michal, as a gift to bring heat to the aged king. The maiden served as King David's bedwarmer during the long months it took the king to die; that service alone made her a royal bequest, a legacy for the next king. And everyone with eyes to see knew that Prince Solomon had already chosen Abishag for his own queen.

Prince Adonijah's arrogant folly had earned him death, death Joab dealt him as King Solomon watched in horror. Joab merely shrugged and wiped his sword blade clean on Adonijah's scarlet cloak. It had been Benaiah who had come forward and quietly ordered his guardsmen to carry out Prince Adonijah's body; who had surrounded King Solomon with men of the palace guard; who had escorted Queen Michal and the king's mother, Bathsheba, safely back to the women's palace. It had been Benaiah who had ensured that before King Solomon again set foot in the throne room, the steps of the throne were washed clean of his brother's blood.

Benaiah had done those things not to win favor in the new king's eyes, but because his task was to protect the king and to ensure peace within the king's house. But King Solomon did not forget Benaiah's quiet support—and with

Great David dead, it was Solomon's will alone that counted. Solomon lifted the burden of command from Joab and gave that power into Benaiah's hand.

Knowing what was due a man of Joab's rank, Benaiah had gone to tell him of Solomon's decision before the change was announced in the king's court. To his surprise, Joab took the news unflinching.

"I thought as much. I am old, and have been David's man these forty years." Joab's eyes seemed to look past Benaiah, into a past the young could never share.

Benaiah shifted, uneasy; more than once, Joab had taken bad news well, then struck down the man who stood in his way. "I did not seek this office, Joab. It is King Solomon's will."

"No need to tell me; I've known you since you were a boy. Deceit isn't in you. Rest easy, Benaiah. Adonijah was the last. My sword days are over."

"I am sorry, Joab." Benaiah studied the impassive man before him. "You are not surprised."

"Nor should you be, unless you do not know Solomon at all. He will never forgive me for slaying his brother."

"But Adonijah as good as demanded the throne. And what he said of the Lady Abishag—"

"Was still not treason," Joab said. "But Adonijah had to die, or Solomon would not know a day's peace on that golden throne of his. Someone had to kill him. So I did."

Benaiah thought this over. "It was murder."

Joab shrugged. "It was necessary. Always remember, King's Commander, that the king must do what is right—and his general must do what is needful." Joab regarded Benaiah steadily, as if over crossed swords. "It will be needful that you kill me, Benaiah. But don't expect me to make it easy for you."

Although Benaiah sensed in his bones that Joab was right, he shook his head. "No. Live peacefully in your own house, Joab; King Solomon is not vengeful."

"No," said Joab, "he isn't. That is why he has you."

"Tell me one thing, Joab—how does a man do what is needful and still sleep quiet at night?"

Joab had smiled, teeth a wolf-white flash. "You learn," he said.

———

Much as he had loathed the knowledge Joab had imparted, Benaiah was too honest to deny its truth: King Solomon would never forgive King David's general. For Solomon had not hated his brother Adonijah—any more than Solomon hated Joab. Solomon did not hate any man.

Sometimes Benaiah thought that was Solomon's greatest weakness. *Wisdom is not common sense.* In a king's world, what was good was not always what was wise.

But as Joab had so truly said, knowing the difference, and acting wisely, was Benaiah's job. King Solomon relied upon Benaiah as King David had relied upon Joab.

And as for sleeping sound—to Benaiah's dismay, Joab had been right. He had learned.

PART THREE

Sow the Wind

Abishag

Before I was brought to King David's court, before I knew her for myself, I had always thought the harpers' tales made Queen Michal sound too good to be true. No woman could be so wise, so virtuous, so tolerant—

"Unless she is simpleminded," I had said one day, when my mother and her friends were telling over the latest gossip from Jerusalem as they filled their jars at the village well. I spoke with the pride and careless arrogance of ignorant youth. "I would never share a husband so, if I were queen!"

Many girls' mothers would have cuffed them for such unseemly words; most would have rebuked them sharply. My mother merely regarded me steadily as she dipped her empty jar into the water and said, "Easy to say now, Abishag. Remember your words, Daughter, and say them again in a dozen years, if they still are true." Then she lifted the water jar to her hip, balancing the heavy vessel as if it were a child. "All women should be as simpleminded as Queen Michal. The world would turn a good deal better than it now does!"

My mother smiled, and her friends all laughed—my mother owned the gift of bringing laughter with her. And as they laughed, I bowed my head and splashed water from the well upon my hot cheeks, knowing I had sounded both young and foolish. But no woman can be so openhearted as men say the queen is!

And so I thought, even upon the day I first met Queen Michal, the day I entered King David's palace.

Baalit Sings

My mother was my father's first wife, the bride of his heart. I never knew her, for she died bringing me into the world. But I knew my father; knew him better than most daughters know their sires, for having lost his most cherished wife, he cherished me in her stead. This was good of him; many men would have blamed the child that had cost them the much-loved mother—and that child not even a son, but a mere daughter.

I was the king's only daughter, the court's only princess. My father was a good man who deserved a perfect daughter, a model of womanly grace and beauty: meek, docile, obedient. A girl who could weave and embroider, knead bread and bake sweet cakes. A paragon of the womanly talents.

Instead, he had me.

Hard as I tried—and I wished very much to please my father—I could not be that perfect girl. My father was handsome as the sun; my mother, so I had been told, had been sloe-dark and shapely, partridge plump. I should have been a beauty too, sleek-haired and soft, wide-eyed and pearl-smooth.

But some unknown foremother had bequeathed me wild hair and restless eyes. Worse, I owned a will as untamed and unruly as my hair, possessed a lust for knowledge as keen as my searching eyes.

Oh, I could weave, and embroider as well as most and better than some; any task is better well-done than ill. But I also wished to play upon the harp, and to dance; to drive a chariot; to read, and to write as well. To have the freedom my brothers squandered so carelessly.

My father did his best for me; treated me almost as if I were indeed a son, rather than a daughter. Bestowed upon me as much freedom as he could.

"Let her learn to read; what harm can come of her knowing?"

"Let her play upon the harp, if it pleases her. She gets that song-love from her grandfather, Great David."

"Let her accompany me in the chariot if it amuses the child."

Although none of them stood in place of my mother, my father's wives objected to each concession granted me, arguing that such indulgent treatment would spoil any girl. That such liberty would turn me headstrong and unwomanly. Unmarriageable.

My father laughed at that, and said only that no knowledge was ever wasted. "Wisdom is better than rubies," he told them, "and as for the rest—when the time comes for her to marry, she will have her choice of the world's kings. Who would spurn the daughter of King Solomon?"

So I learned what I wished, and tried to be what my father desired, what he thought I truly was: his soft, womanly, loving little daughter. I did try. And I did love my father dearly.

But I was not soft, and I was not womanly.

Those things I knew I would never be.

So greatly did my father cherish me that, although I was only the king's daughter, I dwelt in the rooms that had once housed Queen Michal herself. This prize was granted to me by my father the summer I turned thirteen. The gift was generous and the giving of it ingenious; my father had a taste for riddles and puzzles. He summoned me to the women's courtyard, the large one that belonged to all his wives in common, and there handed me a knotted thread.

"Follow this to its end," he told me, "and what you find there will be yours."

The thread he handed me was thick and rough enough to be more rightly called cord; I began to gather its length up into my hands, then saw that the scarlet thread fell to the ground and led off across the courtyard. My father smiled at me, and my heart beat faster, knowing there must be a special gift waiting for me at the end of the trail of thread. I am glad to say that I remembered to thank him before I followed the thread, winding it into a ball as I traced its path.

It took me half the morning to wind along the thread to its end; whoever had laid down the thread's pattern had been industrious, and the course I followed wound about columns and along corridors, traced around fountains and down stairwells, wove in and out of doorways. The game caught everyone's fancy, and so I was watched by smiling women and trailed after by excited children. It seemed I paced every foot of the women's quarters before I at last came to the cord's end at a courtyard gate.

The gate was ebony, dark wood polished smooth and inlaid with rows of ivory plaques. The cord was knotted to the gilded latch. My father stood beside the gate, waiting for me.

The ball of cord I held had grown unwieldy over the course of my quest;

now I set it down before my father. "I am here," I said, and my father looked down at the ball of cord and then at me. "Now I see why it took you so long to find your way to your prize," he said. "You could just have hastened along the cord and left it lying upon the floor, you know."

"Isn't the thread mine too?" I asked, and my father laughed and hugged me, and kissed me upon my forehead. "My clever, careful daughter! I am twice glad to give you this gift; I can think of no one else worthy of it."

He turned and pushed open the ebony gate. "Once what lies behind this gate belonged to Queen Michal," he told me, "and now it belongs to you."

My eyes grew wide, for Queen Michal had been Great David's first wife, foremost among his women, the woman he had won with blood and kept with iron. The woman who had raised my father more truly than had his own mother. My father spoke of her as he spoke of no other woman save my mother. Now he had given me Queen Michal's court for my own. I tried to form words into a graceful thanks, but in my excitement I could say only "Queen Michal's rooms? For *me*?"

But my father seemed to think this enough; he smiled. "The queen's rooms, for you, my daughter. You are no longer a child needing a nurse. You are growing into a woman; it is time you had a court and maidservants of your own."

He said also that I might do as pleased me with these rooms which now were mine, but there was a stiffness in his voice, and I knew he hoped that I would make no changes to this place in which he had been raised. So I thanked him, and said only that the rooms pleased me just as they were.

"If they were good enough for a queen, surely they are good enough for a king's daughter," I said, and sensed my father's pleasure at my answer.

And truly, the old queen's rooms were lovely; the walls painted with swallows and poppies, the courtyard gay with lilies and a fountain whose water sang endlessly over pale stone. I sat upon the edge of the fountain, dipping my hand into the flowing water, and smiled. *Truly I am now a woman grown, and as good as a queen.* So I thought, in my pleasure and my pride, but I did not say so aloud—that much modesty and sense I did possess.

Only later did I wonder why my father had given me Queen Michal's rooms, and not Queen Abishag's. I had received not my mother's rooms but his mother's—or rather, his stepmother's. And so I wondered.

But I did not ask.

That was the night my dreams began, the night I first slept in the old queen's rooms that were now my own.

I held a scarlet thread in my hands, a thread leading into darkness. Behind me a wall of stone stood cold against my back. Light gleamed through chinks between the stones, bright sparks of warmth, but I could not retreat from the darkness that lay ahead.

Slowly I began to follow the scarlet thread, coiling it into a ball in my hands as I traced its path. The thread led me in a long slow dance through darkness into shadow, through shadow into smoke. I followed where the thread led me, obedient to its will.

Darkness lifted; I stood within a vast courtyard, a court whose walls were set with a dozen gates. The gates stood open, waiting for my choice. Trusting my guide, I looked down at the ball of scarlet thread, knowing it would lead me to the gate I must pass through. But I no longer had one strong true thread to follow; a dozen thin lines of red now flowed from my hand, and each new thread led through a different gate.

Now I must choose; choose one path, and see all other gates close against me forever—

I woke weeping. My own sorrow shocked me, for the dream had not been so fearful after all. A thread to follow, a gateway to choose— *Do not be foolish,* I chided myself, *you dreamed because you sleep in a new room, in a new bed. You will forget those dream gates by the morning.*

But I did not forget.

Until now, my dreams had been a child's; bright images faded into nothingness by dawn's light. Never before had I remembered a dream as vividly as if it were true memory.

Never before had my dreams troubled my nights, and my days. Perhaps my passage into womanhood bred these unquiet illusions. Once I would have asked my grandmothers, sought wisdom from their lips. When I was a child, it seemed to me they knew the answers to all questions, the keys to all riddles. But now they were gone, and I must find my answers for myself.

As always, to think of my loss summoned tears to sting my eyes. And just as I had possessed more than most, so my loss was greater. For most girls, if they are fortunate, can claim two grandmothers. I was truly favored, for as I said, I grew up under the guidance of three: my mother's mother, and my father's mother—and his foster-mother as well. These three shaped my dreams, and hence my life.

As did my mother, although her I never knew. Yet she had left me a legacy of love that served me well; better than gold and rubies, in the end.

And of course I owned much that had been hers; all the jewels that had been Queen Abishag's became mine, treasures to serve as dowry, to be handed down to my own daughter in her turn. Thick chains of gold, bolts of cloth fine enough for a goddess, handfuls of rubies and pearls—such things any queen might own. Nor was I too high-minded to spurn gems and silks and gold; always I have liked pretty things.

But I had other treasures from my mother, and these I cherished more than gems or gold, for these she had chosen herself, and given into her mother's hands to bestow upon me, when I should be old enough to understand and to cherish the gifts. This legacy seemed little enough; no more than the contents of a small ivory casket. A spangled veil. A necklace of coral and pearl; a glass vial iridescent as a dragonfly wing, still smelling sweet of roses and sharp of cinnamon. A silver mirror small as a woman's palm. A bracelet, a shabby trinket of worn brass chains and flakes of crystal. An ivory Asherah, an idol carved so long ago its curves had darkened to the color of wild honey.

I did not know why my mother should have kept the Asherah; never had I heard any word that hinted she was less than a good Daughter of the Lord. But there the little goddess lay, wrapped in a scrap of crimson silk.

My handmaiden Rivkah, who once had been my mother's maidservant, had given me the casket the first time the moon's pull drew me into womanhood. "Your mother's mother gave it into my keeping, when she knew she could no longer remain here. She bade me lay it in your hands and tell you it is your legacy from your mothers."

My mother's mother's name was Zhurleen, and even though she was no longer young, she was very beautiful—or knew how to seem so. She knew everything there was to know about women's secrets. She had spent much time with me when I was a small girl, singing me secret songs and telling me mysterious stories. In her tales, girls and goddesses did not sit spinning by the hearth; no, they sought treasures and rescued children, created gardens and ruled the heavens.

She liked best to tell me the tale of the Bright Lady Inanna, who sought her dead lover in the Underworld, defying her sister Death. "There are seven gates one must pass to reach the Queen of Death's palace, and at each gate a treasure was taken from Inanna, until the bright Queen of Heaven walked clad only in her flowing hair. Only that was left to veil her, to keep her safe."

Inanna faced her sister Ereshkigal bravely, but Ereshkigal slew Inanna and hung her upon a tree. And for three days Inanna hung there dead in the Land of No Return—until her servant cunningly smuggled the food and water of life into Death's palace of lapis lazuli.

"And so Inanna returned to walk the fields and touch the flowers, so that the world rejoiced once more in her love."

That I liked, that the Bright Lady returned to smile upon the fruit and flowers. But I liked Lady Death too, who ruled her own kingdom and did not need to bargain away her jewels for a lover. When I told my grandmother that, she laughed.

"You do not understand now," my grandmother said, just as she did at the end of each tale she told me, "but one day you will. Remember, little goddess, that a woman may have whatever she desires, so long as she remains veiled like the Goddess Herself."

And then she would laugh, and feed me pomegranate seeds or bits of honey-cake. "So you will remember wisdom is sweet."

Zhurleen was my laughing grandmother.

Bathsheba was my father's mother; my indulgent grandmother, who granted my childish whims without question. I remembered her as a pair of soft loving arms and an endless kindness. "Of course you may have my necklet, sweetling—there now, little dove—see how pretty you look!" She was never strict, never stern. Even as a child, I knew my other two grandmothers guarded the Lady Bathsheba as if she were their own daughter, rather than the mother of the king.

Queen Michal stood in a grandmother's place to me as well. Although Bathsheba had given birth to my father, it was Queen Michal who had shaped him, and he gave her the honor due a mother—and a queen.

Queen Michal was cool and clever, and sometimes less than gentle, even with my other grandmothers, who were her dearest friends. "Those are not wise songs to sing to a princess of Israel," she would tell my grandmother Zhurleen; and to Bathsheba, "It is not wise to let a girl think she may have whatsoever she wishes merely for the asking."

And then she would take my small hand and lead me off to her own garden, and sit me down beside the fountain, and there lecture me as if I were old and wise as my own father. "Your grandmothers are good women, and kind, and loving, but sometimes they do not see clearly. Remember it is better to keep silent and wait. That is what women must do, little princess. Wait."

"Wait for what?" I asked, but Queen Michal never told me—or if she did, I neither understood her words nor remembered them. I preferred my laughing grandmother's songs and my indulgent grandmother's gifts to Queen Michal's cool warnings.

This sounds like much, as if I spent all my days with them and studied them well; in truth, I barely remembered their faces now, for they were old when I was very young. Queen Michal and the Lady Bathsheba now slept in the burial cave beside King David, and my laughing grandmother Zhurleen was gone as well. Bathsheba and Michal died the year I turned seven, and one day soon after that I ran into my grandmother Zhurleen's rooms to find her maidservants folding her garments and packing all she owned into travel chests. And when I saw that she would leave, and began to weep, she folded me in her arms; I breathed in the scent of lilies and myrrh.

"Someday you will understand," she said, and for once she did not laugh. "Yes, of course I love you, child—but I am old now, and the friends of my heart are gone. I weary of living in a strange land." She set her hands upon my shoulders and held me away from her, gazing steadily into my tear-wet eyes.

"I wish to go home, Baalit. I wish to return to my own people and my own gods. And—there are other reasons." But what they were, she did not tell me then.

"But what will I do without you?" I wailed; then at last she laughed, softly.

"You will do very well, child." She kissed me upon the forehead, her lips cool and soft upon my hot skin. "Now dry your eyes and remember I shall not be in my grave but in Ascalon. Nothing is forever, little goddess."

All three, gone between one full moon and the next. Only their words remained, veiled memories, spoken now only in dreams.

But in the ivory casket I held a tangible past, a gift from the women who had come before me; a treasure given into my hands now that I too was a woman.

Rivkah did not say that the casket was a secret gift, but somehow I sensed that my father would not like to see it, and so I kept the little box beneath my bed—not hidden, but not flaunted either. And from time to time I would pull the casket out and take up my mother's small treasures and hold them, weighing them in my hand, waiting to see if they would reveal her to me.

For what did I know of my mother, after all? Nothing, save what I had been told. Told by my father, her husband, who had loved her well. Told by my father's wives, who had envied her. Neither love nor envy told truly; such emotions created their own reality. Joy and love, sorrow and hate—none of these cast a true image. Passion was truth's enemy.

Gradually it became my habit each month, when the moon rose full and silver light poured down into the courtyard garden that had once been Queen Michal's and now was mine, to lift my mother's gift from where it lay waiting beneath my bed and carry it out into the moonlight. There I would tell over the remnants of her life that my mother had left me, each in its proper order:

Veil, necklace, vial, mirror, bracelet, goddess. Six memories. I would hold each, striving to see the past they embodied. But I never could, and at last I would grow sleepy, and pack my treasures carefully away again.

There was a seventh memory: a spindle of ivory with a whirl of amber. But the ivory spindle did not rest within my mother's treasure box; I had not set eyes upon it since I was seven. I remembered Queen Michal sitting, spinning the pretty toy. "It helps me think," she told me. "Someday it will be yours, and it will help you."

But the ivory spindle had been lost.

I had a spindle of my own, of course, a pretty thing of smooth-polished olive wood. Queen Michal had been right; spinning aided thought. Once I had learned to spin a smooth thread, the steady rise and fall, the endless whir as wool lengthened into thread, calmed my mind. Outwardly I seemed both dutiful and diligent, while my mind roved free.

Sometimes I wondered why Queen Michal had needed such solace, or my mother either, for surely they had not been shackled by custom as I was. I was only the king's daughter, they had both been queens. Surely they had never suffered the restless cravings that ate my peace.

Today I needed the calm spinning would summon. Carrying spindle and wool into my garden, I stood beside the bed of lilies and flicked the whirl to set it turning. Well, and so should I be a queen, one day. For I must marry, and as a princess, I was a playing-piece in the games of kings. A valuable piece, for my father prized me. I would marry a great king, and then I too would be a queen, as my mother had been before me. Staring at the turning whirl, I tried to summon up a vision of myself as a great king's queen. A queen clothed in purple linen dark as storm cloud; a queen adorned with chains of gold and gems. A queen who had only to lift her soft hand to have her lightest whim granted. . . .

But the brilliant image would not form; I saw only the slowly turning disk of wood, the growing length of pale thread. My mind was too unquiet to play that game.

And a queen is more than gowns and gold. The words slid unbidden into my mind, familiar as if I had often heard them said. *You have a woman's power—* A soft voice; a ripple of laughter—my mother? But I had never heard her voice. . . . I shook my head, and that inner voice fell silent.

Then I was sorry, and tried again to hear those faint, laughing words. But the moment had passed. I had no more success listening to the past than I had visioning the future.

I sighed and fed more wool to the spindle, spun the whirl again. Abishag, daughter of Zhurleen; Queen Abishag, wife of King Solomon. Abishag, mother of Baalit. . . . I would never know my mother, she would never speak to me, save in dreams.

The soft voice I sometimes heard was only the whisper of my own heart, the echo of my own longing for a love I had never known. All that remained to me of my mother lay here, enclosed in an ivory box.

In the end, I must live my own life. Not hers.

Helike

Her father was Horse Lord, king over the herds that roamed the windswept plains once ruled by long-dead Troy. Like all his children, she had ridden before she could walk. By the time she was seven, she could control the wildest mare, soothe the most high-strung stallion.

"The girl rides like a centaur!" That was the best her father could say of any child of his. She had basked in that pride as if it were the sun.

Her skill with horses shaped her life. As a child, she had been dedicated to Hippona, goddess of horses; seeing her gift of horse-mastery, her father had fostered her with Doromene, queen of the tribe of women known as Amazons, the Sword Maidens.

With the Maidens, she had ridden before the wind, learning the ways of Hippona's children. She had grown straight and supple as a young cedar, shaped by wind and sun and long hard days into a woman fit to command warhorses, or warriors.

At fourteen, she had vowed herself to the Sword Maidens. She would live all her life calling the wide golden plains home, wedded to no man, faithful to her sisters and her goddess.

I forgot a woman may make only the vows a man will let her keep.

For a faraway king needed horses, and her father needed strong allies. And so one day her father had sent to the Sword Maidens and summoned his daughter. Curious, she had ridden back with the messenger; she had not seen her father in a decade, and knew a wish to stand before him and feel the warmth of his pride in her once more.

Had I known, I would not have gone. Even now, she knew that for a lie; her father would have threatened to seize her by force if he could have had her no other way. The Sword Queen would have defied him— *And I would have obeyed him. I could not let my sisters die defending me.* The Sword Maidens could not withstand the Horse Lord's warriors. *But had I known I never again would set eyes upon my sisters, I would have taken greater care with my farewells.*

When she had ridden into the Horse Lord's city, it had been as a woman of pride and honor, a woman all those she rode past eyed with awe and envy. Small girls stared up at her, their young eyes wide as full moons, longing to become what she was. She rode up the wide king's way to the palace and into the palace courtyard where her father awaited, smiling. She dismounted and bowed before him, and smiling still, her father raised her up and kissed her cheek.

"You have grown beautiful, my daughter. Your foster-mother raised you well; I am pleased."

Her father then asked to see the sword she carried, and she drew the blade from its deerskin sheath and gave it into his outstretched hand.

"I have learned to use it with skill and honor, Father. My queen is pleased with me, too."

"You are a good girl, Helike. You always were the best rider of all my children." Her father smiled again, and she smiled back, pleased by his praise. That was the last moment she had known unblemished pleasure.

"Now go with the women, Helike. They will prepare you to meet the emissaries of King Solomon, who wish to see you before accepting you for their ruler. No one buys a mare sight unseen!" And her father laughed; she did not, staring at her father until his laughter faded.

"King Solomon?" she said, grasping at the hope she had misunderstood. "Me?"

"Yes, you. Who else? All your elder sisters are already wed—to your good fortune now." Her father's eyes shifted, unwilling to meet hers.

She would not collude in his pretense that she must be pleased. "Do you not remember I am vowed as a maiden to Hippona, I am sworn to the Sword Queen?"

"And do you not remember you're my daughter, owing me obedience?" Clever, he said no more, but motioned the waiting women with a wave of his hand. And the women gathered about her and swept her along with them, out of the Horse Lord's courtyard and into their own cloistered world.

Her father had taken her short bronze sword. Now the women took away the rest of the garments that proclaimed her a Sword Maid. Her high laced boots, her doeskin trousers. Her bead-sewn fringed tunic. Her broad belt with its loops for sword and dagger. Her quiver and arrows. Her moon-curved bow.

When they took away the band of silver a handspan wide that protected her throat, the Sword Maid vanished. All that remained was a slender girl whose body was hardened by riding and hunting, and whose pale hair was bound into a single braid.

And then one of the waiting women untied the leather cord and shook Helike's hair free of the tight-woven braid. Her hair rippled down her back like water, washing away the last token of her freedom.

All her life she had ridden one road. Now that high road was barred to her forever.

"Come, Lady Helike," the chief of the women said, "it is time to prepare you to meet those who will take you to your husband."

That evening she had been taken before half-a-dozen men whom her father said were King Solomon's emissaries, been displayed before them like a brood mare. Her father extolled her good points—her long sun-gilded hair, her clear sun-browned skin, her fine white teeth.

"My eyes tell me she's comely enough," the king's ambassador said when her father ceased counting over the charms of her face and form. "What of her character?"

Her father stared at that; if a princess were fair to look upon, what else mattered? "She has lived these last ten years with the Sword Maids, who pledge themselves to chastity," he said at last. "What better guarantee of her virtue can I offer?"

"Not that it matters," her father informed her the next morning, "for King Solomon has such a great need of my horses he would overlook a greater fault in you than wantonness."

She said nothing, fearing to weep before him. She had not slept, but spent the long night vainly seeking a third path for herself.

If she obeyed her father, she violated her vows to Hippona the White Mare, and to Artemis the Huntress, and to the Sword Maidens.

If she rebelled against her father and fled, she condemned her blood-sisters to the Horse Lord's wrath—and King Solomon's as well.

A third path lay between those two choices: death.

And even that was an uncertain road. *I might slay myself; then I would violate no vows.* But the cheated king might still take vengeance against the Sword Maids—and death was hard to face in cold blood. She had lacked the courage to turn a blade into her own flesh.

And so she had wed as she had been ordered, her body offered up to seal a treaty of trade and trust between the Horse Lord and the King of Israel and Judah.

Now she who had ridden the broad plains that flowed across the world like a sea of grass, who had called the wind her home, dwelt prisoned within walls of wood and stone.

Sometimes she wished she had possessed the courage to take the third path. Now—

Now it was too late.

Baalit Sings

But although my grandmothers were gone, and I missed them sorely, do not think I paced solitary as a cat; a princess is rarely alone. Nor was I lonely, which is a different thing. I was fortunate in my handmaidens, for they had been given me when they and I were still in our cradles. Although we were mistress and maidservants, we grew up almost as sisters. And although three girls could hardly be more different, we loved one another dearly.

Nimrah was my elder by nearly a year; sleek and elegant as the leopardess for which she was named. Although her family came from the faraway northern lands—"Or so my father's mother says!"—Nimrah herself had been born in Jerusalem. Nimrah was tall as a boy and pale as bone, and it would be hard to find a good husband for her. I knew I must bestow a dowry upon her generous enough to transform Nimrah from an ugly foreigner to an exotic bride.

Keshet was nine months younger than I, as rounded and dark as Nimrah was slender and fair. Her mother had wed one of my father's brothers, and when he had been killed leading his men into battle, his wife had begged King Solomon's aid and been granted asylum in the king's house. Keshet had been born soon enough after his death to be counted Prince Shobab's daughter—and late enough for it to be whispered she was King Solomon's.

I thought it possible that she was my half-sister; that my father, grieving the loss of my mother, had taken comfort where he had gone to offer it. But I was not sure; my father had never acknowledged Keshet, after all.

Keshet herself seemed untroubled by the whispered tales. "Either I am the daughter of a prince or of a king, and in either case, King David is still my grandfather! That is what counts."

I could not imagine a life without Nimrah and Keshet; I believe they felt the same. I could never have stolen so many hours without their aid, nor wandered so freely.

For it is hard to live one's own life when so much is forbidden; truly, it is simpler to live in memories and dreams. When I was a girl, little had been denied me—or so I thought. For what does a child demand, after all, but childish things—a bright toy, a pretty sash, a handful of glass beads? The year I became a woman, I learned that even a princess is chained. Oh, because I was King Solomon's pampered daughter, my chains were bright with gems and weighed lightly upon my childish will—but they bound me just the same.

That year I learned to loathe the word *forbidden*. For so much was now forbidden to me that my brothers enjoyed at their will. They might run about as they pleased; I must walk modest and quiet. They might learn whatsoever they wished; I must confine myself to those studies thought fit for one who was only a girl. Some traditions bound even a king's beloved daughter. My father indulged me, eased the tightness of the invisible chains that bound me—but even he could not remake the world.

And that was what I longed to do, to shape the world to my desire.

"Why may my brothers choose, and I may not?" I demanded of Rivkah. "It is not fair! I am as clever as they—cleverer! And—"

"And the world is as it is, and no use struggling against it." That was Rivkah's placid argument. Nor were my handmaidens Nimrah and Keshet any less bound by tradition.

"Why do you wish to ride out with your brothers? You will come back covered in dust and your gown will be ruined." Tidy as a cat, Keshet could imagine few worse fates.

Nimrah understood my restless urges better, but she, too, urged prudence. "Do not give your father's wives cause to complain of you, Princess. You go your own way easily enough; why force the king to see it?"

I knew she was right, for my father hated to deny my whims—nor would he forbid activities he did not discover.

That was the year I learned to keep my wild hair smoothly bound and my restless eyes downcast—and my unruly thoughts silent. Outwardly I paced tranquil, the image of a tame and dutiful daughter—for I did not wish to pain my father, who loved me so much and understood me so little.

My true self remained veiled. Veiled from my father, from my stepmothers, from my handmaidens. Veiled, although I did not yet know it, even from myself.

I took care with my secrets, entrusting them to no one. Even Nimrah and Keshet did not know all I dared. More than one person cannot keep a secret, even when life rides upon silence.

And there were things I might dare, and be forgiven, and those I might not. Even my father, who loved learning and who permitted his foreign wives to worship as they wished, would not have been pleased to know his own daughter visited the temples of alien gods.

Oddly enough, it was the woman's veil I so despised that permitted me such freedom, the veil I sulked over when obliged to cover myself with it as befit a king's daughter, complaining that its enslaving folds stifled me.

I learned that while it is true a veil confines, transmutes a woman into a shadow sliding unnoticed through life, a veil also grants freedom.

A veil transforms one woman into any woman. Hidden behind a veil, a woman might pass by unrecognized even by her own brother.

Veiled, I slipped easily from the king's palace. Veiled, I was but one more woman, unknown and unknowable. Veiled, King Solomon's daughter wandered freely, unhindered.

Veiled, I learned the city's limits. Veiled, I studied the life of my father's people, their loves and angers, their hates and joys.

Veiled, I learned myself, and my desires.

King David's City, once the abode of Lord Yahweh only, now held dozens of temples raised to honor alien gods—and goddesses as well. Baal, Anath, and Astarte, Dagon and Bast—all now were housed within Jerusalem's sheltering walls.

The prophet Ahijah raged against these alien idols, but few took notice of his protests. In a time of peace, a time when the rains came in their season and the harvests were bountiful, who could believe the Lord angered? And did not the Lord's Temple, the Great Temple that housed the sacred Ark, crown the highest hill in all the city? Did not that prove the Lord's dominion over all other gods?

So the foreign temples stayed, and their gods flourished. The temples were good for business as well, for travelers to Jerusalem liked finding their own gods dwelling there. Cheerful traders spend more freely than do those who dourly count the days until they see home again. Jerusalem prospered.

Veiled, I visited the forbidden temples, standing silent, seeing yet unseen. At first the mere breaking of the iron taboo thrilled me, and I could barely set foot beyond a temple gate. What unclean horrors would I find within, what bizarre, arcane rites would I see practiced?

Rather to my disappointment, when I at last dared enter the houses of alien gods, I found little that was strange to me, save the images.

Incense burning, priests praying, petitioners seeking favor, acolytes collecting offerings—these seemed the same, no matter what god or goddess was entreated. And always there was a holy of holies, a sanctuary so sacred only the highest ranking priest or priestess might enter.

All that differed from one temple to the next was the face of the god. For all temples save Lord Yahweh's were adorned with idols, images of carven wood or stone. These images varied—some gods were beautiful, winged and smiling. Some wore the heads of animals.

And some were women. Goddesses. Goddesses slim as the crescent moon shining in their curled hair. Goddesses lush and fertile as ripe pomegranates. Goddesses fierce and strong as the great cats fawning at their feet. I liked looking at the goddesses; they reminded me of my laughing grandmother.

It was against those many goddesses that Ahijah poured out his greatest venom. Whoredom was the least of the sins their worshippers were accused of.

But I saw no sign of the bloody, vile crimes the prophet Ahijah preached against. Certainly none of the temples practiced any sacrifice greater than those the Lord himself found acceptable: a bull, a ram, a dove. Some sacrificed nothing at all; Ishtar's favorite offering was the release of songbirds into the air, to fly freely.

There was a trick to that, for the birds, left to themselves, flew back to their home behind their temple, there to be fed and pampered until they were sold to other worshippers. I knew this because I bought my own wicker cage of songbirds from the temple bird merchant, and marked one of the birds before tossing it skyward. The next time I visited Ishtar's temple and handed over a sliver of silver in exchange for a songbird for the goddess, I received the same bird I had marked, the henna streak upon its feathers faded but still rosy enough to see. I laughed as I flung the small bird upward, knowing it would only return safely home once it had stretched its small bright wings.

As for whoredom—in some temples, priestesses offered themselves as mortal mirrors for the goddesses they served. But they were not harlots, and any man who strove to treat them so found little welcome in any god's temple thereafter. And there were festivals held in groves beyond the city upon the great holy days, where all men were deemed gods and all women goddesses, and all love a holy offering.

Or so I heard; I had never set foot beyond the city walls myself, save in dreams. A great chasm separates daring from folly. There were adventures I knew better than to attempt.

Just as for all my curiosity, my restlessness, my daring, I knew better than to cross beyond the brazen gate of the Lord's Temple upon the hill. Once I thought of dressing in boy's clothing to make the attempt, but it was a moment's wild impulse, instantly quelled by good sense. If I were found there, even being King Solomon's daughter might not be enough to save me from the priests' anger.

How strange; the house of my own god was forbidden to me. To all women. Only the outer court was permitted to women. Farther than that, they might not go, lest they defile our god's sanctuary.

No wonder women turned instead to the goddesses who welcomed them open-armed, and offered love instead of wrath. No wonder women baked sweet cakes and poured honey wine for the queens of heaven. And then Ahijah raged, and ranted, and demanded to know what sin women carried, that they turned away from a god who had already denied them!

My half-brothers too helped fill my world; my father's sons, sired upon his foreign wives. I was fond of many of my brothers, indifferent to others. And then there was my brother Rehoboam, the Crown Prince. Him, I loathed, and with good reason.

I do not know what trick of fate granted my brother Rehoboam the honor of being a king's firstborn son. I do know that of all my brothers, Rehoboam was perhaps the least deserving of kingship. Rehoboam could not even rule himself; how was he to rule others?

Prince Rehoboam was neither clever nor kind, and no one knew this better than I. That was why I walked cautious and watchful when Rehoboam was nearby. He liked me no better than I liked him; not only was I our father's pet, but I spoiled Rehoboam's vicious games when I could.

As I did the day I rescued the Lady Nefret's Egyptian cat.

That day I was where I had no particular right to be, as was the cat. I had spent the morning with my brothers' Akkadian tutor, a eunuch who had, by virtue of his maiming as a man, gained unquestioned access to the women's palace. Emneht schooled me in the sacred songs of Ugarit and of Ur; I did not know whether I believed the ancient stories Emneht taught us were truth or tale only, but I found the language beautiful. And my father believed always that knowledge was its own reward.

I was walking back to my own courtyard when I heard noise from a side corridor, sounds like jackals yipping. Since there were no jackals dwelling within the palace, I knew it had to be boys—boys engaged in mischief. I ran around the corner and saw at once that it was worse than that. My brother Rehoboam and his pack of friends had cornered a cat.

The cat's coat was a soft brown tipped with black, like a rabbit's; gold hoops pierced its wide ears, and a collar of red and blue beads circled its sleek neck. An Egyptian cat, a darling of my father's Egyptian wife.

The soft little animal was trapped upon the top of a column; Rehoboam thrust a burning brand at its nose, trying to force the cat down as the others jeered. Unnoticed, I padded up behind my brother; I grabbed his thick curly hair in both my hands and hauled back with all my strength.

Rehoboam yowled and swung around, waving his arms frantically; the burning stick scorched the fringe edging my scarf. Refusing to yield, I yanked again, and Rehoboam stumbled as he tried to dislodge my fierce grip on his hair.

My brother flailed about; he landed a kick on my calf that unbalanced me, but I did not fall. My grasp on his hair kept me upright. None of Rehoboam's comrades interfered, either to help him or to hinder me—they might run and tell tales, but none would willingly entangle himself in the royal family's quarrels.

This knowledge strengthened me; I released Rehoboam's hair and shoved past him, set myself as a wall before the trapped cat. There I waited, permitting my brother to withdraw, if he would. A wise boy would have retreated at this point, but Rehoboam had never been noted for good sense or judgment.

"How dare you attack me, you viper?" Rehoboam glared at me and waved the makeshift torch. Warily, he remained at arm's length. I still had strands of his hair clutched in my fists.

"How dare you torment the Lady Nefret's cat?" I demanded; I thought of spitting at him, but he was too far away for it to do any good.

"The beast's an abomination; the prophet Ahijah says so." Rehoboam waved the torch. "It should be burnt."

Ahijah did rage against the Egyptian queen's cats, but that was not why Rehoboam wished to kill this one. The prophet's decree was only an excuse; Rehoboam delighted in cruelty. "You are vile, and if you harm the Lady Nefret's cat, our father will punish you."

"He won't know."

"Oh, yes he will, for I will tell him." Rehoboam could not prevent that, even if he beat me—and while I knew it would please Rehoboam greatly to beat me, I doubted he would dare. Our father loathed cruelty; Rehoboam had gone too far, and should have had the wit to know it.

He hesitated; the burning brand's fire turned smoky. One day, wit and caution would not suffice to restrain his darker desires—but today those chains still held. Rehoboam scowled and flung the torch aside.

"Oh, go away, you—you *girl!*" But it was Rehoboam who stormed off, followed by his uneasy sycophants.

I waited until I could no longer hear them rampaging down the corridor, then walked quietly to the corner. The boys were out of sight, and the noise of their passage had faded away.

I went back and lifted down the quivering Egyptian cat; the little animal hissed but permitted me to hold her and stroke her soft golden brown fur. Gradually her trembling ceased, and I carried her back to Queen Nefret's courtyard. There I handed the cat over to one of the Egyptian maidservants who served the queen, and who was horrified to learn her favorite cat had roamed so far from the safety of Nefret's quarters.

"The Lady Nefret will be most grateful." The Egyptian maid shuddered, cradling the cat to her breast. "Think what would have happened had some-one else found her! This is a cruel land—why, upon the streets I have seen men throw stones and sticks at cats and dogs! Barbarians!"

While I did not wish to agree that my own people were barbarians, I also did not think they should torment animals that had done them no harm. So I said nothing, save that I was glad to restore Queen Nefret's pet to her.

"The Lady Nefret will wish to thank you, Princess. If you will wait here, I shall tell her of your kindness."

I shrugged this off; then it did not occur to me that one should never re-fuse a potential ally. It did not occur to me that the Princess Baalit, King Solomon's favored child, needed allies.

"It does not matter." I found the Egyptian queen cool and distant, exquisite as Minoan glass. Her quiet elegance made me feel uncouth and unkempt at the best of times; cat or no cat, I preferred to meet the Lady Nefret only when I looked more like a king's daughter and less like a street tumbler.

So before Nefret's servant could delay me, I ran off to repair the damage my struggle with Rehoboam had done to my garments and my person.

And to decide whether I should tell my father what had passed between my brother and me today. No matter what Rehoboam did, he remained my father's eldest son, his proclaimed heir. It would only trouble my father's mind and wound his heart if he knew what Rehoboam were truly like.

So by the time I reached my own rooms, I had settled in my mind that I would say nothing of the affair of the Lady Nefret's cat. Nothing had happened to the cat, after all—

—and perhaps Rehoboam will improve and become a good king after all. Someday perhaps we shall even be friends. I was young enough still to be foolishly optimistic.

Rehoboam

That little bitch! Rehoboam swore inwardly as he led his followers away from his sister and her fiery temper, for it would not do for his companions to hear the king's heir vilify the king's overly-indulged daughter. One of the boys would be sure to run and tell the nearest officious servant, who would tell his father, who would call Rehoboam to him for a somber lecture on the behavior expected of his son. As if princes had no privileges, only duties! But Rehoboam was too conscious of the precarious nature of his position to utter those rebellious words; his mother had lectured him too often on the need for caution.

"Yes, you are the eldest; yes, the king has sworn you are his heir. But always remember, Rehoboam, my dear son, that this kingdom is not like others, that it has no history, no tradition. King Solomon may change his mind and choose another to be king after him. Always remember that, my son, and tread cautiously. When you are king, then you may do as pleases you. But until then . . ."

Until then, Prince Rehoboam must behave himself. Rehoboam's mouth twisted in an angry smile. His mother was right; he knew she was right. He must cage his nature. But he didn't have to like it.

He stopped, turned to his followers. Half-a-dozen boys, sons of servants and concubines, boys hoping loyalty to the crown prince would bring favors when he was king. Boys who would obey his orders, tolerate his whims—and report on him to their fathers or their mothers. *I can't trust anyone,* Rehoboam thought fretfully. Except his mother, of course.

He studied his companions; they regarded him with bright eager interest, seeking to learn what would placate, what would please. But not because they loved him; Rehoboam had not needed his mother's warnings to know *that.* A king's heir had no friends, only flatterers. *They do not like me; they wish to ensure their places in my favor when I am king.*

"Shall we find you another cat, Prince?" Lahad offered, but Rehoboam shook his head. Another cat would not be Queen Nefret's cat; Rehoboam had hoped to make his mother's rival suffer.

"No," he said. "No more cats today."

"No more sisters," Oreb said, and snickered.

Vowing Oreb would regret mocking him, Rehoboam forced himself to laugh. "Who cares what she does? She's only a girl. Come, let's visit the stables. My father the king has promised me a new team for my chariot. I am to have my choice of the new horses."

The appreciative envy on their faces warmed Rehoboam.

"Your father the king is generous," Pelaliah said.

"I am the heir," Rehoboam reminded them. He did not reveal that his father had also promised a new team of horses to all the royal princes who were old enough to handle the reins. At least the king had decreed that Rehoboam should choose first. *But I am Crown Prince. He should treat me better than all the others.*

As if sensing Rehoboam's resentment, Pelaliah said, "You will choose the best, my prince. Have patience, for someday you will be greater than all men." Pelaliah always had the right words ready to his tongue. Rehoboam suspected his mother coached him. But Pelaliah was right.

Someday . . . Rehoboam's eyes gleamed as he contemplated the shining future. Someday he would be king. Someday he would rule over all men.

And someday—ah, someday his sister Baalit would be sorry.

Baalit Sings

In my rooms, Rivkah pounced upon me, demanding to know how I had managed to tangle my hair and ruin my new fringed scarf so swiftly. "You are too old to run wild like a boy, Princess; look at you!" Rivkah thrust my silver mirror towards me. "Now all my hard work to do over again—and what's that upon your gown?"

"Cat hair and claw marks."

Rivkah swelled with indignation. "Cats and claws! And what would your father the king say, if he saw you looking like this?"

"You are a puff adder of righteousness, Rivkah. My father would say nothing, once I explained. I saved the Lady Nefret's cat from my brother Rehoboam."

"That boy." Rivkah's tone of rueful indulgence brought a frown to my brow, and Rivkah smiled, equally indulgent of my foibles. "Now, I know you don't like him, Princess, but brothers and sisters always quarrel. It means nothing."

I thought of saying that I didn't quarrel with my half-brothers Saul and Jonathan, or with Abner and Joab, or Ishbaal and Eliazar—or that Jerioth and Samuel disliked Rehoboam as hotly as I. But I knew such plain speaking would do no good and might do harm, so I closed my lips tightly over the words.

"Now sit down here and let me comb out those tangles." Rivkah did not ask, she commanded. But she rewarded as well, for Rivkah, who had once served my mother, gave me my mother's life as a harpers' tale to ease dull tasks.

"Do not wriggle, child, or we will be here all day. Never have I seen such hair for tangles. Your mother's hair was like silk. So was mine, come to that. We were the prettiest girls in Shunem, Abishag and I."

I tried hard to sit still; Rivkah had a gift with words. "Tell me," I said. "I will be still, I swear it."

Rivkah ran her hands over my hair and sighed. "If only I could curl this, rather than braid it! It is strong and would curl well."

"Comb me curls, then." I had never worn my hair styled in such a fashion—although Amyntor of Caphtor had told me, once, that I should wear it so. *"No point in trying to be what you're not. No, let it curl as it wills—I vow you'd look as charming as the ladies painted upon the old palace walls, back when Knossos ruled the waves."* What would I look like, with my hair coiled long down my back?

"It would not be seemly for the king's daughter. No, it must be tamed and braided. Now, where was I?"

"You were the prettiest girls in Shunem," I reminded her, and Rivkah laughed softly.

"Yes, we were, but that was long ago. Shall I tell you how your mother first saw your father?"

I began to nod, recalling in time that I had been bidden to remain still. "Yes," I said, "tell that." Rivkah had told me the story many times, but she liked to tell it, and I to hear it.

"The day was long and hot," Rivkah began, and I settled to listen to words I could have recited in my sleep. "Abishag and I had walked to the well and tarried there, for the sun was harsh and the road dusty, and we were loath to return home, where all that awaited us—"

"Was the task of pulling weeds in the kitchen garden!"

"Who tells this tale, you or I?" She tugged my hair gently and continued smoothly. "So instead of filling our water jars at once, we lingered at the well, and as we rested there, a man approached. He was a stranger, and he was hot and tired, and dust coated his garments—but we saw at once that his clothes were of fine cloth. And his manners were as fine as his clothing, for when he saw us standing by the well, he bowed and would have turned away, but Abishag lifted her voice and offered to draw him water from the well."

"Like Rebekah and Abraham's servant," I added. "Have you not finished combing out my hair *yet?*"

"Your hair must be combed well or not at all, and if not at all, then you must be sheared like a sheep. Be patient, and I will braid gold flowers in your hair, or silver bells." Rivkah continued pulling the sandalwood comb through my hair as she spoke. "Of course, if my tale bores you—"

I hastily denied that and begged her to continue. Although I knew the story by heart, and could have recited word for word along with Rivkah, it was a comfort to hear her tell it. I sat quiet as stone as Rivkah subdued my unruly hair and told again how my mother had drawn water for a stranger at the well, and taken him home to her mother, where he revealed he had come from King David's great city, Jerusalem—and that he sought a fair maid to serve King David's queen, Michal.

"Well, who would refuse such a chance? Our Abishag was sent off to Jerusalem with as great a dowry as if she went as a bride. I went too, as her handmaiden; in palaces, even slaves have slaves! We traveled in such great state one would have thought Abishag and I were queens ourselves! And then we came to Jerusalem."

"We were taken to the women's quarters of the palace—King David's palace, then. There were fewer women; King David did not marry as often as your father! Where King David warred, King Solomon marries, as they say. So the women's quarters were smaller then—there has been so much built since!"

"That is not part of the story." I had no wish to hear about all the buildings that my father had raised; he was always building something new. "You were taken to a garden—"

"Oh, yes. We were taken to a garden. And there a young man waited for us. He was so good to look upon, so richly garbed, that I knew he must be one of King David's sons—"

"And it was Prince Solomon! And when he and my mother looked upon one another, their eyes turned to stars. Was my father as handsome as the Lord Amyntor, do you think?"

"If you wish to tell the tale to yourself, say so." Rivkah tugged the comb against my hair, a silent reproof, before continuing. "Well, then he took Abishag to speak with Queen Michal, and so there was our Abishag tending old King David, sleeping in his bedchamber too. To say plain, I was troubled in my heart for her. 'You're not even his concubine; what will you do when the king's dead and you branded a harlot?' And do you know what she did?"

"She laughed," I said.

"That's right, she laughed at me, and said, 'When one king dies, another rises!' and went off to sit with Queen Michal, who had taken a great fancy to her. Sometimes I thought Abishag spent more time with Queen Michal than she did with King David!"

When Rivkah told her tales, I felt myself there, as close as if I were my mother's shadow. Now I waited, but Rivkah's fingers were busy knotting the ends of my braids, and she seemed to have forgotten to continue her story.

"And then King David lay dying," I prompted, but Rivkah had finished persuading my hair into tidiness and now said only "There, that looks well. Mind you do not catch your braids and pull out the bells; you are too careless, Baalit." Rivkah held up a mirror so that I might admire her handiwork. I sighed, knowing I would not hear the end of the tale today.

But I remembered to thank Rivkah for her careful work, praising her skill. It was not as if I did not know all my mother's life by heart, after all.

Sometimes it seemed to me that Rivkah no longer cared to dwell upon that part of the tale, of the days between the time Great David lay dying and the time King Solomon stood beneath the wedding canopy and claimed fair Abishag as his queen. And when she did speak of those days now, Rivkah's words held an undertone of censure, as if she no longer thought so well of Abishag's part in that fall and rise of princes.

I was sorry for that, for those hot swift days were what I most loved to hear Rivkah tell. But I would never lose their memory—for so I thought of those images, although I was not born until long after that reckless year. Sometimes, indeed, it seemed I had been there, had watched and listened as my mother had . . .

 . . . listened as Prince Adonijah knelt at his father's bedside and begged the dying king to attend a great banquet "in your honor, Father. In King David's honor—all men may walk through my gate and feast in your name. All the princes and all the great men of the kingdom will be there to praise you."

"To praise me?" The king's eyes, death-pale, seemed to shift: for a breath they glinted keen as blades. "All the great men?"

"Yes, Father."

"Abiathar? The high priest Abiathar?"

Prince Adonijah nodded. "Yes, and—"

"And the high priest Zadok? And Benaiah? Nathan, the prophet Nathan—does he await me at your great feast?"

A pause; Adonijah's gaze slid away from his father's face. "They have not come—not yet. But they will."

"And Joab? My war-chief? Does Joab sit at your table, Adonijah, my son?"

"Yes." Adonijah straightened, smiling now. "Yes, Joab sits at my table, Father."

Then King David smiled too. "Come closer, Adonijah." And when the prince did as his father commanded, the king laid his hands upon Adonijah's sleek hair, in silent blessing. Then King David slanted his eyes towards Abishag. "Adonijah will make a fine king, will he not, girl?"

And Abishag bowed her head and murmured, "As my lord the king says." Then she rose and took the king's water jug away to fill it again with sweet water, pausing only to speak with Prince Adonijah's servant, who awaited his master in the king's courtyard. From the prince's servant, she gleaned bright grains of news, news she carried swiftly to Queen Michal. And when Queen Michal heard Abishag's tale, the queen kissed her and sent her back to King David.

Abishag had learned King David's palace well, could walk its labyrinth of halls and gardens *blindfolded if need be. She returned to the king's side and sat there until Queen Michal came, and when Queen Michal left again, carrying the king's ring with her, Abishag slipped back into her place beside the king. All that long afternoon Abishag sat patient, as if she had never stirred from her post. And while Abishag waited, Prince Solomon set the king's ring upon his finger and the crown upon his head, and rode forth. . . .*

That was how my father had been crowned king. Without my mother's warning and Queen Michal's swift act, Prince Adonijah undoubtedly would have seized the crown for himself.

I was almost as old as my mother had been when she helped make a king of my father. I longed to do some daring, important deed, as she had done. But I knew I yearned to catch the moon, for under my father's wise rule, the twin kingdoms lay peaceful under a serene sky. Nor was there any doubt of who would be king after him. There was little chance I would be called upon to perform great deeds.

No, there was nothing for me to do but wait—wait until my father arranged my marriage.

What else could a girl—even a princess—do?

Abishag

Later I wondered just how much my mother knew, and when she knew it. Midday was no fit time to fetch water, to carry heavy jars home under a high hot sun—or a fit time to wear a costly new veil, either. But as it turned out, my mother was right to send us and right to have me wear my spangled veil, for as Rivkah and I tarried at the well, a man walked up to us.

Although he was tired and dusty from travel, he wore garments of fine cloth and ornaments of silver; the servant who followed him was almost as grand. I looked upon the man and knew I saw the road to my future. As if in a dream, I heard my voice offering to draw him water from the well.

That is how I came to be chosen for King David, by doing as Rebekah did; by drawing water from a well and offering it to a great man's steward. Rebekah gained a husband by her action. I gained a king.

Makeda

Politics made strange marriages; trade made odder couplings. The faraway kingdoms of Israel and Judah craved silver, animal hides, and ivory; the land of Cush required iron and cedarwood. More important even than precious metals and trade goods, a seal upon vows of friendship was required.

"And what better bond than blood?" her uncle demanded, stalking through the women's compound, staring into the face of each wife, daughter, and slave he passed. Until he reached her, and stopped. "You, Makeda. You will go."

A clever choice; with one stroke, her uncle would gain an ally and be rid of the last reminder that he'd severed the royal bloodline of Cush. His only claim to the kingship lay in his marriage to Makeda's mother's sister. Among those Sheso the death goddess had summoned in the plague season had been Makeda's father, the king. Of all those in whose veins flowed the blood of serpents, Makeda alone remained alive.

And that only because my uncle fears to kill me, lest Saa-set and Jangu-set curse him forever. But nothing prevented him from making her life a torment. She had endured, vowing that someday each slight to her honor, each wound to her pride, would be repaid. She prayed each night to the Lady of Snakes and the Serpent King to bring her swift vengeance.

But her uncle prayed too, and it seemed his gods were stronger than hers. For now a solution to this thorny problem had flung itself at his feet.

Nodding his head in agreement with himself, her uncle smiled, showing teeth filed into points. "Yes, Princess Makeda, see what a great marriage I have made for you! You will wed King Solomon. I decree it."

Shock numbed her mind; she remembered thinking only that, not being of the Serpent's blood, he had no right to serpent's teeth. About to utter a damning refusal, she found herself hesitating, as if afraid to speak.

"Good." Her uncle turned away quickly, as if he feared to meet her eyes. "King Solomon's men will take you away with them tomorrow. Be ready."

Tomorrow! She watched him stride away, too fast, a pace that hinted at fear. *Coward,* she thought coldly. *Tell me only now, so that I have no time to work against you.*

As her uncle left, his women began to surround her, all talking at once; she drew herself up straight and tall, to vow that she would not obey, king's command or no.

But something bound her tongue, forbidding speech. This time she knew it must be Jangu-set preventing her from uttering words that could not be unspoken. Makeda ran her tongue over the biting points of her own serpent's teeth, mark of her royal blood. If Jangu-set wished something of her, she had better find out what He had to say before she made plans of her own.

The shallow crystal bowl had been held by her mother's hands, and her mother's, and her mother's before that, back through time to their first mother Saa-set, the Lady of Snakes. Makeda unwrapped the bowl from the snakeskin which shielded it and set it upon the leopard's hide spread before her on the floor.

Her serpent's basket she set gently beside her before she lifted the lid. The cobra had been hers since she had hatched the egg which nurtured it. The egg had warmed between her breasts as the cobra grew inside the leathery shell; the snakelet had struggled into life with the aid of Makeda's gentle hands. She herself had woven the basket in which the cobra slept.

Now the deadly serpent flowed out of its home and coiled placidly about her arm. Makeda stroked the cobra's dark brown scales, soothing her mind as she soothed the serpent. Calm, the snake obediently gave up its venom as she pressed its fangs to the lip of the crystal bowl. When the milking was done, she permitted the cobra to glide away and bent forward over the scrying bowl.

The serpent's venom coiled over the crystal, oily and iridescent. Makeda touched the liquid with her forefinger; touched her fingertip to her brow, to her lips, to her heart. Then she waited, watching as images began to swirl over the poison's gleaming skin.

A man, a golden man. A woman black as midnight. A crown fading from her brow. . . . Anger and fear stirred; Makeda forced herself to ignore them, to summon the calm needed to see with the Lady's eyes. *Ships blown before the wind; a journey. A child, a boy. A boy with her proud face and clear serpent's eyes. Twin serpents flowed towards him; he held out his hands and the serpents glided up his arms, wound themselves above his brow. Crowned in serpents, the boy stood tall. He spread his arms and a wind rose and carried him south, and as he flew a false serpent shed its skin and fled before him. . . .*

Makeda's eyes burned; she blinked and the vision faded, leaving an after-image of a serpent's skin, empty now, its gold dull, dimming. . . . Then that image too faded, and she saw only the shallow pool of venom in the crystal bowl.

Shaking, she pressed her hands to her eyes. She had her answer, clear and unambiguous. She must consent to this exile—but she would go with Jangu-set's promise that the future belonged to those who carried the blood of serpents in their veins. To Makeda, and to her son.

Serpent's wisdom; the patience of a cobra on a rock, waiting for its prey.

So. I must go, and wait—and one day my son will return and take back what is ours.
Makeda knew her task now. She must go into exile, endure whatever awaited
her in the unknown north. And she must raise her son in pride and hope;
raise him to one day place the Serpent Crown upon his brow.

*Yes, King of Serpents. I will wait. I will have faith, and I will wait upon Your will. Your
will, and mine.*

But already she knew her patience must be counted out in years. Jangu-
set had not promised a smooth path, or a short one. Nor would Makeda
ask such a promise. But one thing more she must ask.

*However long this task may take, I will not lose faith. But please, Lord of Serpents, let
this King Solomon be a worthy father for my son!*

Cush lay far to the south of Israel and Judah, beyond even the Land of the
Two Crowns; when she had been carried into Jerusalem and unveiled in the
palace court, there had been silence, for no one had seen a woman like her
before. She had not understood their language then, but she instinctively
knew the silence was one not of admiration but of shock.

But then her new husband had come forward and taken her hand, and
smiled upon her, and spoken words that sang through the tense silence.
Later, when she had learned to speak his language, she found out what King
Solomon had said that day.

"How beautiful you are," he had said, "black and beautiful as night."

And since King Solomon had proclaimed her beautiful, no man dared
say otherwise.

She had tried to thank him, when they could understand one another
with words as well as flesh; he had laughed at her gratitude.

"Why, Makeda, do you not know it is said that King Solomon is the
wisest and most truthful of men? What else could I say, then, save the
truth—that you are beautiful?"

"At home I was thought so. It is different here."

"Yes, it is different. Here your beauty is foreign, surprising the eye. That
is why the other women are jealous of you. Do not let them make you unhappy."

"They do not trouble me," Makeda said, and was rewarded with another of her husband's sweet smiles. *No, they do not trouble me. If ever they do, I myself will make sure they cease to do so.* Makeda was a king's daughter, one of half-a-hundred royal children reared in a court of serpents and shadows. Poison, the silent remedy, was bred in her blood.

"I am glad you are happy here." King Solomon caressed the tight curls of her hair. Once she had seen how he cherished her differences, Makeda had begun to enhance them. And when Solomon came to her, she dressed as a princess of Cush rather than as a queen of Israel, knowing her exotic appearance pleased him. In the silent, bitter struggle his wives waged for the king's attentions, Makeda battled expertly, wielding her dark exoticism as a weapon.

That is why I am hated by his women—because I please him more than they. The thought warmed her blood, just as Solomon's greatest gift to her warmed her heart.

Her son.

As she had known he would be, her boy had been born under the sign of the Serpent, giver of wisdom. And although he had already fathered over a dozen sons, King Solomon rejoiced as if hers was his firstborn.

To reward her for the gift of a son, King Solomon had given her a necklace of brilliant stones the pale pure yellow of a cat's eye, and given their son a cradle carved of cedar and lined in sandalwood. "And he will have all his brothers have, when he is old enough. Horses and servants and land. But for now—"

The king bent over his newest son, offering him a rattle with a coral handle; the baby grasped it and kicked vigorously. "For now, I think he will prefer this." Solomon smiled at the baby and then looked at Makeda. "What shall we name him? Is there some name of your own land that you would have him called?"

"You are kind, my king, but no— I would have him called David, after your own father." For a moment Makeda thought Solomon would refuse her this honor, for his face seemed oddly blank, and his eyes troubled. Then the cloud passed; he nodded.

"Very well, my Makeda—since you wish it, we will call him David. Perhaps he will inherit my father's gift for music."

She bowed, and thanked him, and kept her own wish for their son locked within her heart. It was not Great David's gift for song that she wished his grandson to inherit but his gift for victory. *This David, too, will be a king. I have seen it.*

Smiling, Makeda bent over Prince David's cradle and lifted him into her strong arms. Unlike many of the king's other wives, who relied upon wetnurses and slaves to care for their children, she alone nursed and cared for her infant son. He would suck in strength and courage from her, grow strong and brave and wise. He would grow safely to manhood here, in his father's kingdom.

And then, when the time was ripe, he would return to hers, and claim the throne that awaited him.

Humming a cradle-tune old when the Mountains of the Moon were young, Makeda rocked her son against her breast. *You will never be king in Israel, but the world is wide, my David. It holds many kingdoms.* Her son would wear a crown; she had seen it in the serpent's venom. She could wait.

And if I must wait for my son's future, it might as well be here. Here, far from her homeland, she could raise her prince to manhood, keep him safe for his destiny. She looked down at David's soft face and smiled. *Yes, my son. We will wait.*

It was not a hard thing, to await the future as a queen in King Solomon's palace. If only it weren't so cold in Jerusalem, Makeda sometimes thought she could be perfectly happy here.

Baalit Sings

Within a garden walled in cedar and silver, a woman paced, restless as a caged leopard. Bright silks clothed her body; bright gems adorned her hair, her wrists, her throat. Her hands held a spindle, a pretty thing, amber and ivory, a queen's toy; as she walked, she spun. The wool upon the spindle was black, yet the thread spun from it was white.

I walked through poppies and lilies until I stood before her. She looked at me and smiled.

"Ask," she said, and waited.

The world waited as I formed my question, a question I had not known I wished to ask. "How is it possible to spin darkness into light?"

"The darkness is the past," she said, "and the light the future. I have done all I can, my daughter; now it is your turn to spin."

She held the spindle out to me, and I saw that the gold upon her wrists chained her, bound her to the silver garden. Slowly I reached out and accepted the ivory spindle and its burden. Heavy as stone, the dark wool dragged at me, forced me to my knees.

"It is too heavy," I said. "I cannot hold it."

"It was too heavy for me, yet I held it, and spun it too. Now it is your turn." The chained woman stood and watched as I struggled to my feet again.

"Who are you?" I asked. "Are you my mother?"

"Does it matter? Heed my lesson, Baalit. Spin, or die."

I touched the spindle and began to pull the wool into thread, darkness into light. My fingers began to sting, to burn as if the wool were fire. "How long?" I asked. "How much thread must I spin?"

There was no answer; I stood alone in the sealed garden. I spun thread, and I wept, knowing I could not stop and live. . . .

My eyes were wet when I awoke; the tears were no dream. Nor was the sorrow. *Spin, or die*— I shuddered, and wondered if the woman in my dream garden had been my mother. No, she could not have been, for I had been told my mother was dark and comely, while this woman had been tawny, like a lioness. *Does it matter?* she had asked; I supposed it did not, for whoever she was, her ghost had come to warn me. Now I must interpret my dream, that I might know the danger when I encountered it.

I tried to summon sleep again, but rest would not come. And so I sat and stared out across the city all the long hours until morning.

But dreams that torment us by night fade as the sun's rays touch them—and I was not yet old enough to judge dreams truly. By day's light, the dream that had left me weak and shaking with fear in the dark night hours soon seemed caused by nothing more than my quarrel with Rehoboam, or my encounter with my father's newest bride. The Lady Dacxuri's eyes were enough to cause any number of ill dreams!

So I told myself, and even believed it, for a time. For as I have said, although I was only a girl, I was my father's favored child. From the moment I drew my first breath as my mother drew her last, I held King Solomon's heart in my keeping. And just as whatsoever my mother had desired my father granted without question, so whatever infant demands I voiced were instantly gratified; whatever childish treasures I longed for were mine for the asking. The Princess Baalit was denied nothing.

Now I see that I demanded even my dreams do as I wished, be what I desired.

By the time the Queen of the South rode through the gates of Jerusalem and into my father's life, the Princess Baalit was spoiled with indulgence. Never did it occur to me that what I wished would not be granted.

That what I wanted, I could not have.

For until I looked upon the Sheban queen, and the women who followed her, I had wished only for childish things. Never had it occurred to me that I had not even known my own true desires. Nor that my heart's desire would prove a prize that no man—or woman either—could grant me.

That what I desired so greatly I must claim for myself.

PART FOUR

—— •◆• ——

Better Than Rubies

Abishag

All my tomorrows began in a palace garden where Prince Solomon awaited me. Bright as the sun, beautiful as morning, he looked into my waiting eyes; desire curled, fire-hot, honey-sweet, beneath my skin.

"I have seen you before," he said, and I nodded.

"Yes. Long ago, in Mahanaim."

That was all; he held out his hand and I took it, sliding my fingers over his palm, entwining my fingers with his in a lovers' knot.

Solomon

"This summer seems endless, does it not?" Amyntor turned query into jest, his habit when no answer was sought. Solomon smiled in dutiful acknowledgment, and looked out over the dry gold of the hills.

"The winter was long and summer has barely begun; it will grow hotter soon. And soon after that the year will turn, and then all will once more bewail the length of winter's days." Solomon himself no longer cared if the days were summer-long, or winter-short. He cared only that each task be done properly, in its proper season. *That is the way to peace; that is the course of wisdom.*

"You're thinking again, my lord king, and not of pleasant things. It's an unhealthy habit. You'd think a man with forty wives, one of them still hot as a new-wed bride, could summon up a pleasant image or two while he muses upon the housetop."

"Ah, but I was not thinking of my wives, even of the newest."

"You ought to, my lord king, before they stop thinking of you. Even," Amyntor added, "the newest. Those girls from world's end burn all the hotter for their land's chill."

"I do think of my wives—but not just now." Now, for this shining hour, Solomon wished only to enjoy the sun, and the company of a man whose heaviest word drifted like a feather upon the air, and whose darkest mood gleamed noonday bright. Nothing weighed leaden upon Amyntor; his easy company was anodyne to a king clutched at by men who demanded his wisdom and women who desired his favor. That Amyntor was a foreigner only added to the attraction of his company, for he neither petitioned nor demanded. With Amyntor, he could sometimes be only Solomon, rather than King Solomon the Wise.

"You're thinking again, O King. Trouble in the harem?"

Now Solomon smiled in earnest. "May a king have no other matters that trouble him, save women?"

"None so amusing." Amyntor sat upon the wall guarding the balcony; he drew one leg up and clasped his hands about his knee. "Very well, then— trouble with that unwashed wandering seer of yours?"

Again Solomon denied truth to Amyntor's guess. Nor did he lie in doing so. An uneasy heart was not trouble. *No, there is no trouble—none save that within my own mind.*

For all Ahijah's dire prophecies of the Lord's wrath, for all Solomon's wives' bitter complaints, the princess from Colchis had entered effortlessly into the life of the women's palace, her foreign customs no stranger than any others. But Solomon found himself uneasy, these long summer days, an unease that he laid at the Lady Dacxuri's gate. Not that his newest bride performed evil rites, nor that she defied him, for she did not.

Yet my other wives fear her and complain of her—and for no reason. No reason, save that the Lady Dacxuri was the newest come of the king's wives, and her place in the women's world had not yet become a settled thing. Solomon had done his best, but what lay beyond the Queens' Gate was as strange to him as if passing through the jeweled cedar panels took him into a faraway land, a land in which the laws of men counted for nothing.

Once it had not been so; once to walk through the cedar gate had been to walk into his beloved's arms. But that day's sun had set long years ago—

So long ago, so many years, that Abishag's daughter has grown old enough to marry in her turn. As always, the thought grieved him, although his daughter's marriage was inevitable; a girl's fate was to marry, and a princess's fate was to marry for policy.

Sometimes Solomon toyed with the idea of offering Baalit's hand in marriage to his good friend Amyntor. A royal bond might tether the Caphtoran to Israel's side. Or it might not; Amyntor had a roving heart. He might refuse to wed the king's daughter, which would be a great insult. Or he might marry Baalit and try to carry her off with him when he grew tired of the feel of Jerusalem's streets beneath his feet. Neither course pleased Solomon—nor would wedding Baalit to Amyntor bring any advantage for the kingdom. *Only for the king. And that is not reason enough.*

"Very well, my lord the king is *not* troubled. Still he frowns, and on such a day, too."

Again Solomon summoned a smile. "Ah, well, I confess that I, too, find the summer's days stretch long. The land is quiet, the people at peace—"

"—and the king is bored," Amyntor finished, and Solomon laughed.

But even as he laughed, Solomon heard again Nefret's calm assertion that he suffered from boredom. Now Amyntor made the same claim. *Is it so plain to others that I find life dull? How dare I, with all the world at my command, admit to that sin?* "Not so bad as that, but I admit a diversion would be pleasant."

As if summoned by the king's words, a palace servant emerged from the shadowed room that faced upon the king's balcony and came forward, bowing low before Solomon. "Rise," said the king, forcing himself to smile at the waiting servant, "rise and speak."

"O King, the watchtower sends word that a royal messenger has entered the city in haste, with word for the king's ears."

Solomon nodded. "Tell my Great Officers of the Court to await me by the Lion Throne."

"It shall be done as the king says." The servant padded swiftly off, and Solomon permitted himself to sigh at last.

Amyntor shook his head. "You are too indulgent, King Solomon. The king should bid his royal messenger to attend him here—at your convenience rather than at his."

"Perhaps, but men who labor diligently deserve reward. It pleases them to be received in all honor and glory by the king. And a wise king pleases his servants and his subjects when he can."

By the time the royal messenger had finally passed through the palace gate itself, Solomon sat upon the throne awaiting him, and the Great Officers of the Court—those who were not engaged elsewhere—stood arrayed at the king's right hand. Amyntor stood by the king's left hand, and of all those who attended upon Solomon, only Amyntor seemed truly at ease. *Even now, my people have not grown into empire. I wonder how many kings, how many generations of men, are required to turn tribes to nations?*

The circle of hammered gold pressed heavy about his temples; the lion-headed scepter lay across his knees. When the royal messenger ran into the court, he would see King Solomon arrayed gloriously, awaiting the messenger and his words.

He had judged the time well; before the officials could grow restive—*and begin grumbling that they have important tasks to attend to and no time to waste!*—the sound of bare feet slapping against marble heralded the messenger's arrival. The man burst from the shadowed pillars and ran arrow-straight up the court to fling himself to his knees before the Lion Throne.

"Speak." Solomon smiled, gravely, and awaited the urgent news.

"O King, live forever; I bear greetings from the Lord Esau, the king's governor at Ezion-geber, to King Solomon the Wise. I bear greetings from Hodaiah, captain of the Tarshish fleet. Here are the captain's words: The Tarshish ship has returned, O King—and they have brought with them—"

"Stop." The messenger was so out of breath Solomon found it hard to understand the gasped words. He looked hard at the messenger and sighed. "Come, man, catch your breath; take a cup of wine. The news cannot be so urgent you must kill yourself to bring it."

The system of royal couriers worked well; its only fault lay in the overzealous nature of the runners, who prided themselves on their speed. Each message thus became, for a time at least, tidings vital and urgent.

With a peculiar mixture of gratitude and irritation, the royal messenger accepted wine. "O King—" he began, and Solomon lifted his hand.

"I will not hear one word until you no longer gulp air like a beached eel. Wait; your tidings will keep for a wine cup."

Solomon waited, patient, as the man gulped the wine and wiped his mouth. Then he smiled and said, "That is better; now say the captain's words to me."

Finally permitted to deliver his news, the messenger straightened. "O King, Hodaiah, Captain of the Tarshish fleet, sends King Solomon this news: The fleet has returned from the lands of the south bearing ivory, and spices, and gold, and many other treasures—these things, and more, all sent as gifts by the Queen of the Spice Land to King Solomon. And the queen herself has come as well, to see with her own eyes the glories of the kingdom of Israel, and to hear with her own ears the wisdom of King Solomon, and to bear witness of both back to her own land of Sheba."

Solomon stared, surprised as he had seldom been. "The Queen of Sheba has come here? To our kingdom?"

"Yes, O King—sailed north with the Tarshish fleet." Satisfied with the king's reception of his news, the messenger stood proudly, awaiting further queries.

The Spice Queen, come half a world to my court? Now, why? Solomon had sent his envoys to faraway Sheba in hope of yet another alliance to aid his fast-growing kingdom—this royal response surpassed even his wildest imaginings of the outcome of that visit. *Has the King of Sheba sent his wife as ambassador? Or as gift?*

A puzzle redolent of intrigue and spice; the dull boredom Solomon labored under vanished like mist under strong sun.

"Where is the Sheban queen now?" Sheba—the Spice Kingdom, fabled for its incense—and for the wild tales travelers told of the Morning Land. *Now I shall learn their truth.*

"She and all her attendants wait at Ezion-geber, O King."

The port city of Ezion-geber was Israel's outlet to the southern world and its riches. Copper and iron were mined nearby; Ezion-geber smelted metal as well as expediting trade.

Can Sheba think to spy upon our mines and foundries? To what end? Perhaps Sheba wished to acquire the source of such riches to add to its own and sought to study the defenses there. Perhaps the queen herself had been sent to conceal the true purpose of the visit. Perhaps—

Perhaps I should stop wasting my own time; I can know nothing of Sheba's purpose until I speak with the queen. Suddenly restless, Solomon rose to his feet.

"Well done," he told the messenger in clear tones that carried well through the great court. The man smiled, gratified, and Solomon instructed Ahishar, the chief steward, to see that the diligent messenger was rewarded.

Then Solomon turned to Zadok. "Well, High Priest? What do you think of this news?"

"It is very strange," Zadok said with ponderous deliberation, "for Sheba lies very far to the south. Still, Solomon's wisdom is far-famed; perhaps this Sheban queen truly seeks to learn from you."

Zadok, you have become a true courtier, saying yes and no with the same breath. Solomon smiled. "Perhaps she does," he said. *But I doubt it,* he finished silently, and listened as his officials argued over whether the king should or should not permit the unexpected queen to come before him.

"Strange women cannot be trusted; suppose she wishes harm to our king?" "Folly—but doubtless she hopes to trick him into a favorable alliance. Trade with Sheba comes at a high price." "Perhaps she is not the queen at all but a spy sent to learn our king's secrets."

At that, Solomon lifted his hand. "Enough," he said and glanced at Amyntor, who raised his eyebrows.

"The Queen of Sheba sounds promising," said the Caphtoran. "Perhaps your god has heard and granted your prayer after all."

Solomon smiled. "Nothing can be known until I see this woman and hear her voice with my own ears. I will journey to Ezion-geber to greet her and make her welcome in our land."

"You cannot risk it, my king—this may be a trap," Elihoreph said, and at the chief scribe's solemn words, Solomon laughed.

"A fine trap, to come into my own kingdom and place herself in my power!"

"A subtle trap; women are subtle as the serpent." Elihoreph scowled, and Solomon nodded, grave; it would not do to wound the chief scribe's touchy pride.

"True; like the serpent, women are lovely, subtle, and wise. All the more reason to confront a woman who is also a queen far from King David's City. The king's thanks for a timely warning."

Elihoreph bowed, mollified for the moment; Solomon resolutely refused to glance to his left. *For if I meet Amyntor's eyes, I shall laugh again—* And no wise king humbled his servants before others.

"I have heard your words," Solomon said. "Now hear mine. I shall go to Ezion-geber to welcome the Queen of Sheba to my kingdom. She is a royal guest; we must treat her royally."

Zadok frowned, and slowly shook his head. "I must protest, O King. It does not befit your dignity to go to meet this foreign woman—"

You mean it does not befit your comfort to travel a dozen steps beyond the city gate! But rather than chide the old man, Solomon merely smiled. "Whatever a king does befits his dignity, Zadok. But do not worry; I shall not insist my high priest accompany me!"

"Of course I am at the king's command," Zadok said—but he did not argue further.

Lest I change my mind and bid him come after all. Solomon resisted the temptation to jest further with the high priest. *Rest easy, Zadok; I shall not need a priest to help me greet this wandering queen.*

But there was a man whose counsel he would need. Solomon laid the lion scepter upon the throne, dismissing his chief ministers. *I have heard all they have to say a dozen times. Now I will lay the matter before someone who will not simply recite to me what has always been done—as if that were reason never to do a new thing!*

Benaiah

That King Solomon sought him out did not surprise Benaiah; the king ruled his willful subjects with prudence and care. Important matters he spread before his court officials, soliciting their views.

And once the court officers and the clerks and the priests had made Solomon a gift of their opinions, the king turned to his general. *All things pass beneath the sword blade, in the end.* Soon or late, diplomacy and marriage and alliances must be strengthened by force. And so, soon or late, the king whose name meant "peace" must summon war.

Rumors and whispers fled through the king's palace as swiftly as swallows; by the time Benaiah looked down the walkway that crowned the city walls and saw the king pacing towards him, he had already heard the news of the arrival of the queen from Sheba a dozen times over. And with each retelling, the tale changed.

So when the king began to speak, Benaiah held up his hand. "My lord king, is it true the Sheban queen flew here upon eagle's wings? That she has brought you gifts of forty shekels of gold and more gems than there are stars in the heavens? That she is a djinn who has enchanted your master of ships, a sorceress who can shift her shape at will?"

At Benaiah's dry recitation of the wildest of the tales he had overheard, the king laughed. "For all I know, she may own all those powers. I have not yet looked upon her. As for the gifts—doubtless she has brought what she hopes will please my vanity and incline my mind to her desires."

"And what does this foreign queen desire?"

"That I do not yet know." Solomon smiled. "Perhaps she truly wishes to test my wisdom. What do you think, Benaiah?"

"What do I think? I think no queen leaves her kingdom and journeys across half a world just to play games."

"Perhaps this one has. Perhaps she finds time lies heavy in her hands and wishes me to amuse her."

"Perhaps." Benaiah echoed the king's jest, even as he turned the king's words this way and that, seeking truth. Of course the Shebans wanted something of Solomon— *Why else journey a thousand miles to a strange land?* What Benaiah could not guess was what prize the Shebans coveted. A prize so great that a queen set herself at risk to win it—

"I journey to Ezion-geber to greet her, to see this fabled queen with my own eyes. All my officers of the court have cried out against such an action—they fear for my honor and their own comfort. Now it is your turn to speak."

Benaiah considered, unhurried; King Solomon waited patiently until his general at last said, "I think it a wise course, O King. Better to encounter a serpent in the field than in the house."

"Wise Benaiah! I shall go forth and encounter this serpent upon the road, and you shall help me judge whether her fangs drip venom or honey."

"When do we leave for Ezion-geber?"

"At once, for I wish to meet this venturesome queen while she is still new-come to this land."

"As the king says, so it shall be," Benaiah said, and Solomon smiled grimly.

"Yes, so it shall be—after each man who served my father has explained why I must not and how King David would have managed matters better and dazzled with his splendor besides. Perhaps I should ride to Ezion-geber garbed as my own messenger; judge her before she can judge me."

"That prospers only in harpers' tales." Benaiah wasted no breath deploring such a scheme; King Solomon had no more intention of riding out alone and in disguise than Benaiah did of allowing such folly. *The court officials have been tormenting him again. Pack of idiots—can they not see badgering him's no way to guide his steps?*

Solomon stared to the south, as if his eyes could pierce the miles that lay between Jerusalem and the city in which the Queen of Sheba waited. "Harpers' tales." The king's words were spoken so softly Benaiah heard them as a sigh on the hot summer wind.

Then Solomon turned again to Benaiah. "At tomorrow's dawn, I ride out and travel the King's Highway south to greet the Queen of Sheba at Ezion-geber. If the king's officers and servants cannot be ready to do the same—why, then the king must ride accompanied only by those who best love him."

"Are you going to tell them that, my lord king, or am I?" Benaiah asked, and Solomon smiled.

"Amyntor may tell them," Solomon said. "That should ensure swift compliance with the king's wishes."

Yes, you're Great David's son, all right—and a credit to Queen Michal's teaching. But Benaiah knew better than to speak such words, although he often thought them. Such praises cut keen as a double-edged blade; King Solomon shunned comparison with his royal father.

And it was safer not to speak at all of the king's mother—either of them.

Baalit Sings

I knelt beside a grinding mill, a mill whose upper stone was formed of bright gold and whose lower stone of dull iron. Bracelets broad and thick as manacles circled my wrists, heavy as stone. Time poured into the mill, hours brilliant as crystal, glowing as pearl. Golden chains bound me to the golden millstone; I turned the mill, grinding hours into sand that drifted away like mist. Hour after jeweled hour ground away; hour after hour I turned the mill, endlessly grinding. . . .

I awoke with my blood pounding so hard it shook my skin. A dream; only a dream. Nor had the dream been so terrible that I must wake cold and damp with fear. So I told myself, and forced myself to lie quiet until my blood ran calm.

But after that I dared not sleep again; rather than lie awake staring into darkness, I rose and walked out onto my balcony, moving softly so I would not wake Nimrah and Keshet, who slept peaceful as kittens in the other bed. When I was restless, I preferred solitude.

And of late, I was too often restless. Even I did not know what troubled me; I knew only that I suffered unquiet dreams. Tonight's had truly frightened me, and I did not know why.

"It is only a dream," I whispered. "It cannot harm me." I stared out across the city to the eastern hills. Night paled there; dawn was rising. Sunlight banished dreams, both bad and good. Sunlight would banish the cold weight of dream chains upon my wrists.

Dawn's promise warmed the air and soothed my fears; weary, I padded back to my bed and let sleep claim me once more.

Because I had sat awake from deep midnight until sunrise, I slept far into the morning. Because I was the king's favored child, no one dared wake me.

And so by the time I rose and ate and dressed, and heard from my maidservants that my father had ridden south to greet the queen of fabled Sheba, it was too late to beg to join him. Too late even to follow after him and catch him upon the King's Highway. My status as King Solomon's daughter granted me command only in small things. In greater matters, I stood as powerless as any other girl. No man would risk obeying me were I foolish enough to order horses harnessed and a chariot prepared.

Like all the other women in my father's palace, all I could do was wait.

Wait, and watch—and wonder at the thought of a woman who traveled the world as freely as a man.

Solomon

King Solomon rode out from Jerusalem in royal state, attended by priests and warriors, accompanied by master of horse and master of treasures. A dozen cartloads of rich food and fine garb followed; pomegranate wine and mantles fringed with gold, quail preserved in honey and girdles sewn with pearls—provisions for the journey and gifts to welcome the visiting queen.

He expected to ride through Ezion-geber's gate to find the Sheban queen still a guest of the governor's, resting there after the sea journey from the Morning Land. To have his charioteer draw rein upon the crest of the last of the hills beyond Sela and from that height to gaze down upon a bright splash of color that was the Sheban queen's camp—that, Solomon had not expected.

Oh, he had seen tents before, and dwelt within them too, when he had ventured forth to visit among the tribesmen who roamed his empire. But those tents had been sturdy, workmanlike creations of dark skins and rough cloth. The Sheban tents formed bright rings of color, circled protectively about the central pavilions. Those shone brilliant as moonlight, their cloth bleached white as bone; above the largest stood a tall pole from which banners of leopard skin hung heavy under the hot sun.

"Colorful," Amyntor said, and Solomon could only agree.

"A royal spectacle," he said, and drew laughter from Amyntor and a slight smile from Benaiah. The rest of his entourage stared, solemn as judges, at the Sheban camp. "The Queen of Sheba awaits," Solomon said. "Shall the King of Israel advance at once, or shall he await—"

"Developments?" Amyntor suggested, and Solomon laughed.

"An invitation?" Solomon countered. "Or shall I go forth to the queen's camp in disguise, perhaps surprise her in her bath?"

There was a low cough from Elihoreph. "I do not think that would be wise, O King. We should send forth an emissary to announce the king's presence, and await the queen's petition."

"Yes." As always, Dathan, keeper of the scribe's supplies, nodded agreement with the chief scribe. "Decisions must be made with due prudence and caution—"

Prudence and caution! If I await decisions from Elihoreph and Dathan, I shall wait until the stars grow cold. Solomon held up his hand for silence. "I see no reason not to approach the queen's encampment. She journeyed a thousand miles to meet me, after all."

"But my lord king—" Elihoreph began, and suddenly Solomon could bear no more.

No more pomp, no more high state. No more men solemnly praising my most foolish word. No more women smiling upon my most graceless caress— With that thought, Solomon caught up the reins from the startled charioteer. "My lord king orders his court to continue on to the Sheban camp. Solomon drives alone." He glanced at the charioteer. "Get out," the king commanded and, when the man hesitated, said, "Now," in a voice that fell upon the man's ears like a whip. As the charioteer jumped off, Solomon signaled the restive horses; the matched stallions sprang forward, eager to run.

As the horses settled into a steady canter, Solomon risked one backward glance to see that even this most outrageous order was obeyed—by all but two men. Amyntor and Benaiah had ridden out of the king's caravan and followed, each in his own fashion. Amyntor rode his desert-bred mare as if he raced the wind; Benaiah simply set his horse into a steady, ground-eating pace, knowing sooner or later Solomon must draw his horses to a halt.

I could know each man a league away, they ride as they live. So thinking, Solomon turned his attention back to his team, coaxed the high-mettled stallions to a calmer pace that permitted Benaiah and Amyntor to catch up to him.

"No, I am not mad," Solomon said, before Benaiah could utter the words.

"The king may be mad if it pleases him," Benaiah said, and Amyntor laughed.

"Sometimes it is wisest to be a little mad." Amyntor stroked his mare's sweat-slick neck. "But it's even wiser to keep your friends close—"

"Do not say 'O King,'" Solomon warned. "I am weary of the words."

"Ah." Amyntor and Benaiah exchanged a glance that Solomon under-stood very well indeed; a glance that said, *Our king plays the fool; it is our task to humor him and keep him safely out of mischief.*

Solomon sighed. "No fear, I promise I will do nothing rash—nothing more rash than this, at any rate."

"I don't see what you hope to gain." Benaiah's eyes scanned the hillside, alert as a falcon to any shifting shadow.

Amyntor grinned, teeth flashing white. "Disguised as a humble charioteer, Solomon the Wise hopes to come upon the Queen of the Morning and win her heart—"

"You should be a harper, Caphtoran. My lord, we should go on; the horses need care." Benaiah nodded towards the road that led down into the narrow valley and the Sheban's waiting camp.

So much for my freedom! Sighing, Solomon urged his horses onward, more sedately this time. Escorted by Amyntor and Benaiah, he drove down the dusty road. As the hillside eased into the valley, a dry streambed opened onto the path. Suddenly Benaiah urged his horse forward, barring Solomon's way as a moon-pale beast flashed out of the gully.

The animal checked at the sight of them, stood regarding them with grave eyes the shape of almonds and the color of sloes. It looked back, as if seeking command, and a moment later three riders cantered out of the wadi, dark-garbed figures on light-boned, sun-sleek desert horses. Seeing Solomon and his escort, the riders halted.

Two of the riders were plainly attendants, guardians of the third. And all three were women—

Two warriors, and a queen. Solomon knew beyond doubting that he gazed upon the woman who had journeyed so far to meet him. *Who else would ride guarded by Amazons?* He had heard of the warrior women, but had never before seen one for himself. The queen's warriors caught his eyes, more intriguing at the moment than the queen herself.

The silence was broken by Amyntor's easy laughter. "Welcome, ladies! It seems, O King, that the Queen of Spices owns no more patience than the King of Israel. Neither can wait to set eyes upon the other." Amyntor regarded the Sheban's gaudily-adorned horses and raised his eyebrows. "Such riches; one would almost think the Sheban queen sought to impress Solomon the Wise."

"And is Solomon the Wise so foolish that mere gold will dazzle him?" The voice was rich as sun-warm honey; laughter rippled beneath the mocking words. Solomon looked into eyes bright as sun-spangled amber. All else was concealed by a veil that fell to her waist in front and below her hips behind, sleek black cloth resting in folds upon her horse's rump.

All else, save her hands; rosy with henna, they held the reins lightly, easily; the fine southern horse she rode bowed unresisting to her will.

Solomon looked upon her, and smiled. "No, he is not so foolish as that, O Queen of the South. But he is dazzled nonetheless."

"Take care with your compliments, King Solomon—for you have not yet seen my face."

"I do not need to; are not all queens beautiful?"

"And all kings wise?" she countered, and Solomon laughed.

"Of course. Is your king as wise as his queen is beautiful?"

Now it was her turn to laugh, low and soft behind the veil that hid her face. "No king rules Sheba, Solomon the Wise."

No king— "You?" he said.

"I. Yes, I rule Sheba."

Bred to run, the stallions shifted, restless; he knew they would not stand long. "This is not how we were meant to meet—"

"—but you could not bear another solemn exhortation, another dire caution. No more could I, and so we find ourselves here, playing at freedom."

"Great minds think alike," said Solomon, and she laughed, softly.

"And fools seldom differ." She held out her hand, snapped her fingers; the pale hound trotted to her horse's side. "The King of Israel and the Queen of Sheba will meet before their courts, as is proper. Solomon and Bilqis have met here."

She lifted her gilded reins and her horse wheeled and sprang away, back down the narrow wadi. The Amazons followed, and it was only then, as sunlight flashed from their metal-sewn tunics, that Solomon realized he had forgotten the warrior women as soon as he heard the Queen of Sheba's voice.

"You have royal luck, my lord king." Amyntor, half-mocking, shook his head. "Now, when I drive out, do I encounter veiled beauties and Moon Maids too? I do not. I'm fortunate to meet an ancient goatherd and his smelly flock."

"You might see more if you spoke less." Benaiah's words fell dry and hard. "We should go back, my lord king. It grows late."

The words seemed to warn, to caution; Solomon glanced quickly at his general, but Benaiah's face revealed nothing. Nodding, Solomon relaxed his iron grip on the reins, and the team leapt eagerly forward. He did not need to look to know that Benaiah and Amyntor followed.

So I have met the Queen of Sheba. And seen what? Laughing eyes and painted hands; nothing more. *I have not even seen her face.* But Solomon knew that did not matter—just as he knew that no matter what warning Benaiah's words might have carried, it was too late to turn back.

Abishag

Of course I loved Prince Solomon; what girl would not? From the first sight of his face, I was lost, and I knew it. Had she seen me in that moment, my mother would have despaired of me, for always she wished me to control my own passions. Yet between one beat and the next, I gave my heart into Solomon's keeping.

But my mother's teachings enabled me to smile and speak calmly, as if my heart beat quiet and my blood flowed cool. And so when Prince Solomon told me he had sent his man to seek a fair maid to serve Queen Michal, my voice was steady as I murmured that I hoped the queen would like me.

"She will—and you will like my mother," Prince Solomon assured me, and I smiled and asked, "Which mother, my lord?" for Solomon called two women mother—the Lady Bathsheba, who had borne him, and Queen Michal, who had raised him.

Solomon laughed softly, replying, "Why, both. And they will love you as—" He stopped, but the words he had not spoken hung between us as clearly as if burned into the air. "As I do."

I bowed my head and hoped he was right; if the queen did not favor me, I had little hope of holding Prince Solomon. *She will like me,* I vowed silently. *She must. For I could not surrender Prince Solomon's heart. It had been too late for that the moment our eyes met in the palace garden; he was the beloved for whom I had waited since the day my mother conceived me.*

Bilqis

So now I have met King Solomon, Lion of Israel and Judah. As she rode back towards her own tents, the queen pondered the meeting, wondered if it held portents of their future. *Both of us impatient, seeking to confront our fates. A good omen?*

He had smiled, had spoken to her as equal—that said much of a man. And he was young—not truly young, of course; King Solomon was a man grown, with sons of his own. But he was younger than she. *Young enough to be my son.* The thought flashed through her mind; she banished it. However many years separated them, Solomon was no boy. *He is a man and a king, just as I am a woman and a queen. I must not forget that, nor hold him lightly.* She must remember that this man was called "the Wise."

But I am no fool; doubtless I can deal with him well enough. So thinking, she smiled behind the black veil that shielded her from sand and sun. *I think I surprised you, Solomon the Wise. You greeted Bilqis well enough. Now let us see how you welcome the Queen of Sheba.*

Khurrami

"King Solomon is here? *Here?*" Tamrin's voice rose sharp; his hands grasped each other tight as a lovers' knot. "Has the man no sense? How are we to greet him? Nothing is prepared, nothing!"

"What is good enough for the Queen of Sheba is certainly good enough for King Solomon," Khurrami said. "And once he sets eyes upon our queen unveiled, doubtless he will not care what foods are spread before him! And never have you failed to supply what our queen needs." Khurrami smiled and laid her hand over the chief eunuch's tight-laced fingers. "You will not fail her now."

So she had coaxed and cajoled, and as always, the queen's chief eunuch had managed to create bounteous perfection despite his dark misgivings. The queen's great pavilion spread over a feast fit for the gods themselves— certainly fit for an unexpected guest, however royal. Roast lamb and baked fish; breads stuffed with spiced cheese; sweet wine; pomegranates, grapes, and apricots so perfect they glowed like warm jewels.

And then there was Bilqis herself. Graceful as a panther, she sat upon a chair of ivory; by her right knee sat her white hound, Moonwind, by her left, her favorite hunting cheetahs sprawled in angular grace. Wide collars set with emeralds circled the beasts' necks, collars matched by the necklace that adorned the queen's own throat. She wore few other jewels—a daring choice. But then, Bilqis herself shone like a rare gem—

And if this uncouth king does not have the wit to see her worth, he is a fool—or blind!

"Why do you smile?" Irsiya regarded Khurrami reprovingly; Irsiya, like her brother Tamrin, was ruled by custom and ritual, worried over trifles.

"Because everything under this roof looks just as it should," Khurrami said, "and because I doubt King Solomon has ever set eyes upon anything half so magnificent."

"I hope not. But I think the queen should have worn the leopard crown and the emeralds, and the gown sewn with peacock eyes, and—"

"And I think King Solomon would rather see her without any gems or gowns at all." Khurrami laughed at Irsiya's indignant frown. "Oh, do not worry so—our queen knows how to handle men—even men from this crude hard land. You will see; she will have only to smile upon him, and this king will give her whatever she desires!"

Solomon

Banquets are no place for plain speaking. I am glad we first met as we did—alone save for trusted friends. Solomon regarded the vast pavilion that lay before him, a fantasy of scarlet and indigo, and acknowledged the wealth and will that could create a palace meant to stand for so brief a time. But that the kingdom of Sheba owned great riches was no secret, and luxury had been flaunted at him before. The rich cloth, the gold, the attendants were nothing.

What I wish to see is the Queen of Sheba's face.

Which was doubtless what the royal guest had intended when she contrived to encounter him upon the road. To intrigue him, to waken curiosity. She had succeeded—even knowing he had been well-played, Solomon could not deny his desire to see the woman who owned those sun-bright eyes.

Of course, her people might veil always—Sheba was a strange land with stranger customs. *But surely a king may look upon the face of a queen?*

And then he entered the great pavilion and his question was answered. He paid no heed to the courtiers, the Amazons, the banquet spread down the center of the tent, a river of opulence. He saw only the woman who waited for him upon a throne of ivory. A woman who looked at him with sun-hot eyes.

A woman who smiled upon him, and extended her hand in beckoning welcome. "The king comes to greet me; I am honored."

Solomon strode forward; when he stood before the queen he hesitated, uncertain whether he was meant to clasp her outstretched hand in his. They did not know each other's customs, and it would be easy to offend. Before the moment could become awkward, she swept her hand sideways, indicating a second ivory chair set beside hers.

"Please, sit. That you could not wait to greet me gratifies my vanity; now permit me to gratify yours and treat you as my equal." Laughter danced in her eyes, rippled beneath the solemn words.

Solomon smiled. "Am I not?" he asked, as solemn as she. The queen seemed to ponder the question with great care before answering.

"Oh, here—yes, here, I think we are equals. In our own courts—who can say?" She shrugged, the gesture eloquently skeptical, and Solomon laughed, watching to see how she accepted his tribute to her wit. And to his delight, she smiled.

Clever and at ease, free of arrogance. And proud of her wit—rightly so. A woman worth knowing. Solomon seated himself in the ivory chair beside her, and only then remembered that he had longed to see beyond her veil to discover whether her face was fair to look upon. Now he realized that did not matter; her perfection of face and form was less important than her beautiful mind.

"You have welcomed me to your tent; now it is I who welcome you to my kingdom. You gratify my vanity, for you have traveled far and long to reach me." *Too far, and too long, for this royal visit to have been undertaken to sat-*

isfy mere whim. Only some compelling, urgent matter could have brought this queen here; now Solomon must discover that reason.

"Seeing King Solomon, the journey is forgotten." Bilqis smiled. "Your fame has spread even to the world's end, great King. I knew I must look upon your face and hear your wisdom for myself."

She was richly beautiful, sun-rich, as a ripe peach or a full-blown rose was beautiful. And she was lying to him— *Or say, rather, that she tells me less than truth.*

Solomon smiled in his turn. "And the Queen of Sheba journeyed long days and hard miles only to see King Solomon in all his glory?"

She lowered her eyes, then glanced up at him through heavy lashes. "I have heard King Solomon is all that is wise and just. It is well for a queen to seek wisdom; I have come seeking Solomon's. It is said he can solve the hardest riddles; perhaps he can unravel mine."

Flattering, but a difficult sweetmeat to swallow. This woman treated him as if he were fool enough to fall before honeyed words and perfumed flesh. He had seen too many beautiful women, heard too many flattering words, to be deceived.

"If you truly believe me wise, why do you treat me as a fool?" he asked, suddenly unwilling to play this too-familiar game. "No one travels half the world to ask riddles. Try again."

Without moving, she seemed to straighten, no longer subtly yearning. Now she regarded him candidly, eyes intent. "You seek to trade in Sheba's realm. I would talk of treaties, and of spices, and of profit for us both."

"No ruler leaves a throne unguarded; rulers send emissaries to speak for them—as I did. Try again."

This time she smiled. "It is impossible to hide anything from King Solomon's wisdom. You are right, O King; I have journeyed a thousand miles seeking the answer to a riddle."

"You need not jest with me, O Queen. Ask freely, and I shall freely grant whatever favor you ask—if I can in honor and wisdom do so."

"You are as kind and generous as you are wise, King Solomon, and I thank you. But the riddle is mine to solve, and the answer the gods' to give. Our goddess Ilat has sent me north, to your land; has promised me that what I most desire dwells within your kingdom." She regarded him gravely, as if weighing his worth, then smiled again. "As you say, a long journey. And since I am here, perhaps we can also speak of trade, and treaties?"

"And try our wits with riddles?"

"If that amuses you."

"You think your riddles unsolvable?"

"I think them . . . difficult. At least, men find them so."

"And women?"

"May have better fortune." Supple and graceful as a young cat, the queen rose from her ivory throne. "Now if the great king of Israel and Judah will deign to follow where I lead, he will receive the gifts of Sheba from its queen's hands."

The Spice Queen had brought gifts so extravagant Solomon could only stare, silent in the face of such generosity. Caskets of frankincense, baskets of pearls, chests of Ophir's pure gold . . . any one of which would ransom a king. *Or a queen.* Solomon raised the lid of the nearest gilded basket. Rare black pearls filled the basket; pearls dark as storm clouds, deep as shadows. *Pearls as dusky as my Abishag's hair. . . .*

Silent, he bent and slid his hand into the black pearls, lifted them to gaze more closely upon their midnight luster. *I have never seen such gems.* Slowly, he let the darkly glowing spheres slip between his fingers to fall back into the gilded basket. *Such riches. Such beauty. I wonder what she wants?*

For if Solomon had learned anything during his years as king over the empire his father had carved out of the kingdoms surrounding Israel and Judah, it was that every gift carried a price. The richer the gift, the higher the price.

But to ask in plain words what the Spice Queen wanted so badly she would pay so dearly for it was unthinkable. Protocol must be observed. And so Solomon smiled and said, "The queen honors me beyond my worth. These are gifts fit for the king of all the world."

"Trifles barely fit for the King of Wisdom's eyes to glance upon." Laughter warmed her voice; she smiled, and fine lines creased her silk skin, fanned out from the corners of her eyes and mouth.

She is not afraid to smile, to betray her age. Solomon smiled back. "Then they are not for me?"

"They must be, for I was told Solomon is the wisest king under the sky."

"You have been deceived. Now, had you been told I was the wisest king in Israel—"

To his delight, she laughed. "Well, as I have carried these gems and spices all the way from the land of Sheba to lay them at King Solomon's feet, I suppose I must do so even if he is the most foolish king under the sky."

"As he would be to spurn such gifts, and such a giver." Solomon studied the caskets of gems, the gilded boxes of spices, the chests of gold. *Yes, it would take a fool indeed to scorn such riches. Or perhaps a very wise man. . . .*

The queen rose to her feet, graceful as a cat in sunlight. "If Sheba's tribute to King Solomon's wisdom finds favor in his eyes, Sheba is pleased." She held out her hand; henna patterns scrolled over her skin, roses at sunset. Her face revealed only serene pleasure.

"Be pleased, then, and accept King Solomon's thanks for Sheba's gifts." Solomon smiled and took her outstretched hand. The Spice Queen's generosity was overwhelming; suspect. And now he must somehow offer up gifts that were a match for hers, for it could not be said that King Solomon's welcome was grudging, his gifts miserly. *Although what I can grant to a queen who comes bearing such a weight in frankincense and gems I do not know. But doubtless she will think of something.*

Nikaulis

What am I doing here, in this land of hard men and harder laws? An idle question; Nikaulis knew why she was here: her queen commanded it. And though Nikaulis herself thought this journey odd, and her queen's behavior odder still, it was not her place to question, only to obey.

But she would be less than human if she did not wonder. Of course she did not doubt the queen obeyed divine decree—but sometimes, during the long journey north, Nikaulis had wondered if the queen had misunderstood her goddess's message. Oracles were tricky things. Had the queen's own desire led her astray? Surely not; Bilqis had reigned many years and must know how to interpret her goddess's will. Fortunately, Nikaulis's own goddess was less difficult to understand: Artemis, the Moon's Sword Blade, demanded only chastity and courage of her worshippers.

Nikaulis gazed across the hard-packed earth to the pavilion sheltering the queen and the king she had traveled so far to meet. Bilqis reclined, indolent, against silken cushions; her favorite maid, Khurrami, slowly waved a fan of peacock feathers, creating a soft breath of air that pressed the fabric of the queen's garment closer to her skin. The queen spoke, gesturing with practiced ease, and King Solomon smiled and answered. Nikaulis could only guess at their words; from their smiles, and Bilqis's gentle laughter, the king's wit was to the queen's taste.

Vigilant, even here in the midst of apparent amity, Nikaulis kept her eyes moving, studying those around her for any hint of threat. All seemed peaceful. Then her seeking eyes met another's equally intent gaze; Nikaulis found herself exchanging stares with the commander of King Solomon's guard.

Benaiah. That was his name, a soft name for so hard a man. Nikaulis had learned to weigh and to judge a warrior's worth; this man had fought battles in his day, and fought them well. His sun-darkened skin bore enough scars to prove him a fighter, few enough to prove him a good one. But now he grew old, his hair gray and his body thickened, although he still moved with a fighter's easy grace. His eyes were dark, unwavering—

Heat flooded her face, a strange tingling that shocked her. *I have stood too long in the sun,* she told herself. *That is all.* Unwilling to reveal weakness, she kept her gaze level, her face smooth, meeting Benaiah's keen eyes without wavering. She counted heartbeats; after half-a-dozen, she slid her gaze past the guard, resumed scanning the royal gathering.

For no matter how safe, how civil, this meeting seemed, men carried danger with them like a plague. *Hard men, hard laws. I wish the queen had not come here. This land is not safe for her. For any woman.*

Nikaulis found herself gazing once again upon King Solomon's general; the man's eyes probed the pavilion, judged the men and women gathered there, as hers did. For a breath their gazes met, swept on, seeking danger to the rulers they guarded.

The king's man, too, will be glad when this folly is over and done with. The queen will find what she seeks, and we will return home to Sheba.

Soon.

Benaiah

Benaiah had not been captain of the foreign troops under King David and survived to become commander of the host under King Solomon by being indecisive and trusting. Perhaps this woman, this Queen of Sheba, had journeyed half a world only to behold King Solomon in all his glory.

Perhaps she had not. Perhaps she was not even Sheban, let alone its queen. Benaiah stood ready at King Solomon's side, and reserved judgment. In truth, he cared little about the queen, save as her visit affected King Solomon and

Benaiah's own task. Another woman filled his eyes; had captured his dreams since the moment he first saw her riding beside the foreign queen in the desert wadi.

Now she stood watchful beside the Sheban queen, a woman such as he had never before encountered: slender as a hunting knife, supple as a bowstring. Her plaited hair shone bronze in the sunlight. She wore a short tunic and trousers, in the Scythian style, and a sword was belted at her side. Her eyes, when she turned them upon Benaiah, were gray, gray as a polished iron blade.

Something odd happened as her iron eyes met his. Warmth flowed beneath his skin; slow fire caressed his bones. Time slowed.

Then her seeking eyes slid past him, freeing him. *Who is she? What is she?* Benaiah caught the arm of the nearest Sheban, asked the questions, oddly surprised to find that his words did not burn themselves into the incense-laden air.

"That? Why, that is the captain of the queen's guard, the Sword Maid Nikaulis." Then, as Benaiah stood grim and silent, the Sheban added, "Some call them Moon Maids. Amazons. Do all your people treat guests so coarsely?"

Benaiah released the affronted Sheban and stared at the queen's captain. He had heard of the Amazons, warrior women who had once ruled the open lands, who served kings only at their own pleasure. But that was long ago; the world had turned and changed, and few now living had set eyes upon one of the fabled Sword Maids.

Sometimes Benaiah had dreamed of such a woman. But dreams faded at dawn. Benaiah knew better than to build a house upon dreams.

An old soldier, Benaiah prided himself upon sleeping quick and hard, no matter how rough his bed—but that night sleep was long in coming. Benaiah lay in the darkness and stared at the moonlit plain beyond the campfires. The warrior maid's image trembled before him, a silver ghost in the pale moon's light, a golden flame dancing in the banked fire's depths. *Nikaulis. Sword Maid.*

And when he at last closed his eyes, she burned before him still, an ardent brand upon the darkness before sleep.

Amazon.

Baalit Sings

Mounted on a horse swift as air, I rode a path laid down in moonlight. The horse moved strong between my thighs, muscle slid beneath skin as we fled whatever followed behind. For we were hunted, pursued relentlessly through the sunlit hours of the day into the cool silver night.

I fled an enemy that never paused, never tired. My horse reached a riverbank and checked its headlong pace; before us water flashed bright as glass. We splashed through the bright water, leapt up the far bank. For a breath the pressure of the hunter eased—

—and then my foe slipped across the water; rejoined me. I looked back to face my fear. And saw nothing.

Before me the grass stretched endless, flowing beneath the wind like gilded water. Behind me the river burned, moonlight transmuted into fire. Terror hunted me.

And I ran. . . .

I woke cold to my bones. But when I tried to reveal my dream to Keshet and Nimrah, I found that I could not. Even in memory, my dream hunter remained unseen.

A troubling dream—but night demons flee sunlight, and I soon had no time for dreams, for my father sent messengers to warn his wives that he returned with his guest, the Queen of Sheba—

"Coming here, to stay under his roof. And where are we to put her and her court?" That was the Lady Chadara's question, and I thought it not unreasonable. But then, the Lady Chadara held the duty of managing the supplies and servants. No one else cared—

"So long as she does not think to take my rooms!" said Yeshara, only to find herself scorned by Naamah.

"As if she would desire them! Mine, now—I am the chief wife, mother of the king's eldest son. But if this woman thinks to take my place, she will find herself mistaken." Naamah tossed her head, displaying the clean lines of her chin and throat. Naamah battled time as a mortal enemy; with great effort, she had held her foe at arm's length—so far.

Her claim enticed others into the rising quarrel. "We all know there is no chief wife," Xenodice said; an Achaean, she stood always ready to argue fiercely on any matter or on none. "And if there were, surely it would be Pharaoh's Daughter. *She* is a queen to her very bones."

Naamah's red lips thinned a moment, but she did not retaliate. There was no need; Naamah's cronies rounded upon Xenodice, eager for prey as a pack

of hunting hounds. "So only Pharaoh's Daughter is fit to be queen?" demanded Naomi, whose tart tongue made her name, Pleasant, a wry jest. "Unfit, rather—all these years wed to the king and not one child, not even a girl."

This spiteful comment was a mistake, for it reminded all the women gathered in the harem garden of the only woman who had ever held the king's
heart in her keeping. The woman who had given him a daughter whom he
favored above all his many sons. Now the women all turned to gaze upon
me, where I sat playing cat's-cradle for my baby brother David, the Lady
Makeda's son.

Sensing the pressure of their regard, I paused with my fingers tangled in
the scarlet thread I wove into patterns for my small half-brother's amusement. The stilling of my fingers and thread displeased him; he frowned and
waved his hands and feet, demanding I continue. When I did not, he reached
up and grasped the thread, pulling hard and tangling the pattern beyond all
unknotting. *I will have to begin again,* I thought, glancing down at David's
clutching fingers. I decided to remain silent, not add kindling to the fire of
their quarrel.

And I knew silent observers heard more of interest than those who
wished their own views admired. So I bowed my head over the scarlet thread
and began slowly unplucking the knot, to start the game again. David's
mother sat upon a bench close by; she watched, and slanted her night eyes
at my father's other wives.

"Jackals about a bone," she said, and laughed.

As if Makeda had not spoken, the others lifted their eyes from me, to
continue scratching each other with sharp words. No wife would willingly
retreat a step to grant another pride of place, and on one thing only could
they agree: that the arrival of the Queen of Sheba promised trouble.

Why they should be so sure of that, I did not know. No one had yet set
eyes upon the fabled Queen of the Morning. She might be old, or plain, or
dull-witted. As for why she had journeyed a thousand miles—

"She hopes to wed King Solomon," Arishat said. "Why else would a
woman travel so far and so long? And then she will be the chief lady of the
palace."

"Why else? To glean treasure, of course. Is not Jerusalem the world's heart
now?" That was Marah, spiteful as her name.

I had the scarlet thread smooth, and began twining it about my fingers, weaving the pattern once more. Small David stuck his fist into his mouth, staring wide-eyed as the web grew between my hands. *Why do they hate the She-ban queen so? They have not yet set eyes upon her!* But they were jealous as cats of their place in sunlight—or, as the Lady Makeda had said, as jackals of a bone. I glanced up through my lashes, judging who had gathered to complain and quarrel. Naamah, of course, and Marah; Yeshara and Arishat. That they partook of such bitter bread surprised no one, and any who wished to protest imagined wrongs drifted towards them.

Others avoided the quarrelsome group. At the other end of the garden, Melasadne rolled a gilded leather ball for her two young sons and half-a-dozen small white dogs. Lady Leeorenda and the Persian princess, Nilufer, sat beneath the lemon tree, engrossed in a scroll. Nefret, the Pharaoh's daughter, had not come to the garden at all that day.

And the Lady Chadara had left it. As I studied my father's wives, I realized that Chadara no longer stood within the group of arguing women. *Because she must prepare for the Sheban queen's arrival, and they need only deplore it.* The thought made me smile; David pulled his fist from his mouth and laughed, and once again seized the net of thread I had so painstakingly rewoven for him.

At that, I, too, laughed, and set aside the tangle of scarlet. "So you grow bored, little prince? Come, let us walk about and find something else to amuse you." I scooped him up from the sheepskin on which he lay and kissed his plump neck. He gurgled happily and grabbed one of my braids.

"I will take him now." Makeda rose and held out her hands; I gave David into his mother's arms and then pried his fingers from my hair. And when she had taken him away, I, too, slipped from the main garden.

I wanted to know more about this visitor from a far land, this unknown woman who dared such a journey. *Why has she journeyed so long and so far? And for what?* Trade and treaties could be negotiated by envoys; queens did not travel half the world lightly. *So why has this queen come here? What does she seek?*

But I would not learn what I wished to know from my father's wives. I must wait until the Queen of Sheba arrived, and discover her secrets for myself.

Bilqis

As they rode north from the encampment outside the walls of Ezion-geber, Bilqis studied King Solomon with discreet caution, judging him as if he were a rich gem for which she bargained. *Or say, rather, a treaty which I must ex-amine point by point, lest I be deceived by fine words and a smiling face.*

One thing already she had learned: these men regarded her and her women with both awe and anger; a potent mixture that she must control with great care. Oh, the king was pleasant enough, at least pretending tolerance—but his courtiers were less tactful. *And the king's general never takes his eyes from my Amazons, and never smiles.* Such men could be dangerous—

"What so chains the queen's thoughts?" King Solomon's question summoned her attention back to the moment; she glanced sidelong and saw him trying to judge her mood.

Difficult, with a veil guarding my face. Behind that protective cloth, she smiled. "I think on the king's land, and on his people, so different from my own. I look forward to learning of them both."

"As I do to learning of yours." He hesitated, then said, "And to discovering what has truly brought you so far from your kingdom and your throne. It must be a great matter for you to so risk yourself and your crown."

At first she did not answer; they rode side by side in a circle of silence created by their hidden desires. They crested a hill, and she looked upon a broad river flowing slowly through the valley below. By the river's color and the speed of its flow southward, she judged it not deep. But in this land of golden dust and rose-red stone, the river glowed like a fine turquoise.

"The Jordan," the king said. "Our mightiest river."

She liked the wit that could so describe the shallow waterway, and the patience that let him wait without repeating his question. It was for her to choose when and if to answer. As their horses walked slowly down the hill road, she decided to reveal the truth to King Solomon—*some truth, for the moment. I will see how he accepts a portion before gifting him with the whole.*

"I have come at my goddess's bidding."

Solomon regarded her with interest. "Your goddess speaks to you?"

"From time to time. And your god—does He speak to you?"

Now it was his turn to pause, as if weighing each word before he uttered it. At last he said, "Once. How does your goddess speak with you? In dreams? Visions?"

Bilqis shrugged; the dark veils shrouding her rippled as if lifted by a summer breeze. "She makes Herself understood, if I have the wit to heed Her."

"And your goddess—" He paused, and she said, answering his silent query, "Her name is Ilat. Sun of our Days, Mother of Sheba."

"And Ilat told you to journey north, to see me?"

"She told me to seek to the north. You"—she slanted her eyes at him, shrugged again, creating another subtle ripple of veils—"you were kind enough to provide ships for the journey."

"Charity is a virtue. What is the prize your goddess has promised, that you look upon a thousand miles as if it were a single step?"

"One worth a journey to world's end and back. And you, Solomon? What did your god promise you—once?"

Again he seemed to weigh his words, at last saying only "What I asked of Him." And after another silence, "It is wise to think well before one petitions one's god."

Yes, for She—or He—may answer, and the gods do not think as we do. Time to lighten the mood; she laughed, low and soft, the sound muted by her veil.

"True enough, and enough truth for today." Bilqis tilted her head; the thin gold stars sewn upon her veil shimmered and glinted. "Now the King of Israel has questioned the Queen of Sheba, and she him, and both been answered. Now ask again, any question you desire. Surely there is something the man Solomon wishes to ask the woman Bilqis?"

"Yes," Solomon said. "Why do you hide yourself behind gold and veils—yet ride upon a horse like—"

"A man? Why, I ride because upon a horse one can move freely, without reliance upon others. And I veil"—she glanced sideways, and her eyes met his—"I veil to hide my face from the sun, which kisses too hard and hot. Does that answer please you, Solomon?"

And before he could answer, she touched Shams with her heels; the stallion danced sideways. "I must let him run, or he will give me no peace," she said, and sent Shams cantering off along the road that led north.

To Jerusalem.

Abishag

Prince Solomon left me sitting by a pretty fountain in the queen's own garden to await Queen Michal. Outwardly serene, I fretted over every detail of my appearance, though I knew worry was both needless and useless. Needless, as I had garbed myself with care, ensuring that my gown displayed both my person and my skill at sewing to good advantage.

Useless, as I would face the queen within a few breaths, and so had no time to alter any fault there might be.

I knew I looked well, and I knew I was Prince Solomon's own choice—and I knew, too, those things would count for nothing if Queen Michal did not find me pleasing.

My own troubled thoughts trapped my senses so that I did not hear her approach, and thus did not see her until she stood close. And then I was so flustered I barely managed to bend my head modestly and bow low. All I saw of the queen was her feet, which were slender and pale, and clad in sandals of gilded leather.

"Rise, Abishag," she said, "and sit here beside me."

Hoping the queen did not sense my fears, I forced myself to move with slow grace, as my mother had taught me. Queen Michal watched me with what I knew must be critical eyes as I spread my skirt carefully, so that the cloth would neither pull too tight across my thighs nor trip me up when I must stand again.

"A pretty design. Is it the work of your own hands?"

"Yes, Queen Michal." I brushed my fingers over one of the moons I had so painstakingly sewn upon the fine blue linen. "And the pattern is mine as well." Golden suns and silver moons, set row upon row—my own fancy. This was the first time I had ever worn the gown.

The queen's praise made me bold; I raised my eyes to hers. She smiled, and for a breath looked so like Prince Solomon I found it hard to remember that she was not truly his mother. I am not sure Queen Michal herself always remembered that.

I am sure she knew at once that Prince Solomon had claimed my heart; I think it pleased her. She smiled upon me and kissed my cheek, and unclasped an ornament of fine coral and pearls from her own neck and set it about mine.

I thanked her with a pretty speech complimenting her beauty—and learned that Queen Michal need not be fulsomely flattered. She preferred truth, when it could be safely told.

Baalit Sings

A considerate man, my father sent messengers ahead each day, keeping his ministers apprised of his progress towards the city. He sent orders, too; orders concerning the housing and entertainment of the Queen of the South and her entourage. The Sheban queen was to be given the Little Palace, the wing of the King's House that once had been the king's dwelling place. Now it was the quiet portion of the palace, seldom used and too old-fashioned for Solomon's wives to grace with their presence.

All that had changed, for my father's commands summoned workmen to the Little Palace: men to smooth fresh clay upon the walls, to paint the faded images back to bright life. Once again the Little Palace came alive, re-born to house a foreign queen and her exotic court.

Gossip flew to Jerusalem more swiftly than the king's fleetest messenger, and so long before the watchtower wardens lit the fires that would signal the king's return with his royal guest, everyone in the city, from Pharaoh's Daughter to the lowest beggar in the street, knew that nothing to match the Sheban queen's court had ever been seen in all the land.

Women warriors guard the Sheban queen, the fabled Sword Maids, haters of men sworn to chastity and the Moon. Eunuchs tend her; princes sacrificed their manhood to serve her.

She speaks with birds and with beasts. She can change into a serpent at will.

Half beast herself, the queen dares not display her deformed body; heavy veils shroud her always from men's eyes.

With each retelling, the rumors grew wilder, until the Sheban queen's beauty became more than mortal, her consequence greater than an emperor's. As for the treasures she had brought— *Gold beyond weighing and gems beyond counting. Frankincense and myrrh enough to fill the Temple itself from floor to rooftree. Pearls large as peacock's eggs, rubies large as a woman's heart*—those were the stuff of wild dreams.

As was the queen herself. *Half djinn and half fire. Clever as the Sphinx.* Even the queen's titles sang like golden bells: the Queen of the South, the Queen of the Morning Land. The Spice Queen.

Although King Solomon's wives came from every kingdom from Melite and Egypt to distant Colchis, the Queen of Sheba's entourage promised to eclipse all others that had entered through Jerusalem's great eastern gate. Upon the day that King Solomon and the Queen of Sheba rode through the streets of Jerusalem to the palace, the streets and housetops were so crowded with people come to gaze upon her that no one could move so much as a step for the press of bodies until the royal procession had passed by. And although the Sheban queen indeed had veiled herself, those who had come to watch were not disappointed—

"For a cloak golden as the sun covered her, and a mask of pearls hid her face," Nimrah told me; I had sent her to try to spy out the Queen of Sheba before she reached the sanctuary of the Little Palace. "Her hands were painted with henna and her fingernails painted with gold."

"And her feet?" I asked, for one of the wilder tales claimed that the Queen of Sheba walked not upon a woman's feet but upon little hooves, like a goat.

"The golden cloak hid her feet," Nimrah said, "so we must wait and see. If she indeed possesses hooves, perhaps she gilds them as well as her nails."

"Perhaps she does," I said, and we both laughed. I could not quite believe in the hooves—but who truly knew what might be possible in a land in which trees dripped incense for the gods—and a woman ruled over men?

Bilqis

Against her expectations, her first sight of Jerusalem impressed Bilqis. The city sprawled rich and careless across the hills it commanded; circled by walls high and broad, crowned upon its highest point by a building so clad in gold that it seemed to burn under the noonday sun like a bonfire.

"That is the Temple." King Solomon noticed even the smallest change in her attention; now he named the great building that had caught her eyes.

"King Solomon's Temple—so I have heard it called." She smiled, slanting her eyes towards him. *His lips smile, but his eyes do not. Now, why?* A queen could not afford to ignore subtleties.

"So called because I put my father's plans in motion. The Temple was his dream."

And not yours? She gazed across the valley at the blaze of gold. "It is magnificent. And the city is beautiful." That, too, was a surprise. But even at a distance, the city pulsed with life, shone new and hopeful.

"Yes, Jerusalem is beautiful. So much of it is new, since even my father's time. He conquered an aging town and built a great city upon its foundations."

"The City of David." Jerusalem the Golden. Again she watched as King Solomon smiled—and again that smile did not warm his eyes.

"Yes, the City of David. My father won not only cities but men's hearts."

"And women's too, I hear."

"Of course. How could he not? David was a hero, skilled at war and at love." Solomon's tone revealed nothing.

Which told her everything. *A hero for a father—that is a heavy burden for a man to bear.* It was her turn to smile, to speak lightly. "Yes, even in Sheba we heard of King David. And now of King Solomon. Your land breeds great men."

"And yours clever women," he said, and she inclined her head, acknowledging the compliment.

"So that is the Great Temple. And the king's palace—surely that is as magnificent—or nearly so?"

"Nearly so," he agreed, and they rode on along the valley road, the broad way that led up the hill to the open gates of the City of David.

Just as she had spared no cost, no effort, to bring the glory of Sheba north to the court of King Solomon, so the king had spared nothing in providing for his royal guest. She had been presented with the Little Palace; she was to consider that residence her own during her stay—

"Which the King of Israel hopes will be long," Solomon had said, to which she had replied, "A king's hopes are customarily fulfilled, are they not?"

She only hoped that her sojourn in Jerusalem would not merely seem long. *Three days in an unquiet house is longer than three years in a loving one.* And she had to admit the Little Palace charming, its old-fashioned columns sturdy rather than elegant, its rooms cozy rather than spacious. Even the new-painted walls copied the style of a previous generation, the lilies straight as guardsmen, the swallows flying in neat rows above the rigid yellow flowers.

The oldest portion of the great palace that now covered half a hilltop, the Little Palace could function as its own small world, a private sanctuary against the tumult of the busy court. And before she had dwelt half-a-day within Jerusalem's imposing walls, Bilqis knew that refuge would be vital.

Jerusalem might serve as the world's marketplace, but the city's sophistication sank only as deep as the bright paint upon the palace walls. So new a kingdom that the oldest men and women who dwelt within it had seen its first king crowned, Israel still sought its true balance. Quarrels between the old ways and the new arose constantly, and King Solomon's far-famed court squabbled like a pen of fighting quail.

"—and this is the old palace, the one their great King David built when he conquered the city." Khurrami's tart voice snared Bilqis's attention; she listened as Khurrami went on, "Lodging the Queen of Sheba in these hallowed rooms is intended as a great honor, so I suppose they will have to serve." Khurrami set the queen's mirror upon the glossy surface of an ebony chest; she regarded the silver disk critically and reached out to move it again.

"Oh, leave the mirror there, Khurrami—it will do well enough." Irsiya set the alabaster box that held the queen's eye paints beside the mirror. "And of course King Solomon means to honor Sheba; how could any man doubt it?"

"The men of Jerusalem would greatly enjoy doubting it," Khurrami said. "They don't like women here."

"King Solomon has forty wives," Irsiya countered, and Khurrami laughed.

"Oh, the king likes women well enough! No honor is great enough for the Queen of Sheba, not in his eyes." Khurrami's eyes met the queen's; Bilqis smiled and beckoned.

"You have been working since midday setting my rooms in order. Come and sit by me, and rest—and tell me all you have learned." For Khurrami numbered among her virtues the knack of acquiring information, of gathering gossip as easily as she gathered flowers in a garden.

Now Khurrami sat and retold all the tales she had already gleaned from the palace slaves and servants—and the insults and complaints as well. *Unpleasant, but no surprise, not after what we encountered upon our journey here.* Sheba clung to ancient ways, followed a path fewer and fewer now walked. Khurrami's report distressed Irsiya; the queen listened unmoved to relayed comments disparaging her wisdom, her demeanor, and her character.

At last she said, "Thank you, Khurrami—and do stop widening your eyes and shaking your head, Irsiya. Of course Israel is nothing like Sheba; we are the crown of all the world and can hardly expect other kingdoms to equal us." *They are both tired, my girls; I must send them off to rest.*

She smiled and reached out to tuck a straying curl back into the coils of Khurrami's shining hair. But before she could speak, Khurrami said, "There is one thing more, my queen. King Solomon has ordered a second throne set beside his in the great court, the one circled by so many columns of cedar they call it the Forest of Lebanon. The throne waits to receive his royal guest—even though she be a woman."

"Has he?" Bilqis said. "Has he indeed?"

A good sign—at least, she would accept it as a fair omen. At the very least, King Solomon proved himself more open-minded than many. Kings rarely counted tolerance among the royal virtues. *A paragon among men—or he wishes to seem so.*

"So King Solomon will set the Queen of Sheba beside him as an equal. Now, how is the queen to garb herself to repay that compliment?"

In answer, Khurrami and Irsiya happily debated the virtues of each gown and veil the queen possessed, each gem and girdle, each diadem and cloak. "Gold," Khurrami said, "gold only for your clothing and jewelry. Gild your eyelids and fingertips—and sprinkle your hair with gold dust. You will outshine the noonday sun." This shining image failed to appeal to Irsiya, who favored more colorful raiment. "Tyrian purple—that always shows one's wealth. Gold fringe, yes—but for your ornaments, your finest gems. And the Phoenix girdle."

"Not that thing!" Khurrami recoiled as dramatically as if Irsiya had dropped a viper into her hands.

My poor Khurrami; her taste is so delicate! But truly, Khurrami's objection was not without merit. Ancient, yes; a treasure beyond price, yes. But as an item of apparel—the vastly admired Phoenix girdle proved difficult to love. Row upon row of pearls, each perfect as a full moon, each as large as a cherry, formed the fabled girdle; those pearls alone created a matchless prize.

But it was the pearls' color that rendered the Phoenix girdle priceless. Fire gold, ember red—Sheban legend swore each pearl had formed from the broken shell of an egg of the fabled phoenix, the bird of fire. Pearls the color of dying flames—

—crafted into a girdle two handspans wide, the rows of pearls caught up at intervals by claws of gold. The girdle's original simple moon-knot clasp had been reworked a century ago; now two phoenixes with ruby eyes and bodies of gold faced each other, their grasping claws serving as hooks to close the girdle. Two tassels as long as a woman's arm hung down from the phoenix clasp, as if serving as the birds' tails. One tassel was formed of white pearls, the other of black.

"It's traditional," Irsiya said.

"It's atrocious," retorted Khurrami. "And far too heavy as well. These court functions go on for *hours*—do *you* want to wear ten pounds of pearls about your waist for hours?"

"What could better display our queen's wealth?" Irsiya countered. "The Phoenix girdle, and the Slave King's emeralds, and—"

"And what could better display dreadful taste?" Khurrami cut in. "She is Queen of Sheba, Queen of the Morning—not a plaster idol in a second-rate roadside temple! Tyrian purple and emeralds and the Phoenix girdle as well—do you want King Solomon to think she's blind?"

Irsiya glared back. "Well, if you had *your* way, he'd think she owned less than a beggar by the road! She is Queen of Sheba, Queen of the South, ruler over all the Spice Lands. Do you want these unshaved barbarians to think she's poor and weak?"

The queen laughed, and both handmaidens turned to face her with identical expressions of aggrieved indignation. "Peace," the queen said. "As always, both of you are right—and wrong."

"What then will it please the queen to wear to King Solomon's court?" Irsiya asked. "Plain gold and the Phoenix pearls?"

"The queen is not wearing that ghastly girdle," Khurrami said flatly.

I must not let them quarrel like cats simply because they amuse me. Curbing her urge to laugh again, Bilqis merely smiled. "Again, you are both wrong—and right."

That caught their attention; they stared at her, plainly trying to solve the riddle she had set them. After a long pause, Irsiya said, rather plaintively, "The queen must wear *something.*"

"For this occasion, yes." She smiled at Irsiya, the easily shocked, as Khurrami regarded her queen with growing suspicion. "Now do not glare at me like that, Khurrami, I do not order my affairs—or garb—only to suit your pleasure. And Irsiya, do try to remember you are a queen's lady and not a virgin priestess dwelling alone in a cave. Now do not sulk, for truly you both have aided my decision. I now know exactly what I shall wear to be welcomed by our royal host."

She looked upon her doubting handmaidens and smiled. "And I swear to you by Ilat's eyes that not a man there will ever forget the day that the Queen of Sheba first entered King Solomon's court."

Baalit Sings

The Queen of Sheba might as well have dwelt upon the moon, for no one saw her or the exotic court that accompanied her. Protocol must be observed; the royal guest must petition for guest-right and the royal host offer welcome in approved and formal fashion. Until that ritual had been accomplished, the visiting queen remained secluded in the Little Palace. And for once, no amount of cajoling upon my part gained me my own way.

My first confident request to my father that I be allowed to visit the queen had gleaned only a smiling refusal. Unaccustomed to being denied, I asked again, this time arguing that, as the king's daughter, I had a duty to make the foreign guest welcome.

"Yes—once she has rested. The journey from Sheba is long, and hard on a woman. Do not trouble her now."

"I would not trouble her, I swear I would not. Surely she will think me ill-mannered if I do not greet her and offer a welcome gift!"

"No, Baalit," my father said in a tone I had never before heard from him, a tone which warned that I must not argue.

So I bowed my head and went quietly away, chiding myself for having asked his permission at all. Had I simply gone to the Little Palace by my own will, my father might have scolded me afterward, but I would have met the Sheban queen before anyone else. But I could not now pretend I had not heard or understood my father's order.

So I must find another path to my own way. A little thought provided an answer, for while I might be forbidden to go uninvited to the Little Palace, surely the Queen of Sheba could see whom she wished. After all, my father visited her, as did the palace steward, Ahishar; and the Lady Chadara, overseer of the women's palace—and my father's friend, Amyntor of Caphtor.

I smiled, and sent Nimrah to summon Amyntor to meet me upon the wall above the palace gate. As I waited there, gazing over the busy city, I told over to myself what I would say to Amyntor. I knew he would come to me; everyone wished to please the king's favored child.

I was so intent upon my own plans that I did not hear him approach; only when his shadow fell over me did I turn to see him standing tall and glittering before me. Under the midday sun, the long ringlets of his black hair shone with blue glints. Today a sprig of jasmine gleamed behind his ear, white stars against midnight. Amyntor always wore flowers.

"Princess," he said, and bowed low; when he straightened, I saw laughter lit his eyes, spangles of gold dancing in dark amber. "You summoned me and behold, I am here."

And as I smiled, he added, "Now, *why* am I here, Princess?"

"I wished to speak with you," I said, lifting my chin to regard him with what I hoped was royal composure.

"I'm honored—and at least you had sense enough to choose a very public place for our tryst." Amyntor waved a hand, indicating the open sky above us and the city below. "Far less suspicious than meetings in shadowed corners and dark gardens."

His tone mocked, but I decided it wisest to accept his words as praise. I smiled again and said, "I thank you for answering my summons, Lord Amyntor. I have a favor I would ask of you."

I paused, but he said nothing, merely raising his eyebrows, and after a moment I spoke again to fill the silence. "You visit the Sheban queen," I said. "Will you take her a message from me?"

"That depends on the message," Amyntor said, and as I stared at him, he added, "Now, don't bristle up like a cross cat—never vow you'll do something until you know what's truly being asked." He smiled, a flash of teeth. "What message, Princess?"

Reminding myself that I wished to ask a favor of him, I bound my temper before I spoke. "My greetings to the queen, and my welcome to King David's City," I said, my voice calm. "And my wish that she ask I visit her, to present her with a gift." This last I added lightly, as if it mattered little.

Amyntor laughed—and then shook his head. "My apologies, Princess, but you'll have to find another to carry that message—or wait until your father permits your visit to the Sheban queen."

Chagrined, I made myself ask, "How did you know?"

"If he'd permit you to visit her," Amyntor said, "you wouldn't need me to carry messages for you."

And from that refusal Amyntor would not be moved, although I argued and cajoled as persuasively as I could. What harm could there be in indulging me in this? Sooner or later I would meet the queen; courtesy demanded I welcome her, greet her with gifts. My father was rightly solicitous of his royal guest, but I swore I would not tire her—

Amyntor listened, and laughed. "You'd tire anyone, Princess—even the Queen of Sheba, and I doubt she's easily wearied! Sorry, but the answer's still no. Your father doesn't give you many orders, so you'd best obey the ones he does."

"Oh, he will not be angry with me," I told Amyntor, confident of my father's indulgence. Never before had my father denied me anything. "He will forgive me."

"Perhaps he will, but he might not forgive me. No, thank you, I shan't risk it. I'm not yet weary of Jerusalem's pleasures. And besides, I like your father; I won't slink about behind his back."

"He would not know you had helped me," I argued. "No one would know."

"Wrong, Princess," Amyntor said. "The Sheban queen would know, and you would know—and *I* would know. Now run along and play like a good girl."

"I am not a good girl!" I said without pausing to think how my words would sound, and was paid for this carelessness with Amyntor's easy laughter.

"Run along and play like a bad girl, then," he said, and as I gaped at him, he flicked the tip of my nose with his finger and strode off, leaving me standing there furious with both him and myself—and not one step closer to the Queen of Sheba.

For once I held no advantage over the other women in my father's palace. Like all the others, I must wait until my father chose to reveal his queenly guest.

I strove to conceal my avid interest, feigning indifference when the gossip in the women's palace turned endlessly to the visitor from the south. But in truth, I was no better than any other woman; like all the rest, I was wild with curiosity to see the foreign queen who had traveled half the world only to see King Solomon with her own eyes. A foreign queen for whom King Solomon had set up a throne beside his own.

And I owned a coign of vantage my father's wives did not.

Concealed behind my father's throne was a secret chamber; from its recess, one could view the king's great court without being seen. I had found the secret room when I was very small. I had been more willful than usual that day, and sought to hide from my nurse, and had crossed from the women's palace to the king's world. My wayward act yielded unexpected treasure—behind a heavy leather curtain painted with scarlet poppies, I found a private sanctuary.

The room behind the curtain was small and dark, for the only light came through a latticed window. Later I saw that lattice from the other side, from the king's great court; only then did I learn how cunningly the spy hole had been wrought. For from the court, all that could be seen behind the king's throne was a wall of painted tiles. Bright reeds and lotus flowers fooled the eye, masked the secret room beyond.

Someone had set cushions by the latticed window—someone long ago, for the cushions were dull with dust. A faint scent of cinnamon clung to the cloth. The hidden chamber had delighted me; within it I felt safe, as if held in my mother's arms. There I spent a pleasant hour hidden from all the world, until I grew hungry and decided I was no longer cross with my nurse.

Of course my nurse was cross with me, but as no one dared treat me harshly for fear of angering my father, she only threatened to tell him I had vanished for hours— "And King Solomon will not like that, Princess. Why, anything might have happened to you! Where did you go?"

"Nowhere," I said, for I had no intention of sharing my secret. But then I smiled at her and begged her not to tell my father, for I did not wish to grieve him. My nurse made me promise that I would not wander off and become lost again; I was able to swear that with a clear heart, for I had not been lost. No one within its walls knew the king's palace better than I.

And so I claimed that secret chamber for my own. When I grew older, I cleared the dust and took away the old cushions with their dirt-rotten cloth, replacing them with new. I did not tell even my father that I knew the secret of spying upon the throne room—although I think perhaps he guessed. It was not, after all, a very great secret. He might himself have used the room when he was a boy, learning kingship from Great David's acts.

Now, while my father's wives watched the Sheban queen from behind the screens of the queens' gallery, I sat in my hidden room; from that spy post, I could look past my father's throne straight into the court. No one but my father himself commanded a better view of those who came before the king.

I do not think anyone who watched in King Solomon's court that day ever forgot the moment the Queen of Sheba stepped into the courtyard and set her feet upon the path to the king's throne. She knew the tales that had flown from one ear to the next, knew how eagerly all men wished to set eyes upon her, to judge her for themselves. She knew, and she made them wait for what they desired.

Before men saw the Queen of the South, they saw the treasure she had carried with her from Sheba. Bearers clad as finely as princes bore in litters upon which rested open caskets of pearls and incense; these men were followed by others drawing a cart piled high with nuggets of gold. It was no short task for the Shebans who displayed the queen's gifts to my father's waiting court, but at last the final gift had been set before the Lion Throne. Then, and then only, did the queen herself come into King Solomon's court.

Two handmaidens entered before her, women garbed and gemmed so richly the greatest queen might envy them. Gowns of Tyrian purple, shawls of scarlet fringed with pure rich gold, veils sheer and glittering as moonlight. One woman was adorned with emeralds about her throat and arms and wrists; the other wore about her hips a wide girdle of pearls crimson as sunset. That pearl girdle alone would purchase a kingdom.

As they drew closer to the throne, I saw that their faces glittered jewel-bright. The paint that gleamed upon their eyelids and mouths, their cheeks and brows, had been mixed with crushed gems. Still more precious stones had been threaded upon silver chains and woven through their intricately braided hair.

The two jeweled handmaidens walked to the foot of my father's throne, bowed low, and backed away to sink gracefully to their knees on either side of the marble steps. While they waited there, still as the carved lions that guarded the throne, the Queen of Sheba showed herself at last.

She walked slowly through the shadows of the cedar columns into the light. There she paused for a heartbeat, and I saw her eyes seek my father's. And then she began to walk towards him, smiling—and I do not think a man there could tear his gaze from her, or a woman either.

Ivory silk flowed over the curves of her body like rich cream. Two pins of gold formed in the shape of leopard paws clasped the simple gown at her shoulders; two ivory combs held back her heavy shining hair. Thin chains of gold hung with tiny bells circled her ankles. Her feet were bare.

As she paced towards my father's throne, the only sound in the great court was the sweet small chimes of the golden bells that hung about the Queen of Sheba's ankles.

I had never before seen a woman like her.

She walked straight and tall, and when she stood before his throne, her eyes met my father's and did not waver. She was a true queen, a woman who ruled by right. I had thought she would appear hard, mannish, unwomanly. But I was wrong.

The Sheban queen was beautiful; beautiful as summer afternoon when the shadows grow long. Beautiful as wind and rain and stars, as all things ripe and warm. As beautiful as my mother in my dreams.

I could not tell her age; it did not matter.

"Bilqis, Queen of Sheba, greets King Solomon of Israel and Judah." Her voice rang clear; like my father, she knew how to send her words across a vast room so that all might hear. She did not bow to my father; she was his equal.

He rose and descended the steps of the Lion Throne, his hand out-stretched. "Solomon, King of Israel and Judah, greets Bilqis, Queen of Sheba," he said. "Be welcome to my court and sit beside me as long as you desire."

She put her hand upon his, and he led her up the steps, to the new throne set beside his. The Lion Throne of David was formed of carved and gilded cedar, ornamented with solemn lions, footed with lions' paws. For the Sheban queen, he had ordered fashioned a throne upon which leopards adorned silvered wood. Only when the Sheban queen and my father both sat upon their thrones did I pay any heed to the warrior who stood behind the queen. *Ah, that must be the Sword Maid, the Amazon.* But even so odd a sight as a woman warrior could not pull my eyes from the queen for long.

She is truly a queen—as much a queen as my father is a king. This I knew in my bones; a truth I had not dreamed could exist. And I knew another thing as well: I must meet the Sheba queen—*no matter the cost.*

Even as the words flared like fire in my mind, I wondered why I thought that meeting would cost me anything.

Ahijah

Even of King Solomon, I would not have granted this tale's truth—save that I have looked upon this corruption with my own eyes.

When he had heard that the king had raised up a throne beside his own and set a pagan queen upon it, Ahijah had doubted. Even Solomon, whose House of Women sheltered idols within its walls, would not dare do such a thing. *But he has. Now no one can doubt this king's love of vice and iniquity.*

Ahijah stood in the shadows cast by the pillars of cedar ringing the great court and watched as the Sheban queen walked in brazen wantonness up to the steps of King Solomon's throne. She did not bow. The king came down the steps to offer her his hand and lead her to the silver throne placed beside his own.

And as King Solomon announced to all the court that the Queen of Sheba would sit beside him at her own pleasure, Ahijah drew in his breath and stepped forward, out of the shelter given by the cedar pillars. *You see me, King Solomon. Heed me.* But as Ahijah drew in his breath, the king's gaze slid over him, swift as a falcon's shadow. As if Ahijah were no more than a servant or a dog.

As if he could no longer be seen by the king's eyes.

No. Silent, Ahijah stepped back between the pillars. *No. You will not laugh at me again, O King. Not again. I am Yahweh's prophet, and I will not cast Yahweh's words upon deaf ears. I will wait—wait until the day Yahweh sets the weapon in my hand that will destroy you.*

Helike

Although she cared nothing about the Queen of the South, she had followed all the rest of the king's women to the gallery overlooking the great court; compliance was easier than thought. She had not dreamed that she would regret this choice so bitterly, that pride and passion long chained would be unleashed by the sight of a foreign woman.

But it was not the Sheban queen—a creature sun-kissed and lush; she plainly worshipped an easy goddess of day and laughter—no, it was not the queen who captured Helike's eyes. For a pace behind the Queen of the South stood a warrior. A tall, supple figure clad in a leather tunic sewn with bronze disks and scarlet leather trousers tucked into high laced boots. A figure whose strong hand rested on the hilt of a short iron sword and whose hair fell down her back in a single braid. A band of silver a handspan wide guarded her throat. . . .

No. No. Surely my eyes lie. But she knew they did not. Behind the Sheban queen a Moon Maid stood sword watch. Pure and straight; a reproach from the Huntress, keen as an arrow in the heart.

I was that once. And now— Helike bowed her head, sick disgust pushing against her throat. *Now I am nothing. A man's wife; his vessel to fill as he will. Chattel.*

Others pressed forward, pushed her towards the rear of the queens' gallery. She allowed herself to be shuffled back; she would not struggle to retain her place. *What place? What does it matter what I do here?*

But once her sight was barred by the bodies of the king's women, terror rushed through her. If the Huntress had vouchsafed a sign—*a sign to me, after all these long cold moons*—how could she refuse to accept it? *Even though it means my death, I must look again upon my sister-in-blood.*

Deaf to the protests of those she brushed aside, Helike fought her way back to the cedarwood lattice that hid the king's women from view. There she clung, staring through the screen, filling her eyes with the sight of her unknown sword-sister.

She could not tell which clan had reared the stranger; she knew only that they were moon-kin. For now, that was enough.

And for once she was glad of the seclusion the king's women kept. She could feast her starved eyes upon the Sword Maid unseen, without risk that the Queen's Blade would see her— *And if she did?* Bitter thought; Helike tasted bile on her tongue. *And if she did, what would she see? Nothing. Nothing but a palace woman.*

Tears bit at her eyes; Helike lifted her gaze from the Amazon and stared at King Solomon where he sat upon the great gold and cedar throne. *What would she see? One of King Solomon's queens.* The golden king upon his golden throne blurred, became a golden haze before the bright mosaic on the wall behind the throne. The Spice Queen moved, radiance incarnate, towards the golden glory of King Solomon. The Sword Maid stood, spear-straight, her scarlet leather bright as blood, never flinching.

No, I am wrong. She would see nothing. Nothing at all.

Abishag

The queen's truth was that I had been chosen to act as her eyes and ears in King David's chambers. For Queen Michal meant the next king to be Solomon. To that end, she must know all that passed between the king and those who visited him as he lay cold in his bedchamber. And so I had been chosen—a young maiden to tend and warm the dying king—and to carry all that was said or done in his presence back to Queen Michal.

But she left the final choice in my hands; I weighed all she had said, and remembered all my mother had so carefully taught me, as if she had prepared me always for this task.

And I thought of Solomon's sun-bright eyes. "Yes," I said, and lifted my hand to curl my fingers about the cool coral and warm pearls the queen had set about my throat. "I will be your gift to King David."

"My last gift to him," the queen said, and smiled.

And so I became one of the king's many women—and one of the queen's shadows. The second task was harder than the first.

Bilqis

She had been royally housed and greeted—greeted as an equal, a ruler to set beside the king himself. In this land, Bilqis knew that was no small gift.

Already her servants brought her rumors of outrage that a mere woman should be so honored. *Let the men and women of this kingdom protest; I shall not remain here long enough for it to matter to me.*

One thing only mattered: seeking out the promised queen she had journeyed so far to claim.

If she indeed is here. If she exists at all. For now she had met King Solomon, and looked upon the City of David, and upon the Great Temple as well. But she had not yet discovered, in this royal city, the daughter that Ilat had promised.

"Cultivate patience and reap riches," she reminded herself, but the old proverb failed to soothe her unquiet heart. Somewhere upon her long journey she had begun to doubt, not only her goddess but herself. Had she mistaken Ilat's words, heard only what she had longed too greatly to hear? *Have I traveled half the world only to fail?*

She pushed the thought aside; worry was weakness. *If I have erred, I must correct the error.* Her goddess had led her here, had promised a daughter for Sheba. *Now I must unravel Her riddle and find the girl.*

But perhaps there was no girl—not yet. Suddenly she saw another way— *We are far from Sheba; we will not see Ma'rib's walls again for a year.* She had young women attending her, women whose bodies were still fruitful. *Get one of them with child by the king, and claim the babe as my own daughter, goddess-granted. I shall have one of them take Solomon to her bed. A child of his to fulfill Ilat's promise—*

No. The denial rang clear. That path was wrong; she knew it in her bones.

Then I must wait. Wait and see what Ilat sends. Only please, Mother, let it be soon! Seeking ease from her fears, she went to stand before the altar, facing the ivory image of the goddess. Crossing her hands over her breasts, Bilqis bowed her head and then looked into Ilat's lapis eyes. She did not petition, she merely stood awaiting whatever Ilat might deign to send her. But she felt nothing, and after a time she bowed her head again and backed away.

"The gods aid those who aid themselves," she told herself, and heard a soft laugh; Khurrami came towards her, bearing an alabaster bowl in her hands. Pomegranates glowed red and perfect against the pale stone.

"A gift from King Solomon?" the queen asked, and Khurrami shook her head.

"No," Khurrami said, holding out the alabaster bowl. "A gift from King Solomon's daughter."

The words seemed to echo in the warm scented air; she stared at the crimson fruit, reached out and took a pomegranate in her hand. "King Solomon's daughter," she said slowly, and then, "Khurrami, I am a fool. Send word to King Solomon that the Queen of Sheba wishes to walk and talk with him this afternoon. And tell Irsiya to come to me and help me dress to meet with the king."

Khurrami set the alabaster bowl upon a carved cedarwood chest and went off to perform her tasks; Bilqis cradled the pomegranate in her hands. *You knew the king had a daughter, yet it did not occur to you that she might be the girl you seek? Did you think your prize would be set before you upon a golden tray with the king's other gifts?*

And why had the king not offered to show her his wives, his children? Of course she had met Prince Rehoboam—who had greeted her with a sullen courtesy that boded ill for his future reign did he not improve his manners—and such of the king's sons as were old enough to have left the women's palace and have quarters of their own. *But Solomon has not shown me his women's world. Why?*

Perhaps it was Ilat's doing, to remind her that even a queen could be a fool. "Did I expect a slave girl or a novice priestess to cross my path in the street and have my crown fall at her feet?" Her fingers closed over the pomegranate's smooth tough skin; she laughed softly. "I have listened to too many harpers' songs."

She gazed at the fruit that shone like rubies within the moon-pale vessel. Still smiling, she set the pomegranate she held back in the bowl and then carried the princess's gift to lay before Ilat's ivory feet.

"Thank you," she said. She had asked for guidance—and what clearer sign could the goddess have sent her? Soon her quest would be ended and she could return home—home with Sheba's future safely in her keeping.

When she asked King Solomon if she might see the queens' palace, she made her request light, half a jest. "Forty wives, and all of them queens! Now that is a sight worth setting eyes upon." Bilqis slanted her own eyes at the king, teasing glints half-veiled by her lashes. "Why do you hide them from me? Are you afraid of what they may reveal?"

Solomon laughed. "A man afraid of his wife—"

"Or wives," she said.

"—or wives, is a man who wed the wrong woman—or women," he added. "No, I thought only that such a visit would bore you."

"Because I rule a kingdom and they do not?" So that was the reason, no more—and had she had the wit to ask at once, she would not have wasted a week once she arrived in Jerusalem! She tilted her head, letting her tiered gold earring brush her cheek, light as a dragonfly. "Tell me, O King, do you speak only with kings and princes? Or do you learn from all men?"

He did not spend breath on an answer they both already knew; he smiled and held out his hand. "Come, then, O Queen, and look upon the world of the king's women. Although what the Queen of the South may learn from women whose only interests are their garments, their gems, and their children, I do not know."

O Solomon, you are called "the Wise"—yet you are as blind as any other man when you look upon your own women. But she only smiled, and laid her hand over his. "Of course you do not know; you are a man. Show me your women, reveal to me the living treasures of your palace, King Solomon, because I ask it."

"Whatsoever the Queen of Sheba desires, that she shall have," the king said, and Bilqis smiled, the curve of her lips as meaningless as his extravagant ritual promise.

As they walked through the courtyards and corridors, Bilqis noted each fruit or flower painted upon plaster walls, each emblem carved in stone, that might serve as a clue to guide her should she ever need to walk these halls alone. The Palace of the Sun and Moon in Ma'rib rose seven stories into the sky and spread its brick skirts wide—but King Solomon's House of Cedar was a match for it in size and splendor.

And like all kings' houses—and queens' too—Solomon's palace coiled about itself like a serpent. Without quick eyes and mind, a stranger would lose his way by the third turning. *Labyrinth,* such royal puzzle-houses had been called when Knossos still stood and the Bull-King and the Lady of the Labrys ruled all the world washed by the Great Sea.

And like all palaces, King Solomon's offered hidden vantage points from which to spy upon those the king wished observed. A long gallery shadowed one side of the women's quarters, its windows veiled by latticed screens delicately carved in stone; from that private spot, shielded from their eyes, the king could watch his women—

"Secretly," King Solomon said, and she sensed hidden amusement beneath his blandly correct tone.

"And does King Solomon the Wise often watch here in secret?" Her own voice gave no hint of her distaste for such enforced seclusion of royal women; this land was not hers, and its ways were strange. She must take care not to give offense.

Solomon smiled. "King Solomon is too wise to think his presence here is ever truly secret. My women know more of what happens in Jerusalem than do my spies!"

Blind you may be when you look upon your wives—but at least you are wise enough not to despise women as so many men do in this land that reckons lineage by fathers instead of mothers. She allowed her own lips to curve in an answering smile, but said nothing. Instead, she moved forward to look down into the garden below.

Clearly the common ground of the women's palace, the garden spread wide, offering both sunlight and shade, fruit trees and fountains. Flowers, too, and neat-laid paths to walk upon, and benches to rest upon set beneath olive and lemon trees. And for all the garden was set within palace walls, and all the women who walked within it were a king's wives, the queens' garden court seemed in truth no more than a village gathering place, the grand fountain no more than a village well.

Here is the heart of King Solomon's world. The women at the well, and their children. Here is where I shall truly learn to know him. Any man can play the hero to a guest. His women—ah, they will know him better.

In the garden below, a woman strolled past, half-a-dozen tiny white dogs trotting along with her, their fur swirling about them like water. Two women sat upon the fountain's edge, their heads bent close in quiet talk. Several small boys kicked a gilded leather ball back and forth.

"Your sons?" she asked, turning away, ready to go on. *If I do not see his daughter soon, I will ask. Patience has limits.*

"Some of them." Solomon gazed down upon the domestic scene and smiled. "And there is my daughter." His voice changed as he said the words, love and pride haunted by sorrow.

At last. Bilqis turned back and looked down into the women's garden once more, and a wave of gratitude swept through her, heating her blood and turning her bones to wax.

Forgive me, Mother Ilat; never again will I doubt.

A girl ran after the gilded ball, caught it up, and tossed it for the little boys to chase. As they ran, she laughed, pushing unruly hair from her face. Then, as if she knew herself watched, the girl looked up, and all Bilqis's lingering fears fled as she stared down into sun-bright eyes.

Yes. Yes, this is the daughter I have come for. She is Sheba's next queen.

A great queen, too, for the girl was a fire-child; born under the stars of the Phoenix, the sign that claimed kings and queens as its beloved children. Her birth-stars blazed in the red that rippled through her dark hair, flames born of the sun's rays. *Yes. That one.*

"That one." Nothing of the triumph and delight soaring through Bilqis touched her voice. "A lovely girl; what is she called?"

"Her name is Baalit," King Solomon said.

Baalit; little goddess. Pain grasped her heart; she closed her eyes against bitter memory. "*Baalit . . . my goddess-child. Sheba's queen, Mother. . . .*" Her daughter Allit's dying words, naming a child who had lived to draw only half-a-dozen breaths— *No. I must think not of what was but of what will be. You were right, my Allit— Baalit will one day be Queen of the Morning.*

"It is a good name," she said at last.

"It is a strange name for a girl of our god's people to bear, but her mother desired it."

Now the pain rang sharp in his voice; clearly the girl's mother had been dearly loved. Bilqis laid her hand upon his. "You are a good man, King Solomon. Many would not have honored such a desire." She did not give him time to answer but spoke swiftly on. "Let us go down into the garden, for I would meet your wives and sons, and your daughter."

"If you wish it," he said, smiling, and she managed to smile back as if she made only the lightest, least vital, of requests.

"Yes, I wish it."

"Very well; come with me, and I shall present my daughter to you. But I warn you, my Baalit is a clever girl who asks as many questions as—"

"As her father does? Do not trouble yourself, King Solomon. Questions amuse me." And she laughed, easy and soft; she dared not betray strong interest—not yet.

But she is the one I have been sent here to find. She is. I know. She is a queen already, and does not yet know it.

This wild girl burned with the passionate fire that once had blazed through Bilqis's blood. Bilqis did not need Ilat's whisper telling her this girl was the one for whom she had come so far, and at such risk. Baalit was the daughter of her soul; whatever the cost, Sheba must have her.

Solomon held out his hand, and Bilqis laid hers upon it. Despite her exultation, her skin was cool, her face calm. And her steps matched his; she would not ruin all by undue haste. Behind her tranquil eyes, her mind began telling over what she now must do.

She permitted herself a soft laugh, as if at the small jest King Solomon was telling her over the flowers in his garden. *My true daughter, my gift from the Queen of Heaven. I must return great offerings as thanks for this favor.* Prayers were so rarely answered so clearly; Bilqis was truly grateful.

"Such serenity," the king said, pausing at the gateway to the garden. "A rare quality; I would give much to possess it for myself."

She noted the hint of doubled meaning, gratifying to know she could still bring fire to men's eyes. *Or say, rather, warmth; I do not think this man sparks to fire.*

"Yes, true serenity is a rare gift; the gods do not often bestow peace upon us. Ah, what lovely carving upon this gate; you are fortunate in your craftsmen, King Solomon. Now let us enter your garden that I may meet the fairest flower within its walls."

When she and the king entered the garden, all the women ceased to move or speak. They stared at the queen— *As if turned to salt by my gaze.* Bilqis kept her face bland; she must not laugh at King Solomon's women.

"Here you see some of my good wives and my fine sons." The king smiled upon the women and then led her to where his daughter stood, hands still lifted to catch a gilded ball. "But you shall meet them in a moment. First, I must show you the most precious jewel in the king's palace."

Solomon smiled, and his daughter smiled back, meeting his gaze squarely. "See, O Queen of the South, the treasure of the north. My daughter, Princess Baalit."

As the king held out his hand, the princess crossed her arms over her breast and sank to her knees, head modestly bowed. "Greetings, my father; I am honored by your presence. Greetings, Queen of the South. Welcome to my father's kingdom, on his behalf—and on mine."

Graceful as flowing water, she rose to stand straight before them, her clear bright eyes intent upon Bilqis's face. Looking into those eyes, Bilqis offered up silent thanks to Ilat. *Yes. This girl is the one. It is she whom I have traveled half the world to claim.* Exaltation burned her blood, dizzying her; she forced herself to speak calmly.

"You spoke truth, O King, when you claimed your daughter as your most precious jewel. The Queen of the South thanks the Princess of Israel for her welcome—and Bilqis thanks Baalit. You are indeed the treasure your father calls you." Light-headed with joy, Bilqis smiled, and watched in delight as Princess Baalit smiled back.

The girl was all that first glance had promised, and more. Oh, there was nothing outwardly odd about the princess, nothing strange to make others point at her, weave hissing tales of her as she passed. Indeed, she was everything King Solomon's daughter should be: poised and comely, with a graceful wit that adorned her character as the gold and gems upon her arms and throat adorned her body. King Solomon had raised his daughter well; she owned pride without arrogance, generosity without foolishness.

And within her, fire burned, fire the gods gifted upon those they loved well. Baalit's feet touched the threshold to womanhood, and the rising flames within her licked well-seasoned timbers, ready to burst into glorious light.

But that fire was but a little thing as yet, as easily banked as kindled.

I must open her to that fire; such a gift must not be wasted. Still smiling at the princess, Bilqis extended her hand and touched the king's wrist. "You are fortunate in your children, King Solomon. You must grant me your daughter's company."

"Granted," he said, "if it pleases you both."

"It pleases me," she said, and looked to the princess. "Does it please King Solomon's daughter to bear the Queen of Sheba joyful company?"

Princess Baalit clasped the queen's outstretched hand and bent to press the queen's fingers to her forehead. "If my father wishes it, and you wish it, there is nothing that would give me greater pleasure," she said, and Solomon laughed.

"You see what a gem she is—a more pious and proper answer I could not desire." The king smiled at his daughter, who displayed enough pleasure at his praise to show she valued it, but not so much as to show his praises were seldom spoken.

"Thank you, my father. I hold myself ready to do the queen's bidding."

Each of the princess's answers seemed to confirm her as the goddess's choice. *A thousand praises, Mother. I shall set a cup of pearls before You as thank-offering before the moon turns again.*

A few more words were spoken, and then King Solomon moved on, leading her away from the princess, seeking to display his wives and sons for her approval. Smiling, Bilqis followed him. And without looking back, she knew that Princess Baalit stood and watched—and waited.

Solomon

Although he knew he was being elegantly, skillfully, flattered, Solomon still warmed to the queen's approval of his daughter. *After all, it is something to my credit that the Queen of the Morning feels the need to flatter me.* And he was no besotted fool; he knew his own child's virtues. Abishag's daughter was indeed a jewel worthy of a queen's praise.

He watched the queen smile upon Baalit, watched as the queen stooped, graceful as water, to kiss the girl's smooth forehead. Ripe beauty greeting the ripening; pomegranate fruit and flower. . . .

An image worthy of a song. A thousand pities I am only King Solomon and not King David; my father's skill would have been equal to the task of creating a song from such beauty.

Suddenly he seemed alone; queen and princess stood before him in a circle of silent understanding Solomon knew he could not enter. Sunlight gilded their skin, sparked slow fire from their hair; they dazzled his eyes, bright as fire from heaven—

As he led the queen towards his waiting wives, he chided himself silently. *I wax poetic,* he told himself, mocking his much-lauded talent with words. *King Solomon the Wise, King Solomon the Great, the writer of proverbs*—

But proverbs were cold things, weighed against songs.

His father had composed songs that men still sang. *No doubt men still will sing them in a thousand years.* Whatever King David had touched turned to gold; whatever sin King David committed became virtue.

Had any other man and woman done what King David and the Lady Bathsheba dared, they would both have been stoned at the city wall. Queen Michal had prevented that tragedy; that much of the affair Solomon knew. But he knew there was more, something darker even than the tales that his father had murdered his mother's husband. But what that dark secret was, Solomon had never learned. . . .

"Return to us, O King; we wait upon your pleasure." Laughter warmed the Spice Queen's voice, rippled beneath her words; a subtle caress.

Caught back from the past, Solomon countered by returning the queen's own words, always a useful ploy. "No, it is the king who waits upon the queen's pleasure. What is your will, Queen of the South?" He smiled; another useful ploy when one had not been attending.

But the Sheban queen was as adept at this game as Solomon himself. "King Solomon has been elsewhere in his thoughts. Doubtless the words of mere women bore him." Wicked pleasure glinted golden in the depths of her eyes.

Warmth kindled Solomon's blood; he smiled back, this time without calculating the effect his expression would have. "Never," he said, and the queen laughed.

"The proper answer, Solomon the Wise," said the queen, "is 'Ah, but the Queen of Sheba is not a mere woman!' "

"Perhaps it is, but as Solomon the Wise is but a mere man, he can speak only what is true, and not what is proper. And the truth, O Queen, is that your words could never bore any man."

Their slow pace had brought them to those of his wives who had chosen to amuse themselves in the garden; Solomon presented each to the Queen of Sheba, taking care to do so in the order of their marriage to him. He would not set any one woman above another, but no one could argue that this method exalted one queen over the other. Even Naamah, mother of the crown prince, must wait until those who had wed the king before her had bowed before the Sheban queen.

The Queen of Sheba spoke pleasantly to his wives, affectionately to his small sons. Then, with a sidelong glance at the watching women—*huddled together like a covey of quail; do they think Bilqis will turn them into sand with a touch?*—the queen said, "And now the Queen of the South claims the Princess Baalit to amuse her for an hour."

"As the queen wishes." There was no other answer Solomon could make— *Nor should I wish to.* Yet as he watched the Sheban queen walk back across the garden to Baalit, and saw the delight upon his daughter's enraptured face, he forced down an urge to call them back to him.

Do not be foolish. What harm can come of letting Baalit chatter to Bilqis?

Baalit Sings

When my father entered the harem garden leading the Queen of the South by the hand, I stared at her and thought only *I am not ready!* I had no idea what I meant; ready for what? And why should I tremble as if I faced some great danger? I had longed to meet the Spice Queen since I had watched her in my father's great court; had schemed, without success, to meet her. Now my father himself brought her to me.

Seen close, she was still beautiful, although clear sunlight revealed lines shadowing her eyes. She did not strive to conceal the fact, and I admired her the more for such courage. All my stepmothers labored mightily to hide the least sign of time's passage.

My heart pounded so I could scarcely think; I hardly knew what she said, or I answered, but it pleased both my father and the foreign queen, who said, "You are indeed the treasure your father calls you."

I felt my face grow hot. "My father praises me too highly, for he loves me too well to say I am less than perfection."

"Do you say, then, that King Solomon—the Wise—errs?" asked the queen.

My father said, "I often err, but not in praising my daughter, who is better to me than forty sons."

"And who should know better than a man who has forty sons?" the queen replied, and my father laughed.

"Oh, I have not quite so many as forty! Come and meet a quiverful of them before they go mad with waiting."

My father led the queen off to present my brothers and his wives. I watched the queen speak kindly to each; she even bent and fondled the Lady Melasadne's frolic of dogs. *How they will queen it over the others who have not met the Sheban!* I foresaw a fresh crop of vigorous quarrels in the days to come.

As I watched, the Sheban queen smiled up at my father and laughed, softly; I saw my father smile, gazing fondly upon her. Jealousy bit sharp; until now, only I had ever brought that look of loving amusement to my father's face. Then shame flooded me, washed away the unworthy emotion. How dare I deny my father pleasure? *If he has found a woman who can make him truly happy, how dare I object?*

And as I thought this, the queen left him and came walking back towards me; she moved easily and quietly, as comfortable in her body as a cat. I stared, unable to think what I should say. How could I impress a woman who ruled the world's most fabulous kingdom? So I waited for the queen to speak first.

"So you are King Solomon's daughter." Her voice was soft, husky; it seemed she spoke for my ears only. "Truly you are worthy of such a father."

"You cannot know that yet." I had not known I would speak so frankly until I uttered the words. Horrified, I tried to form an apology, but there was no need, for the queen smiled, and suddenly I felt I had known her all my life, might speak my mind freely to her.

"You have a sharp wit," the queen said, and I felt myself grow hot.

"I try not to," I said, and she smiled again.

"Keep the wit; at times it serves well. But remember that wit is a blade." The queen paused, as if waiting for me to finish her thought; I did.

"And a blade may be turned against its wielder," I said.

"Ah, so Solomon's daughter is wise as well as clever."

"Not yet," I said, "but I try to be wise. And it is not wise for a girl to seem too clever."

She sighed. "Here—no, here it is not wise for a girl to seem too clever. Come sit with me and talk awhile."

I sat with her on the bench beneath the pomegranate tree, casting swift glances back at my father and his wives. I knew my stepmothers would count each moment I spent alone with the Sheban queen, her attention sparking envy in those who most loudly scorned her foreign wiles. "What does the queen wish to speak of?"

"Why, of you." She smiled upon me as fondly as if I were her own daughter. "And I wish to thank you for your gift."

"A small thing, compared to my father's gifts," I said, and she laughed.

"A charming thing. And your father is the most generous of kings—but one cannot eat gold or gems!"

Much relieved, I too smiled, and clasped my hands in my lap to keep from fidgeting with my sash. I wished to seem calm and royal, to be even half her equal. "I am pleased that my gift pleased you." I had longed to gain her regard, and had first thought to send her a cup of embossed gold filled with pearls. But something had stopped me; almost against my will, I had chosen an unadorned alabaster bowl and ripe pomegranates to send as my greeting to the Queen of the Morning.

And my gift had pleased her.

"Yes, I was most pleased to receive your gift, and am even more pleased to meet you at last. I have been waiting a lifetime to meet you, Baalit."

That day, I thought this only a polite Sheban phrase, a meaningless compliment. So I smiled, taking her words lightly, and said that I, too, had longed to meet her, and that I hoped I did not disappoint, now that she had met me.

"You are all I thought you would be, and more. You are a worthy daughter; I see your father and your mother in your eyes."

"How can you? My father stands there, across the garden. My mother has lain long years dead."

"Nevertheless, she too created you. She is there, Princess. She will always be there in you."

Did the Sheban queen know somehow of my dreams—dreams I often thought were sent by my mother's ghost? *No, she cannot.* Not unless she were the sorceress some called her—

"A pinch of incense for your thoughts, Princess," she said, and her eyes were so kind I found myself saying, "Is it true you are a djinn's daughter?" I was horrified the moment the words left my lips, but the Sheban queen only laughed and shook her head.

"No, nor am I sprung from an eternal flame, nor is my true form that of a white serpent. Do not look so startled; I would be a poor ruler did I not know what tales were told of me. But no, I am a woman like any other."

"No," I said, "you are unlike any other. You rule a kingdom."

"So does your father."

"Yes, but he is a man. Men are born to rule."

"And women to be ruled?" the queen asked, and I could say only "And women to be ruled. That is the way things are done."

"That is the way things are done here. But Israel is not all the world, little goddess."

"*Little goddess*—" No one had called me that since my laughing grandmother had left me to return to Ascalon. I blinked back a sudden sharp press of tears.

"That is what your name means, is it not?" she asked, and I nodded. "A strange name for a daughter of the god Yahweh. But your mother wished it?"

"Yes, my mother wished it. I do not know why." Even my father did not know. Perhaps to please her own mother. Perhaps as a dying vow. I would never know. To my horror, more tears stung my eyes; I looked down to hide them, but I knew I failed.

The queen put her fingers under my chin, lifted my head until we looked straight into each other's eyes. "Why does not matter, not now. What counts is that your mother's love flows in your blood. Never doubt that."

She glanced across the garden; I saw my father turn his head and smile at us. The queen touched my cheek, her fingers soft as a dove's feathers. "And now I must return to your father. But I will be back, Baalit. Do not doubt that either."

"I won't," I said, and rose as she did, watching her walk back along the path of white pebbles until she stood at my father's side once more. As they left the garden, the queen glanced aside and smiled at me. I would have done anything for her in that moment; I knew that somehow I must repay her for opening a gate in my mind that I had not known was closed and barred.

Israel is not all the world, little goddess. . . . Always I had known that.

But now I believed it. A world lived strong and joyous beyond Jerusalem's walls. And even if I never saw that bright world, I would know always that it waited there.

Bilqis

Now that she had looked upon the prize, the fulfillment of Ilat's promise, Bilqis forced herself to remain outwardly calm, cool as water in a deep untroubled well. Her exultation, her joy, her relief—those she must conceal. *Another riddle: how to hide one's heart?* But hide her desire she must, until the time was ripe. And that would be soon; she sensed a turning point had been reached and passed in the garden of King Solomon's women. *Tomorrow. Tomorrow I will begin a riddle game that only I shall know I play. And I shall win. I must.*

The next morning Bilqis retraced the web of palace halls that King Solomon had led her down, until she stood once more in the king's gallery, looking down into the queens' garden. There she watched, and told over what she knew of this kingdom to which she had been summoned. For it was folly to act rashly; her goal was too vital to risk losing by moving too swiftly in this royal game.

So I stand here, where the king stands—not often, I think. But sometimes. Her host struck her as an odd man to rule over such stiff-necked, unruly subjects.

However smooth his face, however evenhanded his judgments, his eyes betray a troubled mind. This kingdom was no easy one for any man to rule—*let alone one who thinks too much and feels too deeply.*

For herself, Israel's court was a revelation, and not a pleasant one. Oh, she had always known Sheba was of a different world, a world in which women and men joined as partners in life's dance. She had known that beyond the northern sands men ruled by force rather than by right. But until she saw for herself, she had not known what that truly meant.

Here no woman governed her own life. Always it was given in charge—to a father, a brother, a husband. A son, if he were the only man alive to command her. Nothing belonged to her; all her riches were granted her as a gift—no, as a loan, a loan which must be constantly repaid with labor and obedience.

Worst of all, her children were not her own. In defiance of all sense, all decency, in this land a woman's children belonged to the man who claimed her as chattel. *As if the mere scatterer of seed has more claim than the woman who conceives and bears the fruit!*

But that was law here; the father's right prevailed. As if any man could truly *know* he had sired a child! Always, always there was the possibility of doubt: a woman might be unfaithful, or merely mistaken. Only a mother could be claimed beyond any doubt.

She leaned her forehead upon the cool stone latticework and looked down into the harem garden. Today only half-a-dozen of the king's women sat there, chattering to each other and trying on trinkets. One, more industrious than the rest, stitched spangles to a garment; the cloth flashed as thin gold disks caught sunlight.

How can they be content with their lives? They do nothing, their words count for nothing. These northern women were less free than chained slaves, for their shackles were invisible—

And so they swear they wear none. A chill slid over her skin. *I would rather wear fetters openly. How can they live so, weighing each word to please a man, never setting a foot where man forbids it?*

And yet these women were happy enough—or, if they were not, were unhappy for other reasons. *My desires are not theirs, nor theirs mine.* She stared down at the women in the garden. Now one of them leaned close to her neighbor, whispered in her ear; they both laughed. For a moment Bilqis envied them, so placid, so content. *They have so few worries!*

There were two sides to any wall. While no woman here was truly free, their men were also bound—bound to care for the women they had entrapped. *Pity the man who owns too many women; he will know no peace in this life unless they choose to grant it.*

Now the women rose and drifted off into the shadows of the harem. Only the diligent seamstress remained. She did not sit long alone; a woman carrying a baby upon her hip and leading a small boy by the hand entered the garden. The seamstress set aside her cloth and held out her arms, and the boy flung himself into them. Bilqis sighed and turned away.

That young mother would never bear the weight of a kingdom upon her shoulders, never make a choice greater than that between one jewel and another. She would never be treated as an equal. But she would be cared for, spared the harsh freedom of choice.

Perhaps she has made a fair exchange. Bilqis knew such thoughts sprang from weariness and fear. She could not live as such women did; she would die.

Just as they would recoil in horror if told they must rule their own lives. She alone ruled hers—and so must govern herself more harshly than another would. She chained and veiled herself with law, with duty, with honor. Never could she think only of herself and her desires.

These women are not free because they are chattel. I am not free because I am queen. She set her hands against the cool unyielding stone curtain and thought of what she must do before she might see home again, and be released from these dark thoughts, these troubling doubts. What she must do, and what she must persuade King Solomon to do.

What we both must do, whether we will or no.

In the end, no woman was ever free. And no man either.

PART FIVE

---·◆·---

Pomegranate Seed

Abishag

The hardest task I faced in the king's house was hiding my true heart. I had been brought to Jerusalem to minister to Prince Solomon's father. That the prince and I loved swift and hot as fire did not matter. I knew that, even as I listened to Queen Michal tell over my duties to the old king—and to the new. For she made it clear that Solomon was to be king, when Great David at last abandoned his grasp on life and throne. And King Solomon would need loyal hearts about him—and who more loyal than I, who already loved him more than life?

I would become a legacy from the old king to the new. I was promised to King Solomon in his turn—

Oh, Queen Michal knew how to sway one to her wishes; she was guileful as a serpent. Even then, I knew a queen needed such talents. I admired her skill.

Baalit Sings

Later, when she told me all that was in her heart, I knew that Queen Bilqis had hunted her quarry soft-footed, courted and seduced my mind. I do not blame her; how could I? For she set nothing in my mind or heart that had not lain sleeping there like a shy bird, awaiting a morning upon which it might awake, and spread its wings—and fly.

But at the start, I knew only that the Queen of Sheba sought my company, and that flattered me. To my credit, I did wonder at her attention, but then I thought, *She sees my father favors me, and wishes to please him.* Well, that, too, was true enough.

It began simply enough, those first steps upon the path the queen wished me to tread. She would send for me, and I would go to the Little Palace, entering Sheba's kingdom as I passed through the gates, for all within the Little Palace was done as it was in the Morning Land. And I would watch, and listen, and talk with the queen and her servants. No hardship; I sought knowledge even then, gathering facts as other girls might flowers.

The Shebans had created a world within a world, one exotic and compelling. The women moved within it as freely as men— "Or at least, as freely as we can, here in this strange land," the queen's handmaiden Khurrami told me on one of those first visits, as I awaited the queen in the small courtyard that had once been King David's private sanctuary. "How do you endure it, Princess, trapped always within these walls?"

I slid my eyes aside, not yet trusting enough to reveal to her that I slipped custom's bonds as I wished—something even my father did not know. "I am accustomed to it, I suppose," I answered, and Khurrami said, "Of course," but her eyes seemed to regard me keenly.

"And the men here are so—" Irsiya sought for a word that would express her feelings without harshness; unlike Khurrami, bright and sharp, Irsiya was as softly pretty as her name, which meant "rainbow." "So rough and hard. Have they no—"

"Manners? No, they have not," Khurrami finished, and Irsiya glanced at me; Khurrami laughed. "Oh, the princess does not mind plain speaking, and truth is truth."

"Our manners and customs here are not those of Sheba." I kept my voice smooth, for while the Shebans were guests here, I still did not like to hear my own people mocked.

"A good answer." The queen came forward into the little courtyard, and we all bowed. She beckoned to Khurrami and Irsiya, and smiled at me. "Forgive me, Baalit, but I must give these idle girls of mine some tasks to perform for me." She took them aside and spoke softly to them while I waited beside the small pool, watching dragonflies dart over the water's surface. The day was warm, the queen's voice a murmur blending with the buzz of insects seeking sun and flowers.

"And Irsiya, set out my jewels, for I dine with the king. Khurrami, take Moonwind out to run." The queen's voice rose for me to hear these last orders; she turned and walked towards me, smiling. "There, that is done.

Now I may rest and amuse myself for an hour. Come and sit with me, Baalit, that we may talk."

I did not know what I could say to amuse the Queen of Sheba, but I sat beside her on the garden bench. As she did not begin to speak, merely smiling at me and waiting, I said, "I hope your visit to my father's court goes well?"

"Oh, yes. We have much in common, he and I, and I think Israel and Sheba will be good friends in years to come."

"With good trade," I said, and she laughed softly.

"Of course. If I succeed here, Israel shall be Sheba's most favored market."

"That will please my father greatly. And our kingdom itself? I know it is very different from Sheba; our ways must be very strange to you."

"I will not deny that—just as our ways are strange to you. But if you dwelt in Sheba, you would easily learn to live as we do." She turned her gaze to the flashes of green and gold skimming the pool's surface. "But not all is strange. We have such insects in our gardens in Sheba. And Jerusalem is magnificent, its Temple one of the world's wonders. When I rode up the Hill of Olive Trees and first looked upon it shining under the sky, it so filled my eyes I could not speak. I had not thought so much gold existed in all the world. And when the noonday sun strikes it, the whole city seems to blaze with the Temple's fire."

Of course the Temple was a wonder, but I had grown up seeing it always; I was accustomed to its fiery grandeur. I tried to think what setting eyes upon it for the first time must be like. *Yes, to come over the hills and see the Temple shining upon the high hill—that must be wondrous.*

"Jerusalem is a city of temples." The queen leaned to trail her fingertips across the pool's serene surface. "A holy city indeed."

"It is only the Lord's Temple that matters." I was not sure if I sought to warn the queen or myself. "The other temples are full of priestesses and idols and—" I stopped; better to say nothing more, lest I betray too much knowledge of what lay within those houses of strange gods and goddesses.

"And incense," the queen finished, "which is why Sheba is so fortunate a kingdom. Nothing else so pleases the gods—even your Lord Yahweh."

That was true; every god and goddess I had ever heard of craved the perfumes of frankincense and roses, nard and cinnamon and myrrh. And blood. Even the Lord accepted blood offerings.

"So that is all you know of the temples in Jerusalem? That they are good markets for frankincense?" Queen Bilqis turned her serene gaze from the dragonflies to me, and suddenly I knew that when she had taken her hand-maidens aside, it had been to hear what they had learned of me. And I re-membered Khurrami's keen assessing eyes.

Khurrami guessed and told; I betrayed to her that the palace walls do not imprison me.

I sat silent; I would not lie to the queen—and I dared not speak the truth. That King Solomon's daughter had so much as set her feet upon the doorsills of those temples would cause a scandal to rock Jerusalem's hills. But as the queen continued to regard me with steady cool eyes, I found my-self speaking, as if her gaze drew words from my mouth. Few men or women can keep their lips closed when another waits upon their words, a useful trick to know.

"It is forbidden for the Lord's daughters to set foot in the houses of alien gods."

"That is truth," she said, "but not the whole truth. So you choose to think for yourself. Like your father, you seek wisdom."

"Is there any virtue in that, for a woman?" My life was spread before me, fixed as a pattern carved in stone. King Solomon's daughter was a prize playing-piece in the great game of politics. Already men strove for that prize, knowing any man might win me should he seize the king's favor. Had not King Solomon's own father married a king's daughter when he himself had been nothing but a plain warrior?

"There is virtue in all things, Baalit."

Something in her calm acceptance of my unruliest utterances drew un-cautious words from me; I spoke, and she listened as if I, too, were a great queen, and her equal. Her approval was heady as strong wine, and when at last I left the queen, I walked slowly, as if afraid to jar my unsettled thoughts. And later still, when my handmaidens had unclasped my jewels and unbound my braided hair, I stood upon my balcony and stared out over the city, gazing towards the far horizon. A world waited there, beyond the palace gate, beyond the city walls, beyond the life ordained for me.

Perhaps my future was not immutable after all.

Bilqis

Although she had found the girl, Bilqis knew she was still far from gaining the prize she had crossed the world to seek. *Ilat promised I would find Sheba's* next queen. *Now it is my task to win her.* To win Sheba's future. For that, she needed time.

And time I have. She disliked Israel's customs, its harsh laws, its contempt for women—but no one could dislike King Solomon. The most gracious of hosts, the king proved himself a witty and charming companion as well. *He is too good for the kingdom he rules. I cherish his virtues even if his own people do not.* "Ah, yes, Solomon is a good wise king—but what a pity you did not visit Israel when David ruled the land! Now there was a king!"

Her spies had heard that wistful chant forty times over since the day she had ridden into Jerusalem—still called the City of David. "King David's Day" had become a jest to her handmaidens, a catchphrase to her servants. "That water jug would not have broken if David still ruled!" "If David were king, grapes would be sweeter this year!" "This wine stain would wash out if David sat upon the throne!"

She had laughed herself, the first time she heard it. She no longer laughed. *No matter what he achieves, still the people sigh for David's time. Poor Solomon.*

Solomon ruled a people unused to dominion, to edicts, to taxation—to the daily demands of a government that oversaw an empire. *He gives them roads and peace, and they long for the disorder of a day long past.*

And distance lent enchantment to fading memory; transmuted chaos into sweet freedom. Bilqis sighed, and set aside thoughts of Solomon. It was not the king but the king's daughter that she must lure to her.

I do not think that will be hard to do; already she flexes her wings. This land cannot hold her—not and let her remain what she is.

Then she set her thoughts of Baalit, too, aside. Even here, a thousand miles from Sheba, its queen must work. Bilqis cleared her mind and called her scribe to her; a morning's work meant an afternoon's freedom for her—and for Baalit.

When she had earned her liberty, Bilqis called a slave to her and told him that she wished word sent to the princess; the eunuch smiled. "Easily done, Sun of our Days. Princess Baalit awaits you in the room of the blue monkeys. Shall I send her to you?"

"No, I shall go to her." Bilqis walked through the line of rooms that led to the one in which Baalit waited. In the doorway she paused, watched

Baalit pace before the long wall painted with blue monkeys plucking yellow crocuses. As she passed each monkey, Baalit reached out and stroked its painted tail.

"Old-fashioned, but pretty," Bilqis said, and Baalit stopped and turned. Bilqis was pleased to note that the girl did not blush or attempt to explain away her idle gesture.

"Yes. Are there really blue monkeys somewhere?"

"Only upon painted walls."

"So many things exist only in dreams."

"Yes—but many things exist in this world. We need only reach out and accept what the gods give."

Baalit set her hand upon the wall, traced the curving line of a monkey's upturned tail. "Truly? And if we are given nothing?"

Ah, she begins to see what awaits her here. Knowing she must spread her net with care, Bilqis said, "Nothing? You have youth and health and high rank—and that is not a small thing in this world. And you rejoice in the best of fathers."

Baalit shrugged. "Oh, I know my father loves me—but sometimes I think he loves me too well. And sometimes I think he fears to love me at all."

As Baalit stared at the painted monkeys, Bilqis remained still, fearing an ill-chosen word would silence the girl.

After a moment, Baalit sighed, and came and knelt beside her. "You see, he loved my mother greatly—she was his first wife, queen of his heart."

"And she died."

"Died bearing me. He lost her, and in exchange received only a girl."

"You think he would have grieved for his wife less had you been born a boy? You do your father's love for her no justice."

"At least a boy, a prince, could hope to be king." Baalit hesitated, then said, "I know my father swore his eldest son would be king, but—"

"But he thought his first wife would bear him his first son," Bilqis said, "and even when she did not, kings have changed their minds before. Yes, had you been a boy, Baalit, I think it very likely you would have been king in your turn. But you are a girl, and you can never rule here." She stroked Baalit's close-braided hair. "You are the first wife's child, you are the wisest child—" *And you are the oldest girl, the only girl, but that counts for nothing here.* "—and your father's favorite. Yet—"

"It is Rehoboam who is heir. That scorpion! He will rend the kingdom like a rotten rag." Baalit's eyes stared, cloud pale, into some future she alone could see. "And I—I shall be married to some pompous official who will be so awed at wedding the granddaughter of King David that he will not even beat me!"

The disgust in the girl's voice made Sheba laugh. "Do you wish to be beaten, then? An odd desire!"

"No—but—"

"But you will be tied to a man who regards you as a prize, rather than as a woman. Why do you fear this? You are a princess; surely King Solomon plans a royal match for you."

"He wishes to keep me close—and we do not marry our women to un-circumcised outlanders." She shook her head, smiling wistfully. "If I were wed to a foreign king, I think I should not mind so much, for I would live far from Jerusalem, in a strange land, and—"

"And you would be one wife among many, wed to a man too old and too tired to be of use to even one woman."

"Oh, I know that. But no one there would have known me since I was in swaddling clothes—and there are ways men may be of use other than in bed!"

"So, you would be queen and run affairs—and your husband—to suit yourself," Bilqis said, and Baalit laughed.

"I know these are a child's fancies; you must forget them." Baalit rose to her feet, adjusting her bracelets as if they were her only care in the world. Sheba was not fooled; Baalit's will burned fiercely bright; Solomon's daughter would not prove an easy pawn to play.

But in some ways, Baalit was a child still, as she herself had just claimed; Bilqis smiled and offered a new temptation, one held in reserve until she knew the girl could judge new things fairly. "A child's fancies are easily for-gotten. Now come—child—for I have someone for you to meet, and some-thing new for you to try, if you dare."

Baalit Sings

Darkness clung to me like a heavy veil that day; all that morning it seemed my father's wives had nothing better to do than debate where and when and to whom I should be married. Even Keshet and Nimrah caught that fever, arguing over whether my wedding dress should be of scarlet or of saffron, and whether my bridal gems should be jacinths or rubies. At last I could not endure it and fled to the Little Palace, prepared to remain there into the night to see Queen Bilqis. She at least did not treat me as no more than a bride in waiting.

That was the day the Sheban queen opened a door to a freedom I had not dreamed existed—not for a woman. First she charmed me into better humor, and then she presented me to Moonwind.

I say it so because the queen's hunting hound claimed better breeding and far better manners than most princes—and because he looked down his long nose at me as a king might at a grubby beggar.

A dog, yes; a dog that stood aloof, proud; an image glowing in alabaster and silk. Moonwind bore no resemblance to the pariah dogs that scavenged the streets, slinking creatures near kin to jackals.

"Dogs are unclean animals." So I had always been warned, save by the Lady Melasadne, who came to Jerusalem from a faraway island and whose whole heart was given to the tiny white dogs she cosseted, caring more for the small creatures than for her rough sons. But Lady Melasadne's dogs had as little in common with street-dogs as did this elegant creature, whose sloe eyes regarded me doubtfully—as if it were I who were unclean.

"Folly. Moonwind is as clean as you or I—and certainly cleaner than that seer who complains so loudly of him." Bilqis stroked the hound's silken ears. She looked at me, clearly expecting me to touch him as well. Cautious, I extended my hand, an action that would have had all Lady Melasadne's doglets flinging themselves upon me in a wave of fur.

Even more wary than I of an alien touch, Moonwind recoiled slightly; the queen laughed. "You must win his regard, but the prize is worth the effort. Moonwind has a true heart and is a loyal beast—and useful, as well."

"Useful?"

"Of course. Do you not hunt with hounds in this land?"

"Hunt? With dogs?" Laughing, I shook my head. "Do you think a girl is permitted to hunt? Perhaps they do so in your land, O Queen, but here in Israel men alone hunt. And they do so on foot, or sometimes from chariots, but I have never heard of hunting with dogs. How is it done?"

The queen smiled and stroked Moonwind's slender head. "Come and see for yourself. What true objection can there be? You will be under my eye, and surely the Queen of Sheba is a fit guardian for Solomon's daughter!"

"Hunting is for men."

"Hunting is for hunters. Dress yourself in sturdy clothing, and come and learn."

I hesitated, desire battling caution; dared I violate custom so greatly?

Then the queen gave aid to desire's force. "Your father the king has sworn I may do as I wish, act as I would in my own kingdom. To hunt with the queen is a great honor. Surely you will not refuse?"

She raised her eyebrows; her face became a haughty mask, stiff with pride. Playing her game, I smoothed my own face to meek obedience and bowed before her. "If Sheba's queen commands, how can Solomon's daughter do less than obey?"

My false meekness fell away like a dropped veil as the queen laughed. "So dutiful! Go change your clothing—no, wait. You will own nothing suitable." She turned to her waiting handmaiden. "Khurrami, gather clothing from my captain for the princess. I am sure Nikaulis's garments can be persuaded to fit you, Baalit."

Just as I had never seen such a dog as Moonwind, I had never seen such a horse as Shams. The horses my father dealt in were small fierce creatures, pullers of war chariots. They were never ridden, nor used for any purpose less noble than warfare, or the hunting of wild beasts.

Shams was different: tall, sleek-muscled, sweet-tempered. When he saw the queen, the stallion's ears pricked forward, tips almost touching. His nostrils flared wide, and he uttered soft whuffling sounds.

The queen laughed and cupped her hands over his soft muzzle. "So you have missed me? Or is it what I bring that you yearn for?" The queen pulled a dried apricot from her pouch and offered it upon her palm; Shams took the fruit delicately and nudged her, plainly hoping for more.

"No, that is all." The queen stroked his gleaming neck and said to me, "And that slothful creature is for you to begin upon. She is both gentle and patient; heed her and you will learn much. Will you not, Dawn?"

I drew my eyes from the glory of Shams and studied Dawn. Smaller than the queen's stallion, plump and sturdy and gray as her name, Dawn regarded me with soft dark eyes. "I am to ride that one?"

"Of course; did you think to begin upon a horse like Shams? Your first ride would be your last, child, and you lucky to escape shattered bones."

Then she nodded and a groom came forward, knelt and cupped his hands. The queen set her foot in the man's hands; sprang from them onto the horse's back. Shams danced impatiently as she settled herself and gathered up the gilded leather reins. "Well, Princess?" she said, looking over at me, "do you wish to remain at home after all?"

Not only had I never flung my leg over a horse's back in my life, I had only rarely even ridden in a chariot. But what the Queen of Sheba did, I swore I too would do. And so I drew a deep breath and walked up to Dawn; as the queen had done with Shams, I laid my hand upon the mare's thick neck.

"I am to ride you," I said, feeling no shame at talking to a dumb beast. "Be kind, and forgive my ignorance." Swallowing hard, I nodded to the groom as the queen had done. And just as he had done for the queen, the groom locked his hands together for me to set my foot upon.

This is the last chance to turn back. I ignored my fear and its coward's warning and forced myself to forget I wore leather trousers that showed the shape of my legs to all the world. Trying to pretend I had some notion what I did, I grasped Dawn's mane in both my hands and placed my left foot onto the groom's waiting hands. A heartbeat later I sat upon the mare's back, hardly daring to breathe.

"Are you well-settled?" the queen asked. "Then come, follow me—slowly and gently; you must learn balance and judgment to ride well." Shams walked forward at the queen's signal, a signal invisible to my uninitiated eyes.

Slowly, Dawn followed; I clutched the mare's mane in both my hands and pressed my thighs against her broad sides so hard my muscles ached for three days after. But the cost in aches and effort was as nothing compared to the joy of sitting tall upon a strong beast and guiding it as one willed.

And as the queen instructed me in how to sit properly, to relax into the trot and urge the placid Dawn past that rough gait into the smooth delight of the canter, pleasure spread through my body, warm and sweet as summer honey.

Upon a horse, I could see far as a falcon; upon a horse, I could challenge the wind. Upon a horse, a girl became a man's equal.

Such pleasure, potent as any wine—no, not mere pleasure. As I reined

Dawn to a halt at the crest of the hill leading away from Jerusalem, I named the emotion that so elated me.

Triumph.

Forgiveness for transgression is easier to obtain than permission. I asked no one whether I might venture forth with the Sheban queen. Nor did I tell anyone where I was bound. The king's palace sprawled, a maze of courtyards and corridors, over more land than did the Great Temple. Even if I were sought, I could easily explain away my absence.

But I returned from my first ride out with the Sheban queen to find Keshet and Nimrah frantic and furious with worry; I had been asked for by my brother Caleb, who wished me to play with him—

"And you know what Prince Caleb is like when thwarted," Keshet said. "He howled like a paid mourner when you were not here—"

"And like an entire pack of mad jackals when we could not find you." Nimrah regarded me steadily with her pale cool eyes. "Of course you are our mistress, and our lives are yours—but we cannot serve you with our eyes bandaged."

"Yes—suppose it had been the king who desired your presence, rather than Prince Caleb!" Unlike Nimrah, Keshet burned hot when angered. "And you nowhere to be found, and we able to say only that we knew not where you might be. You leave us as ignorant as—as—"

"As Prince Rehoboam?" I tried to jest her into better humor, with no success.

Keshet stamped her foot. "Even Prince Rehoboam might have better sense! Where were you, Baalit?"

"And with whom?" Nimrah's voice cut sharp with a disdain I could not understand.

But their mistress or no, I knew Nimrah and Keshet had good reason to be angry. My follies rebounded on their heads. Still, I was a princess and they were not; I lifted my chin and said, "If you must know, I was with the Queen of Sheba. She showed me how to ride a horse, as she does."

"The Sheban queen. Oh, I see." Relief softened Nimrah; I had not seen until she slackened her hold on her temper how truly fearful she had been. I put my arm about her waist and said, "Why? Who did you think I was with?"

Nimrah turned her head to look straight into my eyes. "A man, perhaps," she said, and I gaped at her. "What man?" I asked blankly. After a moment, she smiled. "Any man. But I see I was wrong."

"Of course you were wrong; she does not yet think of such things, even when she ought," Keshet snapped in a tone that made me feel myself still in swaddling bands. Then, lest I think she had forgotten my transgressions, Keshet turned on me. "Riding upon a horse? Are you mad? Far better if you *had* been with a man. He could marry you, but what can a horse do, save toss you off and trample you? How came your father to permit such nonsense? I suppose you teased at him until he gave in."

Within the circle of my arm, I felt Nimrah's silent sigh and knew she already guessed the truth. So before either girl could berate me further, I said, "I did not tease him. I—I did not ask him."

"Oh, Baalit, *why not?*" Keshet half-wailed.

"I was with the Queen of Sheba," I offered, "and some of her servants rode out with us as well."

"Suppose you had broken your neck?" demanded Keshet, unmollified.

"I didn't. And it is my neck, not yours!"

"Yes, it is—and if you break that neck, you will be dead, but we will still be alive to bear the king's anger." Keshet glared at me, her eyes as hot as mine.

Nimrah slipped from my embrace and set a pale hand upon Keshet's arm. "Peace, Keshet; Baalit has returned safely to us." Nimrah slanted her glance towards me. "And the two of us can ensure she rides no more without the king's consent."

"And yours too, I suppose!" *Someday*, I swore to myself, *someday I shall be served by men and women who have not known me since I lay wailing in my cradle! Truly you would think I could not walk safely across the garden without their guidance!*

"Why, Princess, we are but your handmaidens. Who are we to say to our mistress yea or nay?" Nimrah's voice was smooth as cream cooled in the well; Keshet giggled. Then, relenting, Nimrah smiled, and said, "But if your father the king grants you leave to ride with the Sheban queen—why, then what happens is no fault of ours."

And so, to placate my handmaidens, I had to beg my father's consent that I might learn to ride a horse. Such permission proved harder to gain than I had foreseen. Like Keshet, my father seemed to understand only that those who rode upon horses often fell from them onto the hard ground. Since he himself shocked the traditional by riding horses when he chose, I thought him unreasonable. More, he proved stubborn in the face of my entreaties.

"I will be careful," I swore as he continued to shake his head. "Please, Father, grant me leave to do this."

He sighed heavily. "My dear child, it does not please me to deny you, but such an endeavor is far too dangerous for you. Horses are not suited to women's guidance; they are too powerful and unpredictable. You are not strong enough to control a chariot team. How could you control a horse once upon its back?"

Much as I longed to beg, I knew better than to continue to plead in that fashion. Such a tactic would only grieve my father, who truly hated to deny me anything, while failing to convince him to grant my request. Instead, I met his objections with the only arguments he respected: logic and reason.

"I know I cannot control a harnessed pair, my father, but that, as you say, requires great strength. Upon a horse's back, it is skill that counts, and that I can acquire." Then I offered my strongest counter to his fear. "Horses cannot be so very dangerous, Father; do not the Shebans ride them? Have we not seen the Sheban queen herself upon a horse?" And then, the final shot: "You ride horses yourself, and care nothing for what people say of its perils."

I knew he could not deny that; my father never refused to acknowledge truth.

Nor did he now. "It is as you say. But—" He paused, and I waited, regarding him steadily. At last he sighed. "Very well. You may try—but cautiously, under Semorn's eye."

"The master of the king's horses will be delighted to learn of this new honor you bestow upon him," I said, and as I hoped, my father laughed.

"But remember, Baalit, you are to be careful," he added, and I bowed my head. "Yes, my father. I will be careful." Then I flung my arms around him and kissed his cheek, and thanked him a dozen times before running off to tell the Queen of Sheba that my father had granted permission for me to ride upon a horse, just as she did.

———

At first I had merely wished to try a strange new custom, expecting only to be amused, and to anger my brothers. Instead, I discovered a true joy.

Mounted, I possessed freedom I had once known only in dreams. To sit astride a horse, to send the great beast racing across the plain until my hair pulled loose from its bonds to stream like a banner behind me—that was indeed delight. I exulted in the horse's strength as if it were my own; in a sense it *was* mine, mine to command, if I owned the skill to do so.

And I did, for my mastery of riding had been rapid; the Sheban master of horse had regarded me closely the first time I was set upon a gentle mare, and called me a born rider. My prowess proved him right, and never did I feel uneasy upon a horse. True, I tumbled off often enough at first, but falls never troubled me; I also owned the knack of rolling soft and springing up again like a cat, ready to try again.

After she observed my talent for riding, the queen bestowed a great gift upon me: a horse of my own, a sleek-muscled stallion sired by her own favorite, Shams. I named him Uri, for his fire-bright coat and hot courage. Uri seemed to fear nothing; upon his back, I was swift and free as wind.

Of course there was a great uproar about my riding at all, let alone riding out beyond the city walls. Our people used horses only to draw chariots; to ride a horse seemed an unnatural risk even for a man. To have the king's daughter riding out, bold as a boy, was scandal indeed. But I had my father's permission, however grudgingly granted, and needed no other's approval.

This was indeed fortunate, as no one else would have granted it. Even my dearly-loved handmaidens did not understand why I risked my neck only to dash about on a beast that might do anything at any moment.

"Horses are stupid, chancy creatures; you cannot trust them." Keshet could not be moved from this belief. And Nimrah failed to grasp my reasons for wishing to ride beyond Jerusalem's walls. "It is not as if you journey to another city. All you do is ride in circles."

"I am learning to control a great creature," I said. "When I ride with the wind blowing through my hair, I feel free."

But that only reminded Keshet that I returned from my rides with my hair a-tangle and my clothing awash in dust. And if Nimrah grasped what I revealed when I spoke of freedom, she betrayed no sign that she understood. What I sought, I sought alone.

Abishag

King David himself was little trouble to me, and my duties were not hard. The past was all he cared for, now. When I first stood before him, and the ancient serving woman who attended me unpinned the brooches at my shoulders so that the bright thin gown slipped down my body like water, I knew I was safe. Even the sight of my body gleaming in the late afternoon sunlight could not brighten those old eyes. King David wished only for someone to sit and listen to his endless tales of war and conquest and men long dead.

But I did my best to please him; I had been well-taught by my mother, who was the wisest woman living and knew everything about men and their ways—or so it seemed to me, when I was young. So I comforted the dying king, listened to him tell of the days when he was young and his world bright. I coaxed him to eat slices of melon from my fingers; I laughed at his jests.

And I slept beside him, offering my young heat to warm his fading body. But King David had grown still and cold as a lizard; I lay untouched.

Nikaulis

Familiarity breeds content; so claimed an old proverb. Until she had come to Jerusalem, Nikaulis had never questioned that proverb's wisdom. But now she knew the comforting words lied, for no matter how long she dwelt here, she never became content to do so. *This city grows worse, not better. I loathe it more each sunrise. And today—*

Today, she had learned what it was to be less than dust, helpless before the force of men's lusts.

She had passed through a street in which a crowd had gathered—a crowd of men noisy and excited as small boys tormenting a lizard. And she had made the mistake of pushing past, refusing to allow their presence to alter her course.

The object of the men's torment had been driven with stones and shards towards the Dung Gate, the gate in the southern wall that night soil and other refuse was carted through on its way to the city middens below the walls. At first Nikaulis thought the woman old, but a moment later she saw that what had seemed age was only dust-streaked hair and a body drawn in upon itself, seeking to escape the small stones and bits of broken pots that struck unprotected skin.

A mob and a woman—Nikaulis grabbed the arm of the woman standing in the nearest doorway, forcing her to turn from the deadly gathering of men in the street. "Summon the king's guard. I will stop them. Go."

The woman stared at Nikaulis and then laughed. "Summon the king's guard over a whore? Stop them? You? I can tell you're a stranger, so I'll give you a guest gift—go away before you're next." She pulled out of Nikaulis's grasp and backed into the house; the leather door-curtain fell across the opening a moment later.

So brief an exchange, but by the time Nikaulis looked back to gauge her chances of aiding the woman, she saw only the backs of the shouting men. The fleeing woman and her tormentors had reached the inner gate; the bulk of the men stopped there, content to allow the woman to escape if she could. They milled about, restless and looking for more amusement. Nikaulis knew if they spotted her, she would be their next target.

And that would bring trouble crashing into her queen's courtyard. Her first duty was to the queen; Nikaulis retreated calmly, moving with quiet ease that would not catch a watcher's eye. Once she turned a corner, she moved more quickly, for now she did not care who saw. And she wished to return to the Little Palace as swiftly as she could. Only there would she be able to know peace—as much peace as she could in this city of stone and hatred.

Walking through the city's narrow, dust-hot streets, Nikaulis felt trapped—worse, she felt outcast, unclean. Even the women glared at her, or slid their eyes away as if she were filth to be avoided. *Especially the women.* The women of Jerusalem despised her—even the temple harlots watched her pass with wary eyes.

But it was the men who troubled Nikaulis most. The women would glare and spit and mutter—but that was all. Chained and bound by tradition to meekness, they would not act. Action was for men. It was the men of Israel who sparked Nikaulis's warning sense.

Many of the men watched her with guilty greed, anger and lust kindling a covetous desire she felt as slime upon her skin. Seeing her freedom, they thought her free with her body as well. Her denials angered them—and her ability to enforce those denials with sword and strength frightened them. Anger and fear, a potent mix that brewed hatred.

So. The women despise me and the men hate me. Well, I shall not be here long to trouble their small worlds. And until my queen departs for her own land, I shall walk prudently.

So she told herself, knowing that prudence and caution would not be enough. Soon or late, some man here would challenge her chastity with a force that could be denied only with heart's blood. *Soon or late, I must kill a man—unless I can avoid the trap.*

But how, when this city, this very land, was such a trap? *To be a woman in Israel is to be a pawn forever.* In this land, even queens were nothing but the king's women.

She could not imagine such an existence. *How do they endure their lives?*

So thinking, she passed beneath the gate into the women's palace, noting as she did so how little regard was taken by the guardians of that gate. Soft men, eunuchs, who cared nothing for man or woman, having no future to ensure but their own. As Nikaulis strode by, they never ceased their low-voiced gossip, nor did they give her more than fleeting, scornful glances. Tempted to shake proper caution into them, she regarded them with cool disdain; incompetent servants were worse than none at all.

She strode on—and as she turned the corner into a colonnaded alley and disappeared from the eunuchs' sight, she heard one say, "And *we* are called unnatural!" and then high-pitched giggling. *So they took notice of me after all. Someone should warn them that high voices carry like arrows.*

But she would not be the one to deliver that counsel. She was the target of enmity enough without seeking more. She walked on, through the shaded portico, debating whether to tell her queen what she had seen that day in the city.

Perhaps I need not, for she must know as well as I what this kingdom is like— No, *that is coward's logic. She counts upon us all to serve as her eyes and her ears. I must tell her; then the matter rests in her hands.* But what could the queen do? The judgment had been passed, the unlucky woman already thrown out the Dung Gate with no more than she wore upon her body. *Still, she is fortunate not to be now lying dead beneath a pile of sharp stones. What kind of king permits others to act so? No judge, no court—only hatred.*

Again Nikaulis asked herself what she was doing here, in this land of hard men and harder laws, knowing the answer would never change.

The queen commands; I obey. That was *her* law. Too late to wonder if her choice had been for good or for ill. Vows bound her. Life was duty; duty was honor.

For Nikaulis, Queen's Guard, there was nothing else in life.

Benaiah

She did not see him as she walked by—paced by, sleek and lithe as a panther. Nor did Benaiah call to her; what would he say? For now, watching contented him. It was always wise to study an opponent before engaging.

Benaiah gazed after her, noted how she slipped effortlessly through the crowded street. *She moves like a wolf, like danger. How did she transform herself into such a creature?*

Even the Queen of Sheba, a woman ruling a kingdom in her own right, was easier to understand than the captain of her guard. There had been queens before, and all men knew the kingdoms of the south had strange customs. But Nikaulis—she was beyond easy comprehension, for there had never been anything like her in any land men knew. A woman keen and shining as a sword blade.

A woman strong and fierce as a hard campaign.

A warrior.

Never before had Benaiah seen such a thing. No doubt the prophet Ahijah would rage and call it abomination. But Benaiah's blood heated, his bones yearned, at the thought of her.

Warrior and woman both. *Sword-bride.*

For the first time in many years, Benaiah permitted himself to dream. Allowed himself to wonder if there might be more awaiting him than dry old age, and a soldier's grave.

Benaiah knew himself a good commander, fair and just. He knew also that he lacked greatness; that swift fire from heaven did not burn within him. But he soldiered competently, and if he did not blaze star-bright, he led men to frugal victories. Benaiah disliked losing battles or men, fought prudent campaigns. Nor was he overcautious, a trait which in the general's seasoned opinion cost more men than daring.

Men respected Benaiah. His soldiers trusted him not to spend their lives heedlessly. But what would a woman think of him? What would the Sheban queen's captain think?

What would the woman Nikaulis think of the man Benaiah?

Would she think of him at all?

Baalit Sings

Womanly crafts were regarded highly in King Solomon's palace; Queen Michal had set that fashion long ago. Although each queen, each concubine, had her own servants and slaves, few settled for merely overseeing their handmaidens' work. In King Solomon's court, even queens spun and wove and sewed cloth into garments for themselves and their children.

There was a great deal to be said for the custom, as it brought together women who owned nothing else in common save their husband. On fine days, groups of women would choose places in the garden or upon the rooftops; on unpleasant days, the chosen venue might be the queens' gallery, or one of the long pillared porches. Each woman would bring the work of her hands, and there sit and spin and sew—and gossip. Malice created true amity.

That summer there was only one topic spoken of when women gathered: the Queen of Sheba. Nothing else was worth words; the southern queen was too enticing a subject.

Today's gathering was no exception—save that today no one had a good word to say about the Sheban queen or her kingdom—or its gods and goods, its spices and servants. Nothing Sheban pleased. Well, that was not hard to understand; since Queen Bilqis had set her jeweled feet upon King Solomon's land, he had had eyes for no one else.

It was the first time I had ever known my father to set aside his own iron rule—to favor no woman above another. The Spice Queen sat beside King Solomon in the great court, rode out with him to oversee the building of new roads and fortresses. Bilqis and Solomon walked the palace gardens; close as lovers, they strolled among the roses and lilies. She sat beside him at banquets, tested his wit against hers. Riddles, too, became the fashion.

And he visited her in the Little Palace, and no one knew what passed between them there. Sheba's servants did not gossip—at least, not about their queen and our king. Solomon's wives did not curb their tongues when discussing either.

"The king sees no one but her, hears no words but hers," Dvorah mourned. "It is not fair; it is not just; it is not as if she is his wife!"

"She is too old to be his wife," said Jecoliah, "too old to give him children." She looked down at her spindle and sighed; her attention had wandered from her fingers, and the thread had thickened and knotted.

Yeshara jerked her thread so hard it snapped. "That woman! Queen of Sheba—who among us has even *heard* of the place? She's nothing but a harlot, flaunting herself, making a fool of our king! She should be stoned from Jerusalem, she and all her unclean followers."

"I have heard they sacrifice children to the sun." Rahab frowned. "Or was it to the moon? That is why she has come—seeking children, as they have slain all their own."

"She sleeps with dogs!"

"Better dogs than some men."

"Do you call King Solomon lower than a dog?"

Long practice kept me smoothly stitching, red silk pulling through creamy linen, filling in another pomegranate in my design. I did not leap to defend the desert queen, or even my own father. So long as I remained silent, occupied, none of the women would notice I was there. And they would speak freely, without weighing their words—something I instinctively knew was always dangerous, a risk taken only at need.

"I do not say so! But how wise is it for our king to consort with that woman? She will corrupt him with her foreign ways."

As if half the women in this courtyard were not foreign to Israel, and their ways likewise! No sign of thought marred my face, nor did my eyes leave the pomegranate growing, blood red, upon my cloth.

"What do you think they do, when they are alone?"

"I have heard she knows tricks of love unknown even to Asherah's priestess."

"She was raised by desert ghosts, and is half ghost herself, and so her feet are like an ass's. My serving maid had it from the slave who tends the Sheban's bath."

"You are such a fool you'll believe any tale—we've seen her feet for ourselves—*and* we've seen you copy her sandals, as well! Pearls on your feet, as if they were worth staring at—"

"She conceals her hooves with magic," Halit said, stubbornly refusing to concede the point.

Yes, never allow truth to impede your argument! I pressed my lips together, and knotted off the red silk; I pulled too hard and the thread snapped off short. *That is what comes of too much anger, too much haste.* Sighing, I rethreaded my needle and then, slowly, began outlining another pomegranate in gold.

"Perhaps she is a sorceress," Ruth said. "No man spends so many hours with a woman only to hear her talk—however clever he thinks she is."

"She has snared him with her quick tongue," Rahab said, and half the women laughed; others' cheeks reddened. Dvorah shook her head, as if in reproof—but a smile shadowed her lips.

I hoped that the veil self-control wove hid my face; hid it well enough that no one watching me would know that, in truth, I was as curious as any other woman in King Solomon's palace. That I, too, wondered what my father and the Queen of Sheba did, during those long hours they spent alone together.

We all thought we knew—and we all were wrong.

Bilqis

Although no man and few women would have believed it, King Solomon and the Queen of Sheba had not yet touched more than each other's finger-tips. True, the air trembled between them; fire kindled beneath those courtly brushes of hand upon hand. But that was all, and there might never be more. For fair though Solomon was to look upon, Bilqis knew him young enough to be her son—which mattered nothing to her, but she feared those years between them meant much to him. Although she knew it for vanity, she did not wish to look into his eyes and see an old woman mirrored there.

Or even worse, a son's respect for her greater years. *If there is anything I may ever wish to be to you, Solomon—it will not be your mother!*

And so their meetings sparkled, bright as crystal, and they curbed whatever desires smoldered within them as strongly as they would unruly stallions. Friendship alone must suffice—and even that seemed false, when she knew herself the thief who would steal away that gem he valued above all others.

But I will think of that later. Today friendship still glowed golden as the summer light over Jerusalem; she smiled as she walked through Solomon's rooms, out onto the king's balcony that overlooked the houses below. As she came out into the open air, she paused, for the song of a harp lifted wistful and lilting, and white doves wheeled and swooped over the rooftops as if they danced to its music. She stepped out onto the sun-warm stones and saw that the harper was Solomon.

Surprised, she walked across the balcony and sank down to sit coiled at his feet, as if she were a young girl still. "So you play, and no doubt sing, as well as you do all else, O King?"

Solomon smiled and shook his head. "No, you think of my father, King David. He was the songmaker, not I." He made as if to set the harp aside; she laid her hand upon the smooth gilded wood.

"You sing far sweeter songs than his." Flattery, honey-smooth. *Is Wise Solomon vain enough to eat empty praise?*

"And the Queen of the South knows this how?" Solomon smiled down upon her, testing her character in his turn. "For if ever you heard Great David sing, O Queen, it must have been in dreams—or perhaps you raised his ghost from the dust, as King Saul once raised the prophet Samuel?"

Wise indeed. Now it was her turn to smile, slanting her eyes at him; studying this man so certain of his own virtues he need not desire or accept false praise. "Just so, O King. Ghosts sing to me in dreams, that I might weigh their songs against your own."

"Then you must know already that the dead sing always sweeter than the living."

Attuned to nuance, she sensed bitterness shadowing his light words. *So there is something that ripples that smooth pond.* Good; she need only discover what djinns haunted this man, and turn them to tools in her hands.

But now she wished to coax him to her will, even in so small a matter as a song. So she laughed, and laid her hand soft upon his thigh; his muscles hardened beneath her fingers, but he did not flinch away—nor did his expression change. Still he smiled down at her with gentle courtesy.

"The Queen of the South tries to lure Israel's king? He is honored."

"Of course," she said. "Your harp is too well-formed to lay aside."

For long moments he stared down at her, studying her as she had studied him. Then he laughed. "My gracious thanks, O Queen. Now may we speak plainly?"

"Plain speech between man and woman?"

"It is unusual, I know—but I am not a boy, and I weary of eternal games."

Yes, this man is weary—and lonely. She permitted herself to open her senses, seeking to understand, but she knew him too little as yet. *Soon.* For now, she would offer him small comforts. "I care nothing for your father's songs; I would hear yours. Sing for me, Solomon."

"The queen commands?"

"Bilqis asks it."

"Then Solomon cannot refuse." He lifted up the gilded harp and balanced it across his thigh. Then he set his fingers upon the tight-drawn strings, and began.

"Where is she whom my soul loveth? Whither has my beloved gone, the fairest among women? I have threescore queens and fourscore concubines and maidens without number, but I seek my fair one, my bride. Where is she who shines fair as the moon, clear as the sun—" The words poured from his lips; sorrow flowed through them like bitter honey. "My beloved is gone, gone into the garden, to the beds of spices, to feed among the lilies. Thou art a seal upon my heart, for love is strong as death. Thou art fair, my love, thou art fair—" He fell silent, his eyes gazing into yesterday; Bilqis knew he dreamed of the past, of Abishag.

"Sing more," she said, but Solomon shook his head.

"No, it is too unformed, too wild. I sing it only for myself."

"And for her," Bilqis said, gently touching the gilded harp.

"And for her."

Solomon laid the harp across his knees; knowing she would gain no more, Bilqis merely said, "It sounds well enough to me; it is plain you inherit your father's gifts."

To her surprise, he laughed. "Not all of them. But to sing as well as Great David—yes, that I would wish. And I have some small gift with words. But if you would hear David's inheritance, you must hear my daughter sing."

"The princess sings well?"

"Yes. She has the song-gift." For a moment he was silent, as if weighing his next words with great care. But then all he said was "If only she were a boy."

Bilqis knew he did not wish this because a man longs for sons; King Solomon had sons aplenty. Nor did he wish it because he favored the child of his truly loved wife above all his sons. *He wishes this because he is wise enough to know that his daughter is born to rule—and his sons are not.*

"Yes," she said. "My nephew Rahbarin, my sister's son—he is good, he is kind, he is brave. If only he were a girl!"

"We understand one another, I see." Solomon shook his head; sunlight danced over his hair.

"Of course. We were born to know one another. Our stars sang to each other when we were born."

"I hope the stars sing better than I," said Solomon, and set his harp aside.

Someday I must make you sing again, Solomon. Bilqis knew he would sing no more today. But she was patient. She could wait.

Solomon

Have I gone mad? For madness seemed the only explanation for unveiling his heart to the Sheban queen as he had done. No one but Abishag had ever heard that still unfinished song—no one until the Queen of the Morning had smiled at him, warming his cool blood as if she were the sun, life-giving radiance.

She is nothing but a foreign ruler come to bargain with me for her land's sake. So Solomon reminded himself, knowing already he did not believe that comforting lie. The Spice Queen had traveled long and hard to reach King Solomon's court; no light matter had driven her to his side.

There is something she desires, something only I can grant her. He had read that in her sun-warm eyes, heard it in the rich low murmur of her voice. With look and word and gesture, she had implied she desired him; Solomon was too wise in the ways of women to believe that either. Perhaps he found favor in the queen's eyes—but that was not why she had traveled half the world. *I am not so vain as to swallow that sweet lie.*

Nor was he so cold as to discount it utterly. For a spark kindled when their eyes met, heat flared when their fingers touched. *There is some bond between us, some invisible chain that links us.* Only time would unveil the nature of that bond: lifeline—or shackle.

In the meantime—

—I must take more care, Solomon told himself. For kings, head must always rule heart. But even as he chided himself for folly, he felt again the queen's touch upon his hand, heard her warm husky laugh. And to his surprise, he found himself caressing words in his mind as, for the first time in many years, a long-neglected song began to shape itself once more to his desire.

Abishag

The queen's service proved more challenging. To be ready to aid her at need, I set myself to learn the palace as if it were the palm of my hand; my goal was to walk its labyrinth of halls and gardens blindfolded if need be. Many times I blessed my mother's teaching, which might have been designed with this very life in mind. I knew enough to say little and listen much, to lower my eyes and pass for a foolish girl who saw nothing and understood even less. A girl whose only passions were sweet cakes and bright sashes; a girl who giggled and sighed, bored, whenever King David's officials talked with him.

Such a girl was ignored, too foolish to notice. Such a girl was far safer than a quiet, dignified maiden would have been. Such a girl was too foolish for men to fear.

Amyntor

It is time to journey onward. Amyntor always heeded that inner command; he had remained in Jerusalem longer than he had sojourned in any other land. Now, at last, his heart told him it was time to go— *Just when things grow interesting, too. Ah, well; this, too, is at the roll of the gods' dice.*

Still, it seemed a pity—the pitting of the Sheban queen's seductive despair against King Solomon's sorrowful principles promised fine entertainment. Or rather, it would be amusing to observe if Amyntor hadn't become fond of both combatants. *It's always a mistake to have friends on both sides of a stone wall.*

No point in putting off the inevitable. Amyntor sighed, and went to seek out Solomon, knowing already what the king would say, and what he must answer.

As the king's intimate friend, he had access to the king's chambers; now, as he walked through those rooms, a wayward breeze carried the fragrance of frankincense and amber to his nose. The Spice Queen's scent. Amyntor savored the dark perfume, and smiled as he strode on.

He found the king standing on the balcony that overlooked the city, apparently intent on a flock of doves that swooped and whirled above the dust-gold rooftops. A harp lay upon the nearby bench, silently waiting for a hand to draw music from its taut strings. For a moment Amyntor studied his friend, reluctant to disturb the king's peace, however illusory that peace might be. But as he hesitated, Solomon turned and lifted his hand in greeting. "Amyntor."

"I do not intrude, my lord king?" Amyntor asked, and Solomon laughed softly.

"No," said the king, "not now. Come, be welcome." Then, as he gazed at Amyntor, the king's smile faded; between one breath and the next, weariness seemed to drag at his shoulders. "What is it you have come to say?" he asked.

Never a fool nor a coward. Poor king; you'd be happier if you were both. Amyntor did not try to honey his words; Solomon would not thank him for false kindness.

He walked over to stand beside the king. "I've tarried long enough in your house. And I thank you for your kindness—but it is time for me to go."

For a few breaths, Solomon said nothing. "Why?" he asked at last, and Amyntor shrugged.

"Because the road lies open beyond city gates. Because the setting sun beckons. Because I must." Amyntor smiled. "And because Jerusalem grows a little crowded these days."

He saw the king's eyes flicker; Solomon understood, but did not wish to concede the fact. "A king cannot afford to lose so good a friend as you, Amyntor."

"And you won't. I'll always be your friend, King Solomon. But we're wanderers, we sons of the Sea Kings. Someday I may wander back to Jerusalem. Today I must travel on and see where the road takes me."

"Stay," Solomon said. "I need you here, Amyntor."

"No, my lord king, you don't—not anymore."

"I don't understand." There was a knife-edge of despair in the king's voice, the hopelessness of a man who no longer dared look into tomorrow.

Amyntor laid his hand on Solomon's shoulder. "You don't want to understand, my friend. Let me gift you with one last piece of advice—forgive yourself."

"Forgive myself? For what crime?"

"Being human," Amyntor said. "Remember, O King, you too are but a man."

But Amyntor had little hope that his friend would accept that gift. *Ah, well, perhaps the Queen of the South will do for him what I cannot—free him from himself.*

Early the next morning he rode away from Jerusalem accompanied by a dozen slaves and laden with silver and gold; Amyntor had accepted the king's gifts gracefully. He did not expect to retain either slaves or riches long. Those who traveled far, traveled best alone and lightly burdened. *But only a fool despises wealth; it's so useful!*

At the crest of the long hill that led up out of the Valley of Kidron, a rider waited. Clad in a sky-blue tunic with suns stitched upon the cloth in golden thread and leather trousers the color of pale honey, Princess Baalit sat upon the desert horse the Sheban queen had given her with the ease of one born to ride the wind.

Amyntor smiled and waved his servants onward. "Go, I'll catch up to you," he called and drew his horse to a halt beside Baalit's. "Running away with me, Princess? I'm honored, but is this wise?"

"Do you want me to ride away with you?" A challenge, swift and keen. "My father might not forgive you."

Amyntor laughed, and after a moment her eyes softened, and she, too, laughed. "I might risk it," he said. "You're wasted here, you know."

"Yes," Baalit said, "I know." Her lips curved in a smile as sweet and subtle as those painted upon ivory goddesses. Her eyes glinted, blade-bright.

What a girl! In Minos's time, she would have sailed her own ship beyond the horizon—or danced to death or glory in the bull-ring. *No wonder the Sheban queen has chosen her. A fire-bride to wed the land of spices. She's going to be glorious.*

But he would not tempt the gods by saying the words aloud. Instead, he laughed again. "Modest as well as maidenly. What are you doing here, Princess? Come to change my mind?"

"Could I?"

"You might."

"I doubt it; men's minds may change, but not their hearts. No, I came to say farewell." The princess regarded him gravely; Amyntor smiled.

"No need to be so solemn about it, Princess. I'm riding the King's Highway to the sea, not the Dark Road to Hades," he said, and she laughed again, and held out her hand.

"My father will miss you, my lord Amyntor. Come back to us, if you can."

"If I can," he said, and touched his fingertips to hers. "Fare well upon your journey, Princess."

"And you on yours." She hesitated a moment, then said, "Perhaps someday you may even journey as far as Sheba."

"If the gods permit it—someday I'll sail to Sheba to pay homage to its queen."

"Farewell, then, my lord Amyntor. And remember—Baalit will always smile to see your face."

"Oh, I'll remember. I never forget a pretty girl!" he said, and winked at her and touched his heels to his horse's sides.

At the bottom of the hill, he looked back. Baalit still sat upon her horse at the crest of the hill, watching him ride down the road south. In the slant-ing rays of the rising sun, girl and horse blazed fire; a trick of morning light sent those illusory flames soaring upward, bright wings.

Yes, our little fire-goddess is wasted here—but I hope Sheba knows what she's claiming for her own!

Someday he must journey to the kingdom of fabled Sheba. It would be amusing to see how the queen's game played itself out.

Bilqis

Vaunted for his wisdom, King Solomon had so far displayed no more than common sense and a generous heart; enough, surely, for any man to possess—or for any king, come to that. On the days she sat beside him in the court of judgment, Bilqis observed and admired, but she had not yet seen evi-dence of more than mortal wisdom. She expected no more of today's court; she sat beside King Solomon today only because she stalked him as a cat might a tame bird, with endless patience and a steadfast intent.

It was that one day in each seven when any man or woman in the king-dom might freely come before the king and demand his judgment upon any matter, small or great. A dozen cases had been heard by the king; Solomon had listened to each with attention and with the appearance of true inter-est. But Bilqis sensed that he tired, that the endless proofs of stubborn folly his subjects spread before him wearied him.

As they weary any man or woman of sense. But he is more patient with them than I would be. A sudden deep fondness for him warmed her; she lifted her hand to her cheek to catch his eye. When he slid his glance towards her, she smiled; a warm promise.

"Soon," he murmured, so softly even she, seated beside him, caught only a hint of the word. Then he turned to the royal herald. "Let the next case be brought before this court."

Two women walked forward amidst a jangle of brass ornaments; their gaudy striped veils proclaimed them harlots, as did the garish paint about their eyes and upon their mouths. Two men-at-arms followed, each carrying a swaddled infant. The infants were laid at the foot of Solomon's throne; when the swaddling clothes were thrown back, one child kicked vigorously. The other lay stiff and cold in death. Both were boys.

Solomon stared at the infants lying before him, then lifted his eyes to the two women. "What is your quarrel?"

The herald glanced at the women, plainly disapproving. "O great King, these women are harlots, and both bore children the same day."

Solomon lifted his finger; Bilqis leaned towards him. "Rather careless harlots," he murmured, his lips barely moving. She pressed her own lips firmly together and nodded gravely.

Waiting until the king sat attentive again, the herald continued. "Three days later, they awoke, and one child was dead."

"That is a grief, no doubt," Solomon said, "but how is it the business of the king's court?"

"Each claims the living child, great King."

"And no one save the king can undo this knot? Is there no one who can say which child belongs to which woman?"

"No one, great King; they dwelt alone and aided each other in their need. No one else had yet seen the infants."

"And so you have come to the king's court for justice." Solomon pointed to one of the women. "You, tell me what happened."

The woman bowed low. "O King, this woman—whom I had thought my friend!—she lay upon her own child in the night and smothered him. And when she woke and saw what she had done, she switched our children while I slept, so that I found her dead child lying beside me, while she suckled *my* son!"

"She lies! *She* is the one who smothered her own baby, and stole *mine!*"

"*You* are the liar! You who—"

"Silence." Solomon's voice cut through the women's shrill cries; they fell silent, glaring at each other.

So much hate; so little love. They have not even glanced at the children. It seemed impossible that either of these women should be mother to either infant. And how King Solomon was to decide between them, Bilqis did not know. *I would give the child to neither woman, for neither seems to care one heartbeat for it.*

"Have each woman in turn hold the child," Solomon commanded.

That test revealed nothing; lifted from the floor, the infant began to wail, and neither woman could soothe its cries. At last, when they began trying to snatch the child from each other, Solomon rose to his feet and descended the broad steps of the throne.

"Give him to me."

To Sheba's surprise, Solomon rocked the indignant baby to silence within a few moments.

Of course; he is calm, and the women are stiff and harsh with anger. I wonder how he will end this? The child must be fed soon, if nothing else.

Solomon looked down at the baby in his arms, then studied the two women. "Come closer," he said after a moment, and when they obeyed, he stared hard at their painted faces.

At last he said, "Will either of you relinquish claim to this child?"

"Never! He's mine!"

"I will not give up my son!"

"And you can come to no agreement? No, I see that you cannot. Very well. Benaiah, come forward."

Looking slightly puzzled, the commander of the army walked forward to stand beside the king. Solomon thrust the child towards Benaiah; surprised, the general grabbed the baby awkwardly; it began to cry again.

Solomon turned and pitched his voice to carry throughout the court: "Each woman claims the living child; each disavows the dead one. Neither will relinquish her right. They have come before the king, asking justice be done." He glanced at the two women, who stared at him, greedy as sparrows.

"Hear, then, the king's decision: you shall each have half of the child." He turned to the women. "Do you find the king's words fair, his decision just?"

The two harlots stared at him. Then one stiffened and nodded. The other drew in her breath sharply.

What does he play at? Then the king's scheme became clear; Sheba smiled, waiting.

"Very well. Benaiah, take your sword and cut the child in two, and give half to each woman."

As those watching gasped and Benaiah stared suspiciously at Solomon, a wild scream slashed through the rising clamor and the baby's wails. *"No!"* The second woman flung herself forward, clutching at the child Benaiah held. "Please, you can't! Don't kill him!"

The baby screamed and struggled; Benaiah tried dutifully to hold on to the wriggling child for a moment, then allowed the woman to grab the baby. The harlot clutched the baby to her breast; Benaiah slowly put his hand on the hilt of his sword.

Solomon lifted his hand, and Benaiah stepped back, looking relieved. Solomon raised his voice to be heard over the baby's outraged screams. "So you would surrender the child to the other?"

"Yes, my lord. Only don't kill him."

Solomon turned to the other woman, who stood stiff and angry. "And you? Would you say the same?"

She tossed her head; her harlot's veil shuddered. "He's mine, not hers. I'd rather see him dead than at *her* breast!"

As the whole court watched and waited, the king spoke softly to the sobbing harlot who rocked the crying baby in her arms; she nodded and pressed the child's face against her breast. The noise abated, muffled by the woman's gaudy clothing.

"Then hear the king's judgment in this case." Solomon pointed at the dead infant that lay still before the throne. "There is the child you will carry away from here. The living boy I give to his mother—she who holds him now."

Scowling, the denied harlot turned away; Benaiah drew his sword and barred her way with the blade. She glared, and he pointed at the small body that lay before the king's throne. Reluctant, the harlot picked up the dead infant and then was hustled out by guardsmen. Almost unheeded, the harlot who had been granted custody of the living child hurried away with her precious burden.

As men's voices rose in awed questioning and retelling of the judgment just witnessed, Solomon ascended the marble steps and sat upon the Lion Throne once more. "Well, O Queen? What is your judgment of my justice?"

"I thought you mad, at first," she murmured. "But then I saw the beauty of your plan. Having Benaiah hold the child was indeed clever; the poor man did not know whether to obey you—or how, with his arms full of a screaming baby!"

She slanted her eyes at him in shared amusement, and touched his hand gently. "For the rest— May I praise the great king's wisdom?" Then, in a voice that could not be heard beyond the throne's step, she added, "For you know no more than I which woman bore that child."

"What I know," Solomon replied in an equally practiced undertone, "is that the true mother is the one who cared more for the child than for her pride."

Bilqis smiled. "And what did the great King Solomon say to the harlot, when he whispered in her ear?"

"I told her," Solomon said, "for the love of peace to shut that baby up!"

Baalit Sings

That day I had not troubled myself to spy upon the king's court, and so I did not see King Solomon's most famous judgment handed down for myself. But I heard of it within an hour of the decision—and then it seemed everyone I met repeated the tale. The king's act had snared people's minds, and no one could speak of anything else.

So clever. So wise. Surely no other man could judge so justly. Surely no other king could so clearly see past lies to truth. All that day I heard nothing but praise for my father's judgment. No one spoke of the two women, or of the desperation that must have driven them to demand the king's justice.

Bone-deep fear for their futures, for what future did a harlot possess? Once she grew too old to sell her body, she would starve, unless she had stored up wealth against the harsh years.

Or unless she had a son who would care for her when she was old.

Later I asked my father about his choice between the two women. "How did you think of such a plan?" I asked, and he smiled.

"Necessity," my father said. "If I did not think of something, anything, those two women would have screamed curses at each other until sunset."

That, of course, was what made my father great; necessity always made him think of the right thing to do. "But, Father—wouldn't any woman cry out if a babe were about to be slain? I understand that the child's mother would give him up rather than see him dead, but how did you know the false mother would not object as well?"

My father shook his head ruefully. "Now there I was fortunate; one woman's heart was stone and one was soft. But if both had cried out against the sword, I would have been forced to think of another test—now do not ask me what, Daughter, for I know no better than you what it would have been. Thank our Lord in His mercy that I did not have to try!"

Of course I said he was too modest, and of course my father said he was only truthful. Then I asked what he would have done if neither woman had objected to the division of one living child into two dead ones.

"To tell truth, Daughter, I do not know." He smiled. "I suppose I would have had to claim the child myself!"

I was proud of my father's goodness and wisdom, and never doubted his choice was the right one. The Sheban queen saw another side to the judgment of King Solomon.

"Yes, I grant you it was clever, Baalit," she said. "And it gained the child a great-hearted mother." Something in her voice made me look at her closely; she seemed almost to mock the decision.

Now, why? I thought for a few moments, playing over the judgment in my mind, seeking the weakness in the king's ruling that the queen seemed to see. Two women; one child. One woman crying out against the king's sword—

"Surely only his mother would save his life even if it meant giving him up," I said, and the queen smiled.

"I forget how young you are," she said. "Child, there are women who would slay their own infant rather than see it sleeping happy in the arms of another."

"Then—do you say the woman to whom my father granted the child was *not* his true mother?"

"Oh, yes, she is his *true* mother—whether she bore him or not. For she cared enough for him to wish *his* good rather than her own."

I stared. "Do you mean to say," I said at last, "that you do not know which woman's child still lived? That my father may have judged wrongly?"

For a moment, she said nothing. Then she answered my question with one of her own. "Do you think he judged wrongly, Baalit?"

Somehow I knew my answer was important to her, so I thought carefully before I spoke. "I think he may have given the child to the wrong mother," I said at last, "but not to the wrong woman."

The queen laid her hand upon my cheek; I smelled honey and roses. "You are truly Wise Solomon's daughter," she said. "Happy the land over which you will rule."

I stared at her, and saw she did not jest but spoke in earnest. Well, in her land, what she said might be true. But this was Israel, not Sheba.

"The Queen of Sheba is kind," I said, "but I will never rule. Kingship is for men—and queens do not rule here."

"Never is a long time, and some women are true queens wherever they dwell. Rule yourself, Baalit, and you rule all." She drew breath as if she wished to say more; I waited, but then she merely laughed and shook her head.

"I grow too solemn," the queen said. "Come, let us walk in the garden, and you will tell me of the flowers you grow. Perhaps some of them can be carried back with me to Sheba. I think they might grow well there."

I cared little for flowers, but I walked with the queen and showed her the roses and lilacs and lilies. "But if you wish to know about the flowers and the gardens, I am not the one you should ask. The Lady Nefret loves flowers; her garden is a wonder. And the Lady Leeorenda grows herbs and can speak to you of their uses."

The queen laughed. "And you guess—rightly—that I wish to speak to you of other things than roses and lilies. Still, I find their scent pleasing."

"Yes." I waited, certain that she would speak when she judged the moment right.

In silence, we walked the garden path, until at last the queen said, "You think it strange—a land in which women rule, and men do not."

It was not a question, so I did not answer. *You know I think it strange—yes, and wonderful, too. What is it you would ask?*

"For a thousand years, a queen has ruled in Sheba. Mother has passed the crown to daughter, aunt to niece, sister to sister. Until at last the burden was laid in my hands. I think I have discharged my duty well—save in one thing. See the lovely blossoms here; what are they named?"

"Hyacinths," I said. "They come from Achaea. They have bloomed overlong this year; perhaps they too wished to greet the Queen of Sheba."

"And waited until I came to admire them?" She smiled and bent to the hyacinths, cupping her hands about the rich blossoms. "So sweet a perfume. Almost too sweet. Ah, well. As I say, I believe I have ruled well, but—" She stopped and turned to look at me, squarely, as if I were her equal.

"But I have no heir, Baalit. There is no queen to follow me, to set the crown upon her head when mine goes down to dust. My own daughter died bearing my granddaughter, who died before she had drawn a dozen breaths. My nearest kin is my sister's child, who cannot rule."

"Why can't she—" I stopped, thought a moment. "Your sister's child is not a daughter."

"But a son, my nephew. Yes. And even were he a girl, I would be loath to see him on the throne of Sheba."

"Is he so unfit to rule?"

The queen sighed. "Yes, alas. For Rahbarin is pure as rain and good as bread, and two more deadly faults a queen—or a king—cannot possess." Then she smiled. "But as a queen's sword, he is flawless. He guards my throne while I am gone, and so I know I will find it waiting for me when I return."

"You trust him so greatly?"

"He has given his word. And so I know I will return to an unchallenged throne, or to find his body laid down in forfeit."

"That is great trust indeed." I waited, but although we walked among the flowers, the queen spoke no more of her country or her crown, or her sister's son. Whatever she wished to ask of me, she would not ask yet.

Later, in my own chamber, I took the small silver mirror out of the ivory casket and stared into it as I pondered the Sheban queen's words. That she had her own reasons for praising her nephew to me I did not doubt. And after thinking hard upon all she had told me, I believed I knew what they were.

She wished me to think well of Prince Rahbarin—because she wished me to marry him. And before she asked my father for me, she wished to ensure my willingness to do so. I stared into my eyes in the silver disk cupped in my hands, and saw only brightness.

King Solomon's daughter, wed to the Queen of Sheba's sister's son. Fit mother and father for a girl who could be named heir to the Sheban throne. Yes, that could be the future the queen wished to summon.

Or did she spin some other plot? For the queen was no fool, and even a fool could see that my father's line bred sons. My father's father, King David, had sired many sons and few daughters. My father, King Solomon, claimed a dozen and more sons, yet only one daughter. Perhaps the Sheban queen relied on her own blood's power to breed girls, counted its strength greater than that of David's lineage?

And does she think I will meekly wed where I am bid, even if it is she who orders the match? As my father's daughter, I would have little enough choice. Did the

Queen of Sheba offer me more? How much of what Queen Bilqis sang of her nephew's virtues was unpolished truth, and how much gilding over less desirable traits?

I was not fool enough to believe all a desperate queen, a doting aunt, said of the man. But deeds carry more truth than words. Whatever her sister's son was or was not, he had been left to guard Sheba's throne in its queen's absence.

That fact alone vouched for him in a way no fulsome praise could. Tired of looking into my own eyes, I set down my mother's silver mirror and went to lean upon my window ledge. There I gazed out over the rooftops of Jerusalem, past the houses and temples, past the wide walls, my eyes searching south. Of course I saw nothing, save the darkness beyond the city's walls and watch fires. Even had it been bright day, Sheba lay far beyond the horizon.

In the southern sky, the stars of the sign called the Huntsman burned. "Rahbarin," I said, tasting the foreign name, savoring its strangeness on my tongue. I could put no face to the sound, but somehow that did not matter. . . .

I stared at the Huntsman until my feet grew cold. I took that as a sign and went to my bed, to sleep.

And, I hoped, to dream. Truth whispered dreams into sleepers' ears; I hoped to be granted certainty. But sleep refused all my coaxing, and I lay long awake, gazing out upon the rising moon through my open window. At last, when the moon soared high and cast black shadows over moon-pearled rooftops, I abandoned my quest. If sleep would not come to me, I would waste no more time courting its illusions. And the moon called to me.

So I rose hot and rumpled from my bed; pulled my sweat-damp linen shift off and dropped it to the floor. As if I had done this many times, I lifted my hands to my hair and unbound the plait that confined its unruly mass by night. Naked, I walked out of my room onto the queen's balcony.

There I stood in the moon's cool light and gazed out upon Jerusalem. Far above the moon sailed high, pale as pearl, pouring light over the city. By day, Jerusalem glowed golden in the sun. By night, the city shone pale, moon-silvered.

I looked over housetops, clustered flat shadows; between wove the city streets, dark as the bottom of a well. Although it was deep night, I could see small flames, lamps still lit. Torch-fires danced endlessly at the faraway gates in the city walls.

Jerusalem. King Solomon's treasure.

The Lord's city, rich and powerful, a lion dreaming under the radiant moon.

The moon's shadows grew long as I stood there; night's wind flowed soft and cool over my skin. One by one, the little bright lamp flames went out. *One by one, fires died, one by one lights vanished, until all that remained was darkness, black and cold as the bottom of a well. Cold night, moonless night. I stood alone within that cruel darkness; even the stars had gone. I alone against the cold and the dark, without a path upon which to set my restless feet.*

No light, no path. Yet I must venture into that deep night, or forever remain frozen in shadow. I stepped forward and darkness clung like black water to my skin. Darkness flowed over me; I strove to move against its icy current, move forward into deeper night. And as I paced through that black force, setting one foot before the other with stubborn care, light kindled, silver and slow, warmth sliding over my body as sweetly as a mother's caress.

I sought the source of the silver light, but there was neither sun nor moon; at last I looked to myself and saw that the soft radiance glowed forth from my own skin, granting light against the endless night surrounding me, allowing me to walk forward, warm against the dark—

Until I woke, I had not even known I slept. Moonlight had summoned me into dreams, and I had fallen asleep leaning against the stones of my balcony wall. Now my bones were stiff and my skin chill, and my eyes itched, sleep-sanded. I straightened and stretched and looked out again over Jerusalem, and saw that night was over; the sun pushed golden against the eastern hilltops. Before me, Jerusalem's rooftops glowed like pearls in the pale dawn light. All that was left of night was blue shadows in the city streets and darkness falling in the west.

I looked across the city to the great brass-bound gates in the city wall. There the torches guttered dim, their fires fading against the dawn like ancient eyes closing against the rising light.

Abishag

Now I blessed my mother's long, careful schooling that had fitted me to take my place within a royal household. But I knew I still had much to learn, and so I studied Queen Michal. She ruled the women's palace, knew everything that passed within its gates. Nor did she waste her strength in foolish struggles. Kings will always have many women; a woman who refuses to acknowledge that will break her own heart and destroy the happiness of all the court. Queen Michal knew this well, and never did I see her look upon any of King David's other women with anything but serene acceptance.

I vowed I would do the same, when I was queen. For that was the path to keeping both peace and my husband's heart. Although it was not easy, Queen Abishag kept the vow the maiden Abishag had made. And I was right to do so.

For however many women King Solomon possessed, he always, until the end, came back to me.

Baalit Sings

That night changed something deep within me, altered the way I saw my world. Some veil seemed to have slipped away and I no longer looked upon life with a child's eyes.

I had always been my father's favorite child, had accepted that status as my right. For was I not his only daughter, his only bond to his beloved, my mother Abishag? Now I began to study that bond, to see how a king's favor served as a trap for the unwary. For Solomon was not only my father but my king—and a king's lightest glance carries the weight of stones.

Only when that royal glance lifted, only when his eyes turned upon the Sheban queen, only then did I even know I had labored under such a burden.

Of course I had known my brother Rehoboam loathed me. But Rehoboam was born covetous; lay all the world in his hands and still he would grasp for more. Others of my brothers looked upon me as a pet, or as a pestilence, depending upon their age and their character. To those brothers younger than I, I was another playmate; I can at least lay in the scales to my credit that I never shirked my duty to my little brothers.

Now I saw that even those of my brothers who regarded me with tolerant eyes resented the lion's share of our father's love that he bestowed upon me. I could do nothing to lessen that regard, nor did I think it my fault. But that resentment, hidden as smoldering coals are hidden beneath ash, awaited only new tinder to flare into malice. In a crisis, my brothers would not stand for me; I would find no champions among them.

Nor would I find supporters among my father's many wives. To my stepmothers, too, I remained a pampered doll—the king's beloved daughter, who drew to herself the favor they wished for their own children. Had I been blessed with sisters, perhaps they would have carried some of the burden that now pressed upon me alone. But King Solomon's wives bred sons; most would call him the most fortunate of men. A king must have sons, of course—but too many princes bred trouble both within and without the household. Even though Rehoboam had been hailed as crown prince at his birth, destined from the moment he first drew breath as king to come after Solomon, his half-brothers looked on him with cool assessing eyes. And his stepmothers studied him, avid and covetous for their own sons' futures. One misstep, and the pack would tear Prince Rehoboam down into the dust.

That knowledge tormented Queen Naamah; she had long years to walk before her son placed the crown of Israel and Judah upon his brow. She must wonder all the hours of each day and each night if Rehoboam would safely walk the blade-edged path that lay between him and his promised throne.

Now I acknowledged a truth my heart already knew: that peace was not to be snared within halls of ivory, love not to be bound even with chains of gold and gemstones.

And that contentment fled before ambition as swiftly as swallows before a storm.

I said as much to the Sheban queen, one day when I rode with her out to the plains beyond Jerusalem's hills. "And I fear I am too ambitious to be happy; I have become"—I struggled for the right word, and settled upon—"restless. I know other girls desire only to marry and bear children—but I want more than that."

"What more?"

"I do not know; what is there? I wish—I wish I had been born a boy; I would make a better king than Rehoboam!" I had not intended to say so much; the words burst from me, and the queen laughed.

"Yes, you would, child. Do not look so troubled—you would be a fool not to know your own worth, and even ambition prospers in its proper season. As for your restless heart—your childhood lies in ashes now; soon you will be a woman. We all emulate the phoenix, we women."

She saw that I did not understand and said, "What, you do not know the phoenix, the bird of fire?"

I shook my head, and the queen smiled. "The bird of fire is a fabulous creature formed of sunlight and of clouds; her crystal eyes see the past and the future. The phoenix lives a thousand years, and when she grows old, she builds herself a bed of spices, a pyre of frankincense and sandalwood and cedar. There the phoenix burns to ash, and from those ashes is reborn to live another thousand years."

"She?"

"Yes, for what else could the bird of fire be? She is her own mother and her own daughter, never and always changing."

"Like the moon."

"Yes, although the phoenix is the sun's creature. Ah, look, the hounds have sighted game. Come!" And she set her horse into a gallop, leaving me to follow or not, as I chose.

Though I did not then know why, the Sheban queen's tale of the bird of fire caught my mind and my heart. That night I dreamed of fiery birth.

I stood upon sand, sand so hot and clear it might be glass. Above me the night sky arched, and across it poured a river of stars, stars that blazed like gems in firelight. The falling stars drew me up after them, embraced me as if I too were a burning star. We flowed across the midnight sky, down into the rising dawnlight. The stars fell and fell, gathering in a great ball of fire, and at last I knew that burning lodestone was the morning sun and that I feared to follow the stars into its light.

Something flashed by me; a bird, its fire-bright feathers streaming stars. As it soared past it turned its head and I looked deep into crystal eyes. I reached out my hand and the bird slowed, curving back to land upon my wrist.

Its scaled feet were gold and its claws silver; the bird's feet circled my wrist and I felt its pain and knew that pain could consume me. And I knew, too, that the bird summoned me, demanded I dare the fire.

As I hesitated, the bird spread its burning wings and soared into the cascading stars. I watched it fly, watched it fall, watched it vanish into the rising sun.

The stars were nearly gone; my time to choose was nearly gone. I took a deep breath and flung myself after the last stars, following them into the sun's fire.

I burned; pain demanded I surrender, disappear within the endless flame. Surrender would be easy—but there was a prize beyond kingdoms to be won if I could claim it. I fought pain's dark power, seeking beyond sorrow to fire's heart.

Peace glowed there; eternity bound in flames. I could rest here, forever unchanging. But before me another pyre burned with clear pure light, and I knew I had one last choice to make. This time I did not falter.

Within that secret flame I died and was reborn, reshaped for new tomorrows. Glorious, I spread my wings and flew into bright morning. . . .

When I woke, my skin seemed to glow hot, as if little flames clung to it still. But the dream-heat faded quickly. The phoenix was gone, banished by harsh day. I closed my eyes hard against sharp tears. But the temptation to weep soon passed; I told myself that I must not weep for a bird seen only in dreams.

But I did not forget the firebird and its crystal eyes. Something in that fiery image ensnared me; I would not give it up. Somehow I must keep faith with the phoenix, if only in my dreams.

To remind me of this private vow, I decided I should have a seal ring to wear; my own token, carved to my desire. I knew who I would have work the seal: Yahalom, a widow whose husband had once carved seal rings for the court. Now Yahalom worked at the trade he had taught her, forming signets for those who cared more for a good price and good workmanship than for whether a man's hands or a woman's created the object.

I might have gone to her shop, dealt with her there. I was often in the marketplace, after all. But after a moment's thought, I played the princess and sent one of my maids to summon Yahalom to the palace. When the woman arrived in my garden courtyard, she bowed to me, and I smiled and thanked her for coming to show her wares.

"It was no trouble, Princess," she said; I knew she would have said the same words had she walked barefoot across hot coals to come to me.

I smiled and bade her sit. "I am glad; I thought it would do you no harm to have it known your talent is demanded by the king's household."

She smiled then. "What does the princess desire? For I can create whatever you wish—"

"A seal ring," I said. "You carve them yourself, do you not?"

"Yes. And I do it well; few know this, but long before my husband died, his hands stiffened and would not obey his will, and it was I who carved the seals for those who came to him." Yahalom began to undo the bundle she carried. She spread the cloth smooth before my feet and set varied gem-stones upon its surface.

"No one guessed?" I asked, and she shook her head.

"Indeed, some said his work had improved." She finished arranging the precious stones she had brought and then looked at me. "A seal ring, you said? What jewel do you favor? Is there a stone that brings you good fortune, or luck in matters of the heart?"

Shaking my head, I stared down at the gemstones laid out in neat rows upon the dark cloth. The jewels gleamed in the sunlight; Yahalom had brought her finest wares to the king's palace. I knelt, studying my choices. Turquoise rich as sky; crystal clear as rain. Cat's-eyes and jasper; onyx and jade.

"It is hard to choose, is it not?" Yahalom murmured. "Perhaps—a favored color?" She watched my face closely, shifted a stone forward. "I see fire colors draw your eye. Look upon this one, Princess; hold it in your hand and note the fine hue."

I picked up the stone: a sardius, its color warm and true as honey in the sun.

"That is a fine stone, without flaw. It can be shaped into whatever design you desire."

Sardius, stone of concord and peace. Yes, that would do. I nodded. "I will have the carnelian, then. It will do well."

"And the seal itself? Does the princess know what she would have carved upon the stone?"

"Yes," I said. "The seal is to be a phoenix. A phoenix rising from a bed of flame."

As if the phoenix ring I wore upon my finger possessed a charm to unseal my blind eyes, I now saw all my world clear as a pure winter's day. And what I saw angered me; how had I ever borne such servitude? Ever caressed such chains?

For now I knew what I had valued as comfort and as treasure to be bondage and dross metal. Each gem my father had set upon my brow was but another burden I must carry. Each wall he had set between me and the world was but another bar between me and true life.

The palace was but a prison, my rich robes and splendid jewels but chains to bind me. How was it I had been blind until now?

Myself now freed of blind content, I could not understand how the other women of the king's palace could endure their gilded captivity. *Perhaps they do not,* I told myself. *Perhaps they, too, burn.*

But if others suffered as I did, I saw no sign of it; not yet.

Restive, I paced the harem courts, silent and critical as a cat. How could I ever have dwelt content within this pretty prison? How could my father's wives endure their lives, trapped by walls, by custom, by fear?

I paused in the gateway to the courtyard before me. Within its confines the Lady Melasadne sat, laughing as a dozen tiny dogs white as cloud capered about her. Their eyes shone obsidian-bright, their tongues flickered at her hands like small pink snakes. One of Melasadne's sons crawled through the pack of dogs, intent upon a gilded leather ball near his mother's feet. When he came close enough to the toy, he smacked it hard with his hand; all the little dogs ran about the ball as it rolled across the courtyard's smooth stones, barking in high little yaps. My half-brother crawled after the dogs; he, too, uttered high-pitched yelps, as if he too were a little dog.

Laughing, Melasadne rose and scooped up the gilded ball. Her dogs swarmed about her ankles, danced upon their hind legs; her son sat up and waved his hands. About to toss the ball for them, Melasadne glanced towards the gate and saw me watching; she paused and smiled.

"Come in, Princess, and join our play."

But I could not bear to surrender my solitude. I shook my head and backed into the shadows beneath the roof. Behind me a woman's laughter mingled with shrill barks and delighted shrieks; the cheerful noise echoed from the sun-warm stone walls of the Lady Melasadne's courtyard.

Little dogs and babies. How can she be content with so meager a portion?

All that long day I spied upon my father's wives. I told myself I sought knowledge, yearned to understand how a woman might endure a lifetime spent in bondage, never once daring to see her bounded world as the cage it truly was.

But the truth was less worthy. Anger drove me; anger at the women I knew, whose happiness mocked my misery. And anger at myself, that for so long I had dwelt content in a paradise created for fools.

And so I roamed the corridors and courtyards, seeking proof of the folly of my father's wives—and of my own wit and virtue that set me above them.

Long years later, when I sorted my memories of those passionate young days, I saw that I found proof only of the quiet strength of the human heart. The only folly had been my own, in thinking that all women must dream as I did. Most women, like most men, contented themselves with the common stones that built a wall of life. A husband, children, friends. A task to perform, however simple. Common stones, easy found if one were easy pleased—so I thought then, and despised them in my heart. I yearned for rare gems, longed to perform great deeds.

Only in age does one cherish the simple pleasures, those common stones polished by love to outshine gold. Still, I suppose I was no more foolish at fourteen than any other girl; it is always ourselves whom we judge most harshly.

But I had good teachers, and I can at least say with truth that I paid close heed to their lessons. When those I admired talked, I had wit enough to listen; when they acted, I studied what they had done, and why.

As I did the day I watched the Sheban handmaiden Khurrami catch up a runaway puppy—and gain an ally for her queen.

I had been granted the privilege of walking Moonwind; Khurrami accompanied the sleek hound, serving as elegant escort and drawing all eyes to her as we strolled through the palace gardens. Although the Sheban queen might be resented, Sheban fashions were not. The looped braids of Khurrami's hair, the drape of her veil over her breasts, even the lines of paint about her eyes would be studied and copied.

I thought of Lady Halit flaunting Sheban style while vilifying Sheba's queen, and as I laughed silently, Khurrami slanted her eyes at me—but she did not speak. And before I could decide whether to share my private jest, a scrabbling sound caught Moonwind's notice; his ears lifted and he turned his head, staring down at the ball of white fluff dashing towards him. The puppy bounced to a stop when it saw Moonwind and began to utter sharp chirping barks. Moonwind tensed, as if he sighted prey; I caught the hound's collar, coiled my fingers about the gold-sewn leather.

"It's only one of Lady Melasadne's dogs," I said, and Khurrami laughed.

"Truly? I thought it a handful of wool rolling in the breeze." Khurrami crouched down and held her hand out; the puppy dashed up and licked her scented fingers. She laughed and scooped the puppy up. "So small and valiant—and so lost, I think."

"Yes; give the pup to me. I will take it back to Lady Melasadne's courtyard." I stroked Moonwind's head; the elegant hound seemed as appalled by the wriggling puppy as Queen Naamah would have been by mud upon her gown. Still, I did not laugh, for I did not wish to offend the hound's pride. "Take Moonwind back to the queen; he does not care to be barked at."

Khurrami held the pup up in both her hands; it stared down with bright black eyes and tried to lick her nose. "No, I will carry it. We will all return this small wanderer to his home. You, Princess, may guide me to Lady Melasadne's courtyard, and as for Moonwind—it will do him no harm to learn tolerance."

Lady Melasadne's handmaidens greeted us with cries of delight that brought Melasadne herself hurrying up, her dogs dashing ahead of her. "Oh, you have found my lost one! My thanks, my deepest thanks to you!" She held out her arms, and, smiling, Khurrami set the tiny puppy in Lady Melasadne's hands. Melasadne cuddled the puppy to her cheek; the pup began chewing upon her dangling pearl earring. "You are the Queen of Sheba's handmaiden, the one called Khurrami? A thousand thanks; how may I repay your kindness?"

"Oh, it is not I whom you should thank, but my mistress, the Queen of the South." Khurrami did not make the error of saying more; as she told me later, too many sham details bred traps for their creator. *Just as a half-veiled face entices and a half-shadowed form lures, so a half-truth beguiles. Why spend useless effort creating a tale that does not matter anyway?*"

Now Khurrami smiled and said, "My queen cherishes her dogs and values those who do likewise—although I do not think this proud hound favors his small cousins here."

We all looked down, watched the Lady Melasadne's pack of dogs swirl about our ankles like little breaking waves, weave about Moonwind's feet. Moonwind stood aloof, staring down his long nose in apparent disdain. I laughed.

"He looks as disapproving as the prophet Ahijah himself," I said, and the others laughed with me.

"Truly he does." Melasadne began chirping commands at the small white dogs, which blithely ignored her, engrossed in their investigation of the tall newcomer who stood in their midst like an alabaster statue. "Ah, well, they will come away when they are ready," she said, and then smiled upon Khurrami.

"Tell your mistress, the Queen of the South, that the Lady Melasadne is most grateful for her kindness." Melasadne lifted her hands and unhooked the ocean pearls that circled her neck like a collar of cloud. "Tell her I send this small token of my friendship. I would give her one of Miri's puppies, but I do not think the queen's hound would take kindly to such a rival."

Khurrami received the pearls with smiling grace. "My queen will be pleased to own such friendship, which is a jewel past price."

As I watched, holding Moonwind's collar close, Khurrami bent and caressed the small dogs that milled about our feet. And when one of the pups set its tiny teeth into the hem of her gown and tried to run off with it, ripping little holes in the deep blue cloth, Khurrami only laughed and called the puppy charming and the gown too old and worn for the damage to matter.

As I walked on with Moonwind and Khurrami, I glanced sidelong at her. "Your gown is new; the blue still unfaded. You took its ruin lightly."

"Oh, I can mend the rents, cover them with embroidery. To have the Lady Melasadne's goodwill and friendship—that is worth a few rents, even in a new gown." Khurrami slid the rope of pearls through her fingers, slowly, as if she counted and judged them. "My queen likes to be on good terms with all. It is a wise policy, Princess."

"Certainly it is a pleasant one," I answered, and we continued on. And as I walked beside Khurrami, my hand resting upon Moonwind's silken back, I wondered why a woman as powerful as the Queen of the South should care what one of King Solomon's wives should think of her—and that wife not even the mother of the heir.

When I returned Moonwind to the queen's care, I asked if I might speak with her.

"Always," she said, smiling as she cradled Moonwind's long head between her hands. "What is it, Baalit?"

So I told her what had happened, and how Khurrami had granted the credit for the puppy's rescue to her, rather than claiming it for herself. And I confessed myself surprised that so great and powerful a queen strove so hard to please my father's women. "Why? Are they not your rivals?"

"Why not? Are we not all sisters under the moon? And is it not better to own friends than enemies?"

And even a slave girl can cause trouble if she cares nothing for consequences.

And as I thought this, the queen said, "I am not their rival, although I suppose no one in all Jerusalem believes that." She sighed, and shrugged. "Well, I cannot control others' thoughts or tongues. No, I am not their rival—but it makes them happy to think so. I am someone they can strive to defeat, after all."

I did not understand, and something in her tone and in her eyes made me hesitate to ask for enlightenment. I did not fear that she would not tell me; I knew that she would, if I asked plainly. But somehow I feared to hear her answer.

"So you are pleasant by policy?" I asked, and the queen smiled again.

"Partly—and partly because it is indeed more pleasant to dwell in peace. And partly because I am sorry for them; so many of your father's wives are unhappy."

Startled, I stared at her, then said, "Of course they are not! How could they be unhappy here?"

She looked at me for a long moment, her hands resting upon Moonwind's head as if in blessing. "How indeed?" she said at last. "Go and learn, Baalit, and return enlightened. Your own happiness rests in the balance."

And she would say nothing more. I went off hurt and puzzled to contemplate this new riddle she had posed.

Never had it occurred to me that any of my father's many wives might be less than content with him as a husband. All the world knew King Solomon was wise and just; all the palace knew King Solomon was also kind and generous. Each wife, each concubine, he treated fairly. Not one of King Solomon's women could honestly complain that another received a gift she herself did not receive as well. Nor could any complain that King Solomon favored one wife's bed, favored one wife's son, above any other's.

Why, then, should any of King Solomon's wives weep?

So I had thought, heedless as any child is heedless; who, as a child, thinks upon her elders' sorrows? But I now balanced upon the threshold between girl and woman. Before, a child, I had been blind to what I thought did not concern me. Now, as if the Queen of the South had torn away a veil that had long shrouded my eyes, I began to see clearly.

And to my new eyes, it seemed only regret and sorrow dwelt within the women's palace. Suddenly each quarrel, each spiteful word, I took as proof of a heart's misery. But when I said as much to the Spice Queen, she laughed. "Better, but you still see only with one eye. Come back again when you can see with two."

At first I did not understand her, nor could I understand why a woman whom I knew to be kind could so lightly regard the suffering I had spoken of. But never yet had Sheba offered me less than wisdom—if I had the wit to hear it.

So I began to study the women's palace as intently as if it were all the world, striving to see all its faults and virtues unveiled before me. And I began to learn that all that men and women did concerned me.

Abishag

All that long summer I sat quiet beside a dying king and listened as those who thought I was too foolish, and he too far down the path to death, to notice or to care, spun their plots. For King David had not yet declared his heir, and so men thought the crown a prize any prince might yet win.

Only a few knew that the next king had been chosen long years ago. Chosen, and trained, and now waiting as time spun out like smooth thread between Queen Michal's restless fingers.

When I think of her, it is always that image that I see: a woman spinning. Endlessly spinning—I can count on the fingers of one hand the times I saw the queen without her ivory spindle. To spin wool into thread quieted her, Queen Michal said. Soothed her restless mind.

"Spinning frees me, permits me to think calmly." Smiling, Queen Michal continued her endless task; her fingers pulled soft wool from the basket, twined the wool onto her lengthening thread. Thread coiled above the amber whirl; the spindle dropped from her hand, swinging as it fell, pulling new thread with it. Queen Michal spun as well as a spider; her thread wound thin and smooth about her ivory spindle.

I spun, of course; what well-reared girl did not? But I had no love for the craft, no sweet soft touch upon thin thread. Bearing Queen Michal company, I too spun, and bemoaned my lack of skill, compared with hers.

"Skill grows with time," the queen said, "and I have had many years to learn the art. When I was young—when I was young, I found no joy in spinning. That I was taught by hardship, and by sorrow."

"When King David fled before King Saul's army, and you sat prisoned far away." Later I would have known better than to speak of such old memories at all, unless the queen herself did so. But at least I had sense enough not to call King David's adversary "Mad Saul," which is how he was always spoken of in King David's court. Mad Saul was Queen Michal's father, after all.

Queen Michal looked long at me; her fingers never faltered on the slender thread she spun. At last she said, "Then, and after."

I realized I had erred, misjudged what she had wished to hear from me. Although I longed to know her meaning, I would not learn it now; her face betrayed nothing, the past hidden behind her steady eyes. So I said, hoping to please, "I too hope to learn the joy you found."

"Do you, Abishag?" she said. "I wish you better fortune than that, my child—but since you will always be a king's beloved, I do not think my wishes will count for much."

Baalit Sings

"If you had not wed my father, what would you have done?" A simple enough question—but the answers, I had learned, were not simple at all.

Some of my father's wives merely stared at me when I asked that question of them. Others laughed. But the answer seldom varied: "Oh, I would have wed another king." "I would have wed a prince, a great warrior, a wealthy merchant." One or two answered differently: "I would have become a priestess, had I not become a queen."

And when I asked if they were happy, even those wives who admitted they might have become high priestess of a rich temple eyed me warily and murmured platitudes: "A woman's happiness is in her children." "A woman's happiness is in her husband's happiness."

Most of my father's wives refused to admit that life might offer anything to them other than what they possessed. At least, they refused to admit it to me. Most of my father's wives answered as if they had all learned their responses from the same strict and pious teacher.

And then there were those like the Lady Citrajyoti.

The Lady Citrajyoti had been sent to my father from a land far to the east, farther even than Sheba; she had come to him bearing a dowry of sea pearls and sapphires, and the right to moor his ships at the Indus ports, and to trade there. She was small as a child and dark as amber and her hair fell in a long plait nearly to her gilded and jeweled feet.

When I was admitted into Lady Citrajyoti's rooms, I found her standing before a window, a vivid green parrot perched upon her wrist. Like many of King Solomon's wives, she followed the customs of her own country; she wore only trousers of some cloth so thin she might as well have been wearing water, and all that covered her breasts was a long strand of moonstones as large as doves' eggs.

She and the parrot both tilted their heads and stared at me, studying me with bright opaque eyes. "Princess Baalit," she said, and inclined her head. "You are welcome, of course."

Instantly I sensed that I was not. But neither was I unwelcome; Lady Citrajyoti merely waited to learn what I wished of her.

I looked at the parrot waiting upon her wrist. "Did you bring your bird from your homeland?"

"My home, yes." She spoke with slow care; our language strange to her tongue. She stroked the parrot's breast with one finger; from knuckle to fingertip, her skin was rose-red as a sunset, henna-dyed. "The Princess wishes?"

"To ask—" Suddenly my desire for knowledge seemed merely a rude curiosity. But the queen had commanded, and I knew I must obey or fail some unspoken test. "You are happy here? Pleased?"

She and her parrot stared at me with seemingly identical incomprehension; she continued to stroke the bird's emerald-bright feathers.

At last she said, "Pleased. Yes." Then, as if feeling she had been less than generous, "King Solomon, he is kind." She stopped caressing the green parrot to wave her hand in a gesture that somehow gathered up her rooms and the little courtyard beyond and offered them as proof. "Kind," she said again, and that was all.

I thanked her and went away, my thoughts unsettled.

Had Citrajyoti meant to shock me, outrage my modesty? No, for she had not known I intended to visit her; her garments were simply what a lady from her own land wore. Just as all my father's foreign wives and concubines wore the dress of their own land, followed as many of their own customs as they chose.

Now patterns I had never truly noticed sprang out in bright relief to my opened eyes. In the great courtyard of the women's palace, I saw that those wives and concubines chosen from among the people of Israel and of Judah formed a separate world. They clung together like a bevy of quail surrounded by falcons, turned their faces from the foreign wives as if the very sight of them would breed plague. Their disdain hovered, almost palpable; a murmur of distaste, like insects' buzzing, hung low upon the heavy air.

And for their part, the foreign women flaunted themselves, preening before the chastely covered Daughters of the Law, swearing by their idols with every other breath. Never would one permit a chance to affront the Hebrew women escape.

It seemed to me that the women of Israel and Judah affected more iron virtue than they would have displayed had they gathered at a public well instead of in the king's house—and I suspected that the foreigners feigned more wanton display than would have been permitted in their own lands.

Nor did I spy—for that is what it was, although I neither came in secret nor disguised my interest—only upon the foreign women. My father had also married wisely among his own people; each tribe had given a bride to the king. As I say, the Hebrew wives clung together, creating a tribe of their own within the women's palace.

As a child, I had thought only that they were too bonded by blood to befriend those who were not of their lineage. Too, they had spoken loudest against the freedom my father had always granted me, and so I had not sought out their company.

But when I spoke to them now, I listened with new understanding. For now I knew that these women fought a battle they had lost before ever they set foot upon the cool polished floors of the women's palace. Trained up to be frugal wives, strict mothers, and pious women, as their mothers and their mothers' mothers had been before them, they had married not a shepherd or a farmer or a merchant, but a king. They dwelt not in a good plain house or in a desert tent, but within the walls of a great palace.

And their sister-wives were not others who had been raised as prudently and as strictly as they—but foreigners. Women who had been trained to strange ways, who dressed in alien garments, who worshipped distant gods. Women as exotic and dangerous as bright serpents.

The Hebrew wives feared and envied the foreigners, who embodied the changes time had swept over our land. They could not banish the foreign queens from the women's palace, or from King Solomon's bed.

Some had yielded to the alien lure and adopted those habits and fashions that pleased them. These spoke overlong of how they still truly obeyed the Law—"There is no law to say a woman may not wear Colchian black if it pleases her. And who is to know, after all? I do not flaunt this in the marketplace!" This was said with an uneasy laugh; the speaker sought to convince herself as well as me.

Some strove to dwell within the women's palace as if it were a plain man's house—and as if the other wives did not exist. These spoke little, but their words cut like poisoned blades. "It is better to stay far from them; I never cross the courtyard to their side. And they know better than to so much as touch my gate with their unclean hands."

And one Daughter of the Law had surrendered to neither temptation nor hatred. The Lady Dvorah somehow trod a middle path.

Although she owned as many fine garments as any of the others, they were of a cut and color suitable for a modest woman in her husband's house. In the Lady Dvorah's courtyard, the Law was meticulously observed and the Lord was honored. But that observance did not prevent Dvorah from gossiping with women who neither dressed nor worshipped as she did.

"Of course I keep our Lord's Laws," she told me. "But I cannot keep them for others, nor is His Law binding upon those not of His Covenant. Try one of the little cakes; it is a recipe of my own. I use apricots instead of figs."

So bidden, I tasted the cake and praised its rich flavor. I admit I had a second motive for visiting the Lady Dvorah at midday; she was renowned for her skill as a cook. "So you do not think my father's foreign women unclean?"

"Well, of course they are—they eat impure food and worship idols. But that does not mean I cannot be civil to them when we pass in the garden or the courtyard. Now tell me truly, do you like the wine? I spiced it with clove and cinnamon, but perhaps I should add more honey?"

Again I swore the taste perfect. "Do you not think them immodest?" As if the notion had just occurred to me, I added, "Why, the Lady Citrajyoti walks about in less than I wear at night in my bed!"

"Oh, I think sometimes she only does that because Paziah and Leah and the others turn to salt at the sight of her—as if we had not all seen as much in the bath. She does not walk about half-naked when the winter winds blow! Another cake, child?"

Since she insisted, I took another of the sweet, chewy little cakes. "But the idols?"

Lady Dvorah shrugged. "What can you expect from foreigners?" she said. "They do not compel me to bow down before their gods, and I would not even did they ask me. Which they do not, for they know better than to try."

Yes, for if they offend you, you will no longer offer them cinnamon wine and apricot cakes! The unworthy thought made me laugh; I managed to turn it into a cough and hastily asked if I might take some of the cakes to offer to my maidservants, which pleased the Lady Dvorah.

"Of course you may, and you must send word to tell how they like them." She summoned one of her own servants and bade her fill a bowl with the cakes for me. She sipped from her own wine cup and then asked, "Why are you asking such questions, child?"

Although I had created an explanation for my curiosity, her own question surprised me. The Lady Dvorah was the first who had asked. I smiled and said, "Why, because someday I must go from my father's house to dwell among strangers. I wish to learn how to live in peace there, and be happy."

"You have your father's wisdom," Dvorah said, nodding approval. "Well, I shall tell you what I have learned: keep your own household in your own fashion, and let others do as they please—so long as they let you do the same."

I thanked her and said that sounded wise to me. "Is that all?" I asked.

She considered the matter, and finally said, "Always smile upon your husband, and serve him what he best likes to eat. And make sure that dish is one of your own devising so no other woman can copy it. Your goblet is empty; let me fill it."

As she poured more spiced wine into my cup, I thought on what she had said. Then I asked what trial she found hardest to endure, living among so many foreigners.

She sighed. "Truly? My greatest regret is that I cannot eat their food, and so cannot learn their secrets."

"Can you not ask for the recipe, and alter it to suit the Law?" I asked, and was surprised when she laughed.

"Oh, child, you are so innocent! As if a cook would tell *all* she knows!" She shook her head. "No, to truly obtain knowledge of a dish, I must see it prepared, and taste it, too. So I shall never know that joy.... Do have another cake, child. You are too thin. Men like plump girls."

When she sent me off to learn what I could of men and women, the Sheban queen had laughed. And when I returned to tell the Queen of Sheba all I had done, and what I had learned, she laughed again, and said only that all my effort was a good start.

"For if you are to rule women, and men too, you must know them for what they are."

"I do know them," I said, and she smiled.

"And what do you know, my Baalit?"

"I know that all women and all men are different—and they all are the same. Some would be happy anywhere, and some happy nowhere," I said. "And not one is other than queen in her own life, or king in his."

I expected her to laugh again, but she did not. Instead, she smiled and laid her hand against my cheek, her skin cool against mine. "Yes, in our hearts we all are kings and queens. You know at fourteen what many never learn." And then the queen spoke words whose sound poured through my veins like hot wine. "One day you will be as wise as your father, little goddess. You are fit to rule; you were born to be queen."

For a dozen heartbeats, I basked in her praise as if it were sunlight. Then I curbed my dreams sharp and hard, as if they were bolting mares. "You are kind. But it will not matter, not here. I am only the king's daughter, after all."

And to that, the Queen of Sheba said nothing. What was there to say, when we both knew I spoke iron truth?

Solomon

He could not resist watching his Sheban guest, delighting in her rich beauty; a beauty unforced and unpracticed, as if beauty were but a veil she wore easily and with grace. And often, now, when he came upon the Sheban queen, his daughter too came under his eye. Today he stood in the long gallery above the garden in the women's palace, and once again he watched both Bilqis and Baalit. *They have become as close as sisters—no, not sisters—they share a different bond.* But he could not yet put a name to whatever bound the two.

Below him in the women's garden, his daughter sat close beside the Sheban queen—close as a daughter to her own mother. The queen spoke, and his daughter laughed; the queen reached out and touched Baalit's hair, curled a fire-bright strand about her fingers. Then the queen said something that caused his daughter to smile, and then all expression left her face. For a moment both sat unmoving, and in the rich honey sunlight they seemed caught in amber.

Then Baalit shrugged, and laughed; suddenly weary, Solomon closed his eyes rather than look upon his daughter's enthralled face any longer. *I am glad to see her so happy. Of course I am glad. But—*

But what, O great King? his inner voice mocked. *But your daughter cares more for this foreign woman than she does for you? Finds more pleasure in another's company than she does in yours?*

And then, with deadly precision, keen as a new-whetted blade, *Did you think to keep her always?*

He recoiled from the dark, tempting thought. No, of course he had not thought that! His beloved daughter must have what all women desired: a home, a husband, children of her own. A father's love must not smother a daughter in its embrace. *But Baalit is so young—*

She is near fourteen. Her mother wed you when she was little older than her daughter is now. Solomon had been trained to look clearly on truth; now he forced himself to gaze again upon the scene unfolding in the women's garden below. Clearing his mind, he studied Baalit as if his daughter were new to his eyes.

And he looked upon a stranger: a girl grown tall, lithe and slender as a palm; a girl whose once unruly hair had been tamed into smooth coiled braids. A girl whose fine linen gown clung to curving hips and rounding breasts.

She is no longer a child. Solomon allowed the truth to sink into his heart. *My daughter still—but soon another man's wife.*

In the garden below, the queen spoke on, a passionate intensity radiating from her that Solomon noted without understanding. As if entranced, his daughter's eyes never left the foreign queen's face; his daughter's eyes shone bright as twin moons—

Ah, Sheba, you have stolen my heart—will you steal hers as well? For the Spice Queen must, in the end, return to her own far kingdom. Grief would be her parting gift.

Must she return? the inner voice demanded. *You are king of Israel and of Judah, and of many lands besides—can you not hold one mere woman if you desire her?*

No. No, I will not even think that. Never before had Solomon truly understood how a man could act counter to his own wisdom; in ignorant vanity, he had prided himself upon acting always with cool judgment. Upon doing always what was right, what was just, what was politic, his decisions unpoisoned by folly or passion.

Because I knew not what temptation was. Now—now I am repaid for my arrogance. For the temptation to yield only to his own desires clawed at him, savagely demanding as a leopard.

You are king. Do as you wish. Temptation hissed like a serpent, coiled beneath his heart. *Do as you wish. Your father King David denied himself nothing. Are you less a king than he?*

Yes, hissed that dark serpent's voice. *You are less; you know it to be true. A great king would take as pleased him. What matters save your own desires?*

Below him in the women's garden, the queen and the princess sat untroubled beside the fountain, untouched by the darkness calling to him. Baalit spoke, earnest and eager. Bilqis nodded, and listened, and toyed with a handful of small crimson roses that lay in her lap.

You want her, and you are king. Take what you want. Who can deny the king's desires?

"I can." Spoken in a whisper, the words echoed against the cool stone walls. "I can," Solomon repeated.

He closed his eyes against temptation's brazen light. When at last he dared look again upon the garden below, his daughter and the Sheban queen had gone. All that remained was sunlight upon water, and the rising scent of roses.

Bilqis

Later, when it was too late to call back the words, Bilqis knew she had moved too swiftly, counted too greatly upon Ilat's gift and promise. *Our Mother promised the girl, revealed her to me. But it is I—I who must obtain her. Did I think Ilat would waft the girl from Jerusalem to Sheba in Her arms?*

She had been overjoyed and overconfident— *But had I not been both—ah, had I been as wise as I thought myself, I never would have lain in King Solomon's arms.*

She had looked upon Jerusalem from afar and from its streets; she had seen all the riches the king could spread before her. She had even been permitted to view the Great Temple that crowned the high hill, to walk its outer court and gaze upon the brazen sea resting on the backs of a dozen bronze bulls, and to look upon the two pillars that held up the doorway to the Temple itself.

But of all the riches Jerusalem held, it was within the palace she had found the greatest prize. A pearl of such great price that she had permitted her greed for the treasure to overrule her reason, asked too much too soon. Ever after, when haste tempted her, she would sing that small story to herself, a silent warning.

She had thought herself patient as time, subtle as desert sands. For once she had seen Baalit, she had waited, smiling and serene, as if the king's daughter held no more interest than did the great palace, or the golden Temple, or the grand marketplace in which merchants offered up treasures from lands beyond counting.

But at last it seemed the king had spread before her all that Jerusalem had to offer, and he himself gave her the chance she had sought. That day they had ridden to the valley north of Jerusalem so Solomon might show her his famous stables. She had admired the vast horse farm and the fine horses bred there; King Solomon's horses were prized by generals and kings.

Upon the ride home, they had talked of horses, arguing whether size and strength were more to be valued than speed and suppleness. At last she had said, "Perhaps one could breed a horse possessing all these virtues. When I return to Sheba, I shall choose three of Shams's colts to send you. Put them to your largest, strongest mares—"

"—and in time, we shall see if such a breeding produces that ideal horse. I will accept such a gift eagerly." Solomon had leaned over to touch Shams's arched neck. "I have coveted your horse since I set eyes upon him; now I shall have such a beast for my own pleasure."

She had laughed; they had ridden back along the Jerusalem road well pleased with one another.

Once they had returned to the city, and to the king's house, Solomon had escorted her back to the Little Palace. At its gate he said, "Now you

have at last seen all my treasures, O Queen of Queens." He smiled. "Tell me
your thoughts. Is my kingdom as great as yours?"

Warmed by the undertone of laughter in his voice, she smiled back.
"Your kingdom is great indeed. But true treasure is a companion whose wit
matches one's own."

"Yes; laughing at my own jests grows tiresome."

"What, do your courtiers not laugh when their king smiles?"

"Too much. Do you not know that I am wise and given to clever jests?"

"And so they laugh at whatever words come from your mouth." Mocking, she shook her head. "How sad, that your reputation causes all men to
laugh at you!"

Solomon turned and took her hand. "But you do not laugh, or frown,
save as my words truly move you. You are right; you yourself are your kingdom's treasure." A moment's silence, then he added, very softly, "I wish your
kingdom's treasure were mine."

"You flatter me, O King; I am old enough to be your mother."

"What does that matter? Your mind matches mine; what more could I
desire?"

"A great deal," she said, and laughed. "But you are right that our minds
match, for while you wish my kingdom's treasure, I in turn desire yours."
She kept her tone jesting light. She had lured him to this point with care; he
must not withdraw his words now.

"What can King Solomon possess that the Queen of Sheba could possibly covet?" His tone matched hers; the hint of dark longing had vanished.
"Whatever it is, it is yours."

"Do you not wish first to know what it is I will ask of you?"

"Greed is not in your nature." Solomon smiled again. "Ask."

This was the moment, she felt it in her bones. "King Solomon has sworn
to grant me all I desire. Yet of all his treasures, there is only one that I
would have."

"Whatever treasure Queen Bilqis names shall be hers. Although what
Israel can grant that Sheba does not already possess is a true riddle." Solomon's
voice was tolerant, amused, as if he waited to hear what trinket had taken her
fancy.

"What Israel can grant is what Sheba can no longer provide," she said.
"The riddle's answer is the Princess Baalit."

Silence; the golden amity shattered as the air between them turned cold and hard, and she knew that she had erred. *Too soon; I asked too soon—*

"I do not understand," he said at last, plainly offering her the chance to soften her desire.

But that she could not do; she must have Baalit. Sheba must have Baalit. "You know why I have come so far, and what I seek. Now I have found her. All I ask of you is one girl—"

"I am no Jephthah, to sacrifice my only daughter."

"Sacrifice? To you, to your people, she is only a girl—what life will she have here? In Sheba, she will be queen, Solomon; she will rule Sheba after me."

For a moment he said nothing, his mouth closed tight over harsh words. But when he replied, his voice was flat, his calm worse than anger. "No, O Queen, she will not. She is my only daughter, my kingdom's only princess. She will not be sent to a land half a year away."

"She must leave you someday, O King." She kept her voice as level, as calm, as his. "She will go to a husband, or to a temple. You cannot chain her to childhood; even Solomon the Wise cannot command time itself."

"That is someday, not now. And as you say, she is only a girl. This is not the Morning Land, this is the land of the Lord's Law. Here, girls are not raised up to rule over men."

"No. But even your girls can learn. They raise up the men who rule the kingdom, after all." But her words did not move him; she sensed his withdrawal. And when he claimed urgent tasks demanded him elsewhere, she knew she must concede defeat for the moment. "Of course," she said, and smiled, and before she returned through the gate into the Little Palace, she held her hand out to him as if they had spoken only sweet words, shared only laughter.

But it was the first time he had left her before she ended their encounter; that alone told her how much her request had troubled him. *So much so that he revoked his king's word—whatsoever I desired—* Suddenly weary, she leaned against the window, its stone cool against her cheek. Whatsoever she desired— *Men say such things easily, and kings more easily still.*

Granting her desire would cost Solomon dearly; she did not deny that, even to herself. *But I have been promised that girl, and if King Solomon denies her, his refusal will cost him more dearly still.*

Therefore he must not refuse, must grant what she desired of him. *I must bend him to my will. But how?*

Suddenly she laughed, gay as a girl; how could she have forgotten? *Is not the king a man, and the queen a woman?* Men were ruled by their bodies—and by women's bodies. Even Solomon the Wise was no exception, cool and passionless as he might think himself, for he was ruled by the memory of a woman's body, by the shadow of his beloved, his Abishag.

I must battle a ghost for Solomon's heart. Far easier to fight a living rival— Sober again, Bilqis stood before her mirror, judging herself in the polished silver.

How best to entice him? *Shall I let him catch me bathing in the sunlight, as his father did his mother?*

No; that was a young woman's trick. She was beautiful still, but she was no longer young; the sun no longer stroked her kindly, promising her lover fire's passion. The Sun Goddess had fulfilled Her promise by guiding her here, to this land ruled by men.

So I must seek the blessings of the Moon God, now. Shadow, and moonlight, and her own skilled desire—these would bring Solomon to her. *So much will be easy. To gain the promise of his daughter, his Abishag's child—* That would prove difficult.

But not impossible. *It cannot be impossible. Our Mother led me here, set the girl before me. She would not have promised me what I could not achieve.*

To win her battle, she needed weapons, and those she could forge only when she knew her rival as well as she did herself. Bilqis sent her maidservants and eunuchs to glean old tales from the harem women and the palace servants. She winnowed ancient gossip and rumor, seeking truths she could wield against Solomon's cool armor.

"Abishag? A pretty enough girl, but too quiet."

"Almost a foreigner—I am sure she had foreign blood."

"She was kind, and her voice was soft."

"She bewitched him. There were a dozen more comely than she!"

"She laughed a great deal."

"No modest woman walks as she did—like a cat in heat. And she wore bells about her ankles; she did not learn that trick from a decent woman!"

"Abishag? I remember her; she smelled of cinnamon. Of cinnamon and roses."

Solomon

For seven days he had not seen her; the Queen of Sheba had remained closed within the Little Palace, a stranger to him. At first he had sent servants to her, bearing gifts of fruit and flowers, coaxing. Later he sent messengers to her, asking what was wrong. *No, demanding. How did she become so needful to me?* Lying unquiet in his bed, Solomon smiled into the darkness of the summer night. *You know how; your minds match. She is someone you can talk to, and be understood.*

Even his friend Amyntor could not fully comprehend the weights that pressed upon a king—and now Solomon could not call upon even such comradeship as Amyntor could grant, for the Caphtoran had gone. Always Solomon had known his friend merely paused, like a bird of passage, before continuing a voyage that had no end. *But I miss him all the same—and now Bilqis has taken herself from my sight as well. She is angry because I refused her—but even as Amyntor asked too little of me, Bilqis asked too much.*

Deep night, hot as black fire; how could he sleep when the very air burned his skin? Impossible. Solomon abandoned his dutiful effort to rest and rose, measuring paces to the window. There he sat upon the broad ledge, leaning against stones warm as blood from the day's raging heat. No sleep again tonight; he would be good for nothing in the court tomorrow.

Solomon sighed and rubbed his temples. The hot wind blew hard this season; hard and cruel as law. In just such a summer season his father had seen his mother bathing upon her rooftop, and fallen in love with her on sight. . . .

If you believed the pretty tale now sung by court harpists. Other tongues also told a tale, not so pretty, of passion, of adultery, and of murder. But that tale was whispered in corners, and in secret.

They call mine a court of Law; in truth, it is a court of Secrets.

His father, king, had sent for a woman only because he desired her. *I am king; I can do the same. I could order her brought to me because I will it. Because I desire her.*

Even if she did not desire him? *What is lust worth without love? Without even passion?*

A whisper behind him; a susurrus of air, as if a serpent flowed through the hot night. Solomon remained still, knowing if he turned, he would succumb to temptation, and to sorrow.

"I did not summon you," he said.

"If you had commanded me, I would not have come." There was a ripple of slow laughter in her voice. "How did you know it was I?"

"Your scent; you are fragrant as a heap of spices."

The air swayed about him as she approached. "Your words are sweet as frankincense, and honey is under your tongue."

She stood close behind him, now; he judged her to be no more than a hand's span away. "Words are easy to sweeten."

"So are heavy nights."

Hot night air pressed him; dark perfume stroked his senses. *I should send her away. I shall send her away. This is folly, folly as great as my father's when he took my mother.*

He turned, cautious, avoiding her body. Facing, they were no more than a breath apart. "My queen—"

She smiled. "Yes, your queen—for this night. Come, Solomon, let us rule night together."

Heat molded the robe she wore; silk clung damp to her ripe body. Perfume rose from her skin: frankincense and cinnamon, sweet hint of rose. The scent of love.

Folly. But a folly he could no longer resist.

PART SIX

A Bed of Spices

Abishag

"I wish you better fortune——" Sometimes, during those first months in the king's court, Queen Michal's words left me uneasy in my mind, but I knew the fault lay with me. I was too new to the king's court to play the great game in which the queen so excelled. Queen Michal was wise and just, and well-loved by Solomon; I sought to learn all she could teach.

And I strove too to learn what the Lady Bathsheba had to teach. The Lady Bathsheba was not very wise, as Queen Michal reckoned wisdom, but she was kind and patient; sometimes the Lady Bathsheba could teach what Queen Michal, for all her iron wit, could not.

When I asked Queen Michal why she, a great queen, wore always about her wrist a cheap chain of brass and spangles, she looked at me with eyes cool as crystal and said, "To remind me of the cost of a queen's friendship." It was the Lady Bathsheba who smiled and said, "Long ago it was all I had to send in return, when Michal sent me a gift of oranges. I still remember how their juice flowed over my tongue, both tart and sweet at once."

It was to the Lady Bathsheba I turned when I wished to learn any task I found tedious, for she owned the skill of liking whatever work to which she must set her soft hands. I strove diligently to learn that subtle skill, for I knew already that King Solomon's queen must undertake many tasks that would bore or vex her.

So between Queen Michal and the Lady Bathsheba, I was well-taught. But some skills cannot be taught, only learned. Learned through pain, through hardship, through sorrow.

And, sometimes, through joy.

Rahbarin

As a thousand years of custom demanded, the queen's court was held each new and each full moon. With Queen Bilqis gone, her nephew, as regent, sat upon the Sun Throne and received petitions and granted justice. And answered questions, or tried to. After half-a-year, answering the ever more frequent questions about the queen's continued absence grew not only difficult but tedious.

Why do men ever wish to wear a crown? That, too, was a question Rahbarin could not answer. Serving as the queen's substitute nearly drove him mad; no longer was his time his own, his actions unfettered. Each word must be carefully weighed, each woman or man who petitioned be granted scrupulous justice.

Now he strove to achieve justice once again, listening intently as two women quarreled over the ownership of a white camel's calf. "The camel is mine, her calf mine as well!" "Yes, Qurrat, but who twice lent you gold to breed her to the swiftest racer in all Sheba? I, and what have I seen for it?"

"Enough." Rahbarin lifted the leopard-headed scepter; with the movement, the golden pard's eyes flashed emerald. "This is the camel's second calf of a second mating? Answer only yes or no."

The women eyed each other; greed and misgiving warred at his curt tone. At last one said, "Yes, Prince."

"And has the loan been repaid?"

"Half, Prince," admitted the other.

"Then Qurrat, as the owner of the camel, keeps the other half of the gold but gives this second camel calf into your keeping. Scribe, set down the judgment." *And our Mother spare me from any more cases that could be solved by a village idiot!*

The case of the white camel settled to everyone's partial satisfaction, Rahbarin nodded, and the herald granted the next petitioner permission to approach the Sun Throne. A stout woman dressed in the neat robes of a cloth merchant came forward and planted herself before Rahbarin.

"I am Hawlyat," the woman announced, "I speak for the Cloth Traders' Guild."

"What does Hawlyat of the Cloth Traders' Guild ask of the Sun Throne?" Thus far both petitioner and ruler spoke by rote, the form laid down many lifetimes ago.

"I ask a question."

"That is your right." Rahbarin studied the woman's face and sighed inwardly. The set of her jaw boded nothing but trouble; even before she spoke, Rahbarin knew what her question would be.

"O Prince, our queen has been gone many moons. This is the thirteenth queen's court without a queen. When will she return to us?"

I knew it, Rahbarin thought grimly. The same question had been raised in each of the last half-a-dozen courts. *Who can blame them? She has been gone long months without a word of her return.* No, he could not blame his aunt's subjects for asking the same question to which he himself longed to know the answer. *But I am tired of hearing it!*

He was even more weary of returning evasive answers. But reply he must, so said court etiquette.

"The Sun Throne thanks the merchant Hawlyat for her question." That much came easily, words laid down for the ruler's response. The rest was harder, for he had nothing to give but soothing ambiguities. Now the woman—and all the rest who had come to this day's court—waited to hear what he would say. And Rahbarin had run out of excuses.

So he told the truth. "I do not know," he said. "Our queen sends word each new moon that she is well—and that she will return when our Mother Ilat wills."

"And when will that be, O Prince?"

"I have said already that I do not know," Rahbarin said. "Shall I sit upon the Sun Throne and speak falsely to you? Our queen's task was set her by Ilat Herself, and the queen will return to us when that task has been completed."

"What task?" the merchant Hawlyat demanded.

Rahbarin hesitated, weighing choices. The queen had kept the true purpose of her visit to King Solomon secret, known only to her most trusted court officials; now Rahbarin wondered if that had been wise. The queen hoped to return bringing the next queen as her gift to Sheba. Perhaps it was time her subjects knew what their queen endured on their behalf.

Act as our Mother Ilat directs, and as seems best to you— The Queen's own command; now he must decide what seemed best. *Play for time.* The words seemed to slide into his mind, serpent-subtle. Mother Ilat directing his actions? A djinn seeking to trick him into folly? Or his own reluctance to utter yet another placating half-truth? And how was he to tell the difference?

I must say something. At last Rahbarin said, "The queen will return—"

Voices began to call out "When? How long?" and Rahbarin raised the scepter. Sun-fire flashed from the golden leopard; the great court was silent again, and Rahbarin continued.

"Our queen will return bringing our next queen to us; Ilat Herself has promised us this gift. As for when—I do not know. I have told you what Ilat Sun-Eyes revealed to the Sun of our Days, and if you do not like what I have said, you are welcome to tread the path to the Inner Temple and ask the Queen of Heaven for yourselves. And if She answers you, come back to the next queen's court and tell us all what She has said."

Silence; at last the merchant Hawlyat said, "I ask that our prince send word north to our queen, telling her we are troubled by her long absence."

And urging her to come back? Do you think I have not longed to do so these many months?

"Are we fools, that we cannot govern ourselves for a time? Are we infants, that we wail at our mother's stepping out of the courtyard for an hour? No; I will not send her such a message." A message that would in any case prove useless. Rahbarin had no doubt whatsoever that the queen would return only with the queen to come after, or she would not return at all. "I take orders from our Mother Ilat, and from the queen. I do not take them from my own fears—or yours."

After the queen's court finally ended, Rahbarin rode out into the quiet land past Ma'rib's walls, hoping to find peace in the placid countryside. But although the land stretched green and fertile from the road to the far horizon, the sight failed to soothe his troubled heart. He turned his horse towards the hill road; the mare cantered easily up the slope to the crest, and there Rahbarin reined her in and dismounted. He laid his hand upon her sleek warm neck and stared out over the land, looking to the north.

Below him stood one of Sheba's famed incense forests, rows of trees more precious than gold. Beyond loomed the bulk of the Great Dam, the wonder that granted Sheba water for city and for crops. And beyond that—

—beyond the Great Ma'rib Dam stretched the wilderness of sand and rock that guarded Sheba.

Somewhere beyond that expanse of deadly desert lay the kingdom of Solomon. *And that kingdom now holds our queen.*

A chill slid down his back, soft and irritating as grains of sand. His sudden tension troubled his mare; she tossed her head; the long tassels dangling from her headstall brushed his cheek.

"Softly, my lady," he told her, and caught her reins beneath her chin and touched his fingertips to the hot velvet skin of her muzzle. "You are right, I worry over nothing. King Solomon will not hold our queen against her will. She will return to us safely."

The mare pricked her ears and lipped at his hand; Rahbarin smiled and stroked her muzzle once more. The queen would return; of course she would return. *But when?*

Already she had been gone half a year. *Does so long an absence mean she has succeeded—or failed?* Rahbarin could not imagine his royal aunt failing in any task, goddess-given or not. Bilqis reigned always victorious.

Shadows began to stretch longer; the sun nearly touched the western horizon. Rahbarin stared at the rose-gold fire the setting sun sparked in the western sky and tried to summon up an image of the new queen who might even now be traveling the Spice Road to Sheba. But he saw nothing in the flaming sky, nothing but clouds spreading out across the horizon like burning wings.

Perhaps that phoenix-flare was a good omen; perhaps it was only a trick of the dying light. Rahbarin decided to believe it a good omen. For surely Ilat would not send the queen so far if the quest were hopeless.

But that night he did not lie down with an easy heart, and sleep did not grant him its dark caresses. At last he gave up and rose, and went to walk the wall, pacing the time-worn stones, restless as a caged panther.

She has been gone too long. No matter what pieties Rahbarin mouthed in court, here on the wall he could at least speak truth to himself. *Half a year, and no word, save "wait."*

Beneath his feet the wall's stones glowed warm, still holding the day's heat close. Above him arched the night sky, the Queen's Crown a blaze of white fire over midnight. Rahbarin searched the crown's brilliant stars; vainly, for the cold gems revealed nothing to him.

Please, Bright Lady, guide me. He had made every offering, every prayer, and still no sign was granted. Why would Ilat not speak?

Because you know already what you must do. Abashed, Rahbarin bowed his head. *Have I grown so weak I ask the Lady's aid to do what I should achieve myself?* He knew what his aunt would say to such foolish queries.

"The Lady has granted you a mind and a body. She expects you to use them!"

And had not the queen's last orders been that he should do as seemed best to him? *What seems best for Sheba, for our kingdom. Not what I wish to do.* For if he did as he wished to do, he would ride north and carry their queen back upon his saddlebow. But that would solve nothing.

No, his duty lay here, guarding Sheba and the throne against the queen's coming.

And if our queen never returns?

Rahbarin stared up at the white fire of the burning stars. *If she never returns, she will send us our new queen. And I will hold the throne safe against her coming.*

And when my new queen rides through Ma'rib's gate, she will find me waiting here to serve her.

Baalit Sings

Whenever I think of those days now, my skin always grows hot, and shame at my ungracious actions burns me. I prowled about like a hungry leopard, refused to admit even my handmaidens within the iron circle I drew about myself—and Nimrah and Keshet were dear to me as sisters. I made myself lonely without cause, and let anger eat away my peace. But I was young, and the young are cruel, even to themselves. And I was unquiet in my mind, for no matter what I did, whether I walked in Queen Michal's garden or rode out upon Uri, spun or studied or tossed a ball for my little brothers, Queen Bilqis's words sang silently to me,

"You are fit to rule; you were born to be queen."

Those words had opened a door to thoughts I had long ago forbidden myself even to dream. Now I remembered why I must not listen to that siren-song; it summoned nothing but sorrow.

"Fit to rule"—without conceit, I knew that was true. I had known since I could walk that I was better fitted to rule than was my brother Rehoboam. Rehoboam was stubborn where I was firm, cruel where I was kind; his temper sparked like dry tinder. And he had no skill for judging men, and even

less for judging women. Rehoboam despised women, thinking them weak—and I suspected he secretly despised our father. Rehoboam mistook tolerance for weakness, patience for fear, compromise for failure. His scorn for others was Rehoboam's greatest flaw.

Fit to rule—now I saw that all my life I had studied to become so, had seized all the chances my arrogant brother had thrown away. I had hearkened to my tutors, and I had listened well to my father, studying his court as intently as I did my histories. And I listened to all my stepmothers, even the silliest of them. I had lived fourteen years in my father's palace, and now I knew I had not wasted a day of that time. Each day I had been learning, seeking. Without knowing my goal, I had trained myself for queenship.

"Born to be queen."

But Queen Bilqis was wrong. My years of instinctive study did not matter. Nor did my skills, my wits, my talents—nothing that I was mattered, set against the fact that Rehoboam was the king's son, and I—I was only the king's daughter.

Never would I be such a queen as she. At best, I would become a king's wife.

That was all I would ever be. And that was not enough.

Keshet

"Something is wrong." Nimrah paced the garden; at the path's end she turned and stalked along the bed of lilies, her long braid swinging back and forth across her back.

Keshet watched Nimrah's restless strides and sighed. "What could be wrong? Come and sit here beside me." She patted the broad edge of the fountain, but Nimrah would not be coaxed.

"I don't know. But the princess is troubled."

"What does she have to trouble her?"

"I don't know," Nimrah said again. "But whatever it is, she will not share it with us. Surely you have noticed that she vanishes for hours?"

"She has slipped out of the palace before." Keshet smiled. "We all have."

"Yes—together. But now—wherever it is she goes, she does not take us with her. That troubles me."

Thinking over the days since the last new moon, Keshet realized Nimrah was right. Too often Baalit simply could not be found; she no longer confided all her secrets to them. "You are right," Keshet said. "She leaves us behind; that troubles me also. Do you think she meets a lover?"

Nimrah shook her head. "Who? And she would tell us *that*, I think. This must be something else, something even more dangerous." Nimrah frowned. "It began when the Sheban queen came here."

Keshet considered Nimrah's words. "Yes, I think you are right. And she is not with the queen, or at least, not always. Now, where?"

"And why will she not trust us?"

"I don't know," Keshet said. "Why don't we ask her?"

"Yes," said Nimrah, after a moment's thought, "we will ask."

But asking brought them no peace of mind, for when they claimed the princess's attention that evening, as they brushed out her hair and folded away her garments, Baalit listened to their troubled questions and then said, "I walk to clear my thoughts. That is all."

Her eyes do not meet ours; she lies. That their princess should lie to them shocked Keshet. That their princess thought they would swallow so foolish an excuse angered her. "That is *not* all," Keshet snapped. "Baalit, we know you as well as we know ourselves, so if you are going to lie to us, at least come up with a better tale than that!"

She had hoped such tart words would call forth an unwary response; Baalit's temper burned as hot as her loves. But the princess only looked at Keshet, and then at Nimrah, and at last said, "I cannot. And so rather than tell you lies, I will tell you nothing at all."

And nothing that either Keshet or Nimrah could say pried another word from Baalit's lips. At last they abandoned the effort—at least for that night.

"But we will find out her secret," Keshet whispered to Nimrah as they lay in bed, awake and listening for any sound from Baalit's bed. "We must. How can we protect her if we do not know?"

"We can't. Go to sleep, Keshet." But although she lay silent, Nimrah's breathing did not alter. Later Keshet wondered if any of the three of them had slept that night. If she herself had, she had dreamed only of lying awake, waiting to hear Baalit's soft footsteps as she left them in the dark.

Benaiah

When men asked his opinion of the Sheban affair, Benaiah always merely shrugged. If a man pressed him—and few men dared challenge the king's commander—and if Benaiah felt loquacious that day, he might add a few words to the silent gesture.

"A great queen, fit match for a great king. Not much of an army, though."

And once, when King Solomon himself asked Benaiah's thoughts on the Sheban visit, Benaiah had said, "The Sheban queen desires something of you; perhaps you'll find out what it is, in time. Women are fools at war and cunning at politics."

King Solomon had laughed, and called Benaiah an oversuspicious skeptic.

"No bad thing in the commander of the king's army," Benaiah had said. "I pray you, my lord, to take care how you deal with the woman."

If only he had remembered his own words, taken his own good advice, he would not now suffer the pains of uncertainty and indecision. But once he had seen her, his heart flew to her in an instant—

And your brain followed after, Benaiah told himself. He possessed no strength, no guile, against this opponent. Benaiah fought a war he feared he could not win, a war that could end only one way: badly.

If only I had never set my eyes upon her. If I had never seen her, I would be spared this torment. I wish— But Benaiah stopped short of wishing he had never seen her. That would have spared him—and denied him as well. *It is sheer folly, to love at my age, and to love such a woman.*

A foreigner, and an idol-worshipper, and young enough to be his daughter besides all else— *No, tell the truth, if only to yourself, old man. She is young enough to be my granddaughter.*

But against this enemy, the great general Benaiah fell, powerless before a strange woman's fierce eyes. That was why he now stood before her gate, impatient and inarticulate as any youth fresh from the hills, waiting upon the pleasure of his beloved.

Nikaulis

"That man is here again," Khurrami said. "He asks for you. Shall I tell him to go away?"

"The king's general? Do not be such a fool, girl. I will speak with him." Against her will, Nikaulis's blood beat hard, sending a quiver through her body. She rose and strode towards the door, only to have Khurrami dash past her and bar her way.

"Go like that?" Khurrami demanded. "And go so quickly, as if you leapt to his bidding? Let him wait while you change your garb and dress your hair. And perhaps some paint—"

Shaking her head, Nikaulis attempted to sidestep Khurrami. "Benaiah knows very well what I look like and how I dress. And I will not play foolish games; he asks, and either I come to him or I do not. Now step aside, for I do not wish to keep a good man waiting."

Khurrami sighed and stepped aside. "Oh, very well—but I do wish you would permit me to make you as beautiful as you truly are. No man wishes to wed a warrior!"

"Perhaps not—but then, I have no wish to marry a man, either."

Nikaulis strode off swiftly, hoping to outpace her own unease at uttering such words, words that trembled on the precipice between truth and falsehood. For warrior or not, she knew Benaiah wished to wed her. He had said nothing, he had never so much as touched her hand—but she knew he desired her past reason, past sense. And vows or not, such strong desire tempted her.

But I will not yield. Her virgin body might play traitor, but her will was still hers to command. A Moon Warrior did not marry, did not surrender herself to a man's dominion. But no law, no vow, forbade her to speak with Benaiah, or to walk with him, or to match her strength and skill against his in the training ring.

But no more than that. There must be no more than friendship between us. I must not let him ask for more. If the words were never spoken, there need be no refusal. And refuse she must. She had vowed her chastity to the goddess, and her fidelity to the Queen of Sheba. She could not add a third vow without breaking those two chains of honor that bound her.

So Benaiah must never be permitted to ask for what she must never grant. Must never say words Nikaulis knew a traitor's yearning to hear.

Benaiah

I should stay away from her. But when Benaiah saw Nikaulis walking towards him, moving with the easy grace of a hunting cat, he knew he could not. For once, his desire ruled his common sense and his iron will. And had her will not been as hard as his— *We would have already committed folly a dozen times over.*

Nikaulis stopped before him; her eyes were level with his. "You wished to see me. I am here."

"I am glad." Benaiah thought of saying more, but he was no David, to sing a woman's heart to honey. Or a Solomon, to win her mind with wise words and gentle wit. *I am only a plain warrior, and speak only plainly.*

But the lady of his heart did not seem to care, for that was how she herself spoke. *Neither of us spills easy words; what we say, we mean.*

"You smile," she said, and Benaiah answered, "I thought of what another man might say, facing a woman clad in leather and carrying a sword."

"I have heard what other men say of me. They undervalue their opponent, always a fool's error."

"That is truth. But no woman can stand against a man in battle," Benaiah said, and Nikaulis smiled, a warrior's smile.

"You think not?" Her chin lifted; the wide band of silver collaring her throat glinted bright as her proud eyes.

"I do not think, I know. Oh, I'll grant that a woman may fight well—I am not blind, I have seen you practice with your bow, and your sword. But against a man as skilled as you, your skill must yield to his greater strength."

"So you say strength must always defeat skill?" Nikaulis's eyes met his, clear and unflinching. "What will you wager on that, King's Commander?"

An odd sensation slashed through Benaiah, a traitorous desire to match swords with this warrior girl, to set his body against hers until one proved victor.

"Or are you afraid to challenge me, knowing I may best you?"

"I fear no challenge," Benaiah said. "As for the stakes"—words sprang from his lips before he could consider them, or call them back—"a kiss."

She stared at him; Benaiah stared back, refusing to surrender to his own warring emotions, or to alter his challenge.

"You do not speak. Do you fear you may have to pay the wager, Queen's Guard?"

Pride stiffened her back, as it had forced his words. "I fear no man. The wager stands."

They walked side by side to the practice yard Benaiah had long ago ordered built behind the weapons storehouse. The training ground was deserted at this hour, Benaiah's chief reason for choosing this time and place. Nikaulis looked, and nodded approval. Neither desired an audience.

In the center of the hard-packed earth, Benaiah stopped. "Do you wish to yield?"

"Before we have even drawn our swords? No. I fight fairly."

"Good. So do I. And I will make no allowances because you are a woman."

"Just as I will make no allowances because you are an old man." Nikaulis's eyes gleamed in the sunlight, and Benaiah smiled and drew his sword.

"Until you yield," he said, and Nikaulis laughed.

"Until you do," she said, and drew her own weapon.

And so they began.

Metal against metal; clash and retreat. Within the first half-dozen sword thrusts, Benaiah knew victory would not be won easily. That quick knowledge burned like hot wine; it had been long since he had faced an opponent whose skill so truly matched his own. Each thrust parried instantly, each clash of blade on blade caught and held. Nikaulis moved swiftly, leopard-lithe, serpent-supple. He himself moved more slowly, bull rather than leopard.

Swing, block; turn, thrust, and swing again. The sword-dance, always different, always the same. At first he thought his strength might outlast her swiftness. But as they fought on, blade to blade, Benaiah slowly began to understand that she would not falter.

She was good; as good as he.

Thrust and retreat; advance and swing, bracing against the crash of iron upon iron. And again, hard, neither fighter granting a breath's respite. Benaiah knew he would pay for this in aches and in raw pain—but payment would fall due later.

One last good fight, I and my true equal. How many men could claim that? What matter that his opponent, his peer in skill, was a woman? *Ah, if this could only last forever—*

But he was too experienced a soldier to think this contest could endure much longer.

Sweat glistened on his Sword Maid's face and arms; her breath came hard and fast. Benaiah knew she must be weak with weariness—as was he. But she would not yield. Nikaulis would fight on until her very bones trembled and her traitor body no longer obeyed her will.

As will I. Benaiah knew he could not surrender, not so long as he still breathed. But their battle must end, and soon, lest in their utter weariness, one should wound the other. . . .

Before him, Nikaulis half-turned, and swung her sword high. Benaiah began to lift his own sword to parry, then swept down just as Nikaulis shifted her sword's rising arc to a falling one. Their blades met in a clash of iron; held. Benaiah stared into Nikaulis's eyes. They glowed, battle-hot; she smiled, a feral flash of white teeth.

"Nikaulis." Benaiah struggled to keep his voice low, to speak softly though he longed to gasp for air. "Nikaulis, we must end this. Lay your sword aside."

"Never. I do not yield."

"I do not ask it. Nikaulis, neither of us can win this battle. Lay your sword aside, as I will mine."

For long heartbeats Benaiah feared she had not heard, or understood. Then the fierce gleam faded from her eyes.

"I will lay my sword aside," she said, "when you lower yours."

Strained with long tension, her muscles quivered; her blade shuddered against his, sending tremors up the battered iron. Benaiah could no longer tell whether the trembling he felt in the sword's hilt was from his exhausted muscles, or from hers.

"Together," he said. "We will lay them aside together."

She hesitated, and he added, "At your word, Warrior."

She nodded. "Now," she said, and Benaiah opened his fist and let his sword fall to the hot sand. Her sword fell across his, iron ringing against iron. They looked at each other across the blades.

"You did not win, King's Commander."

"Neither did you," Benaiah said.

To that, she said nothing. In silence, they went back to the arena gate; in silence, they wiped down their swords' blades with linen cloths. At last Nikaulis said, "Fair day, Benaiah," and walked away.

Benaiah watched her until she had turned onto the street that led back to the Little Palace gate. He looked back into the arena where they had fought. Their struggle had forced the pale sand into hollows and ridges; the surface was marred by imprints of their feet. *The sand must be raked smooth again.*

Benaiah sheathed his sword and went off to find a soldier with not enough to do; that careless unknown was about to learn that loitering earned extra duty. Good soldiers always looked busy.

Bilqis

"O Queen—" Khurrami slipped into the chamber in which Bilqis sat dictating messages to send home to Sheba; Khurrami let the gilded leather fall closed behind her. "O Queen, some of the king's women have come to speak with you. Will you see them, Sun of our Days?"

Bilqis stopped, and she and the scribe both stared at Khurrami. "The king's women have come *here?*" That could mean only trouble. "Who has come?"

"Queen Melasadne—she has brought only one dog, which she carries in her shawl as if it were a babe—and Lady Gilade. And Queen Ulbanu and Lady Dvorah have come also. And the Lady Leeorenda."

An embassy from the queens' palace, in fact. Bilqis lifted two fingers, indicating to the scribe that she might go. "I will see them. Escort them to the garden—and have strong wine brought."

"As the queen orders, so it shall be." Khurrami eyed her swiftly. "Before she sees these women, will the queen garb herself more—"

"Royally? You begin to sound like Irsiya. No, plainly the matter is urgent or they would not have come at all. I will see them as I am." As she walked through the Little Palace to the old garden, she tried to deduce what could have brought half-a-dozen of King Solomon's wives to beg audience of their greatest rival. *Something dire, of course, to bring out so placid a lady as Leeorenda. But the Egyptian and the Cushite have not come.* Doubtless Pharaoh's Daughter ignored whatever unpleasantness occurred, while Makeda— *No one with even half a wit would cross the serpent's bride.*

Nor had Naamah come, nor the Colchian, Solomon's newest-wed queen. *So, the battle lines are drawn. And I—I am to act as peacemaker between their warring factions and the king.*

By the time she walked into the garden, the rich wine she had ordered was being carried in; she smiled upon her unexpected guests. "I am honored. Please, take wine, and tell me how I may serve you."

And let us pretend we are all equals and dear sisters here. Bilqis allowed a slave to hand her a filled wine bowl; she lifted the bowl to her lips as if she drank. Encouraged, the others also took wine and drank, which would encourage them to speak freely. They had come to her in haste and distress; Lady Gilade's hair hung down her back in unbound braids, while Ulbanu's feet were bare. Tear-borne kohl smeared Melasadne's cheeks, and the shawl in which she clutched one of her tiny dogs was torn. The puppy itself peered out of the folds like a soft pearl, eyes and nose shining like polished jet.

"Drink," Bilqis said again, and once more feigned sipping her own wine. Then she set the bowl aside and smiled; she moved forward and tickled the puppy's chin and let it lick her fingers, took each woman's hands and kissed her upon the cheek. "Now, sisters, tell me what troubles you, and how I may ease your hearts."

All the women looked at Melasadne, who caught back a sob and then spread the tale before Bilqis. "It all started when Pirip ran off after Prince Caleb—Lady Dvorah's boy—he is a fine boy, too, good with the dogs—"

Long years as queen and judge had trained Bilqis to extract a story smoothly; she understood what had happened even as she uttered soft queries and words of encouragement. Prince Caleb and the puppy had run off to play, and encountered Prince Rehoboam; Rehoboam had snatched up the pup and decided to present it to Queen Dacxuri. "She worships a god who demands dogs each dark moon!"

Of course Prince Caleb had fled back to his mother, who had hastened to Melasadne, who had braved Dacxuri's courtyard to snatch back Pirip from the Colchian's hands. The ensuing quarrel set Melasadne and her friends against the crown prince's mother and her allies, and swiftly grew so bitter that no one within the queens' palace could stop a battle that promised only to worsen. "And no one can force peace. If only Queen Michal still lived!"

From what I have heard, Queen Michal would have sewn you all into sacks and flung you from Jerusalem's walls rather than permit you to trouble Solomon! The thought brought a grim smile. But Bilqis said only "This is very bad, sisters. What would you have me do?" The women all smiled, relieved to have someone take command. Queen Melasadne cuddled the bright-eyed puppy to her breast and said, "Speak to the king. His heart loves peace above all things; he will put a stop to this."

And how will he do that, sister? Bilqis did not speak the words; instead, she nodded and promised to do what she could, a vow that sent Queen Melasadne and Lady Gilade away smiling. Bilqis sighed. A stranger's meddling often brewed more strife than it quenched. But she had given her word; she would speak with King Solomon, and hope what she had to say did not grieve him too deeply.

———

She told the story as gently as she could, but there was no way to sweeten what she must say. And as she had feared, Solomon heaped the blame not upon Rehoboam, or upon the Colchian princess, or upon any of the women who had no better sense than to pour oil upon a hearth-fire until it blazed up as a holocaust, but upon his own head.

"Somehow I have failed them, Bilqis. Truly, I do not know what is wrong—I treat each woman fairly, favoring no one more than another. I treat all my sons equally. Why then is my house no more peaceful than was my father's?"

"Oh, Solomon, my dear—" The word *boy* trembled on her lips; she ate it back, not wishing to remind him how young he was in her eyes.

"Bilqis, you are a woman, and a queen; enlighten me. Wherein do I err? Do I not deal with my household justly?"

"I would say that I am a queen, and a woman." She stroked his arm, caressing away the tension beneath his skin. "As for where you err—perhaps you treat them too justly."

"Another riddle, O Queen of the Morning Land?"

"No, or Solomon the Wise surely would know its answer."

"Perhaps King Solomon is not so wise as his reputation boasts." Solomon set his hand over hers; her skin was cool as morning. "How is it possible to deal too justly?"

She smiled. "My impartial love, my wise king, you have left them nothing to strive for. Or, rather, you have laid before them a prize none can win."

"And what is that?"

"The king's favor."

"I will not exalt one and diminish the rest."

"Once you honored a woman above all others."

"That was long years ago; I was younger then."

"And in love."

"Yes. I was in love." *Abishag*, he thought, and tried to summon her face. Vainly; Solomon closed his eyes, and rested his cheek upon Bilqis's hair. Cinnamon scented her sleek tresses. Cinnamon, and roses.

The scent brought memories rushing like spring floodwater. Abishag waiting for him in the garden, sweet honey in sunlight. Abishag risking all to warn him when his faithless brother Adonijah usurped the crown. Abishag standing upon the king's balcony on their wedding night, clad only in starlight and her unbound hair. Abishag glowing like a golden pomegranate as her body at last nourished their child, the child that would kill her. . . .

Abishag.

"You see?" Sheba's voice was soft as night wind in his ear. "They struggle against a ghost, Solomon. And the dead always win."

Abishag

So I sat quiet beside a dying king and listened and learned. Listened as Prince Adonijah begged his father name him heir—"I am the eldest prince now; my mother was a king's daughter! Who better, Father?"—and as King David smiled and uttered vague soothing words that sounded like promises yet meant nothing.

I looked on as the high priest Abiathar pressed Prince Adonijah's cause, and the dying king swore all would be as Yahweh wished—which Abiathar was canny enough to know for no promise at all.

And I learned as I watched the king's general, Joab, sit by his uncle's bedside and speak plainly. "You should have chosen before, David. Now it is too late; others will choose for you." So Joab said, and to my surprise the dying king laughed, a low harsh sound cut off as he struggled to draw breath.

"Will they, Joab? We shall see. I am not dead yet."

"You will be soon," said Joab.

"Soon," King David said. "But not yet."

Joab shrugged and went away again, but not before I had raised my eyes and found myself looking into his. Joab's eyes shone hard as iron blades; blades that guarded his thoughts, shielded long years of memory. I do not know what he saw in mine.

"You tend the king well," he said, and I lowered my lashes, veiling my eyes, and murmured that I did my best.

King David laughed again, softly. "Is Abishag not a treasure, Joab? A gift from my beloved queen, a gift chosen by my son Solomon."

I sensed the edge of Joab's gaze upon me; I kept my head bowed. But Joab said only "A wise choice. Wiser than your son Adonijah's" before he went away again.

And after Joab had gone, King David beckoned to me; when I leaned close to him, he caught my hand in his. Dying he might be, but his thin old hand still grasped hard. "Yes, a treasure, a wise choice. I have looked into eyes like yours before, just as you will look into eyes like mine again. We know each other well, you and I."

"As the king says," I murmured; I knew better than to dispute with him. At my soft words, he smiled, his eyes fire-bright. "I have a gift for you, queen's gift, so that you too may see what dwells in a queen's eyes."

He pressed something flat and hard into my palm, closed my fingers over cool metal. "Look," he said, and I opened my hand and stared down into a shining silver circle.

Down into my own mirrored eyes.

Bilqis

But a few days later, Bilqis thought she had been wrong; perhaps, for once, the living heart had triumphed. The day dawned fair, and when the palace settled quiet at noonday, Solomon came to her, eager for once as if he were a boy still.

"A fine day," she said, gauging his mood and matching it. "Since I came to this land, I have not seen so blue a sky."

"Yes." His eyes glowed, as if lit by fire. "A day for—"

"A king and a queen?" she asked, playful; testing.

"A day for lovers." He smiled, apparently heedless of the fact that once again he had been tested. "A day for Solomon and Bilqis."

Tested, and had not been found wanting. Still, she remained wary; the man seemed too perfect, as if he were more than human.

Or less. But he stood waiting before her, his hands held out for hers in patient supplication. And suddenly she was sick of wariness and of prudence, of weighing each word before she spoke it. Sick of constant quiet battle. *I spend all my days and all my nights tending others' lives, thinking of their good, creating their happiness. But for today—*

"Will Bilqis come?" Solomon asked, as if sensing her need of aid in crossing the last barrier, and reckless elation transmuted the blood flowing smoothly through her veins to hot pounding wine.

For today, the Queen of the Morning unlocks Bilqis's chains. For today, the queen sets the woman free.

Slowly, she lifted her hands and laid them in his; his fingers closed about hers in silent caress. "Yes, Solomon. For today, Bilqis will come."

She had no idea what Solomon planned—and neither did he. Or so he said; she doubted that, for even a king's impulsive acts must be ordered, devised with care. *But I will not spoil this day with questions. Today is not a test of his wisdom and my cunning.*

Today was freedom. So she merely smiled, and followed where he led her.

Once again, Solomon surprised her; expecting him to carry her to some secluded spot beyond Jerusalem's heavy walls, she found herself instead following him through narrow corridors to a tower with a stairway curved about it.

"Up here," he said, and led her up the narrow stairs.

At the top they stepped forward into a blaze of pale pure light, and she stopped, dazzled by what lay before her.

Surely we are atop the world! But after a moment, she realized they merely stood atop the king's palace, upon its highest roof. From this coign of vantage, all Jerusalem seemed spread before them, a golden haze dreaming under the summer sun. Beyond the city walls lay valleys silvered by rows of olive trees, beyond them mountains rising to the north and to the east. To the west, the land sloped green and golden down towards the restless sea. And to the south—to the south Sheba lay waiting.

But I am no goddess, to see beyond the world's rim—nor am I a queen to trouble myself over a land beyond my eyes. Not today. For today—

"Beautiful, is it not?" Solomon released her hand and slid his arm about her waist, as easily as if they were in truth free young lovers.

"Yes." She turned into his arms, setting her back to the south, and her duties there. "Once again you have surprised me, Solomon; surely an ardent lover takes his beloved into the secret hills for a tryst such as this?"

"Trust me, the hills have no secrets—not for us. If I so much as ask for my horses to be harnessed, half the palace will know where I go and why, and the other half will know before I pick up the reins. And if I go abroad with a beautiful woman—" He laughed and lifted his free hand to her cheek. "We might as well be an army with banners!"

"So you brought me here." Now she saw how well-appointed this rooftop was; a pavilion shaded half the roof; beneath the pavilion's stripes of purple and gold, carpets woven to resemble desert gardens blanketed the hard stone. Cushions lay piled upon the rugs, promising even more comfort when the time was ripe. A table set with wine and fruits, bread and cheese; flowers in bright-painted pots— *Truly he has labored long to create this garden for us. How does he keep this secret?*

"So I brought you here," he agreed. "As any man might bring his beloved to the housetop."

"And as any might come with her beloved. I am my beloved's and he mine—for this span of time. So many love you, king of my heart."

He smiled; she had not thought he could look so world-weary. "Oh, I am loved, Bilqis—but dutifully. I am loved because I am a just man, and a gentle king, and because I do not trouble the people with things they do not wish to understand.

"But I am not well-loved. Not as they loved my father David, no matter what sins he committed, no matter what burdens he laid upon their backs. Him they loved for no reason other than that they loved him."

She slid her fingers through his. "Forget the people, Solomon; their love is not important. Their welfare, their happiness, their safety—those you give them freely, because you are their king, regent for their god upon this earth."

"Yes. But it would be pleasant to be well-loved, despite my faults."

"Or because of them?"

"That, too."

She laughed, trying to entice him back to sweetness. "Then you are lost, for you have no flaws, my dearest love."

"Then I wish I possessed one."

"I am wrong; you do own a fault."

"And what is that?"

"You are too gloomy, my heart. Come to me; forget your ungrateful subjects for an hour."

"They are grateful enough; they give me all their obedience and respect."

"And their daughters, too, when you will have them. You are too moderate, Solomon—a lesser monarch would have a harem of a thousand beauties to cheer his nights."

"Moderation—is that a fault?" He shrugged. "Perhaps it is. I am moderate, and tolerant, and am called Solomon the Wise. Solomon the Just." His eyes studied the city below them. "But this city—this they still call the City of David."

"That will change—"

He shook his head and turned from the city below. "No, it will not. A thousand years from now, they will still call this King David's City."

There was a dull weariness in his voice that chilled her; as if he had abandoned a long-held hope. She did not wait for him to embrace her, but gathered him in her arms as if he were a hurt child.

"Never mind, my love," she whispered in his ear. "Never mind that. I tell you that a thousand years from now King David will be remembered only as the father of Solomon the Wise."

Solomon pulled back and took her face between his hands. "Beloved, your wisdom is as strong wine—and you lie like a queen." Before she could deny this, he bent and kissed her. "And your kisses are honey on the tongue. Come to me, my fair one, my only beloved—"

"Only? How many have climbed those tower stairs with you? I ask as any woman might ask her beloved, whose housetop seems so well-prepared."

"How many do you think?"

"I think—only one other." For a heartbeat she thought she had erred. *Free or not, I should have weighed my words thrice over before reminding him of his lost love!*

But he did not cool, or withdraw. Instead, his eyes softened, glinted crystal-bright. "Only one other, and since her, no one." His hand slid into the soft coils of her hair. "Until you, no one." His fingers sought and found the first of the jeweled ivory pins that bound up her heavy hair.

He drew the pin free so gently she knew it was gone only when she heard the gem-studded ivory chime against the hot smooth stones beneath her feet. "No one at all."

Solomon

Long after the queen had drawn her garments over her body once more— she had permitted him to clasp the jasper brooches upon the shoulders of her gown, to slip the jeweled pins back into the coils of her soft hair—long after she had gone, leaving behind her only the faint perfume of roses and cinnamon, Solomon remained in the rooftop sanctuary he had long ago devised. Here he could rest untroubled. Here he could embrace his beloved.

Here he owned solitude and peace.

Of course the peace was false, the solitude illusion; kings possessed all a man could desire—save privacy. But this retreat gave at least the illusion of that humble luxury.

And he had labored hard to achieve even that. True, his servant Tobiah had aided him; it would have been difficult—nay, impossible—for Solomon to acquire all he needed, and to carry it to the rooftop alone. But Tobiah would never betray the secret retreat; Solomon had no fear of that. And it would be the worst sort of arrogant folly to truly disappear, for not even one man to know where the king might be found at need.

But all else Solomon had done for himself.

No hands other than his had arranged the cushions that awaited them. Just as no servant had carried the fruit and the wine, or spread them out upon the low mosaic table.

The flowers pleased him the most, for they had cost him the greatest skill and effort. Scattered about the rooftop were bright-painted clay pots in which grew iris and hyacinths, roses and lilies; sweet strong perfume drifted upon the heated air. A small garden, but Solomon's own.

And to think I re-created this sanctuary only now, returned only now to this peace. Only because I wished a private tryst with my beloved queen. . . .

Another gift for which he must thank Bilqis. For here, in the aerie devised for a lovers' meeting, Solomon could rest, knowing he would not be interrupted for the minor, the trivial. Only urgent need would bring Tobiah up the winding narrow stairs to the king's secret garden.

Here I may do as I please, without wondering if it is wise, or just, or prudent. Smiling, Solomon tore the round of bread into small bits and flung them out across the sun-hot stones. The sparrows descended promptly, grabbing and squabbling over the king's bounty.

So like my courtiers—save that the birds are more honest. Were men honest, before they set a king above them to bear their burdens and their sins upon his shoulders?

Perhaps it had been better a hundred years past, better when there had been no rich empire, no kingdom. When there had been no king in Israel or in Judah; no court, no subjects, no government. Only a proud, spare people holding themselves aloof from those about them, dwelling as farmers and shepherds and merchants.

No City of David. No Temple.

Such great change; such swift change. Within the space of a single long lifetime the very land upon which men walked had altered beyond recognition.

When Queen Michal was a girl, only judges ruled our land, laid down what law there was. It was still said, of that wild time, that then each man had done what was good in his own eyes. *And that road leads to chaos.* But Michal had lived to

see her father rule those proud, wild men as their first king, and her husband as their second, and had herself raised their third. Now Solomon
ruled not only over Israel and Judah but over Edom and Moab, and half-a-
dozen kingdoms beyond. And his influence swayed royal decisions from
Egypt to Tyre and Babylon.

*Saul ruled one kingdom, and David two. I rule an empire. I wonder what my son will
rule over in his turn?*

The silent question shadowed the day; even a father's eye could not find
a true king in Rehoboam. But the boy was young yet— *I must give him time.
Time and training.*

*But I will not think of that, not here, not this hour. I will not think of the future, or of
the past, or of anything but now. Now, when I once again can lie within this garden, and
look into a woman's eyes, and see love shining there.*

The sky shone blue as a faience bowl above his head; all about him rose
the perfume of the flowers he had brought here. The tower's height muted
all sounds, and beyond the walls he could gaze into the uttermost distance, to the silver haze that veiled the world's end. Beauty, and silence,
and for once, peace. Gifts given, all unwitting, by Bilqis, and her loving
heart.

Even without her, all this gives pleasure. And with her here— Ah, then this rooftop
garden was paradise.

Abishag

*Yes, Solomon's choice proved wiser than Adonijah's. Thinking his father already within the
gates of death, Adonijah chose to hold a great banquet, asking all the princes and all the great
men of the court—all save Solomon and those who favored him. And somehow Adonijah had
persuaded the high priest Abiathar to anoint him as king.*

*Joab sat at Prince Adonijah's table as well. When I told my news to Queen Michal, I
thought Joab's action would be the stone that hit hardest. Instead, her eyes glinted; a smile
shadowed her face. Then she kissed me and bade me return to King David's side. There I sat
beside King David's bed as if I never had left my post until Queen Michal herself came and
sent me away.*

*Sitting silent through the long afternoon, pretending I knew nothing—I was glad, then, to
take up a spindle, and busy myself turning thread. Queen Michal was right.*

*Spinning calmed the hands, and soothed the mind. When all one could do was wait, that
was indeed a blessing.*

Bilqis

Their trysts in the tower garden took place by day, during times when each might be assumed by those who sought them to be somewhere else, somewhere chaste and prudent. But today she had received a silent message from Solomon, a gift of a pearl pure and perfect as the full moon folded in a black cloth sewn with spangles of silver. And she had known that for once—perhaps for the only time—they were to share the paradise of night.

This time, when he climbed the stairs to the tower garden, it was she who awaited him. During the long afternoon, she had bathed in water scented with oil of roses; her handmaidens had smoothed ointment perfumed with her own scent of frankincense and amber into her skin and drawn sandalwood combs through her hair until the fragrance clung to the long gleaming strands.

But to Irsiya's pleas to paint her eyes with malachite and with kohl, to redden her lips, Bilqis shook her head. She merely had Khurrami stroke her throat and the palms of her hands with Abishag's perfume of roses and cinnamon, touch the scent to her breasts and knees and belly.

Nor would she accept any of the massy gold ornaments Irsiya urged upon her, the rich gems Khurrami wished to twine through her hair. And when Irsiya and Khurrami protested, she said only "No. Tonight Solomon sees the woman who loves him—not the Queen from the South."

That silenced them. She stood quiet as Irsiya knelt and wound thin chains hung with golden bells about her ankles, as Khurrami draped a cloak of black linen over her. When they were done, they gazed upon her as proudly as if she were a bride and they her doting grandmothers; their eyes glistened bright with unshed tears.

She drew them to her and kissed first Irsiya and then Khurrami in silent thanks. Khurrami pinned the embroidered veil to the cloak, hiding her face; Irsiya held the heelless slippers for her to step into. And then she moved silent from her rooms, from the Little Palace, through the maze of corridors and courtyards to the king's tower. Cloak and veil concealed her; she moved through the night palace as if she had become a shadow, or a ghost.

When she had climbed the stairs and reached their garden, she unpinned the veil and let it fall from her face, let the cloak slip away. Clad only in the night air, she savored the rising breeze upon her body. To the east, the moon rose full as the pearl Solomon had sent her; above, the stars blazed across the endless darkness. And below—

She walked slowly across the rooftop to the wall that shaped the limit of their solitude; the golden bells about her ankles chimed low and sweet as she moved through the cool air. Below, Jerusalem crouched like a great beast, tawny-dark; torches and hearth fires flared, wrathful eyes. *This land does not love me; I will be glad to abandon it to its anger. But I will miss its king—no, I will miss Solomon. My dearest love, and my last.*

She closed her eyes against pain; and when she opened them again, she turned. Solomon waited there, a shadow among shadows.

As the moon climbed high, they lay in each other's arms, warm against midnight's chill. She cradled him as if he were son as well as lover, and listened as he talked.

For tonight, as if sensing their time grew short, Solomon spoke of the deeds that had brought him here, to this night, and the circle of her arms. He spoke of his mother, and of the queen who had raised him up to be king. And he spoke of guilt, legacy of a child's grief.

"You know I should never have been king, Bilqis? I had a brother—a good man, a brave man. Even Queen Michal praised him, spoke of him with fondness. His name was Amnon, and he was King David's eldest son. Amnon was born to be king. And I had a sister, too. Tamar."

She had heard the tale of Amnon and Tamar as it now was told: rape and murder and war. "There was another brother," she said, as Solomon paused, remained silent so long she feared he would not go on.

"Yes," he said. "Absalom. Our father's favorite, the Lord alone knows why." He twined his fingers through hers, lifted her hand to his face; she knew he breathed in the scent of cinnamon and roses that clung to her love-warm skin. "Absalom and Tamar shared a mother, Maachah; Amnon was Ahinoam's son. And Amnon loved Tamar, and she him; they wished to wed."

"That would have been a good match." *Twice good; a brave prince to please those who swore only men counted in this changing world—and a royal daughter to carry the legacy of the mother, and the past.*

Solomon shrugged. "Perhaps. Queen Michal approved; she promised to speak to King David on their behalf, to urge his consent to their marriage. I loved Tamar and Amnon too. Amnon was always kind, and Tamar gave me a toy horse. Its mane and tail were scarlet wool. I do not know why I remember that."

"You remember because your sister gave the toy to you, and because you loved her." She stroked his arm; his muscles strained tense against his skin.

"But Absalom—Absalom hated Amnon, and Tamar too, when she chose Amnon for her lover. He slew them."

"Yes, my love, I know. The tale is no secret."

"It was not rape. That was Absalom's lie."

"Lies live long, Solomon. Truth—truth is a thing of the heart." She stroked his hair. "There is more; tell me."

He told the rest in slow hard words, as if he feared to utter them. "Queen Michal vowed to aid Amnon and Tamar when Absalom stood there too. He had struck Tamar, you see, and Amnon swore to beat him bloody. I listened as Queen Michal and my mother Bathsheba spoke of what had passed, and of how they favored Amnon and Tamar over Absalom, whom they loathed.

"Later that day I taunted Absalom, rejoicing that my brother Amnon and my sister Tamar would be king and queen, and Absalom less than nothing. Absalom told me our father David would never let them wed, and then—and then I said that they must wed, for they already lay together as if they were husband and wife. And that night Absalom went to Amnon's house and slew them both.

"My words sent him there. My words slew Amnon and Tamar. Amnon should be king today, not I—and Tamar—"

"Might have lain these twenty years dead of bearing her first babe." She stroked Solomon's hair, gently, as one comforting a hurt child. "My dear love, do you think their deaths lie at anyone's feet but Absalom's? Surely half Jerusalem knew Tamar went to her brother's house; do you think they all held their tongues? It takes but one unwary word from a servant to send news flying from one ear to the next. You take too much upon your shoulders, Solomon. Remember you are but a man."

"No, I am a king. And a king must not make such errors."

She laid her hand upon his cheek. "A king—or a queen—is greater than a man or a woman, and so makes greater errors. We do the best we can, my love. That is all anyone can do. That, and beg our gods for aid."

"Oh, I have done that too—and you see how well I am repaid for my efforts." He turned his head; her hand slid away from his cheek. "Ever since I was a small boy, I knew—I *knew*, Bilqis—that I would be king after David. I knew Queen Michal desired it, and she owned the strongest will I have ever known. She was stronger than King David, in the end, or I would not stand here now, bewailing my faults."

"What you call faults many would vaunt as virtues. You are just, and tolerant, and I do not think I have ever met anyone, woman or man, who cared more that he should do what is right." She sensed something still troubled him, something that had long gnawed at his heart—sensed, too, that tonight she could breach the last barrier between them.

She looked up at the night's brilliant sky, and for a moment longed to ask for Ilat's aid. Then, abashed, she thought, *Can you do nothing for yourself, Bilqis? You know your own heart, and what weighs heavy upon you as guardian of your own people. In this, you are Solomon's sister; you have suffered as he does. Tonight be clever— no, be loving—and truly know his heart at last.*

"You are silent, queen of my heart," he said, and she brought her gaze down from the crystal stars and looked into his eyes. He smiled, and brushed back her hair, unveiling her breasts to the night air. "What do you think of, Bilqis, when you gaze up at the stars over King David's City?"

Now, or never. "I think of you, Solomon. What is it that truly torments you? You are too wise to tear yourself over long-ago griefs for which you know you are not to blame. Tell me, my love. Tell me, and be free."

She lay in his arms and counted her heart's slow beat. When she had counted forty, Solomon spoke at last. "I will tell you, since you ask it, and then you will know what a fool I truly am. Would you know what grieves me? A dream, Bilqis. One I dreamed long years ago, when I was newly king."

And your Abishag still lived and life stretched before you like a carpet of gold. "A dream that still troubles you? Perhaps I can interpret it for you, my love. It is one of my duties as Mother of Sheba."

He smiled and touched a stray curl that spiraled down over her breast. "You seem to have many duties, Bilqis. Have you no pleasures?" Laughter rippled beneath his words; she answered in kind.

"With you, my love, duty is pleasure."

"So long as pleasure is not duty."

Her turn to laugh, to touch; she laid her fingertips on the soft skin beside his mouth. "Tell me your dream, Solomon. A queen commands it."

"And a king must obey?" Then he sobered and shifted away from her, stared off into the distant heavens. "It was a night like this one, Bilqis. Beautiful and black, but the moon new and the stars so bright they seemed ripe to fall from the sky and burn the world with their fire. Abishag and I came up here to sleep—to rest, to escape, for my father had died and I alone was king, and—"

He fell silent; she finished for him. "—and the crown weighed heavy and all men about you clamored for you to decide this and command that."

"And then wished to argue my decisions. Yes. So we climbed the tower steps, my wife and I, and I lay with my head in her lap, and for once we were alone and at peace."

As he spoke, she saw that night as clearly as if time fell away, releasing the past. Solomon, fretted by care and weary almost past sleep, unable to find ease; Abishag, looking not up at the stars in burning glory but down into her beloved's troubled eyes, her cool hands stroking his aching head. . . .

Bilqis reached out and gathered Solomon into her arms. *I will care for him, Abishag. I will do what I can. I swear it.* As she made her silent promise, Solomon settled into her embrace, rested his head upon her shoulder. "And you slept," she said, stroking his hair, "and you dreamed."

He hesitated, then seemed to shrug, as if what he would say mattered little. "Yes. The Lord came to me as I slept, and asked what gift He should bestow upon me. Riches, honor, long life, victory over my enemies; whatsoever I should ask. And of all things under heaven and upon the earth—of all things, I chose wisdom."

Again he paused, as if words for once came hard to his tongue. "The Lord proclaimed Himself pleased with me." Solomon stared up at the river of stars splashed across the midnight sky. "But sometimes I wonder, Bilqis—was it my god who so admired me? Or was it only my own pride?" He groped for her hand and laced his fingers through hers; his skin hot against her cool hand. "That is Solomon's dream. How do you interpret it? Am I indeed so wise? I thought so once. But there is one thing upon this earth a king cannot obtain, and that is a truthful judgment of his virtues—and his faults."

"Speak carefully, sister." Bilqis knew the silent voice was Abishag's; tonight her ghost sat beside them, longing to touch her beloved once more. "You

asked your god for wisdom? Do you remember the very words you spoke to Him?"

"As if I dreamed them an hour since. *Give me an understanding heart, Lord; let me judge aright between good and evil.*"

"And your god promised—?"

"He said He granted me *a wise and understanding heart.*"

"Your god did not lie to you, Solomon; such a heart you have. I have met no man so truly good as you." But there was more; she did not need the whisper of Abishag's ghost to tell her that. "How did your dream end, my love?"

For a long span of time he did not answer; she waited, patient, and counted stars. At last he said, "The Lord granted what I had asked of Him. And then He said that He would grant me also that which I had not asked, all a great king could desire in riches and glory and length of days. But as He spoke, He shone bright as polished silver, as a mirror before me. And it seemed to me that I looked upon—"

"Your god?"

"Myself." Solomon closed his eyes and leaned his head wearily against her breast. "Only myself, Bilqis."

And you think that means you dreamed a lie, that your god has deserted you. Ah, my love, how many times I have thought the same thing of my goddess, and never has it been true. She pressed her lips against his forehead, smoothed his night-cooled hair. "Then you have been greatly blessed, Solomon. Few are granted so clear a vision of their god's favor."

"How so?"

"At last, a riddle Solomon the Wise cannot answer." She allowed laughter to ripple beneath her words. "Then it is my turn to reveal truth to you, O great and wise King."

"And what is truth?"

"Why, that you need only yourself to fulfill all your desires. What could be plainer, what sign clearer to read?"

"Nearly anything," Solomon said with bitter humor.

"Now, did I not know I held King Solomon the Wise in my arms, I would think I embraced a fool." Smiling, she pushed him back and took his face between her scented hands; the perfume of cinnamon and roses coiled between them. "Tell me again what you asked of your god, my love."

"Wisdom, and the ability to judge rightly."

"A proper petition, from a new-made king; of course such words pleased your god greatly."

"What else should I ask? Did I not already possess gold and gems beyond counting?"

"You might have begged for great glory, or the death of your enemies. You might have entreated Him for a great name."

"To what end? Without the wisdom to govern well, to judge fairly, a king is no more than a fool—a fool who soon will forfeit whatever riches and glory he may possess."

His cheeks burned beneath her touch, as if her fingers drew fire upon his skin. "You might have asked for happiness, Solomon." She slid her fingers over the corners of his mouth, traced the curve of his lips. "You might have asked for love."

He sighed, and caught her hands in his. "A man must win his own glory, Bilqis, and create his own happiness. And as for love—I fear even the Lord cannot grant that."

She drew him back into her arms, and for a span of time they lay together in silence. Above them the stars blazed white fire; below the palace walls the sounds of night rose as whispers, ghost-song. At last she said, "And knowing all that you have told me, you still doubt your god's favor?"

"What favor? For all the Lord's promise, I have had to struggle to know good and to judge rightly, just as any man must."

"And that is what your dream meant, Solomon. When you looked upon your own image, it was your god's sign unto you—that you yourself already possessed that for which you had asked. You do not need to seek wisdom, for you possess that quality in abundance."

"And that is how you interpret my dream?" Solomon stared up into the eternal night sky. "That is kind of you, queen of my heart."

"It is not kindness, beloved, it is truth." She touched her fingertip to his forehead, to the spot between his brows that hid the third eye, the orb that saw beyond this world into past and future. "You see clearly; too clearly, perhaps. Solomon, my dearest love, do you truly think fools and knaves beg to be granted wisdom? For if you do, you are a greater fool than they!"

At last he smiled, turned for a time from his ghosts to her. "The greatest of kings is always the greatest of fools, Bilqis. And the greatest folly is to speak when it is better to be silent."

And knowing what he desired, she opened herself to him, set herself against the dream-fear which haunted his nights and shadowed his days. Silent, she strove against that demon; silent, she offered him the only shield against those doubts. *Here is love, Solomon. Take what love can give. And trust in yourself as your god so manifestly trusts you.*

And when I am gone, remember me in this garden. Let my ghost walk here with Abishag's. Let us both wait under the endless stars until you come to us at last.

Baalit Sings

Part of what followed began because I underestimated Rehoboam. Regarding him as dull-witted and stone-hearted, I did not realize how keenly jealousy bit him, how bitterly he craved what I possessed—our father's love.

That he begrudged me my intimacy with the Sheban queen as well I did not know. I never once thought of the queen and my brother in the same moment. The queen filled my mind and my heart; I thought of Rehoboam only when I must.

I always knew Rehoboam lacked wisdom, but even I did not think him fool enough to steal my horse—fool enough to think he, who thought force ruled all, could ride Uri, whose pride was as great as Rehoboam's, and whose heart was far greater.

Always I had obeyed my father's admonition to treat slaves and servants with as much courtesy as if they were my equals; at first I had done so because my father wished it, and I wished to please him. As I grew in understanding, I saw other reasons for treating menials with kindness. First I saw that servants wished to please more, that I was better served. Only later, as I reached womanhood, did my eyes open wide enough to see that, in treating others with respect, I ensured that I respected myself as well.

I wish now that I had been wise enough to apply this advice to my relationship with my brother Rehoboam. It might have helped. But I was still only a girl, no matter how well I thought of myself and of my wisdom. And Rehoboam—well, even as a man, Rehoboam remained a fool. Ask any of those who ever served him.

Nimrah and I were playing toss-bones with my brothers Mesach, Eliakim, and Jonathan; I had just thrown sevens—luckiest of all tosses—when Keshet came running into my garden. This alone made us all look and stare, for Keshet was always prim as a pigeon and neat as a cat; when we wished to tease her, we would pull her hair out of place or tug her shawl awry and watch her tidy herself back to perfection within moments.

"Princess, you must come at once," Keshet said, and I looked regretfully at my matched sevens. But I leapt to my feet, telling Jonathan he might play my throws for me, and went at once to Keshet.

"What is wrong?" I asked, and then all the blood seemed to drain from my body; I swayed. "My father? He is hurt?"

"No—oh, no." Keshet caught my arm. "It's Prince Rehoboam— Come with me." She led me to my courtyard gate, where a slave girl I did not know waited. "This is Miri," Keshet said. "Tell the princess what you told me."

Miri ducked her head, and although she mumbled, plainly shy at being in the queens' palace rather than the kitchens, she told her tale simply enough. "The boy Reuben who works in the stables told me to come tell you—tell the princess—that Prince Rehoboam's in the stables and has ordered the princess's horse made ready for him. Reuben says to tell you he's stalling, making him wait, but he can't do that forever, so you must come at once."

I am glad to remember that I thanked Miri before I fled off to the stables; later I gave her a present large enough to buy her a good husband when her seven years' servitude ended. I rewarded Reuben as well; his quick thinking saved us all from disaster. Had he been able to ride out upon my horse, I do not know whether Rehoboam would have ruined Uri's mouth and spirit, or Uri would have thrown and killed Rehoboam. But in either case, I would have lost Uri forever.

I reached the stables just as Rehoboam lost what little patience he possessed and began striking Reuben with his whip. To his endless credit, Reuben stood firm, accepting the blows as the price of time. Still, he was glad to see me; the moment he set eyes upon me, Reuben grabbed Rehoboam's whip, stopping my brother's effort to beat him into submission.

"Here is the princess, Prince Rehoboam. Ask her yourself."

Rehoboam spun around as if he suspected some trick; I summoned up enough breath to speak without gasping. "Brother," I said, "why are you beating Reuben? You know our father does not like—"

"*I* do not like rebellious servants! I am Crown Prince, and when I order a horse brought, it should be brought!" Rehoboam sounded as breathless as if he, not I, had just run half the length of the palace.

"Not," I said, "when it is not your horse." I see now that I should not have said that, should have pretended ignorance and granted Rehoboam a graceful escape. And that course would have kept him from knowing that the servants would do for me what they would not for him: a favor, with no thought of reward.

"I am Crown Prince—my wishes are commands. And you—you are—"

"Only a girl; I know. But girl or not, Uri is mine and mine alone, a gift from the Queen of Sheba, and I forbid you to lay your hands upon him."

"Forbid? *You* forbid *me*?"

"Yes, I do. And I forbid you to beat the servants. And if you won't obey me—because I am *only a girl*—then come with me to our father the king, and we will lay the matter before his judgment. And he will forbid you as I have just done and you know it, Rehoboam!"

We glared at each other, hot as fighting quail; Reuben later said that he thought we would snarl and leap at each other's throats like feuding dogs. Rehoboam was older and larger than I, but I would neither shift my gaze nor retreat so much as one step. I knew our father would back me up, and so did Rehoboam. That was the festering heart of his grievances, after all.

Rehoboam lifted his hand as if to strike me, then glanced at his fist, seeming to realize that he no longer held his whip. He rounded upon Reuben. "Give me that!" Rehoboam snatched back his whip; having ceded ground, he fell back on bluster, and on threats. Reuben was to be flogged and thrown out of the king's stables, Uri to be set to drawing a millstone—

"Like Samson? Go away, Rehoboam. Go away, and never come near my horse again or—"

"Or what? What can you possibly do? I am Crown Prince."

I looked into his handsome cruel face and knew he was right; he was the next king, and it would be hard to do anything to him. And then I knew what a girl could do; a soft young voice seemed to whisper to me, telling me what to say, giving a sure weapon into my hand. Words fell cold as stones from my lips, in a voice I hardly knew for my own.

"I can lie, Brother. I can rend my gown and loosen my hair, and I can go before our father and tell him that you tore my clothing. That you tried to force me to your bed. He would not forgive you that, Rehoboam."

He stood there bending the whip in his hands, glanced past me towards Uri's stall.

"Never touch my horse again. Never whip a servant again for doing his job well. Never make me tell that lie, Brother. Never. Now go away."

And to my relief, he did. Rehoboam stalked off, whip clenched so tightly in his hand that his knuckles paled to bone. When he was gone, the strength that had let me set myself against him flowed out of me like water; I staggered, and Reuben grasped my shoulders and pressed me against the wall.

"Don't sit down, Princess, your gown will be ruined. Stay here and I'll get water. Are you all right?"

I nodded. "Uri?" I asked, and Reuben smiled.

"Fine; the prince never got near him. Seth's bathing him down by the stable well. I had to do something to stretch the time until you came. Now wait here."

As he turned away, I caught his arm. "Rehoboam will not be pleased to be defeated—by a girl. If he tries to harm you, or Miri, you must send word to me at once."

"No fear, Princess. Now let me get you that water. Can't send you back to your handmaidens looking like half-cold death. That Lady Keshet's got a tongue on her sharper than yours."

Reuben went for water, and I leaned against the stable wall and closed my eyes, and thanked that soft sweet voice that had granted me the right words to stop Rehoboam. I tried to care where my brother had gone and who would pay for his anger now, but I found I could not.

For the moment, I was too weary to care—even about Rehoboam.

Naamah

When her son burst unannounced into her rooms, Naamah took one look at his face, fury-darkened, and set aside the perfume vial and ivory stick. "Leave us," she said to the three zealous handmaidens who had been aiding her as she painted her face and perfumed her body.

Paying as little attention to the handmaidens as if they had been graven images upon the wall, Rehoboam burst out, "I hate Baalit. I *hate* her. She gets all, and I nothing. It's not fair." Rehoboam flung himself down upon the carpet, and for a moment Naamah thought he would wave his fists and kick his feet in the air as he had done when, as an infant, he had been denied a sweetmeat. The image made her smile; she bent and stroked his hair.

"What is not fair, my son? Tell your mother—" She wished to add *And she will mend whatever mars your life.* But long years of prudence kept the words from passing her lips. She must find out what troubled her boy before making rash promises to him. She had always taken care never to lie to Rehoboam; as a result, she retained his trust. Naamah would not risk that for a light word.

Rehoboam merely pressed his lips together and shook his head. Silent, he began picking at the threads of her Damascus carpet. So, he must be coaxed, but that was not difficult. Rehoboam's moods were volatile as air.

"Am I to guess your trouble, then? Very well, I shall indulge you. One of your brothers has taunted you? Or—let me see, you have lost a wager? No? Well, then—"

Rehoboam looked up, his eyes sullen with dark anger. "Oh, Mother, you know nothing! What should I care for the words of my brothers, or for a wager either? I am Crown Prince! They are just jealous, for they will be nothing when I am king!"

"So they will," she agreed, smiling. "You will be a great king, my darling boy."

"Greater than my father," Rehoboam said. "Greater than *his* father. Men will never forget *my* name!"

Naamah made a hasty vow to offer a perfect bull up to Milcom if her son's wild boasting would be pardoned. "Hush, my son; it is ill luck to tempt the gods."

"Oh, you will make it right with them." Rehoboam spoke carelessly but with absolute confidence; his faith in her warmed Naamah's heart.

"Whatever I can do for you, you know I will do it." Smiling, she stroked his hair again, and Rehoboam leaned his cheek against her knee. "Now, tell me why you came. Tell me how I may help you, my dearest boy."

Now that he had been cajoled into a better humor, Rehoboam was willing to spread his grievance before her. "Unless you can bewitch my sister, I do not know what you can do. Always my father takes her part. It is not fair; I am the next king, and she is only a girl!"

Ah, it was only Rehoboam's constant complaint—a pity she dared not poison Baalit. But that course was too great a risk, and there was no real need to take it. "My son, Baalit is only a girl, as you say. Soon she will marry and travel to a far country, and you need never again be troubled with her."

"No, she won't. My father plans to wed her here. Here, in Jerusalem. She will be always in the palace, taking the place in my father's heart that should be mine."

"That is foolish, Rehoboam—it is your sore pride speaking." Princesses were valuable only as playing-pieces in the games of kings. Princesses married for reasons of policy; even Solomon would not waste his only daughter on a nobody in his own court! Where was the advantage in that?

Rehoboam lifted his head from her knee and glared up at her. "Don't call me foolish—you are only a woman!"

For a heartbeat Naamah's blood chilled; she must not lose Rehoboam! *Nor must I let him see my fear.* She stiffened her back and regarded him coolly. "I am your mother, Rehoboam. Do not speak to me like that. Perhaps you should come back later, when you can control your temper."

His face softened, and a hint of fear shadowed his eyes. "No. No, Mother, I am sorry. It is just—"

"That you are unhappy." Naamah opened her arms, and Rehoboam flung himself into her embrace. She rocked him against her as if he were still a small boy instead of nearly grown. *Can what he says be true? Is Solomon planning to keep his daughter by him always? Then—*

Suddenly the answer to her son's troubles shone before her, clear and bright. She smiled, and whispered in Rehoboam's ear, "Do not worry, my son. Remember, your mother works always for your good. Now, will you promise to be an obedient son, and do exactly as your mother bids you?"

Rehoboam sat back and regarded her suspiciously. "What are you planning, Mother?"

"Something that will make you happy, my son. That is all you need to know." She laid her hand on his cheek. "Now, promise you will do as I say, when I say it, and you will become your father's favorite."

"Truly? He will love me best?"

"Yes." Naamah forced herself to speak with confidence; nothing less would serve her son's needs.

"Better than he loves my sister?"

Warmed by the future she saw unfolding at her command, Naamah smiled. "He will love you at least as well, my son." She bent and kissed his forehead. "Now go and amuse yourself into a better mood. You must be all smiles when next King Solomon lays eyes upon you."

Unsatisfied but obedient, Rehoboam went away, slinking off like a sullen panther. But for once she was content to let him go in uncertainty. He had trusted her to solve all the problems of his youth. Now Rehoboam must learn to rely upon her in greater matters. Her own future hung in the balance.

For when Rehoboam was king, she would be queen mother. At last she would be the most important woman in a king's life.

For a man might have as many wives as there were stars in the sky—but even a king could have only one mother.

Solomon

When told his wife Naamah craved audience with him, Solomon sighed inwardly, for he had planned to spend the afternoon with Bilqis. But he smiled, and bid his servant let Queen Naamah enter. Naamah was his wife and entitled to his respect—and his time.

And it was easy to smile as she walked through the doorway and approached him, for Naamah was very beautiful, and plainly had prepared herself with great care for this encounter. Always exquisitely garbed, today she seemed even more flawless than usual.

Solomon held out his hand to welcome her. "You are truly lovely, Naamah; a work of art." That compliment brought a faint flush of satisfaction to her cheeks; Solomon strove to praise each of his wives for what she most valued in herself.

"If I please my lord the king, then I am pleased." Naamah bowed, graceful as grass swaying in the wind. "And if I please my lord, may I speak?"

I knew she wished some favor; I wonder if I can guess it? Smiling, Solomon gestured to the stool beside his chair. "Do I not always listen? Speak as pleases you, Naamah."

He watched, admiring, as she settled upon the stool and arranged her skirts in elegant folds. Then she looked up at him through her thick dark lashes; for an instant Solomon remembered his first sight of her upon their wedding day, when she had looked at him with just such an intent, seeking gaze. Even as a young bride, Naamah had been perfection, flawless, adroit in all a woman's arts. . . .

Yes, and she meant to raise that memory. So, whatever Naamah's request, she thought it of great import, worth the use of all her skills. *Well, I will not keep her waiting; let us see what she desires so greatly.*

"We have been too long wed to need tricks between us." Solomon made his voice light, lest Naamah think him angered, or herself too blatant. "So do not hesitate to speak plain words; if I can grant your request, I will do so."

Her lashes swept down, veiling her eyes for a moment. Then she looked up again and smiled. "Thank you, my lord; you are always so kind! But I come seeking favors not for myself but for another—or say, rather, for two others."

"That is kind of you. But am I so terrible that you, a queen, must act as envoy? Who so fears to approach me?"

Naamah laughed softly. "I come not as envoy, my lord, but as a mother on behalf of her son."

What has Rehoboam done now? Solomon sighed. "Speak as a mother then; I listen."

She glanced at him again, as if uncertain how to begin, then said, "I will not weigh my words, but say only what is in my heart. My lord, it does not seem so long ago that we two shared our first night together—but it is many years, and now our son nears manhood. He would marry, and I have come to you, his father, to speak on his behalf."

This was unexpected; Solomon regarded her with more interest. "Rehoboam wishes to wed? Well, that is good hearing; perhaps the boy begins to steady."

"There is nothing like marriage to settle a young man," Naamah agreed, smiling.

"Has he chosen a bride?" Hard though it was to think of Rehoboam as anything but a heedless boy, Solomon knew years slid by too easily. Certainly Rehoboam was old enough to think of love— *But doubtless it is Naamah who thinks of his marriage!* Well, she was a woman; it was only natural she should wish to see her son well wed. Solomon smiled. "Or shall I say, has Naamah chosen a daughter-in-law?"

"Yes," she said, and turned a broad gold bangle about her wrist; green fire glinted from emeralds upon her fingers. "And I think my lord will find our choice good, when he has heard my words. But surely my lord's wisdom has already named the bride?"

"Surely my wisdom has not," Solomon replied. "Come, we need not play games. Who is the girl?"

The bangle stilled. Naamah regarded him guilelessly. "It is Princess Baalit. No, my lord, do not speak until I have done; you swore to hear me out."

Baalit? His own sister— Even as he shrank from the image, a memory from long years past rose to taunt him. His sister Tamar, his brother Amnon. Lovers in a garden. Lovers slain by yet another brother using the name of Law to cloak ambition.

And a voice whispering from that dead past that the king would smile upon their marriage, for they shared only a father. . . .

"Can this be true? Does Rehoboam so look upon his sister?"

"His half-sister," Naamah reminded him. "They never shared a womb, never suckled from the same breast. There is no bar between them. Only think, my lord king—is it not the perfect match? Your heir and your only daughter wed?"

Her words tempted, seduced; Solomon tried to weigh them without passion. *To have Baalit always here, to see her wed under my own roof, to see her children playing about me*—That was lure indeed. But was the lure a snare as well?

Knowing he must think carefully, Solomon said, "There is much in what you say, Naamah. But does the boy truly wish it? And my daughter? I had not thought they liked each other's company overmuch."

"Children's quarrels," Naamah said, smiling. "But they are children no longer. Their hearts have changed."

"Truly?" Had Rehoboam and Baalit learned to love one another, as had Amnon and Tamar? *If they have*— If they had, he would find it hard to deny them. *And it would so ease my heart to have Abishag's daughter with me always*— "Can this be true?"

Naamah smiled and patted his hand, a maternal gesture that seemed for once unpracticed. "My dear husband, a mother knows these things—and while I do not know the Princess Baalit's heart, I have seen how she looks at my son. They are both hot-eyed for each other, my lord king."

Solomon sat quietly, but his thoughts were jumbled, unclear. "I will think upon your words," he said at last.

"That is all I ask," Naamah said. "That, and my son's happiness."

"That is all any of us ask," Solomon said. "Our children's happiness."

Naamah rose, and bowed again, and went away on quiet feet. Solomon sat and watched her go. She was right; such a marriage would be ideal. In many kingdoms, such a marriage would be the custom.

Once before in this palace, a royal brother and sister had wished to wed—only to have their love sacrificed to another's ambition.

Amnon and Tamar were long dead; sometimes Solomon thought he alone remembered them at all. Amnon, the golden hero who had tossed him high up into the air, never failing to catch him securely as he fell. Tamar, the fire-haired girl who fed him sweet cakes, who smelled of roses and sunlight, and who once had given him a painted toy horse. . . .

I will not have that past repeat itself. Rehoboam and Baalit— *If they truly wish to wed, I will grant it. I will not drive true lovers to despair and death.*

And perhaps their wedding would do honor to Solomon's brother and sister, redeem at last Amnon and Tamar's doomed love.

Rehoboam

"Marry Baalit?" Rehoboam could not believe his mother serious. "She is my sister!"

"Half-sister," his mother corrected. "You share only a father; that is no impediment."

"And she's a prideful, willful bitch. I hate her!"

"That also is no impediment to a royal marriage." Now his mother smiled. "Remember, my son, that a man may do as he pleases with his own wife."

These words silenced Rehoboam as the truth of this flowed through his veins, heady as hot wine. A man's wife belonged to him; she was his possession just as was a horse or a lamb, his chattel. A wife owed her husband obedience. If Baalit were his wife, she would become his property, would have to do as he commanded.

My word would be her law. And if she disobeyed, I could beat her. Or have her beaten; that would be safer. . . .

"Yes, smile." His mother laid her hand on his cheek. "And remember to keep smiling, for we have not won the princess for you yet. You must convince your father that you yearn for her, that without her your life will be worth nothing to you."

The lovely vision of Baalit weeping at his feet faded. Rehoboam glared at his mother. "My father won't believe me. Baalit hates me as I hate her."

His mother laughed. "Oh, my dear boy, all girls treat their brothers so. Children's quarrels, soon forgotten." She put her arms around Rehoboam and stroked his hair. "But you must put such childish things behind you now, my son. You must win Baalit's heart—"

"She hasn't got one," Rehoboam muttered, and his mother tugged sharply on his hair, forcing him to look at her.

"You must *listen* to me, Rehoboam. Listen, and obey, unless you wish to chance losing all. You wish to be king, do you not?"

"I *will* be king. My father has said so."

"Your father is not yet dead, and you are not yet king. Suppose he changes his mind? Suppose another gains his favor? He is king and may do as pleases him."

Not be king? A chill slid over Rehoboam's skin. *My father might change his mind, might name another son in my place, and I would have nothing—*

"You had not thought of that, had you?" His mother folded him into her embrace; Rehoboam clung to her. "Never mind, my son; I thought of it long ago, and have never ceased to seek a way to ensure King Solomon keeps his word to you. And now I have found it."

Rehoboam rested his cheek on his mother's shoulder; the sweet scent of chypre rose from her skin. *My mother loves me above all things; I can trust her.*

She stroked his hair again. "Now listen, my son. You must marry your half-sister Baalit. Once she is your wife, your place as King Solomon's heir will be carved in stone. We all know he favors her beyond reason; when you wed her, you will become Solomon's favorite son."

Rehoboam saw no flaw in her logic—but he also saw no clear path to the shining prize his mother dangled before him. "Baalit won't marry me," he said. "I told you, she hates me."

"Then you must make her love you. For Solomon dreads losing the girl; he will grasp at the chance to keep her close, and what could be closer than wedding her to the next king? Oh, yes, Solomon's consent will be easy to obtain—" Here his mother put her hands on his shoulders and pushed him back so that she might gaze into his eyes. "But Rehoboam, he will not consent if Baalit speaks against you, if she refuses. So you must woo Baalit, persuade her to look upon you with favor."

"And how am I to do that?" Rehoboam demanded.

"By keeping your promise to do what I say, when I say it. And you may start by speaking fair words to your sister, and showing her a kind, smiling face. Remember, she is only a girl. You are the next king, Rehoboam. What girl does not dream of a crown?"

Which all sounded very fine, but Rehoboam was less certain than his mother that Baalit could be so easily led. "But suppose she won't listen to me? How will you make her obey you?"

"I do not need to make Baalit obey me; she will obey her father. He does not wish to lose her, and so will be pleased to see her wed to you. But you must keep your temper, Rehoboam—and you must smile when you speak of this to your father. Your father likes to see his children smile."

Baalit Sings

To be summoned before my father was no new thing, but to see my brother Rehoboam there as well surprised me. I bowed before my father, and he bade me rise. I did so, slanting a glance at Rehoboam. My brother's face was sullen; he plainly knew no more than I why we had been summoned together. Hastily I searched my heart—no, I had committed no sin against Rehoboam of which he might truthfully complain.

"My children, I have called you before me to learn what is in your hearts." Our father smiled, all kindness. "Do not fear to answer truly."

I began to worry at that. I never yet had feared to speak truth to my father. What could he ask that I would not answer?

"Hard though it is for me to think it, you both are almost grown." He looked us over, as if seeing us for the first time, and sighed. "I do not know where the years have fled. You, my son, are almost a man. And you, my daughter, are almost a woman. There is a time for all things; a time to grow and a time to learn—and a time to love."

His eyes seemed to look past us, into some long-ago time we did not share. Neither Rehoboam nor I spoke, I from reluctance to banish that wistful pleasure from my father's eyes, and Rehoboam doubtless from boredom, for he had little patience with the dreams of others. I glanced at my brother; he hastily smiled, and I wondered what unpleasant scheme Rehoboam now cherished. *Whatever it is, I will not let him torment me—or Ishbaal or Abner, or Melasadne's dogs or Nefret's cats—*

"And a time to wed." My father's voice called my attention back to him; he smiled at me and took my hand. "My children, I am told you both now think of marriage." And as I stared at him, he reached out and clasped Rehoboam's hand as well. "So you must tell me, is this true? Do the two of you desire to be more to each other than sister and brother?"

Rehoboam gazed at our father earnestly. "Yes, just as my mother has told you."

"And you, Baalit?" my father said, and I found my voice again.

"Rehoboam? But he's my brother!"

"Half-brother!" Rehoboam corrected swiftly.

"Such unions are not unheard of," my father said. "So speak freely—is it true that you wish to marry—"

"Marry *Rehoboam*? I would rather die!"

Rehoboam's eyes told me that he, too, would rather I died—long after, I made that hour into a song that always drew laughter. But as I stood before my father and saw the happiness die from his face at my words, I could have wept. Almost I wished I had claimed Rehoboam as my dearest love—or at least had agreed I wished to become his wife.

My father released our hands. "I see I was mistaken. Never mind, my children."

"It was my mother's idea," Rehoboam said. "I told her it was stupid."

"That is no way to speak of your mother, Rehoboam. She wished only to see you well married. Now run along, both of you—and do not tease each other over this. It is forgotten."

Perhaps my father forgot it, but I could not—and neither could Rehoboam. We never had liked one another, but now he truly hated me and I—I had wit enough to fear him. Rehoboam was the sort to hide a scorpion in one's bedclothes; venomous.

When I left my father, I fled to the Little Palace; never once did it occur to me that I should not tell Queen Bilqis all that had passed. Nor did it seem odd to me that she saw me at once—she was as a mother to me now, and a mother's arms are always open to her daughter. She smiled and kissed my forehead, and said I looked troubled, and I poured out all that had happened that day. By the time I had finished, my whole body trembled as if I had just escaped great injury—which I suppose was true enough. I do not think I would have lived long, as King Rehoboam's wife.

"And then my father told us to run along—as if we were small children! To run along and forget. Does he truly think Rehoboam will forget?" And then, to my horror, I began to weep.

The queen closed her arms around me and rocked me against her breast. "No, but you may forget it, Baalit. Weep, and forget, and then listen to me, for there is something I must say to you. A question I must ask."

I dried my eyes, and then she sat me beside her and held both my hands in hers. I managed to smile and waited, curious, for her to begin. And for the first time since I had met her, I saw the Queen of Sheba hesitate, as if she were afraid to speak—or as if she were afraid of what might come after.

At last I said, "What is it? You know I will do anything you ask."

"Do not be so swift to make that vow, Baalit. Listen, and think—and only then answer." And then, speaking slowly, as if she found it hard to choose her words, she told me why she had truly come across the world to the court of King Solomon the Wise.

I heard how she had watched her sisters die, and her mother, and then her daughter and her daughter's daughter. "I alone remained—I alone, and too old to bear another daughter. I tried, I truly did."

And then, when she thought all lost, she had gone to Sheba's greatest Temple, and there received a promise. "A promise of an heir, of a daughter for Sheba. Of a queen from the north. A queen to sit upon the Sun Throne and tend the Morning Land when I am gone."

I stared at her, and all I could think to say was "So you did not come to bargain with my father over the spice routes?"

"Any of the officers of my court could have done that. I came north to claim a greater prize than trade agreements. I came for a queen. I came for you, Baalit."

Fire flowed through my blood; exultation soared through me until I felt as if I could spread wings and fly. *"You were born to be queen—"*

"So you truly meant it, when you said I was fit to be queen? To rule?"

"Yes, my daughter. I truly meant it. You are the queen our goddess Ilat promised us."

"And you did not think I would come with you? Of course I will!" To Sheba, to freedom. To a shining future—

The queen held up her hand. "Wait, Baalit; there is more. Do you think I have remained half a year in Jerusalem judging you? I knew you were ours the day I set eyes upon you, fire-child."

"Then why did you not ask me before?"

"Because I am not all-wise, Baalit, nor all-patient. I am not Ilat Herself, only Her Mirror on Earth. And so I erred." And then, very gently, she told me how she had asked my father to grant me to her—and he had refused.

"I will conceal nothing from you, Daughter; when he denied what I asked, I set myself to claim his heart so that I might then gain you as his gift. But—"

I smiled. "It is all right; I know. All Jerusalem knows. How could you not love him, or he you?"

She seemed to stare into a world I could not see. "How indeed? But once set that spindle whirling, and only the gods themselves can spin its thread smooth and true. And now—"

And now you dare not ask for me again, lest you lose his heart. I caught her hands in mine. "And now I know. And I will come with you to Sheba and learn all you can teach me. And someday—" Someday Bilqis would die, and Baalit would take her place as queen. But I did not have to think of that today. *Today is a day to rejoice in sun, not to mourn tomorrow's night.*

I lifted her hands and kissed them. "I will come to Sheba; I swear it. My father will not stop me."

The queen's gaze returned to me; the shadows vanished from her eyes. "You will find Sheba strange, Baalit. But you were destined for the south— I think you will be happy there. And your father is truly almost as wise as any man can be; sooner or later he will see the truth, and let you go."

PART SEVEN

Seeking Fire

Abishag

After Adonijah's broken feast, and Solomon's anointing as king and heir, it seemed time itself spun faster. Within a hand's count of days, King David died and King Solomon ruled alone; Adonijah dared ask for me as prize, and Joab struck him down before King Solomon's throne. "He'd be asking for the crown from your head next" was all Joab had to say as he wiped his sword's blade clean on Adonijah's gaudy tunic.

Joab was right, for I was one of the last king's women, and to ask for me was tantamount to claiming the kingship. But his brother's death troubled Solomon, and so I did my best to soothe him, as did Queen Michal. Solomon listened to us both, and smiled, and said only "We must have a fine wedding, Abishag. One fit for a queen."

King David had died when the moon lay dark: when the moon rose full again, King Solomon married me. The pearls braided in my hair could have ransomed all Israel, and my veil was woven through with threads of pure gold. Ever after, my wedding was the touchstone my husband's other wives sought to equal.

And upon the day I married King Solomon and became his first queen, Queen Michal unclasped the bracelet that the Lady Bathsheba had given her so long ago, and fastened the thin brass chains about my own wrist.

Baalit Sings

The fault for what followed lay at my own feet. The Sheban queen's words kindled a blaze within me, a flame of pride and desire that burned to ash all lesser passions. Sun-bright, I glowed with pride—and despite what the queen had told me, I believed my father would be just as proud to have such a prize offered to his daughter. All I can say in my own defense is that I was young, and the young are heedless of all save that which concerns them, as if they alone walked upon the earth.

Nor did I then understand how love such as my father endured for the Queen of Sheba turned hearts into adversaries, and love into a battlefield in which neither side could win, or even surrender. They could only lose.

So after I left the queen, I ran to find my father, seeking to lay my wishes before him at once. That haste was my first error; I should have waited, and approached him at an auspicious moment, when he would be already inclined to heed me. But never before had my father long denied me anything—had I not gained even his permission to ride a horse? It never occurred to me that he might deny me this, my heart's true desire.

Armored in that brazen assurance, I sought my father through the palace, only to learn that he had driven out with my brothers Rehoboam, Jerioth, and Samuel down to the king's great horse farm that lay in the fertile rolling plain to the north.

And when I learned that, instead of going within to my own rooms and preparing myself to greet my father upon his return, I ordered Uri to be brought to me and rode out to join him. Before laughing at my folly, remember that I was barely fourteen, and had been much indulged. I was clever, yes—but there is no credit to being clever, for one is either born so or not. But wisdom is acquired only through hard schooling and long patience. And the young have no time for either.

King Solomon's stables could house twelve thousand horses—that is the tale as travelers tell it now. The numbers grow with the telling; when I was a child, the king's stables were vast and grand, of course. But I do not think my father stabled more than a thousand in his much-prized horse farm. Still, a thousand horses is a great enough number to require a dwelling place that stretched over half the broad valley. King Solomon's stables were greater than many kings' palaces.

Stone walls washed with lime gleamed in the late summer sun; upon stable rooftops, the tents that housed grooms and horse-boys flared blue and yellow, bright as desert wildflowers. Beyond the stables, the horse pastures stretched broad. In the spring, mares and their new foals wandered the lush fields. Those foals were weanlings now, and mares roamed the tawny summer pastures alone.

Uri called to the mares; a few answered, but most never looked up from their grazing. I smiled and stroked his golden neck. "Never mind," I told him, "they will be glad enough to see you in the proper season!"

When I rode into the vast stable courtyard, I saw my father's chariot there; its team of horses had been unhitched and taken elsewhere to be watered and groomed. That meant my father's visit was not a short one.

Grooms hurried up to me as I signaled Uri to halt. I slid from his back and handed the reins to the nearest stableman. "I seek my father, the king," I said. "Where is he?"

My words must have sounded both haughty and urgent, and the stable workers must have been eager to make me someone else's problem. Half-a-dozen voices assured me that my father King Solomon and the three princes had walked out to the schooling field, there to watch the newly weaned foals, that the king might judge which to keep and which to sell.

Leaving Uri in the groom's care, I ran into the stables, cutting through the stallion barn and causing the head groom there to speak hard words to me. "Slow down," he ordered, catching me by the arm and forcing me to halt. "No running. Stallions are touchy beasts, fussing like babes if they're upset. Princess or no, you walk quiet and speak soft when you pass by them."

I knew it would do no good to complain of Gamaliel to my father—for he was right and I wrong. So I begged his pardon, hastily, saying I looked only for my father—

"And sought to save yourself a few breaths' time with a shortcut through the stallion court?" Gamaliel shook his head, plainly disgusted with human folly. "How much time have you won with all your haste? None, because you've had to listen to a lecture from me."

"I know; I am sorry."

"Sorry I delayed you, you mean." Gamaliel released me and stepped aside, and under his strict gaze I walked quiet and soft to the end of the stallion barn. Once past the head groom's private kingdom, I walked more swiftly—but I did not run. For Gamaliel was right; it is not wise to race through stables. I could only hope he would not complain of me to my father.

At last I reached the schooling field, where my father and brothers studiously regarded a chestnut colt as a stable-boy led it back and forth before them. None of them noticed me until the youngling stopped flat-footed, staring at me as if I were a djinn whirled from the air itself. My father turned to see what troubled the colt, and then came swiftly to me.

"Baalit, what are you doing here?" Fear clouded his eyes. "What is wrong?"

"Nothing, Father, I swear it. I wish to speak with you."

The anxiety vanished, replaced by rueful amusement. "And I suppose whatever you wish cannot wait until evening, or even until I return to the palace? Well, what would you ask, Daughter?"

I glanced at my brothers; Jerioth and Samuel had taken advantage of the interruption to stroke the chestnut colt and argue over which of them was the better judge of a horse's worth. Rehoboam stood aside from them, wary of my presence; he gazed at me slantwise, jealous as a fox.

"I cannot ask you here," I said, and my father smiled, resigned as always to my whims.

"Very well." He took my hand and led me to an ancient oak that shaded the well serving the weaning stables. "Your brothers cannot hear us now; you may speak freely." Laughter rippled beneath his words. My father thought me a child still; I would prove to him that I was now a woman, a worthy equal.

"To you, Father, I know I can always speak freely." I drew in a deep breath, and began. As I had ridden to the stables, I had chosen carefully the words I would speak to my father: wise, sober arguments that would obtain his loving consent. Now, facing him, I forgot every clever word I had planned to utter.

"Father, I have just come from speaking with the Sheban queen, and—and she wishes me to go with her to Sheba. To learn from her, to work with her. To be the next Queen of the South—and I think she wishes me to wed her nephew, but I will decide that later, the queen chooses her own consort, and—oh, Father, just think of it! King Solomon's daughter will one day be Queen of Sheba."

Sure of his blessing, I was blinded by my shining future. I saw only what I wished to see, that golden vision of me as Queen of the South. I did not see my father's eyes turn cold, his mouth draw tight. But I heard his voice as he answered me, and each of his words struck me like a stone.

"Do not be foolish, child. You are not going to Sheba."

I stared at him, shocked out of my dreams of glory. "But Father—"

"You are not to trouble Queen Bilqis any further; she cannot take you with her."

Thinking I understood now, I reached out and grasped my father's hands. "You think she did not mean it, that she indulged a child with a pretty story. But you are wrong, Father. The queen *did* mean it; she will swear to it with any oath you desire. She wants me. She needs me. I'm going with her to Sheba. I'll make you proud of me when I'm queen."

For long moments, my father said nothing; the very air about us seemed to chill, time to slow. At last he said, "So you wish to leave your home, your god, your family? To travel to world's end, never to return?"

Such harsh words—as harsh as truth. I did wish to leave; I could no longer bear to stay. I knew it would hurt to speak the words, hurt my father to hear them. But I knew also that only truth would serve, kinder in the end than loving lies. So I said only "Yes, Father."

I would have looked straight into his eyes, my will as strong as his—but my father turned away, stared back at my brothers and the chestnut colt.

"You do not know what you ask, Baalit. You are too young to know." His voice sounded distant; a faraway echo. "No. You are too young to decide such a thing."

"I'm old enough to marry," I said. "I am old enough to bear a child of my own."

"That is different," he said, and the chill in my bones melted, rekindled as anger.

"How different?" I asked. "If I am old enough to risk death to give my husband an heir, surely I am old enough to decide I wish—"

"To be a queen?"

"To leave this kingdom." Until the words left my mouth, I did not know I so longed to flee my home. *My gilded cell. My jeweled chains.* Where had those words come from? My father was no jailer, his palace no prison.

Now he turned back, and this time I understood what glistened in his eyes. *Pain. Loss and loneliness.* He had lost my mother to death; he would soon lose Bilqis to duty. He did not wish to lose his daughter as well.

"Father—" My throat tightened until I could barely speak. "Father, soon or late I must go, if only to a husband. Let me go to Sheba."

"Do not be foolish." My father spoke as if to an importunate child. "Why do you want to be Queen of Sheba? You know nothing of what that means."

"I know Queen Bilqis has asked me to come with her. Give me your blessing."

He said nothing; I summoned up another argument, one harder to confess, for I knew it, too, would hurt my father, however much it might be true. "I wish to go, and—it is not safe for me here. My brother Rehoboam—"

"Yes, he has told me what the prophet Ahijah says of you. But he speaks so of all women, Baalit."

In my dread of Rehoboam's vengeance, I had forgotten the prophet. But it was true that Ahijah, too, was a danger. "He speaks so of all women because he hates all women, mortal or goddess. He would see us all stoned at the city wall."

My father managed to smile. "Do not let him trouble you, child. I am the king; Ahijah will rant and rage, but he will do nothing. Do not let him drive you from your home."

"But I wish to go." I spoke softly, but iron lay beneath the words.

My father shook his head. "I will give you whatever else you wish. I can silence Ahijah, I can silence—"

"But you cannot silence me, Father. I am too much your daughter, and I cannot live here in peace. Let me go. Please."

And then my father uttered words I had not thought he ever would say to me. "I forbid it. You are my daughter, and you will obey."

And as I stared at him, unable to believe that my father had spoken so, he said, "Your place is in the women's palace, Daughter. Now go home—and stay there."

At first shock kept pain and anger chained. I walked slow and quiet away from the schooling field, from my father and my brothers and the chestnut colt over which they quarreled; walked slow and quiet past the restive stallions in their spacious stalls; walked slow and quiet to the courtyard where Uri stood waiting for me. Without a word, I took his reins from the stable-boy who had held them. I vaulted onto Uri's back and then walked him, slow and quiet, until we passed through the wide gate and the broad valley lay open before us.

And then I let Uri run.

That was my second error, for Uri was a horse I could ride only when I controlled myself as well as I did my mount. Truly royal, Uri would not suffer a fool upon his back or permit unruly passion to command him. Before he had carried me a dozen strides, Uri knew that anger, not I, ruled him. Anger demanded he run before the wind; Uri tossed his head and snatched at the bit, caught the metal bar between his teeth. Before I understood what he had done, Uri leapt forward and ran at his own will and not mine.

At first the wild motion bespelled me; wind lashed my hair, blinded my eyes. The stallion's muscles flexed and tensed between my thighs as he fled down the valley, urged on by my wild passion. As if he flew, we swept up the rise to the hills, flashed through the narrow defile onto the Jerusalem road. Even then I did not have sense enough to try to stop him; speed intoxicated me like new wine. But then Uri stumbled upon a rock and I swayed and nearly lost my seat upon his back—and I came to my senses just as Uri lost his.

For we galloped full out down a road cut into rock; beneath Uri's hooves lay stone polished slick by long use. A hoof landing wrong and both Uri and I would crash down upon the rocks that waited below.

Even as that thought slashed through my angry misery, Uri slipped, scrabbled desperately to regain his footing, and flung himself forward again. Fear sobered me; I caught up the doeskin reins, seeking to check our wild flight. But it was too late. My anger had tainted Uri as well; he ran as I had longed to run, fleeing a future I did not wish to see. The stallion had become what I asked of him—an escape. An escape I could no longer control. Now it took all my newfound skill simply to remain upon the horse's back.

That we reached the bottom of the road alive and unharmed was due to Uri's clever hooves and to sheer good fortune. Certainly no credit for our safe descent could be laid in my hands.

Where the road down the hillside flattened into the valley, it split into two paths, one leading north towards Gibeon and the other curving sharply towards the south, and Jerusalem. For an instant Uri slowed, as if to decide which path to choose. In that moment, no longer than a quick indrawn breath, I had one chance to regain control of my mount, and I took it without daring to think of the cost if I failed.

Dropping the reins, I grabbed Uri's mane with my left hand and reached for his bridle with my right. I nearly overbalanced and clung hard with thighs and fist—and then my right hand found what it sought and I clutched the bridle's cheekpiece. I flung my weight back and hauled upon the bridle, hard and steady.

My desperate move succeeded. His head curved back, his flaring nostrils almost touching my knee. Uri slowed, shaking his head in a vain attempt to free himself from the weight hauling him off balance.

"Gently, Uri. Gently now." My voice came soft but firm, coaxing the stallion to listen to my commands once more. Uri flicked his ears back and forth; his frantic strides shortened, slowed, until at last he responded once more to my touch upon his reins, to shifts of my legs against his sides.

When his strength and speed were once more mine to command, I pulled him to a halt and slid from his back. My legs seemed to fold bonelessly beneath me, unable to hold me upright; only my arms about Uri's sweat-foamed neck kept me upon my feet.

I stood so until my breathing steadied and my blood no longer pounded against my skin. I looked at Uri; his coat gleamed with sweat as if it had been oiled; his nostrils flared wide as he, too, sought air. His muscles shuddered beneath my hands.

But when I led him forward he walked steadily enough, and I nearly wept with relief. My heedless anger had not lamed Uri, a mercy I knew I did not deserve. I stroked his wet neck and begged his pardon for treating him so, as if he could understand, and forgive. Perhaps he could, for as I spoke gently to him, Uri rubbed his head against my arm as if to console me.

I cupped my hand over the hot soft skin of his muzzle, and Uri lipped at my palm. I knew he wanted water, but I had none to offer. "I know," I said, "I am sorry." Then I took up the reins and began the long slow walk back to the high road that led to Jerusalem.

Abishag

But even as Queen Michal's handmaidens wove my wedding veil and King Solomon's servants laid pearls before me as my wedding gift, envoys from foreign courts had begun to offer up other brides for my beloved's approval. I could not be his only wife; I must rest content with being his first. But to hear other wives spoken of before we had even wed—that burned my heart like strong lye.

I strove to conceal the hurt, but Solomon loved me too dearly not to see my soul was troubled—and was too wise to promise what he could not perform. King Solomon could not swear that he would have no woman save me alone, but he offered all else that lay within his power to bestow. "You are all the world to me, Abishag. Is there anything I can do to please you, my heart?"

I longed to say, "Nothing, save to love me only." But I did not; I remembered one of my mother's lessons. "Never say there is nothing you desire. Men like to bestow gifts, if they are not too costly. And never ask for what you know a man cannot or will not grant. . . . "

I smiled, and took Solomon's hands. "If my lord the king pleases, I would like my mother to see me wed. Can she not be brought here, to Jerusalem?"

I thought I saw a shadow in his eyes; relief, or guilt, or both. "Of course; you should have asked before—and I should have thought of it for you. Of course you wish your mother here. She shall be brought with all the honor due to a queen's mother, and she shall have rooms as fine as—"

He stopped, for I had bent my head to kiss his hands. "Thank you, my love; I could ask for no richer wedding gift. And I did not ask before because"—I looked up into his eyes—"because I know you will deny me nothing, and so I wish to be careful what I ask."

Solomon

Long years of practice enabled Solomon to set aside his anger and hurt, to continue judging the horses paraded before him as if his daughter's visit had not occurred. Not until he returned to Jerusalem did he permit himself to think upon what had happened—and when he did, memory of his own words flooded him with shame. *"I forbid it."* He, who so prided himself on treating all men and women justly, and with dignity, had spoken to his own daughter as if— *As if I owned her, as if she were—*

As if she were in truth the jewel he called her, his jewel, to dispose of at his will. Was that truly how he thought of her?

No. No, of course I do not think that. Still, she is my daughter— No, I will not consider this further. Baalit is a child still, she does not know what she asks. Yes, that was it: a child dazzled by the foreign queen who flattered her. But no matter how he strove to master his thoughts, Solomon could not. The relentless sunlight could not burn away the vision of his daughter's defiant face, her desperate eyes.

Nor could the rising sounds from the city streets drown out the echo of his own voice, harsh as a stranger's. *You are my daughter and you will obey.*

How could I speak so to her? As if—as if I owned her soul, as if she were—

As if his daughter were no more than another of the king's treasures; a possession to be locked away at his whim.

That was what the Law said she was. In anger and sorrow, he had spoken just as any father might chastise a willful girl. Children were a man's chattel, treasure stored up against an uncertain tomorrow. A father might do as he chose with his daughter's future. That was the Law.

So you will cling to cold law now? Solomon demanded of himself. Had he not trained Baalit up to follow her own will? To think herself the equal of any of her brothers? *Yes, Solomon, you did; in your proud folly you dowered her with a seeking mind and a bold heart—* And now that she wished to follow her stars into a future he could not shape, he revoked his gifts.

You dare invoke the Law, when what you chose to do with Baalit's future was offer it to her with open hands?

No wise words flowed into his mind to answer that cold accusation. Sighing, he walked to the parapet and laid his hands upon the sun-baked stones, welcoming the quick heat beneath his skin. Below him, King David's City sprawled golden in the summer light. On housetops, women worked; he saw cloth spread out to dry, watched serving maids dip into cisterns for stored rainwater. *From such a vantage point, my father looked down upon my mother as she bathed upon her rooftop, and thought her fair—*

And when he lifted his eyes, the Temple filled his vision, its gold burning bright under the noonday sun.

The City of David. The Temple of Solomon. He turned his eyes away from the Temple's savage radiance, looked down again upon the hot busy city. King David's City. *How long will they call Jerusalem by that fond name? And will men ever speak of my Temple with the same love and pride as they do my father's city?*

Or will I be forgotten, and all my faults and virtues fade, less than dust upon the wind?

Had his father David ever known such darkness of spirit? Or his mother? Thinking of Bathsheba's sweet nature, her refusal ever to hear a sour comment or to see a mean deed, Solomon found himself smiling. No, Bathsheba never knew fear or despair. *She walked in sunlight all her days.*

And his other mother, Queen Michal? *Ah, that is a different song.* Queen Michal had always shown a warm face to him, her heart's son, but he had always sensed that behind her eyes lay a deep cold well. Never had he seen her look upon his father with soft eyes; always, when Queen Michal looked upon King David, her eyes held the cool patience of a serpent.

She had not been stone-hearted; no one knew that better than he. But her cool eyes had warmed for him, and for his mother. For David, the hero for whom she had defied her own father, King Saul, for whom she had waited ten years married to another man, for whom she had sacrificed her own future—for David, her eyes held nothing.

Sometimes Solomon thought that was only his own wild fancy— *Boys are selfish creatures, boy princes twice so. I wished her to love me best and only, after all!* Yes, perhaps that was it. All the songs swore Queen Michal loved King David more than honor and herself, after all.

"Yes, and songs are very pretty to listen to. But never mistake a harpers' tale for truth."

Queen Michal's cautioning words echoed in his memory. Unlike his mother Bathsheba, Queen Michal heard every word clear as stone upon stone, saw every deed as plain as sunlight at noon. And she had taught him to do the same. *"Know the truth, Solomon, even if you never speak it. Know the good, even if you never do it."*

"But it is better to speak truth and do good?" he had asked, and Queen Michal had smiled. *"Yes, my heart, it is better to speak truth and do good. But for a king, that is not always possible. Sometimes a king must do what is right."*

He had not understood that riddle for many years. Solomon smiled again, this time at his own folly. *Well, I know the truth and I know the good, and what am I to do with this great and powerful knowledge? And how am I to know what is right?*

Solomon the Wise—he laughed, mocking himself. Solomon the Wise, who knew everything except how to pluck happiness from life's thornbush. *And what makes a man happy? Love?*

Unbidden, the thought summoned the images of his women: Nefret and Naamah; Melasadne and Dvorah. *So many wives; do any of them love me?*

Have you ever asked that of them, Solomon? The silent mockery rippled upon whispered laughter; the silent voice that chided him was Bilqis's.

Ah, now there was love. Well-spiced love. Bilqis, Queen of Sheba. So ripe, so warm, so wise. *My last love.*

So different from his first love. *My jewel, my rose, my song made flesh. My Abishag.*

His passion for Abishag had been a young man's love, demanding and hot. Chaining his desire, surrendering his beloved to his aged father's need, had cost him dearly in sleepless nights and restless days.

But King David had lain dying, cold to his ancient bones, and Solomon had yielded to his father's need and to his foster-mother's will. *No, speak truth, if only to yourself. Queen Michal lauded the plan and twined it about her ambition for me. But the mind that devised the scheme was yours.*

Unwillingly, Solomon remembered the words he had spoken to his foster-mother, seeking her approval. *"At first I thought, Why should not my father have comfort? And then I thought, Why should this girl not tell us what he says, and to whom?"* Yes, and more, but those words Queen Michal had said so that he need not.

"If I take this young fair maid to wife after, it will strengthen my claim to David's crown."

That was only good sense, as Queen Michal had said. A spy in King David's bedchamber and a queen in King Solomon's court—it had seemed so prudent, so simple, when he had revealed his plan to Queen Michal.

But that was before he had sought and found the unknown girl for whom he had planned this twice-royal future.

Before he had found love.

And with love, pain. For Abishag had assented to his wishes, served as his shadow in his father's chambers. *A fair maid to tend him, to sleep beside him and warm his cold bones—a king's maiden, to carry the royal succession in her soft young hands from the old king to the new—*

Abishag had done all that Solomon and Queen Michal asked of her and more. And not once had she faltered or betrayed by so much as a flicker of her lashes what truly had passed between her and King David. To this day, Solomon did not know whether his father had lain with Abishag as a man does with a woman he desires.

He did not wish to know.

Upon their wedding night, Abishag had tried to speak of her nights with King David; desired, Solomon knew, to swear to her chastity. But he had refused to allow her to utter the words.

"What passed between you and my father does not matter," he had told her, "so do not utter words because you think I wish to hear them. Whatever happened, happened." Swiftly, Solomon had taken her face between his hands and kissed her soft mouth, tasted cinnamon and roses. "That is past, my heart. Over and gone. This night is ours alone; ours to do with as we wish. Even if King David possessed your yesterday, King Solomon owns to-day and all your tomorrows. Be content with that."

Abishag had looked long into his eyes; at last she'd said, "I can rest content with that, my king. But can you?"

"Yes," he had said, and again, "Yes. You are my heart and my queen, Abishag. Nothing else matters."

So he had vowed upon their wedding night; then he had thought himself magnanimous, great-hearted and generous. Many men would have demanded a bride come to them virgin although they had themselves sent her to another man's bed.

But I vowed it did not matter. I think she believed me. I hope she did.

For now Solomon knew he had not been generous.

He had been afraid of the truth he might hear.

Rehoboam

What did she want? What did my father promise her? The questions pricked at Rehoboam, spoiling his pleasure at being given his choice of the newly weaned colts. The moment his sister arrived at the schooling field, their father had forgotten everything in his haste to indulge her. His brothers had not noticed, of course— *None of my brothers sees that she steals what is mine. I am the heir, not she! This is not Sheba, after all—*

Fear slashed him, sudden ice against his skin. Israel was not Sheba—but his father was besotted with the Sheban queen, and the queen with Baalit. Had the Sheban persuaded his father to exalt Baalit, to set her up as a queen in Israel?

Yes. That would explain everything. His father's indifference, his half-sister's refusal to marry him, her arrogant disregard for his wishes. *And today at the stables she spoke of being queen. I heard her.* Rehoboam's ears were keen, and some of Baalit's words had cut the air like shining blades. *Yes, that must be what she plans—wait until I tell my mother; she will—*

His mother would what? She would be furious, of course; his mother cared only for his welfare, his future. *If my father thinks to set my sister up as a queen—this time Mother will poison her.* The thought warmed Rehoboam; then he frowned. His sister Baalit never suffered from illness or weakness, and if she died suddenly— *Mother might be suspected, and I cannot afford to lose her.* If only his sister had enemies— *But everyone thinks Baalit so clever, so faultless—*

No. Not everyone.

As if his mother stood behind him and whispered in his ear, Rehoboam suddenly knew exactly what he must do to ensure that his half-sister Baalit never again shadowed his future.

Ahijah was not hard to find on market days; the prophet stood in the porch of the Sheep Gate, lecturing those who passed through as if they were erring children. Rehoboam watched as men came and went, most paying no heed to Ahijah's words— *For they have heard the old fool too often.* Rehoboam had no patience with Ahijah's constant rebukes, but at last he saw how they could be useful. So he smiled, and stalked through the crowd of men and beasts until he stood before Ahijah.

"Greetings, O Prophet," Rehoboam began, and Ahijah glanced down at him, frowned.

"You find Yahweh's words amusing, Prince?" Ahijah demanded, and Rehoboam swiftly looked solemn.

"No. I was only glad to find you so easily, for I must speak with you. I— I am troubled in my mind, and desire your wise counsel." There, that should satisfy the prophet's vanity! All men liked to give advice—*especially to princes!* Irritating though the thought was, Rehoboam kept his face calmly earnest.

Ahijah stared at him as if trying to see behind his eyes; apparently satisfied, the prophet nodded. "Ask then, and receive Yahweh's wisdom."

Exulting, Rehoboam gazed for a moment at the dusty stones beneath his feet; it would not serve his need to reveal any emotion other than troubled sorrow.

"Well?" Ahijah demanded, and Rehoboam raised his head.

"I have come to you because a great weight lies upon my heart," Rehoboam began. "It is a matter of the behavior of—of a woman—"

Ahijah seemed to recoil, as if Rehoboam himself might be unclean. "All women are full of vice; it is the way Yahweh made them."

Rehoboam didn't care how the Lord had made women, he cared only that the prophet should listen to him. "Yes—yes, that is so." Agreeing was the surest way to hold Ahijah's attention. Now to bend their talk to the subject nearest Rehoboam's heart. "But my lord Ahijah, are not some women more vile than others?"

"Do not call me 'lord'; I am only Yahweh's mouthpiece." Ahijah's eyes seemed to burn like coals in his thin face. Still, Rehoboam thought the prophet appeared pleased at a prince's regard.

"Some women," Rehoboam said hastily, fearing to lose the prophet's attention, "some women follow evil ways. What should one do in such an instance?"

Ahijah drew himself up, stiffer than ever—*like a dead cedar*, Rehoboam thought, inwardly smiling. Yes, that was how he would describe the prophet later, when boasting to his friends.

"The Law is clear," Ahijah declared. "An evil woman must be given to judgment."

"Even a kinswoman?" Rehoboam asked, thinking himself cunning. Yes, the prophet took an interest in that question! Rehoboam forced himself to pious solemnity; it would not do to appear triumphant.

"Even so. Do you know of such a one? Yes, of course you must, for the king's house stinks of iniquity. Of pride, and lust, and—"

"Idolatry," Rehoboam prompted. So easy, he exulted. So easy to sway even a prophet! *Oh, what a king I shall be! All men shall leap at my bidding!*

The prophet glanced at him sharply for a moment before agreeing. "Yes, idolatry—the sin Yahweh hates above all others. The sin King Solomon countenances, since his foreign wives delight in it."

"Not only his foreign wives." At last Rehoboam could let his sister's good name fall. "But his daughter too follows after heathen idols. And she is no foreigner. She is a Daughter of the Law. It is not fit that she should be seen in the temples of foreign gods."

"It is not fit that she be there," Ahijah agreed, and Rehoboam nodded gravely at the prophet's repetition of his words. Then Ahijah said, "Have you proof of this?"

Someday, Rehoboam swore crossly, *this prophet will address me properly. I am a prince, after all!* But at the moment he needed Ahijah's goodwill, so he said only "I have seen her walk through their doors with my own eyes, my lord prophet. And others have seen her as well."

"Which temples?" Ahijah asked.

What difference does that make? Rehoboam studied the tiles at his feet, as if ashamed of the words he uttered. "That of Astoreth, and of Belitis." He tried hastily to think of others. "And that of Chemosh, and I think—"

"Does she visit the Grove?" Ahijah's voice dropped almost to a whisper. The Grove—that would mean the princess was not only idolatrous but unchaste as well. Girls had been stoned for less.

"Yes," Rehoboam said after a moment's pause, as if he thought hard and long over his words. "Yes, she has visited the Grove."

As soon as he was out of the prophet's sight, Rehoboam permitted himself to smile. *I've done it, I've done it!*

He'd sworn his half-sister would be sorry she had ever thwarted him. Now she would be. The prophet Ahijah would make sure of that. *Now my father will have to turn to me. I'm his heir, after all, and she—she's only a girl.* Still smiling, Rehoboam ran off down the king's great courtyard—one day to be *his* great court. Someday in his bright future, when he was king.

Ahijah

Yahweh has granted my prayers; my god has delivered mine enemy into my hand. The thought came slow, weighted with its import; Ahijah was gratified to discover he did not exult at what he now must do. Nor did he shrink from the task ahead. *Yahweh's will must be done.*

And since the king refused to see the sin dwelling under his roof—and since the high priest refused to act at all—it was Ahijah himself who must act as king and priest would not. *I shall cleanse the king's house of evil.* And then, when the people saw that even their king could not evade Yahweh's Law, they, too, would abandon their evil ways and return to the path of righteousness.

Ahijah began to consider how to bring Solomon to account. There must be no error, no crack through which King Solomon's serpent-mind might crawl to safety. The evil must be exposed in the king's own great court, to which any man or woman might come and demand justice before the throne.

Solomon is soft and weak. I am neither. I will do whatever I must to bring him down to judgment. Even the king is not above the Law!

Zadok

The sacrifices had gone well; the worshippers had been numerous and generous. As always after the ritual had been properly carried out, Zadok departed in a glow of satisfied peace. The serene procession of the ceremony of sacrifice and worship reaffirmed the steadiness of the world and his own place in it. Today the rituals had flowed even more smoothly than usual. His hand had been steady on the knife, the sacrifice had been swift and faultless; his voice strong, the prayers chanted without flaw. *And to think only yesterday I worried that I grew too old to serve!*

So thinking, Zadok bowed to the Holy of Holies and withdrew from the Sanctuary. Serenely contemplating the day's blessings, he did not notice the figure awaiting him just beyond the Temple door until it was too late to retreat. The prophet Ahijah had seen him.

Zadok's serenity vanished like dew under desert sun. Bad enough when Ahijah cornered him in his own house—but this was a thousand times worse. A confrontation at the Temple door, with all eyes upon them and all ears stretched to hear whatever they might say—

How have I offended, Lord? Zadok wailed silently. But he managed to smile upon Ahijah, and even to greet the prophet pleasantly, although he knew his efforts would be in vain.

"Welcome to the Lord's House, Ahijah; we are honored by your presence."

"So as well as having no name, Yahweh now dwells within walls, does He?" Ahijah demanded, and Zadok valiantly tried to smile as if Ahijah jested.

"Of course He does not—but are we to grant Him no honors because of that? Come, walk with me to my own house and be welcomed there." Zadok knew he would regret bringing Ahijah under his roof, but at least then the verbal lashing the prophet was sure to deliver would take place in private, rather than before the eyes of half Jerusalem.

Ahijah regarded Zadok with scorn. "Like Yahweh, I need no house, and no walls can stop the truth of my words. Listen, Zadok, High Priest of King Solomon's Temple; listen and heed."

"I listen, Prophet." There was little else Zadok could do; Ahijah stood between Zadok and the steps down into the Temple court.

"Then for once you show wisdom. Mark my words, for I shall say them once only. This city, once a citadel of holy purity, a woman chaste, now is no better than a painted harlot. Idols pollute the streets; false gods seduce all who pass by. And what is the source of this filth, this iniquity?"

The prophet paused, as if awaiting reply, but Zadok knew better than to speak. Words from him would only be oil poured upon the open flame of Ahijah's loathing.

"From one who should be Yahweh's vessel." Ahijah turned from Zadok to face the courtyard. "The king. The king's palace is a sinkhole of lust and idolatry. And the king tolerates the sin beneath his roof—no, worse, he revels in such vile deeds. Solomon takes strange women to his bed, he worships at their shrines. And his children follow his footsteps through the mud.

"Does not the king flaunt a pagan queen before us all? Does he not bend low before her and grant her all she desires? Do not his own women frequent the brothels of the Queen of Heaven?"

As Ahijah spoke, Zadok grew increasingly uneasy. True, the prophet often raved against the court's vices—but this was the first time Ahijah had dared proclaim them so publicly.

And on the very steps of the Temple, and before me, in the sight of all men. Zadok faced a dilemma he must solve, and swiftly, if disaster were not to crash down upon his blameless head. For Ahijah spoke treason. *If I do not rebuke him, I condone his words.* And if Zadok did rebuke the prophet— *All Israel knows Solomon permits his wives their own gods. If I rebuke Ahijah, I publicly condone idolatry.*

Ahijah had fallen silent and turned back to face Zadok, waiting. When Zadok did not speak at once, Ahijah said, "Well, High Priest? What is the Law? For a daughter of Yahweh who consorts wanton in the Grove, what does the Law ordain?"

With those words, Ahijah's true snare lay revealed. *He speaks of the king's women—but the one he truly accuses is the Princess Baalit. Yes, that is the way to kill Solomon's heart.* Zadok knew he was not a clever man, but suddenly the words he must say flowed smoothly from his tongue.

"For such a one, death; death by stones." *You know that, Prophet, as do all in the Temple court who listen to your poisoned words. Well, I too have words for you.* Zadok drew himself up, filled with an odd sense of power, as if for once he were Ahijah's equal in all things. "But for so grave a charge there must be proof. There must be witnesses—witnesses of untarnished motive. Have you such proof, Prophet? Have you such witnesses?"

"There will be proof," Ahijah said. "There will be witnesses. And then you must uphold the Law, High Priest—no matter who the transgressor may be."

"Bring me such proof, and such witnesses, and I will uphold the Law." Unflinching, Zadok looked into the prophet's eyes. "But remember, Ahijah, that there is another sin the Lord our god hates."

Zadok paused, as Ahijah had before, waiting. At last Ahijah asked, slowly, as if the words were being forced from his mouth. "And what is that, Zadok?"

"False witness," Zadok said. "Be careful, Prophet. Be very, very careful. For I am High Priest, and I will uphold the Law. The Lord's Law, Prophet. Not yours."

Still exalted by that uncanny strength, Zadok stared into the prophet's eyes. And for the first time since Zadok had known him, it was Ahijah who first looked away.

Zadok did not remember how he got home; doubtless the Lord—or long habit—had guided his steps. Once there, he collapsed upon his bed; his body trembled as if with cold. The fiery power that had upheld him as he confronted the prophet Ahijah had vanished. And it had taken all Zadok's own small power with it, leaving him weak and shaken.

Was that the power of Yahweh, of the Lord? Zadok did not know; he knew only that for a shining moment he had burned stronger than the angry prophet. But that moment was gone. Zadok did not know why he had been granted that brief glory, and he was too weary to try to understand.

But there was one thing more left to do. *I must warn King Solomon.* Zadok swallowed the hot spiced wine his wife brought him and held the bowl out for more. *Yes, I must warn the king. As soon as I am able, I will go to King Solomon.*

Ahijah

Proof. Yes, the high priest is right. Grudgingly, Ahijah admitted the truth of Zadok's words; the concession left a sour taste upon his tongue. *Yahweh's Law demands proof.*

But such proof would not be easy to get. Even the princess's visits to the temples of foreign gods would not be enough; many women visited those temples—too many. Well, that must stop. But men would not condemn the king's daughter for doing what their wives and daughters also did, for that would be to condemn their own womenfolk as well.

As they should, as they should— Ahijah forced himself to calmness. First cleanse the king's house, and the others would follow. He must smash the serpent's venomous head. The king.

So mere visits to the temples of strange gods would not suffice. But Prince Rehoboam had also admitted that his sister visited the Grove. And for that, Ahijah could demand her death. *A princess of the House of David wallowing wanton in the Grove, worshipping the Morning Star with her own body, opening herself to all comers!* Disgusted to nausea by the image sullying his mind, Ahijah shuddered and spat.

That was where she must be taken. She must be dragged from that foulness, dragged through the city streets and flung naked before her father's throne. The Law was clear, clear as pure water: for wantonness, she must die. King Solomon would be forced to condemn his daughter or lose his throne.

Ahijah smiled. Let the vaunted wisdom of Solomon show the king a way out of that trap!

Baalit Sings

Later, it seemed to me that Ahijah's secret plan to disgrace me must have been known to half the city. The fault lay in the prophet's own iron virtue; to him, a word sworn was immutable. It did not occur to Ahijah that the men he bound to secrecy would not count it oath-breaking to whisper the matter to their wives as they lay together. Or that Rehoboam would work against his own good by boasting to his followers that his haughty sister would soon be dragged down lower than dust.

As a result, I heard of the plot to violate the Grove of the Morning Star well before the new moon showed in the evening sky. And I was not even the first to know of the matter, for word came to me from Ishvaalit, sister of one of Rehoboam's friends. Her brother Athaniel had listened to Rehoboam's boast, praised him for wisdom greater than Solomon's, and gone straight to his own sister—not to warn me, for Athaniel cared nothing for me for either good or ill, but Athaniel was fond of his sister, and Ishvaalit worshipped in the Grove each full moon. Athaniel cared a great deal for what happened to Ishvaalit, and so he warned her to stay away from the Goddess's Grove at the next bright moon. No fool, Ishvaalit soon extracted the whole tale from her brother, and then came straight to me.

"We must speak," she told me.

"Very well," I said, and invited her into my own courtyard.

But Ishvaalit shook her head. "Come sit with me by the fountain in the queens' garden." The great fountain there was a favored spot; what was spoken beside its falling waters could not be heard three steps away. So I knew what she wished to say was secret—there is no better place to trade secrets than in plain sight—and smiled, and wound my arm about her waist, and walked with her like a sister through the hallways and galleries until we reached the garden.

"Now," I said when we sat beside the singing fountain, "tell me."

"Your brother Prince Rehoboam plots against you," Ishvaalit said, and I smiled.

"Always," I said, "it is the only way he can be happy, by injuring others."

"Do not laugh." Ishvaalit smiled, as if we shared a mild jest. "This time he means your death."

I sat like stone while Ishvaalit told me of Rehoboam's boasts, and her brother's warning. I knew Rehoboam hated me—but so greatly? What wrong had I done him? I was not even a rival for the throne, for, as he had so often jeered, I was only a girl.

Ishvaalit finished her tale, and I forced myself to laugh, shaking my head as if she spun jests too well. "I do not know what the prophet plans," I said, "for you know I do not go to the Grove by moonlight." I had visited the Grove of the Morning Star once, by day, and seen only a well-tended orchard, a vale of pomegranates and olives. The Grove's moon did not call me; I had not gone again.

"I know only what my brother told me," Ishvaalit said. "Now I have told you." She leaned forward, then, and laid her hand over mine. "I do not know what the prophet plans—but until the full moon wanes, do not drink from any cup you do not share with others, and do not go aside with any you do not trust as you trust yourself."

I promised I would not. I knew what Ahijah and Rehoboam thought, that since the wild princess roamed where she would, it would be simple to force a sleeping potion down her throat and carry her off to the Grove, to be found lying naked by scandalized louts—

Well, I knew better than that. "I will be careful," I said. "Go now, and warn the priestesses who serve the Morning Star that this bright moon, their goddess will be best served by chastity. And warn the Daughters of the Law not to go at all."

If Ahijah could not snare me, he still would happily accuse any girl found there and demand she be delivered up for stoning. My father would refuse, I knew that, but it would be best to avoid an open clash between king and prophet.

"I will tell them," Ishvaalit said. And then we remained beside the great fountain, chattering of this and that, until half-a-dozen of my father's wives came to bask in the sun. Ishvaalit and I wove our way into other conversations, as if caught by their gossip, until at last I looked up from the new embroidery stitch Ahinoam was displaying and saw that Ishvaalit was gone. I smiled, and set to praising my stepmother's needlework, and hoped that I was truly as clever as I had sometimes been told.

For Rehoboam's scheme had kindled an answering plan in my own mind. A daring plan; a dangerous plan. But one that might, in the end, hold the key that would unlock the prison enclosing me.

Abishag

My mother walked the corridors of the women's palace as smoothly as if her feet already knew the path. "Daughters spin secrets," say old wives—but nothing compared with those secrets cherished by mothers. The ivory-set ebony gate that led to Queen Michal's courtyard stood open in silent welcome; my mother looked upon the gate and smiled.

Queen Michal sat beside the courtyard fountain, trailing her fingers in the cool water. I led my mother before Queen Michal and bowed. "O Queen, I bring before you my mother."

Whereupon my mother bowed; despite her age, she was graceful as a willow in the wind. Smiling, she rose and said, "O Queen, live forever."

Queen Michal stared at her, and for the space of an in-drawn breath, I thought she would not speak. "So it is you," Queen Michal said at last. "And what are you called now?"

My mother laughed, and then the queen laughed too, and embraced her. "Oh, but I am glad to see you once again!" the queen said. "And this time I will not let you go."

"This time I will not ask it." My mother stepped back and regarded the queen critically, as if Queen Michal too were her daughter, and my mother must pass judgment upon her hair and gown and jewels. "You look well, Michal. Queenship suits you."

"No," said the queen, "but queenship is a gown I must wear, for my—for King Solomon's sake."

My mother stood silent for a moment, then said, "O Queen, shall I weigh my words or speak freely?"

"Had I heeded you when first we met, I would have saved myself a well of tears. Speak."

"Then spare yourself more tears and bow to truth, Michal. Queenship suits you because you are at heart a queen. If you could set aside your crown now, you would not, King Solomon or no."

Queen Michal seemed to turn to glass, hard and brittle; she stood tall and proud, and I thought she would order my mother from her. But she said only "Do you think so little of me?"

"I think so much of you, O Queen. You are the bones that support the kingdom, the heart that holds the crown. You are the goddess who breathes life into the land— Oh, I know you were born a daughter of Yahweh, and I know in what esteem you hold all gods. But truth is truth, Michal, and you now are what I say. Without you there would be no kingdom here, and owls and jackals would feast among the city's broken stones."

Silence stretched long and cold; my heartbeat echoed in my ears. All our futures had been cast before the queen's jeweled feet. My mother and the queen remained motionless, as if time-locked in amber. Then the air seemed to melt and time to flow again.

"Would that be so bad a thing?" asked the queen, and my mother answered, "It would be a different thing," and took the queen's outstretched hands. As relief swept hot through my blood, Queen Michal embraced my mother once more, this time hugging her hard, as if she were a long-lost sister.

After that, the queen laughed and said, "I did not expect quite so much truth!"

"Queens hear it only rarely. Having heard, what now is your will, O Queen?" My mother's words were said lightly, but a sober question lay behind them.

"Why, that you tell me what I should call you now!" said the queen, and my mother laughed once more and pulled off the modest blue veil that had always covered her hair.

"Call me what name you will, so long as you call me friend, and my daughter yours as well." She glanced at the veil and tossed it to the floor as if it were a dirty rag. "Ah, but it is good to dwell once more among riches!"

"If only—"

"No." My mother held up her hand, as if to hold back Queen Michal's words. "Do not lash yourself with that. If is not a word a queen should use when speaking of the past. Only of the future."

"Perhaps. Still, I was happier as a farmer's wife."

"Perhaps you were—but the kingdom is happier with you as a queen. Do not give your-self airs, Michal; all women—and all men too, although the creatures will deny it with their *dying breath—follow the path they must. The gods never meant you to live and die a farmer's wife, or you would not be here in a queen's scarlet and gold."*

"This from you? Did you not once say we all made our own fates?"

"We do—but only as the gods will it. The gods created you to shape a kingdom's future, Michal—and you have. Do you think Solomon would sit upon the throne today had you not meddled in the fates of David and of Bathsheba? So do not speak foolishly; you are not a foolish woman."

And when I asked, later, how it was that she and Queen Michal knew each other so well, my mother only smiled, and said that it was long ago— *"So long ago it is another land, and all its people dead."*

Nor would she ever again speak of it, save to say, *"The past is the past, Daughter. Now I am friend to one queen and mother to another, and if the gods are kind, I shall be grandmother to a third. I am content with that—and you should be content as well. Do not disturb the dead, Abishag. They will not thank you for rousing them."*

Baalit

Only you can free yourself. So the Queen of Sheba had told me, and now I knew that for truth. Sheba needed a queen to rule after Bilqis, not a girl bestowed upon the throne like a child bride upon an ancient husband. But until now, I had not seen a path to Sheba that I might tread with honor.

I could run away, follow the Shebans, and hope they would not hand me back when my father sent armed men after me. *Yes, start a war over you; that would be fine work indeed.* That was no way to repay my father for his love, or the queen for her teaching. Set two nations at each other's throats, cut off the spice trade with the Morning Land—yes, fine work, if one wished to sing a great song of battles and deaths. Not such a fine thing if one wished to rule a land, tend it and nurture it, comfort it with peace.

It would be better to stay than to try, and fail, breaking many lives in the attempt. Mine among them, for my father would be deeply hurt, and it would be a hard thing for him ever to trust me again.

But if I stayed, I must marry, and my father would not marry me beyond his kingdom. He would give me to one of the great men of Jerusalem, to keep me near. That was all very well while he lived—but when King Solomon lay with his fathers, and King Rehoboam ruled in his turn?

Rehoboam hates me. As king, he will at last be able to act upon that hatred. When my father died, my own life would be forfeit to my brother's enmity. There would be no safety for me then in all the kingdom—nor for any man who married me or for any sons and daughters I might bear.

So I must act now—and thanks to Rehoboam, a path lay before me that might lead me to my future. *How he would rage if he knew he himself provided me the key!*

But I must walk this path with great care; one misstep and I would fall before the stones of the Law. I was setting my father's love against Ahijah's hate, and if I were wrong about which was stronger, I would die.

It was the first time in my life that I sat and thought long and hard, the first time I tried to think as a queen must.

As a woman must.

For it was as a woman that I was Ahijah's foe, although he was not mine. I bore him no ill-will—or at least, I strove not to think hardly of him. Unjust, when I plotted to use him for my own purposes as coldheartedly as he himself conspired against me.

So I set myself against him, princess against prophet. *A man must know his enemy better than he knows his friend.* So said the king's general; Benaiah won always, so I knew his advice sound. What did I know about Ahijah? *Who does he love? Who does he hate? Who does he trust?*

I knew nothing of Ahijah's love or trust. But of his hate—ah, that I knew full well. The prophet Ahijah hated all gods save the Lord Yahweh. And he loathed goddesses above all.

The prophet despised goddesses even more than he did women—and feared them too. No man could hate a thing so greatly without fearing it just as greatly. Ahijah raged as if men dragged him in chains to kiss the idols' gilded feet, when all the priests and priestesses of the foreign gods housed in Jerusalem asked was to worship in peace.

So Ahijah hates and fears me, for I represent the goddess in the king's court. This at last was clear to me. I was the child of the king's great love, whom he had set above all others. I was the daughter the king cherished above all his sons. To Ahijah, this stank of evil; to Ahijah, daughters were not a blessing but a curse.

If he only knew how truly I am a daughter of goddesses! My mother's mother had danced before Astarte's altar—more, she had been a king's pleasure, a bound slave, a merchant's wife, a daughter's mother. And had not my father's mother been Bathsheba, "daughter of the seven gods," who had risen above shame to become mother of the king who succeeded Great David?

And then there had been Michal. A woman who wove life into her own pattern, who had raised my father to be a good man and a wise king.

I now knew what to name these women who had formed me: each a true phoenix, re-creating herself no matter how harsh the choice, how hot the fire. Now it was my turn to choose, and I chose to keep faith with my mothers.

Now I too must remold myself, rise from fire to fly again.

The path I chose for myself was not easy; never think I set my feet upon its stones without pain. For my success would hurt my father deeply. And it would cause a scandal, although the shame would be eased by my banishment from the kingdom. I must leave my home, never again set eyes upon Jerusalem, upon its rooftops burning golden under the summer sun. . . .

Every girl leaves her home, I reminded myself. Change was woman's life. And this change would be of my own choice. I must remember that, when the way grew hard.

So I began to shape Ahijah's plan to my own purpose; that was my third error. The prophet sought to catch me in the Grove, expose me in the act of worshipping the Lady of Light. He wished to drag me before my father's court and accuse me openly, giving my father no chance to shield me.

Well, and so I would let Ahijah find me—but not in the Grove. Outside its sacred ground would suit me better. Let the prophet meet me on my way to the Lady's shrine. Yes, that would do; Ahijah would encounter me at a time and place of my choosing, not his.

Nor would I face him alone. He would have no chance to have men grasp me and force me into a more compromising position. I must have attendants—and they must be girls who could not be harmed by the success of my scheme. I could ask no one who would remain to face Ahijah's wrath. So I could not use my own maids, or any of my friends, or even foreigners who dwelt in Jerusalem.

No, it must be girls immune to what may happen afterward— And as I thought this, I knew already that I must ask help from the Shebans.

But not from the queen! This I must do myself. *If I cannot persuade Khurrami and Irsiya to accompany me, then I do not deserve to succeed.*

Once my will had set the spindle of fortune whirling, cold doubts beset me. *This will be disaster,* my fears whispered. My scheme would fail and, failing, carry me down in sorrow and disgrace. And my father—what would this do to him?

He loves me so; how can I hurt him so deeply? How could I condemn my father to certain pain?

But if I did not, I condemned myself to misery. And to danger; I must not forget that Rehoboam's hatred would one day be a real power he would use against me.

And if I do not carry out my plan, I hurt the queen and all her people. For without a true queen to follow her, Sheba's land was condemned to strife. It was to prevent slaughter that the Sun of Sheba called me; who was I to deny a holy summons?

Yes, blame the gods for your own desires. For I longed for the future Sheba promised as some girls yearn for a lover.

In the end, it did not matter if Bilqis's sun goddess summoned me, or if another power commanded me. Whatever force drove me, god or goddess or both—or neither—I knew only that I must obey that call.

Seeking fire, I fly south, to the morning. To the desert, and beyond. Who knows? Perhaps someday a new truth will rise out of these ashes to sweep its wings across the wide world—

We dream hot dreams, when we are young.

Helike

She had fled this doom in her dreams, but now fate's claws had seized her, and there was no escape. *No. No, I am wrong, it cannot be true.*

But as she stared through her narrow window at the rising moon, Helike knew she was not wrong. *Three moons; three since it was the king's night.* Since that night, she had not bled with the moon. *I am with child.*

The knowledge flowed through her veins, cold as slow poison. The thing she feared above all else had happened: she would bear a child to the King of Israel. She had done all within her power to avoid this fate, had shamed herself and asked guidance of some of the older women, had followed their counsel. But for all her care, she had failed.

Now she faced her fear clear-eyed. *If it is a boy, I can endure this.* By the laws of the Sword Maids, sons belonged to the father.

And daughters to the mother.

But here in Jerusalem, the laws of men controlled the fate of women. Even girls belonged to the father.

If you bear a girl, she will belong to King Solomon, to do with as he wills. King Solomon's daughter would be raised within walls, a pawn and a plaything sacrificed on the altar of royal pride. A slave all her days.

No. My Lady cannot be so cruel.

The moon hung low in the sky, no longer a slim crescent but rounding; in a few more days the moon would rise full. Helike stared at the waxing moon until its silver light filled her eyes and she saw nothing. Nothing but a future as heartless as man's law. And as she looked into that clear cold light, she knew what she must do.

She slipped from the king's house unseen, gliding out the great gate as silent as a shadow of the moon. It was the first time she had set her feet beyond the jeweled harem gate since the day she had been paraded before the court as King Solomon's newest bride, but she knew the way. She had stared from the rooftop often enough, stared into the silver path of the full moon's light, following its trail over rooftop and city wall, high road and field, to the brilliance moonlight sparked from the Grove.

The Grove of the Morning Star did not house her own goddess. Never would the Lady of Swords consent to be chained to a Grove. But a goddess dwelt there, and all goddesses were sisters. The Lady of the Grove might carry a message to Her sister of Swords. A faint hope, but that small chance was all Helike had to cling to now.

Desperation carried her to the Lady's Gate; fear halted her there. This was the last step from which she could draw back. Beyond the silver and willow of the Lady's Gate lay the Grove of the Morning Star, and once she set her feet within the Grove, she would know at last how far she had fallen from her goddess's grace.

I had no choice. But Helike knew she lied; there was always a choice, and she had chosen wrongly. Chosen surrender and bondage over honor and freedom.

"Will you enter the Grove, lady?" The priestess's voice was soft and warm. "All are welcome who come with open hearts."

She had hesitated too long, and once more the choice was made for her— *No.*

Helike summoned courage and faced the priestess squarely. "I would enter, but I do not know if your Lady will welcome one who does not serve Her and who comes with an unquiet heart. I would not trouble Her, save that my need is great."

Undismayed, the priestess smiled and held out her hands in welcome. "And to whom should one turn in great need, save to one's Mother? Enter and be welcome."

She was—had been—a Sword Maiden, dedicated to the pure spare Lady of Swords. Never before had she set foot in the Laughing One's Grove, and she feared what she might find there. But it was quiet beneath the trees, the soft ground unsullied. With each breath, Helike drew in the fresh green scent of leaves and the darker tang of earth; as she followed the priestess deeper into the Grove, the heady perfume of incense wove itself through the cool air. And with the scent of incense came soft murmurs from the shadows, the sound of pleasure. Helike kept her gaze fixed upon the priestess's gilded belt, and did not seek the source of those sounds of joy.

At last the priestess stopped. "Here is our Lady," she said. "Look upon Her, sister, and be comforted."

Before them Asherah stood broad-hipped and smiling, her hands cupped beneath her breasts, offering to feed both body and spirit. The pale stone of her breasts gleamed, smooth-polished by the touch of many devout hands. Helike could not bring herself to lay her hands upon the statue; she crossed her hands over her breast and bowed.

"I would ask a boon, and I bring a gift," she said, and offered the necklace she had chosen from those her father had sent in her dowry when he had sold her to King Solomon. Nuggets of amber hung enmeshed in fine gold chains, the amber prisoned in gold just as small strange creatures lay trapped forever within the amber. "Will your Lady find it pleasing?"

The priestess's eyes widened. "Such a gift could ransom a queen. What would you ask, sister, that you offer so much?"

"I would ask the Laughing One to carry a message to Her sister, the Lady of Swords." Helike knelt to lay the chained amber at the goddess's feet; she forced herself to look up into the Lady of Love's jeweled eyes. "I do not ask for myself—"

But for your daughter. Carried on the night wind, the words whispered silver music through the olive leaves.

"Yes." Helike bent her head under the goddess's gaze, cupped her hands over her rounding belly like a shield. "For my daughter."

No man saw her return in the cold clear light that preceded dawn. Even after these years trapped within palace walls, within women's bonds, she still could summon up her hard-won skills.

Those I still possess. All I lack is honor. That lack clung bitter upon her tongue, poisoned her bones.

But that same lack freed her utterly. *What more can I lose? There is no farther for me to fall; I can act freely, caring for nothing save my daughter's future. That she be free— that is all I ask.*

That was all she dared ask. The Lady of Swords might take pity upon her daughter—but Helike did not hope for mercy for herself.

Baalit Sings

As I walked through the passageway that led from the Queen's Gate to the Little Palace, a woman stepped forward from the deeper shadow of one of the cedar columns. Startled, I paused, tense as a deer. But it was only one of my father's quiet wives; no threat.

"Princess, I must speak with you. I must." Lady Helike's words cut the air like blades, glittering and sharp.

I could not imagine what troubled her, or why she wished to speak with me. Still, I smiled, and said, "Speak, then."

I half-expected her to beg me to intercede with my father on her behalf; others had done so before. So I was unready to hear her say, "You cannot achieve your desire alone, and you must not fail. I can help you. I can. I—"

Cold rain seemed to slide over my skin, into my blood. *Does all Jerusalem know Ahijah's plot—and mine?*

"How do you know this?" I did not waste breath denying or dissembling, for I needed to learn where the weak link lay. I could not afford to have my plans common gossip at the well.

"Three can hold a secret close if two of them are dead. What does it matter who told me? I know. Let me aid you. Please."

"Why?" I asked. I barely knew the Lady Helike; she was reserved and proud, turned in upon herself like a mirrored bowl. Nothing seemed to give her pleasure, not fine gowns, not jewels, not even rare foods. Yet she had come to me now, her eyes hot and desperate, her hands tense as a beggar's.

She did not answer but sank to her knees before me. "Princess, I beg of you—"

Seeing her humble herself so chilled me. "Don't," I said, stepping back. "Please, Lady Helike, do not—" Then somehow the right words came to my lips. "Rise, someone will see."

To my relief, Helike stood again at my words; plainly she feared to be seen petitioning me. "If you will not let me help you, Princess, there is nothing left for me."

"Did I say I would not? But first you must tell me why you think I need anyone's aid—and why you are so hot to offer me your friendship now, when we have barely spoken a dozen words to each other since you entered my father's palace." I slid my arm through hers; her flesh was stiff and cool with despair. "Come, walk with me, show me the flowers in your garden."

She turned a tragic face to me. "I care nothing for flowers."

"You should," I said, "for they hear many secrets."

She understood then; hope brightened her eyes. "Come then—but nothing planted in my garden grows as it should."

"Perhaps you have neglected the flowers; that is never wise." Chatting softly, I walked with her, trying to guess how the Lady Helike had learned my plans to escape from my father's world.

"Now," I said when we had reached her own small garden and walked safely alone among lemon trees in painted pots, "tell me what it is you wish—and do not waste my time, or yours, with lies or pretty words. You said you wished to help me—why, and how? And what price do you set upon your aid?"

Lady Helike stopped and looked at me straitly, her eyes cool as winter stone. "You seek to challenge the prophet Ahijah; that is a dangerous game. If you succeed—"

A chill slid into my bones. "How do you know this?"

She smiled, a wry curve of her mouth. "Women here talk; eunuchs talk even more. And men talk most of all. I listen."

"Say you are right." I plucked a lemon flower from the nearest tree. "If I succeed?"

"If you succeed, you will be gone. You will be free of this palace, of these stone walls."

Startled by the bitterness beneath her words, I said, "You are not happy here?"

A moment's pause; she laughed, softly, mocking her own pain. "Happy? Is a prisoner ever happy? Is an oath-breaker less dishonored because forced to it?" She spoke as if to herself alone; long-endured grief soured her words. She spoke of a pain so old and so familiar she had grown accustomed to the dull constant ache in her heart.

It is not pride with her, not pride at all. Shame flooded me, shame that I had not seen this truth long ago. This wife of my father's, this queen, walked the palace halls in sorrow and regret. Now I knew what lay behind Queen Helike's eyes: self-loathing. She hated, not my father but herself.

The lemon flower lay in my hand, petals crushed by my careless fingers; I brushed them from my skin. "How can I help you?" I asked.

She turned to me; desire shadowed her eyes. "If I aid you, will you take—"

"You with me?" Despair swept me, for that I knew I could not do. My father's wives were the knots that bound treaties, the tribute that bought peace. He could not bestow them as handmaidens, even upon his daughter; in a sense his wives were not my father's to give, only to take.

"No. No. It is too late for me. I cannot go back. But my daughter—you must take her with you."

"But my Lady Helike"—I made my voice very soft, gentle, as if coaxing a frightened kitten from a high branch—"you do not have a daughter."

"No. Not yet. But I will." She pressed her hands over her stomach, revealing new fullness still hidden beneath her tasseled skirt. "The Lady has promised me. I shall have a daughter, and she will redeem my broken oath."

I looked at her rounding body; the child would not be born for half-a-year yet. "Even if that is so, I shall be gone before she is born."

Gone or dead.

"You will take her. You will swear it. If you do not, I shall go before King Solomon and tell him what you plan."

"But Lady Helike—"

"You must. She must be given to Artemis-Hippona. If you do not take her, I shall slay her myself. No daughter of the Huntress will grow within these walls, a plaything for men's whims. A bauble for their lusts."

Ice seemed to creep over my skin; I knew I faced madness. "I will help you," I said, "but will you trust me? I must be gone before your child is born—but if it is a girl, I will send for her, foster her in my own courtyard. I swear it."

"She is a girl; she is promised." No doubt shadowed her mind. "You must vow her to the Lady of Swords, the Lady of Horses. You must swear that too."

"I will not vow away a girl's life without her consent. If she wishes it, she will go to your goddess. That I also swear."

I kept my voice calm, my words low and steady. It seemed to be enough; Helike drew in a deep breath and seemed to free herself from the madness caressing her.

"That is enough," she said at last. She smoothed her hands over her gently arching body once more, smiling; her eyes shone bright as full moons. "Yes, my queen; that is enough."

She sounded still half mad; I dared not leave her. And so I spun my mind, trying to think of some diversion that would interest her—and drive that moon-mad sheen from her eyes. What did I know of the Lady Helike?

Nothing, I realized, and shame burned my face. *She has lived here all these months so wretched she wishes to die of it, and I know nothing of her. Nothing at all, save—*

"You are the Horse Lord's daughter," I said, and Helike stared at me as if it were I who trembled upon madness. "Helike, do you know how to ride a horse?"

A moment later I was sorry, for she began to laugh—and then could not stop. She laughed until she sank to her knees and buried her face in her strong square hands, until the wild sound turned to cruel sobs. And I could do nothing to stop her. I could not even pry her hands from her face; she was stronger than I.

At last, desperate, I set my lips close to her ear and said, "My lady He-like, if you do not stop this, I will go to my father the king and ask his aid." I cast my voice to cut sharp.

And it worked; Helike gasped and coughed—and ceased to weep. She let her hands fall away from her face and gazed up at me.

"I am the Horse Lord's daughter and I rode ten years with the Sword Lady's Maidens. Oh, yes—I can ride a horse."

"Then would you ride with me?" I could not offer the Lady Helike much, but at least I could offer that.

"It is forbidden." No emotion colored Helike's voice. "King's wives do nothing."

"Nothing is forbidden if the king permits it," I said. "I will ask my father if you may ride with me—if you wish it."

She looked at me for a long time, then; at first her eyes seemed to look far beyond me, into some shadow I could not envision. Then, slowly, her gaze warmed, softened, and I knew she now saw me, and not whatever demon had drawn her away.

"He will grant me this," I said. "It is not seemly for a princess to ride alone."

"Or at all. Not in this land of a jealous god and greedy men. But you—your father will deny you nothing."

She weighted the words too clearly to mistake her meaning. Her father had denied her everything.

But that I could not mend. I could only offer what was mine to give. "Shall I ask him?" I said, and she stared down at her hands, hands still strong and hard, for all her long months in my father's palace.

"Yes," Helike said, her voice almost too soft to hear. "Yes, Princess. Ask."

When I approached my father to ask this boon, I saw he was wary of me, fearful that I would again beg him to let me follow the Spice Queen south. So when I only smiled and asked whether his wife Helike might ride out with me, his relief was so great he granted my petition without hesitation or conditions.

"Certainly the Lady Helike may ride with you, if she wishes it, Baalit. But do not tease her to accompany you if she does not wish to."

"She does," I assured him. "She told me she once rode from Troy to Damascus and back again. She can teach me much."

"Oh, yes—her father is the Horse Lord; he sends a hundred mares yearly in his tribute."

And daughters whom he regards as less worthy than his mares. But that I did not say. I only thanked my father, and ran off to tell Helike what he had said.

Benaiah

A long morning studying supply lists and judging between the demands of one garrison and another did not improve any man's temper. When Benaiah at last strode through the gateway that led from the guard wing to the open courtyard of the main palace, he thought only of savoring a jar of beer cool from the well.

"Benaiah," Nikaulis said, and all thought of cool beer fled his mind. The queen's captain stood in the shadow cast by the open gate; Benaiah turned towards her and looked into her steady eyes.

"I must speak with you." Although she did not whisper, her words were soft, pitched for his ears alone.

Privately, Benaiah thought, or she would not have asked at all. Now, where?

"Have I shown you the virtues of our city walls?" he said.

She smiled, plainly relieved he had so swiftly grasped her meaning. "Show me again."

Benaiah led the way to the nearest guard tower; Nikaulis followed, silent as his shadow. He refused to waste time trying to guess what she wished to say. Soon enough he would know. Until it was safe for them to talk, it was sufficient to know that Nikaulis thought the matter urgent and private.

They climbed the winding stone stairs within the tower; when at last they reached the doorway to the city wall, Benaiah said, "The walls shield all; here all the city may look upon us and not hear one word of what we may say to one another. So speak."

"The king's daughter courts danger," she said, staring intently at a rack holding spears for the city guard. "She seeks to use your prophet as her tool. She must be stopped."

Damn the girl! But Benaiah's face betrayed nothing; he lifted the topmost spear as if drawing Nikaulis's attention to the weapon. "Tell me."

Nikaulis chose words well and carefully; a few sentences sufficed to enlighten Benaiah. "Princess Baalit desires to return south with Queen Bilqis, who wishes her to rule Sheba as its next queen. King Solomon will not permit this."

No, I don't suppose he will. Too bad. It would be far better to pack Solomon's favorite child off to the farthest end of the world than to keep her spinning trouble in Jerusalem.

"Now the princess seeks to force the king to release her." Nikaulis turned and walked on down the wall. Benaiah set the spear back into its rack and followed without haste.

"Force him how?"

"At the next full moon, she plans to be found in the Goddess's Grove by the prophet Ahijah," Nikaulis said.

"Is she mad?" demanded Benaiah. "Her great-grandfather Saul died mad; it runs in her blood."

"Not mad, but desperate. The end will be the same."

"How do you know this?" asked Benaiah, and Nikaulis smiled wryly.

"I know this because people cannot remain silent even when speech will cost them dear. I remain silent, and so am forgotten. I listen." Nikaulis set her hands upon the parapet and gazed out over Jerusalem. The soaring sun poured light over the city's rooftops and gardens; King David's City seemed formed of gold and fire. "She must be stopped, Benaiah."

"Yes." If Ahijah laid violent hands upon King Solomon's daughter, blood would run in Jerusalem's gutters. "Now I will tell you what I have overheard: it is said King Solomon thinks to wed Prince Rehoboam to Princess Baalit, and so bind the kingdom close." *And there's a marriage made in madness— or in Queen Naamah's mind. Certainly neither of the king's children had dreamed up that pretty plot!*

Nikaulis turned to face him. "Is King Solomon such a fool? The princess will slit Rehoboam's throat in a month."

"Which would be no bad thing, save that deed would force King Solomon to condemn her to death in her turn. Perhaps she had better poison him; poison is harder to prove."

Nikaulis stared at him, plainly wondering whether he jested.

"Perhaps I jest so we may laugh rather than weep," Benaiah said. "How is it that a man as wise as Solomon can deal so foolishly with his own children?"

Nikaulis shrugged. "Is the wedding tale true?"

"That I do not know—but I overheard those jackals Prince Rehoboam calls friends gloating over his victory."

"And how did they know?" Nikaulis asked.

"Some days ago Prince Rehoboam boasted of it to them—and of how he would tame Princess Baalit once she was his wife, to do with as pleased him."

"The prince is twice a fool." Disdain soured Nikaulis's words.

"Yes. And I will say a thing to you, Nikaulis, that I would not say to any other. King Solomon is the greatest fool of all if he thinks he can summon that future." Benaiah sighed. "Well, I suppose we must stop this nonsense. I tell you freely, Nikaulis, that it is not easy serving kings."

"Or queens. No, it is not. How stop them, Benaiah?" Nikaulis then waited, patient as stone, as Benaiah considered the touchy problem.

Some tasks were best postponed indefinitely. Stopping King Solomon's daughter before she challenged the prophet Ahijah was not one of them. While Nikaulis gazed at sunlight burning across the summer hills, Benaiah silently planned his campaign.

"I will need you," he said at last; Nikaulis inclined her head in assent.

"Ask," she said.

"On the night of the full moon, guard the gate to the princess's court-yard. I can trust no one else with the task. No one is to enter it, or to leave, save King Solomon himself."

"Not even Benaiah, Commander of the King's Army?"

He smiled. "I least of all. For were I permitted to see Princess Baalit alone, the temptation to beat her bloody for this trick might prove too strong to re-sist. Now come with me; we must talk to the priestess of the Grove."

Nikaulis

The Grove's chief priestess merely stared at them when told what they knew. "Well, we cannot allow that," she said. "King Solomon's tolerance is great, but not so great he will overlook his own daughter worshipping here—or pretending to."

"No," said Benaiah. "And Ahijah tolerates nothing."

"No, Ahijah tolerates nothing, not even himself," agreed Asherah's priestess. "Poor man; he suffers because he will not yield to the fact that he himself is only a man."

Benaiah shrugged. "Suffer he may, claw down the king's daughter to harm the king he may not."

The priestess inclined her head; long henna-red curls fell across her breasts. "If the princess shows her face at our gate, we will send her away."

"She won't," said Benaiah. "I shall see to that. And you are to see that no woman save your priestesses can be found in the Grove this full moon."

"You would have me forbid women their worship?" the priestess asked, and Nikaulis saw the sly trap in the woman's eyes.

"The king's general forbids nothing." Nikaulis stepped forward, offering herself as a shield between the priestess and Benaiah. "Let women and men worship as they please—only not this full moon."

"Not unless you want the Grove's trees burned and its ground sown with salt," Benaiah finished.

"King Solomon's threat?" the priestess asked, and Benaiah shrugged again.

"Men's folly," he said, and the priestess smiled.

"Our Lady's thanks to you, my lord Benaiah, and to you, Sword Maid. Trust me, on the night of the full moon, no man shall find what he seeks here." She crossed her henna-red palms over her bare breasts and bowed her head; Benaiah nodded and turned away. Nikaulis followed; she glanced back, once, and saw the chief priestess still standing where they had spoken to her before the willow tree.

"She seems a sensible woman," Benaiah said as they walked back down the path through the Grove towards the gate. "If we have good fortune, we shall thwart both princess and prophet. And I don't know which I'd like to beat more. King Solomon should have banned that canting prophet from the kingdom years ago. Prophets are never anything but trouble. Samuel, Nathan—although Nathan could be reasonable. But Ahijah is never reasonable."

Nikaulis had seen the prophet only in passing. But unlike those of the other men here, men who disparaged her skills as both warrior and woman even as lust darkened their eyes, Ahijah's eyes had held only clean loathing. That iron honesty Nikaulis could admire. "No. Whatever his faults, Ahijah is no hypocrite. I could stand before him naked and the prophet would only turn away."

As soon as the words left her lips, Nikaulis wished she could recall them.

But it was too late. The Lady's Grove summoned passion and folly from men's and women's hearts.

Benaiah stopped, touched her arm; she turned to face him squarely. "I would not turn away, Nikaulis," Benaiah said, and then, "Would you?"

Unfair, unjust; how can I answer? At last she said, "You think this a game. I am not a prize to be won, Benaiah."

He said nothing; she counted heartbeats, willing her blood to calm. At last he said, "This is the only game and the only prize, Nikaulis. I know that now, and so do you. Tell me it is not too late for me to do honor to the Queen of Heaven. Tell me it is not too late to win you."

Although his words were humble, his voice rang as firm as if he ordered troops upon a battlefield. Even as petitioner, Benaiah stood straight and strong as a good blade.

I must not soften; he is hard iron, so must I be also. Nikaulis looked into Benaiah's steady dark eyes. He lusted for her; desire burned hot behind his eyes, rippled hot beneath his calm words.

"Tell me," Benaiah repeated. "Tell me, Nikaulis."

As if kindled by his demand, heat slid serpent-smooth beneath her skin, coiled within her loins. Long years of discipline granted her the power to mask response, but not to quench the fire his had kindled within her.

"You do not command me, Benaiah." Moon-masked; such control would serve for the moment. "As for the Queen of Heaven—ask her for yourself. You do not need me for that."

"I command you as you command me." Still Benaiah did not move; did not attempt to touch her. "You are my match, Nikaulis, as I am yours. I have sought you all my life, war-bride."

"But I have not sought you." The words fell from her lips like stones, cold and hard. *How could I seek what I did not know I lacked?*

At last Benaiah reached out to her; she braced herself to repulse an embrace, setting her hand upon her dagger's hilt. *Now he shows himself for what all men are—selfish and greedy.* Such a man was easily denied, easily forgotten.

"Peace," Benaiah said, and laid his hand over hers. His sword-hardened skin touched hers as gently as water. "Never in my life have I forced a woman; do you think I would start with you?"

"Dare, and learn sorrow." Nikaulis refused to shrink from the touch of his hand on hers. *Nothing. It means nothing.*

For long moments, she thought he would not answer. Then, at last, he let his hand slip from hers.

"Dare, and learn joy," he said. And before she could summon an answer, he turned and walked away from her through the Grove, down the winding path back to the Lady's Gate.

Long after Benaiah had walked away, leaving her standing alone within the Grove, Nikaulis still felt his hand press upon hers, an invisible caress. A bond—

Yes, a bond, she reminded herself. *A chain for a soft-witted woman.* Just as Benaiah's words sought to command her mind, his hands sought to command her body. *No one commands a woman's will without her consent.* That lesson Nikaulis had learned before she had breasts, before she had the strength to lift a sword or pull a bow.

Slowly she turned and walked towards the Grove's edge, following the path Benaiah had used. *Benaiah will not command me; I will not be lured by a man's strength with sword and spear. I am not to be won like a warrior's prize. I will not surrender.*

At the Lady's Gate she paused, looking up at the smiling goddess painted upon the gatepost. Lady of Love, fruitful and profligate; alien to a Sword Maid's vows. "I will not surrender," she said to the bright idol above her. "Not to Benaiah. Not to You. Not even to myself."

So vowing, she walked down the path away from the Grove. As she stepped beyond the trees, into the hot still light of midday, she heard a sound behind her. A whisper of leaves tossed by a playful breeze, a ripple of sun-warm laughter.

But there was no breeze. And when Nikaulis swiftly turned to catch the laughing spy, she saw no one.

Only the Lady's Gate, and an empty path, and a painted goddess shadowed by dust-gilded trees.

Later, when she lay alone in the bed across her queen's doorway, Nikaulis found she could not sleep. She had been set a riddle she could not answer, been challenged to a battle she could not win. Turning on her side to stare into the darkness, she tried to think, and saw Benaiah's form in the shadows, heard his voice in the murmurs of the night.

A choice lay before her; a choice between the queen she had served so long and well and the man she knew only as a worthy opponent, a match for her own skill.

I care nothing for him. He does not kindle my blood. Lie; she had only to ask her own heart to know that.

She needs me. Truth; the queen needed her. But needed her as queen's captain, not as Nikaulis. Any woman as skilled as she could serve as well. Or any man. Only custom dictated that the queen's guard be a woman.

And each year it grew harder to find women who owned the needful skills. Women possessed by no one but themselves, who rode and fought and lived as free as any man. Once the Amazons had been a power in the lands, ridden the war-roads, ruled an empire of the wind.

Now the Maiden clans remaining lived hidden, secret; ruled no more than shadows, their ancient customs fading even in their own memories.

A dozen generations ago an Amazon ruled as Queen of Athens beside Theseus Kingslayer. A dozen generations hence, who will remember we once rode beside the kings of men and were counted their equals?

Time rode with iron hooves; no woman and no man could turn its course.

I grow—womanish. A bitter smile curved her lips. Such thoughts could not aid her in the choice the gods had spread before her. Only cold truth would serve.

The queen, or the man? Duty—or love?

The Lady of Swords owned her service, pledged long ago. And all the years since she had taken that vow, Nikaulis had served Her faithfully and well. Now, without warning, the Lady of Love beckoned, and She, too, was owed worship. But just as the Dark Sister and the Bright owned their own realms, so, too, did they own their own servants.

I cannot serve both Duty and Love. Wiser and stronger women than she had torn themselves to bloody ruin in the attempt. Nikaulis could not serve both goddesses; she must, in the end, choose.

Time spread two futures before her, a merchant displaying glittering wares. Upon this cloth, a life cool as a string of flawless pearls: Nikaulis the queen's guard, the Moon Maid, the Amazon walking pure and cool all her chaste life. *And never again to see him? Never again test my heart and will against his?*

Then take up the other offering: a handful of stones bright and dark. The rarest gems glowed beside dull smooth stones; a woman's days, some bright. Some dark. *Become just a woman like all the others? Become nothing more than his prize?*

Neither life held all that she desired; she must choose, knowing that to choose was also to reject.

So which?

Return to her old life, safe and sure?

Or entrust herself to the unknown, and hazard all she was?

So it seems choice, too, is a duty. And whichever course I choose, I choose tears.

Baalit Sings

In my mind, the fateful night unfolded before me as if I alone wove the pattern of its hours. I forgot that other men and women possessed fears and desires. And I forgot that those I expected to dance the measures of my song had not learned their steps.

My father had told me I had many lessons left to learn. He was right. That night taught me again what I had learned but chosen to forget as I plotted to gain my future: that no man sees himself as no more than one spear-carrier standing among many; that no woman sees herself as no more than one spinner sitting among all the rest.

In our own hearts, we all are our god's best beloved. We are all heroes.

So while I laid out my plans in the arrogance of youth, others also prepared for the Night of the Full Moon. Had I thought well upon the matter even for a heartbeat, I would have gone to the Grove by sundown, waited there until full dark. My warning to Ishvaalit had ensured that my plan was now known almost as widely as was Ahijah's. Too many people knew. And there may be a way in which a secret told even to one other may be kept within palace walls, but if there is, I have not yet learned it, even now.

My true folly was to think no one would care, save I—and Ahijah.

But that night only one thing troubled me, and that was the thought that the prophet Ahijah might not come to the Grove. He had sworn he would seek me out there, drag me out of the Grove's darkness into the light of the

Law's justice. Surely he would keep his word. *But suppose he chooses another night? I cannot run to the Grove each moon on the chance that is the night he will appear!*

By the time I had adorned myself in gown and gems befitting a venture to the Grove of the Morning Star, the western sky burned red and gold. To the east the sky deepened to the blue of night; the edges of the eastern hills glowed silver, heralding the rising moon.

I paced my balcony, restless as a caged leopard. Surely Khurrami and Irsiya should have come to me by now. Surely Helike should already be scratching at my gate, ready to set her feet upon the Grove's path once more. I twisted the serpent of gold about my wrist, toyed with the silver tassels fringing my girdle. Over the eastern hills, the moon rose full, a bright shield against the fall of night.

I looked at the moon and knew with chill certainty that the others were not coming, or they would have been here long ago. *So I must do this thing alone.* For a heartbeat the task seemed too hard for me, too dangerous; my courage melted like salt in rain, and I knew I could not do it—

You must. My inner voice sounded unfamiliar, as if a stranger spoke. *This is your one chance. Act now, or lament forever.*

Now I saw that it had been selfish and craven to rely upon the others to risk themselves for me. *It is your life, your future. You must take the risk if you desire the reward.*

I lifted my eyes to the rising moon. Nothing troubled the moon; she soared the heavens free and silent as a swan, following her own path through endless night. So too would I soar. I had only to summon my courage, and fly.

But in the end, I flew only so far as my courtyard gate. As I stepped beyond it, two shapes moved forward out of the shadows thrown by torchlight. For a breath my skin chilled; the forms seemed ghosts in the unsteady light.

"No, Princess," said Benaiah, and a cold stone seemed to settle in my stomach, freezing me where I stood. Benaiah, my father's commander of the army, and beside him, Nikaulis, captain of the Spice Queen's guard—I would rather it had been ghosts.

"What—what are you doing here?" I demanded, wishing my voice did not sound so much like a mouse's squeak.

"Stopping a foolish girl from causing much pain to herself and to her father," Benaiah said, and that was how my daring scheme ended—with an order from Benaiah for me to behave myself and stop acting like a silly child.

I did not even try to elude them; I knew it would be not only useless, but pointless. I would not defy king and prophet this night. And another moon would be too late.

"Nikaulis will make sure you wait until your father comes to you," Benaiah said. "And I grant her complete authority to use any means necessary to keep you safely in your own courtyard. Do you understand me?"

I longed to speak cool, regal words that would shrivel Benaiah's composure, but I retained enough sense to know that any words I uttered now would sound like the mewling of a spoiled child. So I said nothing. I only nodded and walked past Benaiah and Nikaulis, back through the gate into my garden court.

Behind me, I heard the ebony gate close. I stared at the closed gate until my heartbeat slowed again, my breathing steadied. Then I turned and walked slowly across my courtyard and sat beside the alabaster fountain. I could do nothing now but wait.

Ahijah

For all his rage against Asherah's Grove, Ahijah had never before set foot within that ungodly place. Now he must, for the sake of the kingdom itself. Never had it occurred to him that he would be denied entry.

But when he strode up the path of gilded bricks and approached the gateway to the Grove of the Morning Star, a woman barred his path. Her lips were painted scarlet and her eyelids green; a gilded leather belt two handspans wide circled her waist. Her bare breasts rose like twin moons above the gilded leather, and her thighs gleamed white through the ribbons of her skirt. She held her hands out, palms upward, as Ahijah approached.

"Peace, brother," she began, and Ahijah lifted his staff and slammed it into the ground between them.

"Silence, harlot, and let me pass. I am here on Yahweh's business."

The woman did not move. "You may pass when you come here on Asherah's business," she said. "Anger and hatred are not welcome in the Lady's Grove, Prophet."

So the painted strumpet knew him, and still would not let him pass; pain gnawed Ahijah's stomach. *She will beg to do my bidding before the Lord of Hosts is done with her!*

"Step aside, lest the Most High strike you down, and this blasphemous den of vice with you."

The guardian of the gate laughed. "Your god has not struck us down yet; perhaps He is not as offended by our worship as you are."

She shall be struck down; dogs will eat of her corrupt flesh. Ahijah strove to console himself with the thought, refused to falter in his purpose.

"Let me pass, harlot," he said, and walked forward as if the woman did not exist. *Yahweh will uphold me; His strength will support me. His will shall be done.*

He was not surprised when the half-clothed woman surrendered the path to him; he brushed past her as if she were mist, his eyes fixed upon the path into the Grove. But as he passed, he smelled the cassia and nard upon her skin; heard a low ripple of laughter.

"Look well, Yahweh's Prophet. Look well, and learn."

I will look. And it is you who will learn, harlot. You and King Solomon's daughter—all of you will learn the price of mocking Yahweh and His prophet!

He had searched the Grove, looked upon evil and upon licentiousness past bearing. Gazed upon painted idols, upon painted women, harlots offering themselves to any man who passed by. He had endured the pressure of lust, of wantonness scenting the air like heavy perfume.

He had endured the sly smiles, and the soft laughter as he strode through the Goddess's Grove upon his god's work.

For nothing. Knowledge of his failure burned beneath his heart, gnawed fierce and hot. *Nothing.* King Solomon's daughter had not been found within the Grove. All the women who flaunted themselves that night wore the scarlet-tasseled belt that marked them as priestesses, as daughters of lust. As women sworn to lie with any man who desired them.

But the other women who flocked to the Grove each full moon to slake their lusts had not come this night. The only women in the Grove this night were the priestesses, with their whispers and their laughter.

The king's daughter was not there.

Baalit Sings

All that long night, I sat beside the singing fountain. Above me stars slid across the sky, changing with the changing hours. As the night sky paled from black to deepest blue, heralding dawn, the ebony gate opened.

It was my father; I had known he must come. I had been bracing myself to meet his anger.

As my father walked towards me, I rose from my seat at the fountain's edge. When he stood before me, I bowed my head. "Father—"

"Do not waste your breath on pieties you do not mean." Never had I heard him speak to me so coldly. This was not my father speaking; this was the king.

"I do mean them. I do honor you, Father." To my distress, my words trembled upon the air. I bit the inside of my lip hard, suddenly fearing I might weep.

"You choose an odd way of doing me honor. You are not a child, Baalit; you are nearly a woman ready for marriage. And you are not some slave's child. You are a king's daughter. Kings cannot afford folly."

He paused, and I drew a deep breath, readying myself to respond calmly. But I was not given the chance.

"I had thought you well-taught and wise, Baalit. How could you plot such deadly folly? Were it not for Benaiah's good sense and loyalty, Ahijah would even now be dragging you before the wall for stoning."

"I knew you would stop that."

"Yes, if I knew of it. Ah, I see that pricks you. Good." There was no softness in him now, no yielding. King Solomon spoke, his words clear, his wisdom sharp as a well-honed blade. "Daughter, what were you thinking?"

Cold fear sank into my bones. "Father, I—" My mouth was too dry for words; I tried again. "I had thought he would accuse me in your court. That you would have to send me away to ensure my safety."

"Send you away. Send you away with her—" Sorrow shadowed my father's face; never had I seen him look so weary. For an instant I saw clearly how he would look when he was old.

"Daughter," he said at last, "it is not wise to set in motion events you cannot control."

"Father," I said, "you should have thought of that before you taught me that my mind was my own."

It seemed to me that time slowed, stopped. My father stared at me as if I were a stranger to him, stared and said nothing. Then at last he said, "Yes, I should have thought of that." And then he turned and walked away. I longed to run after him, to call him back, but sorrow weighted me like stones, and I bowed beneath its burden, silent.

For a long time after my father closed the ebony gate behind him, I sat upon the carved bench beside the pale smooth fountain and watched the singing water fall from basin to basin until it reached the lowest point and bubbled up to begin again. The water-song was soothing, like a mother's lullaby; while the water sang, I need think of nothing. The endlessly falling water washed away all thought. Or so it had always done, when I had come here with some childish distress.

But in this hour, in the clear light of rising dawn, my mind was too troubled for the fountain to work its magic. Nothing could soothe away this disaster.

Too restless in my bones to sit any longer, I sought out my other talismans. I brought my mother's ivory box out to my garden courtyard and sat again beside the fountain, counting over her treasures. Always before, they had quieted my mind, invoked peace.

This time, I could not summon what I sought. My fingers caressed the coral beads and pearls of my mother's necklace, but the smooth gems remained cool, refusing comfort. I set the necklace aside and took up the ancient Asherah. The honeyed ivory also failed me; the little goddess lay unyielding in my hand.

The perfume vial still smelled of cinnamon, faint and fading. But when I closed my eyes, no dream-memories danced for me. The vial held a dying fragrance, and that was all.

At last I curled my fingers into the brass and crystal bracelet; that shabby bauble that seemed so out of place among a queen's dearest treasures. But had it not been dear to my mother's heart, the trinket would not have been cherished in the ivory casket. The bracelet's tarnished metal did not glitter; the river crystals barely caught the light.

In the hour I most needed its aid, my mother's legacy had failed me. *Oh, that is the easy path. It is you who have failed; do not blame memories and ghosts.* I forced myself to face that honestly, to accept the pain my thoughts brought. For all I could think of was the greatness of my failure. My clever design had brought nothing but disaster.

I had failed the Sheban queen, and the Lady Helike, and all those unknown men and women waiting in the Land Beyond Morning. I had failed my mother's memory. I had failed my father.

And I had failed myself.

This last bit sharpest; I forced myself to look upon my prideful folly straight and clear. For I had not acted with wisdom and courage and honor. My cold fingers clenched, and pain jabbed my flesh. I looked down and saw that a rough crystal had sliced my skin; a little hurt, but enough to sting. *Punishment for folly, and far less than you deserve.* Staring at the tiny bead of blood upon my finger, I told over my faults.

I had not acted with wisdom. My father had spoken truly when he said I had acted with deadly folly. I had assigned Ahijah a role that I had no assurance he would play. I had set in motion events I could not rule.

I had not acted with courage. To dare heedless of the true price is folly twice over. I had seen only my own part in my spinning—but whatever I spun pulled others into my thread. Had I not been stopped at my own gate, I would have dragged others into my disgrace. From the guards at the palace gates to the priestesses of the Grove, not one would have been untouched.

I had not acted with honor. For I had schemed like Delilah, seeking to obtain my desire by deceit.

And you sought to be a true queen! My own scorn burned my throat, sour as bile. Rather than acting as a great queen, I had behaved like a spoiled, willful child. Not once had I thought of the risk my plan brought to others, or of the pain. I had thought only of walking my own path without hindrance.

Worst of all, I had told myself I acted for the sake of others. For the queen, and for Helike, and for the people of Sheba. That was a lie.

I had done it for myself.

Tears pressed sharp and hot behind my eyes; I held my eyes wide open, refused to let fall easy tears. *No, look well upon what you have done. Think well upon what you have done. And then?*

I laid the brass-and-crystal bracelet back in the ivory treasure box. I stared at the blood that shone like a tiny ruby upon my finger.

And then begin again.

But how? The question tormented me; I thought upon it all the rest of that long day, and far into the night. I sat and stared out my window over the roofs of Jerusalem until the dying moon set. Then I sighed and set the problem from me, telling myself I would think better in the morning. I would try to sleep, and hope to dream.

Sleep came swiftly; I slid easily into its quiet darkness. But I could not summon dreams. Tonight the ghosts I desired would not come to me, and even in lonely sleep I understood that whatever I did now I must achieve with my own efforts, relying upon no one but myself.

And when I awoke, I knew at last what I must do.

My grand and glorious scheme to achieve my own way had been the dream of a child heedless of anything other than her own desires. And worse, my success required others to collude in my plans—plans of which they were ignorant. I had thought to dance them like puppets to tunes only I could hear.

I must achieve my goals by my own will. I could not rely upon any other man or woman to achieve my goals for me. My ambitions were my own; only I could summon my victories.

My intrigue to force my father to grant my petition had deserved to fail. *When I asked, and he denied, I should have simply walked out the palace gate and followed the queen barefoot to Sheba if I must. Anything, rather than attempt to trick consent from my father's lips.*

But I had thought only of my wishes, of my freedom. Never had I thought of what my actions might bring to others, what good or ill I might do. *You saw yourself as queen of the world, doing as you willed without thought, without payment.* As if the Spice Queen had hazarded all she treasured only to give a girl heedless freedom.

Heat flooded me; my face burned as if with fever. Never had I known such shame—and that I alone knew of my selfish folly was little consolation. Now I knew what Amyntor had meant the day I had asked him to help me deceive my father, when he had looked at me and said, "*I will know.*"

It did not matter if all the world thought me a paragon of royal virtues, for I knew what a selfish fool I had been. I no longer thought well of myself. And so guilt burned like slow fire in my bones.

Do not give yourself airs, child. The inner voice chided me, echo of words of guidance spoken long ago, almost forgotten. I did not mistake their message.

For remorse, too, could serve as a kind of self-glory; I reminded myself that my sin was one of thoughtless omission. I had not borne false witness, nor done murder, nor even failed to honor my father. I had merely thought only of my own desires.

Well, that would change. If I saw in Sheba's offer only a glorious life for myself, I was not worthy of the prize offered to me. *"A true king thinks first of the future, next of his people, and last of himself."* I knew my father lived by the iron rule of honor. I could do no less.

So I must begin again, facing my father openly and fearlessly—just as any other of his subjects might. For did King Solomon not hold open court one day in seven so that any man or woman who sought the king's justice might come freely before him, and ask him to judge rightly?

Any man or woman. Even a harlot. Even a queen.

Even his own willful daughter.

Bilqis

The queen heard the tale while she still lay abed; Khurrami padded in just as dawn flowed pale and pure over the Judean hills. Sensing the presence of another, Bilqis woke to find her handmaiden kneeling beside the bed.

"What is wrong?" She did not waste words on lesser questions. Khurrami would not have woken her at this hour for any light reason.

"The Princess Baalit," Khurrami began, and Bilqis sat up, fear sinking fangs into her belly. But she kept silent, letting Khurrami tell the tale as she would.

And it was not an easy thing to hold her tongue and allow Khurrami to speak freely. "The Princess Baalit came to me," Khurrami said, "and begged my aid. She wished to visit the Grove of the Morning Star, but dared not go alone. So she asked me to accompany her, and I agreed."

But something had gone wrong. Baalit had been stopped before she set her feet even a pace beyond her own courtyard gate. "The king's general Benaiah prevented the princess from leaving—he and Nikaulis."

Thank Mother Ilat that Nikaulis has sense, even if Khurrami does not! Slow anger crawled through Sheba's bones. Only long training permitted her to control her voice.

"So the Princess Baalit asked you to accompany her to the Grove—and this you did not choose to tell me?" Her voice remained smooth; good. Moving with care, lest her anger overrule her will, she pushed back her blanket and rose to her feet. "No, do not explain; I have no time for that now. Find out where King Solomon is, and bring me back word. Hurry."

Without a word, Khurrami bowed and ran out. Refusing to succumb to the trap of rushing into heedless action, Sheba stretched slowly and then rang the branch of silver bells to summon her maids.

As soon as Khurrami returns, I shall go to Solomon. It did not take a serpent's wisdom to grasp Princess Baalit's intention. *A bold plan, little princess, but also a rash one.* The girl had wit and will and courage— *But she is still too young to know how to shape tomorrow to her own ends.*

For today, someone must unknot this tangled cord, and she would not leave Solomon to face the task alone.

As her maids combed out her hair, Bilqis weighed her choices: appear before Solomon as queen or as woman. Before she had decided, Khurrami returned, plainly bearing unwelcome news.

"Forgive me, O Queen, but no one knows where the king is. At daybreak he went to the Princess Baalit's courtyard. But since he left its gate again, no man has seen him."

"And has no woman seen him either?" she asked coolly. "If that is how you speak now, Khurrami, it is past time we returned home to Sheba."

No man has seen him— She smiled and shook out her hair, letting it ripple over her shoulders. *I know where you are, Solomon my love. And I know how I must come to you.*

She only hoped that Mother Ilat would tell her what she then must say.

She found him where she had known he must be, alone in the tower garden where they had shared joy. Solomon stood at the roof's edge, his hands resting upon the wall between him and the air below. Even as she entered the garden, she saw that he held his body stiff, as if he feared to move, lest movement release more pain.

And she knew, as well, that he sensed her presence— *And fears that I, too, have come to cause him pain. And so I have, but I do only what must be done.*

Silent, she walked across the tower roof until she stood beside him. He did not speak, nor did she; for a time they watched doves circle the dust-gold roofs below, swallows soar in the blue air above. At last she said, "What will you do, beloved?"

Solomon hesitated, staring out over the rooftops of King David's City. "I will do nothing unjust."

"No. You never will do anything unjust, Solomon." She moved, slowly, and laid her fingers gently upon his hand. "My love, it is not a matter of all or nothing. You marry the daughters of other lands to wed their interests to your own. How much more—"

"If my own daughter rules? Do you think me a fool, that I have not thought of that?"

"No, I do not think you a fool. But Solomon, my heart—do not think your daughter a fool either. She is not; she is only young. So young."

Solomon turned his hand, twined his fingers through hers. "Too young. Were we ever that young, dove of my heart? That arrogant? That sure of ourselves?"

"Yes, my love, we were. But that was long ago. Now it is your daughter's turn to dance. Do not shackle her to your own fears, Solomon. Do not sacrifice her to the past."

"I will not sacrifice her at all. Let Ahijah rave. I am king. I can protect my own daughter."

"In the face of that madman's denunciations?" Bilqis shook her head. "Perhaps now, when you are strong. But what of later? Life is uncertain, a king's life more uncertain than a peasant's. When you are weak, or dead— then what becomes of her?"

Solomon stood silent, and she pressed on. "There is only one safety for a woman in your land, Solomon—you must marry her to a husband strong enough to stand against her enemies. And that means—"

"That I must marry her far away from me." The words came slow and hard; Solomon stared at nothing. His fingers slipped from hers, and she let him go. "That I must give her to a king in a foreign land, send her to dwell among strangers. And so lose her forever."

"Yes." She longed to caress his hand again, to stroke his cheek, convey comfort from her flesh. But she did not. This battle Solomon must fight alone, or he would forever regret yielding.

"I had hoped to wed her to a good man of Jerusalem, one whose house was close by." Solomon's beautiful mouth twisted in a wry smile. "I had hoped to keep her my child forever."

"She will always be your daughter, Solomon. But she must live her own life."

Silent, Solomon bowed his head. Then he said, "Where does wisdom lie now? In my heart, or in yours?"

"In both, my love. And in neither." She longed to beg him, to plead for what she so desired. But in the end, she said nothing at all.

For their fates rested now on Solomon's wisdom, and his love. *Please, Bright One, let him make the right choice. For his own sake, as well as for mine—and hers.*

Abishag

As easily as she had flung aside her sober veil my mother shed her life as the widow Zilpah. "Now I may claim myself again," she said. "I may grant Zhurleen of Ascalon life once more."

More than that, she would not tell me. "Later, if you still wish to know, I will tell you what you have not learned by then. But I think I have taught you well enough for you to glean my story for yourself."

Never again did I see the modest merchant's wife Zilpah; that woman was gone forever. Zhurleen of Ascalon painted her face and garbed herself in scarlet and gold—and set up a shrine in her room to an ivory goddess whose outstretched hands held golden pomegranates and whose painted smile seemed to echo my mother's.

Some of her old life I did learn for myself; enough to know that once my mother had dwelt in King David's palace. But that had been long ago, and few women remained who remembered her.

Of course Queen Michal knew, but somehow I never dared ask her to speak of the past she shared with my mother, and the only other woman who might know was Solomon's mother, Bathsheba. She, I am sure, would have told me whatsoever I wished—but the time for that never seemed to be ripe. Later, much later, when it was too late, I realized that never in all our shared days in the king's palace was I left alone with Queen Bathsheba. Always Queen Michal was there, or my own mother, clinging to Bathsheba like her shadow.

Baalit Sings

The next great court lay three days in the future; I had ample time to think, and to burnish my new design until each step I must take shone clear. This time I must make no mistake, for I had to wager all my future on one throw of the bones.

Upon the third day, I summoned Nimrah and Keshet and commanded my finest garments be brought. "Today I go before my father's court," I said, as they exchanged wary glances, "and must not shame him." That was all; I would not burden them with my doubts and fears.

For once I did not fret as my handmaidens fussed and debated over each garment. My patience puzzled them as much as it pleased, but neither questioned me. I stood still as a temple idol as Keshet slid a mist-thin tunic onto my body, as Nimrah offered a crimson gown. She and Keshet held the gown as I stepped into it; they drew the soft rich cloth up and pinned it closed with golden brooches fashioned in the shape of courting bees. I held out my arms, and Nimrah knelt and wrapped the wide girdle about my hips; gilded leather soft and supple as water. Tassels braided of fine wool and heavy with silver beads hung from the leather girdle to my knees.

"And your hair, Princess?"

For once I did not shrug and say it did not matter. All I did, all I was, all I appeared to be mattered. How did I wish to appear before my father—*No. How does the Princess Baalit, who seeks the crown of the Queen of the South, wish to appear before King Solomon the Wise?*

At last I looked at Nimrah and said, "You know where I am going today, and why. Do my hair as you think best."

"Yes, Princess." Nimrah began to tame my wild hair. When she had done, my hair lay in a smooth-woven crown of braids, flowing into a coil gleaming like a serpent at the nape of my neck. When I looked in my mirror, my eyes widened in admiration of her handiwork.

"You have made a crown of her hair," Keshet said, and Nimrah smiled. "It is how Queen Michal wore her hair, when she sat beside the Lady Bathsheba in your father's court." And then, when she saw Keshet and me staring at her, Nimrah said, "I asked Queen Nefret; she remembered, and drew a picture for me. Later I will show you."

"Yes," I said, "Later. Thank you, Nimrah. Now let me see my jewels."

I chose gems with great care; today I must go before the king as his equal in dignity and honor. Earrings of emerald and beaten gold, hairpins shimmering and trembling with leaves of thin gold and silver. A necklace formed of carved ivory plaques and another of golden snakes twined into an endless knot. Bracelets of ivory from the south and amber from the north.

And at last, when Nimrah and Keshet assured me I was adorned as richly as any goddess, I hesitated, and then took up the shoddy bracelet of worn brass chains from my mother's ivory casket. The movement shook flakes from the fragile river crystals, glittering drops of time past.

"This too," I said, and although Nimrah and Keshet exchanged puzzled glances, neither said a word. Keshet merely bent her head to the task of fastening the timeworn bauble about my left wrist.

All that remained was to don the silver veil, pin its glittering mist securely to my smooth-braided hair. And then I was ready, and Keshet held up my mirror.

I gazed upon a stranger in silver, glittering and unreal. No longer a heedless girl, but a woman. A queen in waiting. But pride did not kindle my blood; an odd chill slid through my veins like slow poison.

"So this is what a queen looks like." I tried to make my words light, mocking my silver ghost in the mirror. But Keshet did not giggle; Nimrah did not murmur agreement. Instead, my words fell harsh and heavy into silence.

"Yes, this is what a queen looks like. Does it please you, child?"

Behind me in the mirror, a shadow danced; I flung down the silver mirror and spun around in a swirl of veil and a chiming of golden anklets, to face the woman who questioned me. For a heartbeat it seemed I looked still into the silver mirror, for her eyes were mine. And although I had not looked upon her face since I was seven years old, I knew who she was.

"Grandmother," I said, and she smiled, and opened her arms to me.

At first I marveled over her arrival, wondering how she knew herself needed, only to hear her laugh.

"Dearest child, do you think every prince and pigherd from Baghdad to Damascus does not know how the Wise King and the Spice Queen dally in the Lady's Dance? Asherah's doves carry the new songs almost as swiftly as rumor. Every temple from here to world's end has received the news by now—even those whose birds are too plump to fly farther than across a courtyard!" A dark cloak embroidered with little stars covered her from throat to ankles; now she flung the cloak aside, revealing clothing such as I had never before seen.

A skirt tiered like lizard's scales; a belt of stiff crimson leather two handspans wide; a bodice tight beneath her breasts, pushing them up as if cupped by loving hands. Golden bees hung heavy from her ears; golden doves spread gleaming wings across her bare breasts. Golden serpents coiled about her arms from wrist to elbow—and beneath her skin, serpents inked darkly into her flesh shadowed those of metal. She watched me stare, and smiled.

"This is how a priestess dresses in our Lady's House, for She is very old, and the old grow stubborn in their ways. So to suit Her pleasure, we garb ourselves as if we dwelt in ancient halls. Ah, well—no one ever claimed the gods owned any taste in clothes!" And she laughed, which startled me even more than her seemingly impious words. "Oh, do not look so shocked, Baalit. Do you think my Lady has no better way to pass Her time than eavesdropping on our lightest words? Or that She cannot laugh?"

"I—I do not know." *Your grandmother Zhurleen? I remember her laugh. Yes, that is how I recall her—the Laughing One. Always, always she would laugh.*

"Doubt, they say, is the beginning of wisdom. Now, daughter of my daughter, humor an old woman and tell her just how you plan to unknot the thread you have so thoroughly tangled. And do not tell me you don't know what I mean, little goddess, for I am old, not feebleminded. Sit, and tell me all that has happened to bring you to this threshold."

And so I sat beside my laughing grandmother and told her all that had happened since the Queen of the South rode through Jerusalem's gate, and all the wrong I had done through folly, and how I planned to mend what I had broken. My grandmother listened, and sometimes asked a quiet question, but she did not laugh—or even smile. I did not know enough then to thank her for that great kindness; only years later did I realize how much self-control it takes for the old to listen solemnly to the young. But my grandmother Zhurleen granted me that boon. When I told her all that was in my heart and mind, all I dreamed of becoming, she listened—and did not laugh.

Instead, when I at last fell silent, she took my hands in hers. "A good plan, Baalit; better than many conjured up by older and wiser heads. You do well to approach your father bravely and openly. He is not a man intrigued by shadows."

She paused; her breath seemed to catch, as if on memory. And in that small silence, I sensed she waited for some response from me, some words she hoped I would speak unprompted—

"I do well," I said slowly, "but?"

"But you are young, and the young are impetuous and disinclined to listen to their elders. Still, as you ask my advice, I will give it." Laughter danced like sunlight in her eyes. "I know King Solomon's mind, for I knew the women who raised him to be a man and a king. What you ask for yourself, your father will grant you if he can. But what you ask for others— that he will grant without hesitation. Now do you know what you must do?"

"Yes, Grandmother," I said after considering her words carefully, "I think I do." I lifted her hands and kissed them, as if she were herself a queen and I her handmaiden.

"Wait a dozen years and then thank me, if you still wish to do so." She withdrew her hands and reached down to the star-sewn cloak that lay soft beside her feet. She lifted up a bundle that had been hidden in the folds of dark cloth, red silk wrapped about some small object. She laid the bundle in her lap, stared down at it as if scrying the future—or the past.

Then she raised her head and smiled at me. "I bring you a gift I have held in trust for you these seven years. Carry it when you go before King Solomon, little goddess, and I swear by the Lady's hair he will grant whatsoever you ask of him—even if you ask a boon that carries you to the ends of the earth."

She handed me the silk-bound bundle; I untied it, carefully, and uncoiled the soft red cloth until it fell away from what it had concealed and I looked upon the treasure my grandmother had given into my hands.

A spindle. A spindle of ivory, its whirl a circle of amber.

I stared at the fragile-looking toy, and then looked up at my grandmother, waiting.

"Queen Baalit will find it useful," she said, "just as Queen Michal and Queen Abishag did before you. If you do not spin, you must learn."

I could spin; of course I could spin. All girls learned to spin. I lifted the spindle; the ivory warmed to my hand, waiting. . . . "And if I carry this, I will be granted whatsoever boon I may ask? Is it magic?"

My grandmother laughed, a sound like a swirl of gay music. "Woman's magic, little goddess. And if you do as I say—which is more than Queen Michal ever did—you will achieve your heart's wish before you are too old to take pleasure in it! Trust me, Granddaughter, King Solomon will send you from his court with goodwill and good wishes, and think himself lucky to do so. He has a good memory, that one—for a man!"

I set my fingers upon the amber whirl and set it spinning, watched as it swirled and slowed. My mother had once touched this spindle as I did now, drawn thread smooth from its ivory distaff. I spun the amber whirl once again, and tried to remember Queen Michal turning this same spindle, its ivory warming to the caress of her long clever hands—

"No." My grandmother laid her hand on mine, stopping the spindle's whirl. "Do not use it to summon yesterdays. It is tomorrow you seek. Spin, O Queen, and summon the future."

I looked at her thin hand and saw how delicate the bones were beneath her skin. Then I looked again at her face and saw that, although she was old, she was beautiful still. Always, when people spoke to me of my grandmother Zhurleen, they told me she was beautiful—but like all those who are young, I had thought beauty a thing created by a certain sheen of hair, a curve of breast and hip, a smoothness of skin. A thing of youth. Even the Sheban queen still clung to youth's perfection.

But my grandmother Zhurleen was truly old—yet still truly beautiful. When I looked into her eyes, I saw that beauty was not only an illusion of the body, but a truth of the heart and mind. So long as the heart and mind find joy, that joy will grant beauty, no matter how gray and dull the hair, how lined and slack the skin.

"Someday, Grandmother, I wish to look like you," I said, and at that she laughed again.

"Live long enough, Granddaughter, and someday your wish will be granted. Now let us go to the King's High Court and liven up this dull day for these duller people!"

"Yes," I said and rose, the queen's spindle cradled in my hands. "Let us go to the King's court."

When we reached the gateway to the great court, my grandmother kissed my forehead and sent me on through the gate alone. I longed to cling to her, but I knew she was right. This I must do myself, or not at all. I stepped forward and did not look back.

When I stood between the tall cedar columns of my father's hall of judgment, and demanded to be brought before the king, the royal herald stared as if he had never set eyes upon me before. He stood like Lot's wife, frozen in place.

"Announce me," I said again, "or I will go in and do it myself."

That sparked life back into him; the herald hurried up to the throne. But instead of announcing me as I had asked, he spoke swiftly to the recorder at the throne's foot. My father sat straight upon his throne; his face surrendered nothing. In the throne beside him, the Queen of Sheba waited, silent.

I heard my father ask, "Who next comes before the king for judgment?" and then the recorder's response.

"The Princess Baalit comes before the court, O King," "the recorder said, and I began to walk towards the Lion Throne, keeping my pace steady and my eyes fixed upon my father.

When I stood before the throne, I bowed, and waited. All rested, now, upon my father's wisdom—and upon my own.

Solomon

"Who next comes before the king for judgment?" Solomon asked, and waited dully for the herald to announce the next petitioner. *Even with Bilqis beside me, this day is endless; has no one in all the kingdom anything better to do than argue in the king's court?*

He received no answer to the ritual question; instead of responding, the royal herald hurried up to the steps leading to the throne and was whispering into the recorder's ear, a serpent's swift hissing. The recorder looked stricken, as if whatever he heard were a blow to his belly. Despite his troubled mind, Solomon's interest quickened.

"Well? Who comes?" he asked, and as he spoke, he heard the queen breathe in sharply. He looked down the great court to the high bronze doors and saw a woman waiting there. She was clad in scarlet and veiled in silver, stood straight and proud before the stares of the men gathered in the king's court.

Then she began to pace forward, moving with steady grace. *Like a queen.* She walked out of the shadows at the far end of the court, and as she passed into the sunlight, she lifted her hands and swept back the silver veil. And Solomon looked into his daughter's eyes.

Swift anger fired his blood; how dare she flaunt herself like this? *No.* Any man or woman in all the kingdom owned the right to come before the king for judgment—for wise and true counsel. Was that not King Solomon's proud boast? *Will you offer your own daughter less justice than you would a harlot?*

Beside him, Sheba reached out and laid her hand upon the broad gold lion's head on which his own hand rested, carefully; her skin did not touch his. Before him, the recorder stood silent, appalled.

"Who comes before the king for judgment?" Solomon asked for the third time. His voice held firm and smooth; nothing of his chaotic emotions slipped past the king's mask of control.

The recorder found his voice at last. "The Princess Baalit comes before the court, O King." He lacked Solomon's control; outrage rang clear.

Baalit walked through shadow and sunlight, until she reached the steps of the throne. There she stopped and bowed. Then she stood and waited, head held high, face smooth, her command over herself stronger than anger or grief.

Pride in this fiery creature he had created warmed him; Solomon knew not one of his sons burned half so hot and bright. He inclined his head, acknowledging her presence. "Princess Baalit, what brings you before the king?"

"I come to ask the king's judgment." Baalit's voice held firm and steady, as if speaking before a court full of men were no new thing to her.

"Any man or woman may come to the king and receive his judgment." Solomon knew already what his daughter would ask of him. And he must answer, answer with truth and wisdom. "You have come to the king. Now ask."

She crossed her hands over her breast and once again bowed before him. "I thank my father the king for his kindness. And I ask that he release me to accompany the Queen of the South, that I may rule Sheba as queen to come after."

Silence lay between them, silence so deep Solomon heard Baalit's veil whisper against her skin. Beside him, Bilqis's breath rasped the heavy air as she, too, waited to hear what Solomon the Wise would now say.

"That is what you ask of the king?"

"Yes, my lord king. That is what I ask."

Time stretched long; the sunlight slanting through the windows high under the eaves set the scene in amber, as if the world waited forever for his answer.

"And if the king does not grant what you have asked of him?"

His daughter regarded him with steady eyes. "Then I must go without my king's consent and without my father's blessing. But I would rather go with both."

Well, Solomon? Are you as wise and as just as all men claim? Or are you only another man whose vows do not hold when the cost is too dear? He turned his head and looked into the Queen of Sheba's quiet eyes; she would not interfere, despite her own desires. *This I must decide for myself.*

But already he knew he had lost; even if he prisoned Baalit here, she would no longer be his. *What good to keep her if her heart calls her elsewhere?*

But before I let her go, there is one more question I must ask. And if she does not know the answer—

If Princess Baalit could not answer King Solomon's last question rightly, she would never be Queen of Sheba.

Baalit Sings

I am told, by those who watched that day, that I stood before King Solomon's throne smooth-faced and proud, that my voice rang steady and clear. Doubtless that is what they saw. But I dwelt within my body, and I know that my hands trembled so I kept them clasped tight before my waist, that my blood pulsed so hard my skin quivered with each heartbeat, that my voice sounded high and faint and very far away.

But I remembered what I had come for, and what I must do, and I did everything as I had promised myself I would. No tricks, no riddles. No clever extracting of vows that would bind my father against his will. *"Oh, no, Father; I ask nothing for myself. Only grant me one boon: swear you will grant the Queen of Sheba whatsoever she desires of you—"*

Oh, I had thought of that, of course. My father would have sworn to do so, knowing even as he did what the queen would ask of him. *No. For this, only truth will serve.*

So I am told I stood calm during the endless span of time I waited for my father to speak again. Time seemed to stop as he sat still and silent upon the Lion Throne. At last he said, "Why do you wish to be queen of Sheba?"

And as the simple words fell soft and quiet into the silence, I knew I must find the true answer, or I never would be anything more than King Solomon's daughter.

Why do you wish to be queen of Sheba? This was not the first time my father had asked that—but I knew this would be the last.

His words hung between us, creating a chasm my words must bridge. And as the silent echoes trembled in the heated air, I sought for my heart's truth. No goddess, no woman, could speak for me. I must speak for myself.

But how to begin? At last I said, "I wish to—" Even small words came hard; I faltered and looked into my father's steady eyes. Pain glinted there, and pride. My father would not aid me in this. What I said and did now would be my choice, and mine alone.

Keeping my eyes upon my father's face, I began again.

"I do not wish to be queen of Sheba. I wish to serve, to do the work I am born and bred to set my hand to." Pausing, I took a slow breath to calm myself. "That work I cannot do here. Nor can that work be done by a king's wife, shackled by rank and tradition. It can be done only by a woman who rules in her own right, and for the rights of others."

Now my voice rang steady, my words firm and clear. I knew now that I spoke for my life, and for the lives of many others as yet unknown to me. "I do not wish to be queen of Sheba, but I cannot do my work unless I am, and so that I must someday become. You are called the wisest of kings, Father. You have never judged wrongly, never squandered the riches bestowed upon you by gods and men—and by women. Do not waste my talents."

For long heartbeats my father said nothing. Then he smiled; only I, who stood at the foot of the throne, saw what that smile cost him. And when he spoke, his voice filled the great court, strong and sure. "I am proud of the daughter I have seen today. The Princess Baalit goes with the Queen of Sheba; King Solomon decrees it."

Then my father rose and came down the steps from his high throne; he took my hand and led me up to the second throne, the one he had ordered placed there when he wished to honor the Queen of the South. From her seat there, Bilqis looked upon us, her face serene as the moon.

"O Queen," said my father, "here is your daughter."

She rose to her feet, and my father set my hand in hers. Her fingers closed softly over mine; her blood beat hard and fast beneath her cool skin. "O King," she said, "you know what is in my heart. Whatsoever you ask of Sheba, it shall be granted, in thanksgiving for this greatest of gifts."

For a breath, I thought my father would not reply; at last he said, in a voice so soft even I could barely hear his words, "What I ask, my love, is that you be happy."

Tears glittered in the queen's eyes like stars, blinding and brilliant. But they did not fall; she smiled, and stepped aside, leaving the way to her throne clear. My father caught her meaning and turned back to speak so that those who waited in the great court might hear.

"Sit beside me today, my daughter," my father said, "and watch and learn." Then he kissed me upon the cheek, and when he spoke again, his voice rang out for all to hear. "And when you are queen in Sheba, King Solomon expects better treaty terms than he has yet been able to exact!"

And he laughed, and so those watching in the great court began to laugh at the king's jest also. I sat down in the queen's throne, swiftly, for my knees trembled and I did not wish to fall in an inglorious heap at King Solomon's feet. Seated, I pulled the queen's spindle from my leather girdle and laid it across my lap, my hand resting upon the warm ivory; the movement drew a crystal flash from the old bracelet upon my wrist. The light caught my father's eye, and he gazed for a long moment upon the shabby bracelet, and upon the ivory spindle.

"So," he said, and a shadow seemed to darken his eyes. "Then there is little more for me to teach you, Daughter. You have already learned all you truly need to know."

Ahijah

At the far end of the king's great court, the prophet Ahijah stood as he had throughout the long morning, silent and still as the soaring pillars of cedar. He watched as King Solomon's daughter paced the long corridor of men until she stood before the Lion Throne. Watched as she bent in petition, and as she rose in pride.

Watched as the Queen of the South turned her voluptuous eyes upon King Solomon, and as he smiled upon his willful, lustful daughter and raised her up to sit at his right hand, beside the Throne of David.

For long heartbeats, Ahijah gazed through the incense haze, the golden smoke for which the kingdom whored. *Incense for the gods. Yahweh's people cry out after idols as babes after poisoned baubles. Incense, wealth of the south—Yahweh's children will choke upon it.*

Before the Lion Throne, Princess Baalit stood proud, the veil she wore glittering like a tainted pool. Beneath that brazen veil, gemstones gleamed bright and cruel as serpents' eyes. King Solomon bent his head to the She-ban queen, who rose from her throne like a wanton flame; the king whispered into the queen's ear, and she smiled and slid aside. The king touched his daughter's hand, and she shifted her body like a temple dancer, coiling into the second throne that stood beside the king's.

A second throne where none should be, set there to sate a woman's vanity. Now the king's daughter sat there, boldly meeting men's eyes. *So proud. So shameless. A reproach in the eyes of Yahweh. A girl raised up to think herself a queen—a goddess! See her preen herself, a peacock for pride, as vainglorious as her father.*

Unexpected pain lanced through him, throbbed behind his sore eyes. *Of course. Of course. Why was I so blind? I struck at the hatchling. But I must slay the king serpent to expunge his evil.*

For who had raised up the girl to such wild ways? Who had permitted her to lust after false gods? Who had bestowed upon her a name that damned her from her birth?

King Solomon, you are the cause of this evil; you have cherished it to your bosom. But what Yahweh gives, Yahweh takes. The pain stabbed harder now, but Ahijah refused to indulge his weak body. He remained still, his hands clenched about the gnarled oak staff, waiting to learn what he now must do. Pain commanded him, pain keen as a lion's fangs, the words of Yahweh slicing his flesh.

Leave. Leave this court of filth and corruption. Leave this king to wallow among his harlots, to grovel before his false gods. Go. Go. Go now, now—

The court's cedar pillars swayed before his eyes; the smoke-laden air shuddered like rough water. "Yes." Ahijah managed to choke out the word. *Yes, I will go. Go, and take Your blessing with me.*

Ahijah could never after summon up a memory of his journey through King David's City to the open land beyond the great gate. He knew only that he stumbled up the road to the Hill of Olive Trees, and there his strength deserted him. Cold-boned and shaking, he groped his way to an outcrop of red rock, half-fell to the ground.

Later, when the pain that speared his head had released him, Ahijah lifted his head and found his eyes drawn back across the valley to Jerusalem. The golden city that had been delivered into King David's hands by Yahweh's grace.

Surely we will not lose all that King David gained, only for King Solomon's fault? Traitorous thought; Yahweh would do as He would. Ahijah looked down, and saw that his hands moved of their own accord, his fingers pulling and tearing at his cloak. The dull cloth lay in pieces in the dust. He stared, then took up the torn pieces, counting slowly.

Twelve; there were twelve pieces torn from his clothing. Ahijah gazed upon the sundered garment and understood. *The kingdom will be divided. And in Yahweh's name, it is I who shall rend King Solomon's rotted cloak of kingship as I have rent this garment.*

Moving slowly, as if through deep water, Ahijah gathered up the tattered remnants of his cloak. He smoothed each piece over his trembling fingers before folding it into his goatskin bag.

Yes, Lord. Now I know what it is that I must do.

Peace flowed through him like honey; at last he knew Yahweh's true will. Holding the goatskin bag against his heart as if it were an infant, Ahijah walked back down the hill to the road that led from Jerusalem. There he waited for the man he knew Yahweh would send to him.

"You bar the road, Prophet. You must move to the side."

Ahijah raised his eyes and looked into those of Jeroboam, the stern austere man who had charge of the king's Forced Levy. The sun beat down hard and hot; as Ahijah gazed upon Jeroboam, fire danced about the man's form, burned within his eyes.

Ahijah smiled. "Greetings, Jeroboam. Hear the words of Yahweh, and obey."

"What has the Lord to say to me? Speak quickly, for I am upon the king's business."

What clearer sign could there be? Smiling, Ahijah walked to the side of

Jeroboam's chariot and laid his hand upon the chariot wheel, savored the heat and dust against his skin.

"You speak truly; you are upon the king's business. For Yahweh says, Behold, I shall rend the kingdom out of the hand of Solomon—rend it as easily as this garment has been torn asunder." As Jeroboam stared down at him, Ahijah pulled the torn pieces of his cloak from the skin bag and lifted them up. "Twelve pieces, one for each tribe. They are for—"

As he glanced up, midday sunlight slashed his eyes; pain flared at his temples. *Wrong, somehow I am wrong. . . .* As he clutched for the answer, to know Yahweh's will, two of the bits of cloth fell from his hand; Ahijah stared down at them as they lay in the dust at his feet.

In the dust, as Solomon has brought his kingdom to dust— The pain behind his eyes eased, and Ahijah lifted his head, cautious, to gaze once more at Jeroboam.

"Yahweh gives ten of the tribes into your hand," Ahijah said, and held out the handful of torn cloth to Jeroboam. "And with them, the kingdom."

Jeroboam slowly took the torn pieces of cloth. "I, king?" he said, and then, "And the other two tribes?"

"Those Yahweh leaves to Solomon, and to his son, out of Yahweh's mercy and for the love Yahweh bore King Solomon's father, David, who was our god's true servant." *Yahweh is more merciful than I; I would grind Solomon and all his works into the dust beneath my feet.* Ahijah set his foot upon the two pieces of cloth lying in the road and turned his steady gaze upon Jeroboam.

"But heed this, Jeroboam, king of ten tribes—you must keep Yahweh's Laws if you would keep His kingdom. Walk in Yahweh's ways as His servant King David did and Yahweh will be with you and all your house."

Still staring at the ten pieces of torn cloth, Jeroboam said, "I hear the Lord's words, Prophet." He closed his hand over the cloth, clutching the pieces tight. "Does King Solomon know of this?"

"What matter? Yahweh works as He wills."

"Yes." Jeroboam shoved the bunched pieces of cloth into his belt; they lay dull against his crimson tunic. "Has the Lord any other word for me, Prophet? Shall I be king soon? Must I wait long years?"

Ahijah waited, but no words came; he shook his head. "Only what I have said to you: Keep Yahweh's Laws and keep His kingdom. That is all."

They stared at each other for a moment; then Jeroboam nodded. "I will go before King Solomon learns of this and seeks my life. I will wait, and hold myself ready."

"And keep Yahweh's Laws," Ahijah said, but Jeroboam had already let his horses canter on, and Ahijah spoke only to himself. He was alone, but it did not matter. He closed his eyes against the sun's glare, savored the peace that flowed through his veins, warm as wine.

I have set Yahweh's will into motion. I have done what my god desired of me. Ahijah walked slowly away from the Jerusalem road until he found a gnarled olive tree, fruitless, but its silver-green leaves cast enough shade to shelter a man who wished only to rest for a time. Ahijah accepted it gratefully; sat beneath the waiting olive tree.

Yahweh's power vanished, leaving him weary, but that did not matter, for he had nothing now that he must do. Nothing but wait until Yahweh called upon him again. *And He will call, for who else so clearly hears His voice, understands His will?*

For Ahijah, that certainty was enough. In the shade of the olive tree, Ahijah closed his eyes and slept dreamless, and at peace.

Abishag

I had never thought to keep what passed between King David and me from Solomon; like all who love, I wished to give my mind and heart, as well as my body, into my beloved's keeping. And so upon our wedding night, when we at last stood bared before each other in the king's bedchamber, I held Solomon off with my hand and tried to tell him the truth. But he refused to hear.

"Whatever happened, happened," he said. "It does not matter." I searched his eyes and saw only love there. So for that one night, we both lay together content.

But I woke uneasy next morning, and so I sought out my mother. "I have a question, Mother, that you alone can answer," I began, and my mother laughed, a low, rich ripple of sound; all my life I loved my mother's laughter.

"You should have asked before the wedding night, and not after, Daughter. Now is too late!" Then she sobered. "What happened, Abishag? Did King Solomon chide you for what you were to King David?"

I shook my head. "No—but he would not listen when I tried to tell him the truth. That King David and I—"

"No." Swift as a serpent strike, my mother's hand pressed against my mouth, trapped my words unspoken. "Do not tell me, Abishag. Do not tell Queen Michal, do not tell your

maidservant. Tell no one." She let her hand fall away from my lips. "*Do you understand? No one.*"

Never had I seen my mother so solemn; I stared, seeking hidden laughter in her eyes. I saw none, only a calm sure command.

"*Not even King Solomon?*" I asked at last.

"*Twice never tell him! For he is a man—and for all Queen Michal has striven to create a god in human form, too good for use, he is still only a man. And no matter what you say, he will shape it into a weapon against you.*"

"*Solomon is not like that,*" I protested, and my mother laughed again.

"*All men are like that,*" she said, and took my hands in her own. "*Now listen to me, Abishag, and remember always what I say to you now. Swear it. Swear it on your love for Solomon.*"

Seeing her so solemn troubled me; I swore as she asked.

"*Never give a man everything. Keep something back, always. A woman without a secret is a woman without power. For a man, certainty is the death of love.*"

"*But I love Solomon; all I have done has been for him, and for him alone.*"

"*And so that you might one day be his queen,*" my mother said with calm assurance. "*Well, there is no shame in that; rejoice that for you, love and ambition embrace.*"

Unwillingly, I understood. Love and ambition—how could I not love Solomon, who could set a crown upon my head? "*Then I owe him truth twice over. Whatever I say—*"

"*Will kill what binds you together. For if you say, 'No, King David never touched me,' a part of King Solomon will not believe you. And if you say, 'Yes, your father lay with me,' that knowledge will gnaw your husband's heart. Soon or late, jealousy will eat away his love for you, leaving only cold bones.*"

I wanted to cry out against this harsh judgment. But all of my life, what my mother taught me had proven true in the end. When my heart's desire lay in the balance, did I dare question her wisdom?

"*Whatever the truth is, whatever passed—or did not—between you and King David, never tell it. Cherish that truth; chain it silent within your heart. Always remember that secret is your power. Do not risk everything on a man's good opinion of himself, Abishag. Even when that man is King Solomon.*"

Baalit Sings

In harpers' songs, the tale ends when the great deed is done, the treasure gained, the favor granted. In life, there are no simple endings. I had won for the Queen of Sheba all that she desired, won for myself my father's blessing.

Now I must ask him for more, must finish spinning out the thread I had begun so long ago.

For this, I went to my father as I had always done, freely and privately, as his daughter. The guards at the doorway to his working rooms stretched their eyes at me; I was worth staring at, now. I was the girl worth the world's weight in incense and in gold. I was the treasure King Solomon had given into the keeping of the Queen of Sheba.

Yesterday I was only King Solomon's daughter. Yesterday, no one cared to look, to see me. Anger coiled within my heart at the thought; I forbade it freedom. *"There is a price to pay for every desire, little goddess. If you will not pay the price, do not claim the prize."* I could no longer afford easy anger.

Instead I smiled at the guards as I had always done and passed through the open doorway. In the first room, my father's scribes sat, awaiting his call; again I smiled as I always did, and greeted them by name, and asked if my father was alone in his inner office. When they said he was, I smiled again; I saw the scribes slant their eyes to stare as I walked past them to the next door. Under the pressure of their eyes, I stood calm and knocked before I opened the door and walked into my father's presence.

He stood facing the map painted upon the long wall, the map of all the world that swayed to King Solomon's will. The land stretched yellow from the Troad to Thebes, from Babylon to Damascus; across the yellow lands ran lines of red: the King's Highway and the Incense Road, the Silk Road and the Way of the Sea. Swathes of blue: the Red Sea that led south to Sheba and the lands beyond; the Black Sea, path to the lands of amber, furs, and gold; the Great Sea that stretched from the shores of the Sea-Cities west to world's end.

"All this bends to my wishes," he said, his voice low and calm; he did not move or turn. "All this I rule, and yet I am not master in my own house. Is that not strange?"

That question, I knew I could not answer. I found my voice, but said only "Father."

For a heartbeat I thought he would not turn to me; then his shoulders softened and he faced me squarely. But he did not smile. "Yes, my daughter?" His voice was smooth, even, as I had heard it many times in the great courtyard as he laid down judgments.

"I have yet another boon I would ask."

"And you come silent and secret to ask it? Do you not wish to hold me to account before priest and people?" Bitterness sharpened my father's voice; surprised, I suddenly found myself looking upon him, not as my father but as a man and a king who had been forced before all the world's eyes to yield to a girl. *No, not that. To yield to his own justice.* I remembered how he had smiled and jested in the throne room, betraying no hint of pain or sorrow, and I could only pray that I, too, would someday own a heart as great as his.

"This boon requires the skills of a wise mind and a generous heart, if it is to be granted." I wished I did not need to ask yet another gift of him, but I must.

"And I am to be both wise and generous, I suppose? Well, what else is it you desire, my daughter?"

I hesitated. "Before I ask, I would beg one thing more—that if you cannot grant this, you will never speak of it to—to anyone."

"To whomever you have promised my favor to? Very well; you have my word. Ask."

That was all he said: "Ask." Not "Ask and it shall be granted."

Knowing how my words would be weighed, I hesitated. No longer was I a child to be indulged; I was a woman to be judged. *I do not ask lightly, or for myself.* And I had my father's word he would never speak of this; if I failed, Helike would never know I had even asked.

If I fail, Helike will slay both her child and herself. So I must not fail. I gathered my words with care, and then began.

"My father, you are a great king; your house holds many wives. Your women have been brought from all lands to wed you, to seal treaties and strengthen alliances. And you treat them all as queens—" I stopped in mid-praise, for my father held up his hand. And to my surprise, he smiled.

"Once more you confound me, Daughter. I understand now; you have promised to ask a boon on behalf of another. Now cease coiling words until at last you reach your point. Ask, and if what the Princess Baalit of Sheba asks can be granted by King Solomon—the Wise—it shall be granted."

To my astonished horror, tears burned my eyes; I blinked hard to keep back the tears. "May the Lady Helike come with me to Sheba?"

"The Lady Helike? The Horse Lord's daughter?" My father stared at me, plainly astonished.

"Yes," I said. And after all my planning, all my care composing an elegant supplication, I found that I need only speak plainly, my words unveiled. *No more secrets.* Now only truth would serve. "She was forced to come to Jerusalem, forced to wed. She loathes the palace, loathes—"

"Me?" My father's voice was low; I suddenly realized even a woman he barely knew could wound him.

"Oh, no—no, it is herself she hates. Father—she was an Amazon, a Sword Maiden. She came as a prisoner, her sword-sisters held as hostage for her submission."

My father stood still and silent; I could not read his eyes. At last he said, "I did not know." That was all, but never before had I heard such pain in his voice.

"It was not your fault," I began, and my father laughed, a sound harsh as a hoopoe's cry.

"When you are queen, my child, you will learn that all that passes is your fault. I am king—it is my duty to know, to care. But I did not know; I accepted unquestioning what the Horse Lord sent—a dozen fine stallions and a hundred finer mares. And a princess to seal the bargain. I inspected the horses with great care."

Now I stared, my mouth slack with surprise; never before had I heard my father speak with such bitterness. "You did not know," I managed to say. I could have wept at the anger I saw in my father's eyes. Anger at himself.

"I should have known. Her oath-breaking lies at my feet; she is guiltless. As the Lord lives, Baalit, I am at fault and should beg her pardon upon my knees in the palace gate." He sighed and set his fingers to his brow; I saw the skin whiten beneath the pressure of his fingers.

"You did not know," I repeated, unwilling to see him take such a burden upon his heart. "It is not your fault. But she is unhappy here, and I—I shall need my own captain, in Sheba."

"She may go; of course she may go. And with all honor, as befits a king's wife and a Sword Maid."

"And the treaty with the Horse Lord?"

"Will stand. If I order my wife to accompany my daughter to her new home, where is the disgrace in that?" A pause, then he added, "I am king, after all; who is to say me nay?"

I felt my face grow hot, for I knew I had forced him to my will—we both knew it. Someday I hoped he would forgive me. But now I must plead on another's behalf, and so pretend I noticed nothing.

"There is one thing more." I wished with all my heart that I could remain silent, but I knew I must tell my father the whole truth. "Helike is with child. That is why she came to me. Oh, Father—she swears her goddess told her the child is a girl, a girl to redeem her own broken vows. She wanted me to take the child to Sheba, to dedicate her to the Horse Goddess. She swore that if I did not, she would slay the child herself."

"And did you swear to do so?"

"I swore that I would send for her daughter and raise her as my own. But that I would not vow any child to a god without her own consent."

"And the Lady Helike agreed to this?"

"Yes," I said, "she agreed. She asked for nothing for herself, only for her daughter. It was I who thought of taking her for my own captain. Helike knows nothing of this."

"Nothing for herself." My father seemed to stare beyond me, into some world only he could see. Then he returned from whatever realm had briefly claimed him; his eyes looked into mine, and I saw a glint, brilliant as crystal, as if my father, too, must battle tears. "Nothing for herself," he said again, and then, "Princess Baalit, the king grants your petition. When you ride south with the Queen of the Morning, the Lady Helike rides with you. I am losing my own daughter; I will not force Helike to lose hers."

I would have bowed to thank him, but my father caught me up in his arms and held me close, as if I were a small girl again. Now I did not fight my tears; my eyes were damp as I hugged him hard. "You are not losing me, Father. You are gaining the best of allies." But my words were muffled by the thick wool of his tunic, and by my tears, and I do not know if he heard me or not.

Helike

For her daughter's sake, she had dared hope, dared dream. But not for herself; Helike accepted despair for herself, dared desire nothing more. It was enough that Princess Baalit had sworn to save her daughter; Helike clung to that promise as she clung to a horse's back—with all her strength and skill.

And the princess had kept her oath; she stood before Helike smiling, speaking words that seemed to ring like sword blades in the garden's closed sullen air. "My father frees you, Helike. You are to come with me to Sheba. And more—you are to be captain of my guard. Captain of the heir's guard, just as Nikaulis is of the queen's guard."

As Helike stared at her, Baalit held out the parcel she carried in her arms, a large bundle wrapped in a crimson cloth. "Here, this is for you. Take it, Helike."

Something is wrong; I feel nothing. No joy. Nothing. It is too late—

The princess tried to push the bundle into Helike's hands. "Take it, open it. Here, let me help you."

She is blind; does she not see she tries to touch a ghost?

As Helike stood there, cold and still, Baalit pulled back the parcel and set it upon the ground between them. Swiftly, the princess stooped and unwrapped the cloth that covered what she had brought. She rose and took Helike's hand, pressed an object into her palm. Helike looked down and stared at a dagger, long-bladed and sharp. Upon the hilt a gilded leopard snarled. The leopard's eye glinted green; emerald-set.

"The leopard is Sheba's beast. You see? You are captain of my guard. You are a warrior again, Helike."

The princess closed Helike's fingers over the dagger and stepped back. Helike turned the knife over in her hands, ran her fingertips along the blade, but her hands shook so she fumbled and the leopard dagger fell to the floor; the iron rang against the tiles like a bell.

"The Queen of Sheba's captain told me what you should have, to ride by my side. All is here, ready for you to don—and I had the garments made in my own colors." Princess Baalit smoothed her hand over scarlet leather, traced flames embroidered in golden thread. "My own colors, marked with my own seal. See, I have had a phoenix stitched upon the tunic. Do you like it?"

The princess smiled hopefully, and suddenly Helike saw that the girl was tentative, unsure, her pride a shield. *The phoenix. The bird born again from fire. What clearer sign could I ask?*

All doubt fled, all pain and anger burned to ash. Helike bowed her head, silently acknowledging her Lady's mercy. Then she reached out and accepted the leather tunic from Baalit's hands.

"Yes, Princess." Helike closed her fingers over the fire-bright leather. "Yes, I like it very much."

Bilqis

The day she was to leave, she went to him one last time, climbed the long
stairs up the tower to the paradise he had created for them upon the palace
rooftop. Her heart told her he awaited her there; her heart did not lie.
When she walked into the honey-light the sun poured upon Jerusalem's
rooftops, Solomon stood before her. He held out his hands, and she walked
into his arms.

They stood there until her slow-pounding heartbeat and his seemed one,
until their breath mingled the perfumes of rose water and of myrrh. At last
she knew it was time to speak.

"Solomon," she began, and he said, "No. Let me speak," and she bowed
her head, knowing what he would say, and knowing, too, that his words
would bring only pain to them both.

But it is his right to say them, and my right to hear them. It is all we will ever have.

Solomon slid his hands up, cradled her face between his palms. "My
love, my heart—stay with me. You want it; I want it. You are queen and I am
king, who is to say us nay?"

Who but we ourselves? For a breath, a heartbeat, she let temptation flood her
like hot wine. Then she forced herself to smile, and laid her hands over his,
curled her fingers about his. She brought their hands down from her face,
but she did not release him yet.

"Oh, Solomon, what you want and what I want do not matter, not in
this. And even if they did—my love, you who are called the Wise, you must
know I am old enough to have borne you as my own son. I am too old to
bear you a princess—a prince, here. A barren foreigner—twice folly, and
that is truth." She closed her eyes against the future he offered, the future
she saw.

"And if I embrace folly? If I say, Live with me, my beloved, my dove of
the rocks? Do not leave me, my sister of spices and myrrh?"

"You know the answer already, you know what lies as a sword blade between us, Solomon the Wise—truth."

"No." He turned and set his fingers over her lips; they lay cool over the
words she had spoken. "Do not speak truth to me, my love. For this moment, for this hour, no truth between us. Tell me what I want to hear,
beloved. Tell me lies. Tell me beautiful lies."

Shaken, she coiled her fingers about his wrist; his fingers slipped from her lips to her cheek. "What shall I tell you? What would it please my beloved to hear?"

"Tell me you love me."

"I love you; I have always loved you. I loved you before you were born and I love you with all the years I have left to me. That is truth. Is that not enough?"

"No. Tell me that you love me more than—"

"My crown?" She leaned her cheek into the curve of his hand. "That is a shackle, not a treasure."

"More than your honor. More than your duty. Tell me—tell me that if you were young enough to bear me a child, you would stay." He coiled her hair about his wrists. "Tell me," he said, a king's command.

She looked steadily into his eyes. "To please you, my king. Yes. To please you, I would stay...." She moved into his waiting arms and laid her head against his breast. Beneath her ear, his heart beat a low, hard rhythm, endless and patient. His breath warmed her forehead, his lips brushing her skin.

"My king," she said. "My beloved. Ah, yes, if I could give you a child— yes. Yes. If you asked it, I would stay with you."

His arms tightened around her. "I am a king. I could change my mind, and no one could deny me. I could keep you here with me."

"But you will not."

"I could keep my daughter." His words were muffled by her heavy hair. "Bilqis, I cannot give you both up. I cannot give her up. She is all that is left to me of my yesterdays."

"She is not yesterday, Solomon; she is tomorrow." For a moment, she closed her eyes against the pain in his. "You must free her to rule the future."

"Must. Always a king *must*. So much for a king's power."

"Power belongs to the gods, O King."

"Then what belongs to man, O Queen?"

"Love, and wisdom."

"Love, and wisdom," he repeated, as if weighing the words in an iron balance. Then he smiled, awkwardly, as if the movement of his lips pained him. "And you would have me sacrifice both."

"As I would, because I am a queen. As you will, because you are a king. And because, for us, there is a thing greater than wisdom, and greater than love."

"And what is that? What is so great that I must renounce all I have? All I am? All I desire?"

"You know already. Honor, my love. Honor, and duty. Without those, we are nothing."

"Honor, and duty." He bowed his head; sunlight gleamed gold upon his hair like a crown. She reached out and placed her hand upon his head.

"That is all there is, in the end. Now kiss me, my beloved and my king, and say good-bye. And think of me, sometimes."

He took her hands, his fingers closing over hers so tightly it hurt. He bent and kissed her palms; she pressed her hands hard against his mouth. Then he stepped back and set his hands upon her shoulders. "Whenever I smell roses, and cinnamon, I shall think of you."

She reached out and touched the tips of her fingers to the corner of his mouth. "Finish your song, Solomon. Sing it often. And when you smell cinnamon and roses, think of love."

He leaned towards her; she closed her eyes. His lips brushed her forehead, soft as smoke from a dying fire.

When she opened her eyes again, she stood alone among the roses and lilies of the tower garden. Solomon was gone.

Nikaulis

With Princess Baalit beside her, the Queen of Sheba had ridden out the great Horse Gate, followed by her handmaidens and her eunuchs. The rest of her court came behind, brilliant as peacocks and noisy as jays, pleased at last to be turning south again, towards home. The queen's soldiers rode ahead of the queen, and behind, safeguarding not only Bilqis herself but the treasure that traveled with her. King Solomon sent his daughter south dowered well enough to ransom an empire.

Nikaulis watched the caravan ride past her out the Horse Gate, watching and judging; nothing must go wrong at this last critical moment. *Soon we will be gone; soon Jerusalem's walls will be behind us, and only the road home ahead.*

The last of the servants and provision carts rolled past; the Queen of Sheba's visit to King Solomon ended. *Now. It is time.* But Nikaulis remained motionless upon her patient horse, waiting. *He will come. We must say good-bye, and wish each other well. Then—then we can forget.*

"Nikaulis." Benaiah stood by her horse's shoulder. He laid a hand upon her mount's side, a hand's breadth from her knee.

"So you ride away."

"I serve my queen." She looked down into his impassive face. "So you remain."

"I serve my king."

Benaiah lifted his hand, held it out to her, a comrade's gesture. Nikaulis clasped his hand, and for an endless heartbeat their fingers touched and clung. Neither spoke. Time's sands had run out for them, and there was nothing more to say. Not even good-bye.

Benaiah released her hand. Nikaulis gathered up her horse's reins and rode away, following after the Queen of Sheba.

On the far hill, Nikaulis reined in her horse and looked back at the City of David. So many people; so many walls. So many reasons to ride on and never once look back . . .

. . . and one reason only to stay.

Benaiah. No, not even the man. The love.

She laid their love upon the scales, and knew that love weighed heavier than all the reasons she could summon to balance against its power.

If I stay, I will grieve for all I lose once I am behind those cold stone walls. But if I go, I will grieve for Benaiah, and for myself. And for the future we will not live together.

The choice was hard, hard as bare stone. But the choice was hers.

And now, at last, Nikaulis knew which goddess she would serve.

Abishag

So for all the years I lived as King Solomon's wife and his queen, I never again spoke of the time when I had belonged to King David. Never would I say what I knew Solomon would never ask of me.

"Did you lie with my father as a woman does with a man? Did he teach you love?"

Unspoken, the question shadowed us. Unspoken, the words forever bound us. Never would King Solomon cast Queen Abishag off, never would she be less than his favorite—for if he did cast her off, he would always wonder if it had been for that which he had sworn did not matter.

Silence was hard. Sometimes, lying beside him as deep night paled to dawn, I longed to rouse him with kisses and confess the truth, no matter the price. But always something stopped me. Perhaps my mother's goddess whispered in my ear. Perhaps it was my own fear.

Or perhaps it was Solomon's iron faith in himself that closed my lips over the truth. Let my beloved think himself as great in generosity as he was in wisdom.

Bilqis

One last look, and then I go on. She owed Solomon that; owed herself that last indulgence. And so Bilqis paused, waiting, as her caravan continued slowly on, and stared back at King David's golden city. Jerusalem gleamed untouched as crystal upon its hilltop, safe within its massive walls. Temple and palace glowed sunfire bright, twin beacons.

She could not see King Solomon at all. *But he watches. I know he watches. Only when the dust my leaving raises settles to the road once more will he abandon his post.*

A shadow fell across her hands; she looked aside to see who had broken her vision. "Nikaulis," she said, acknowledging her captain, and was surprised when the Amazon bowed her head in petition.

"Great Queen, if ever I have served you well, hear me now."

"Of course, Nikaulis. Speak."

"Release me from my vow, O Queen."

Bilqis stared, at first unable to summon words. At last she said only "Why?"

"Because I cannot go with a whole heart. And I will not serve half-hearted."

"All or nothing. Yes." For Nikaulis, that was the only way. No half measures. "You go to the king's commander, then?"

"Yes. I go to Benaiah."

"Think well, Nikaulis. Israel is hard and cold, its ways strange and its laws cruel." She tried to keep her voice level, to keep envy from tainting it. "Benaiah now swears to anything to have you; will he keep those vows once you have given yourself into his keeping?"

"I will be not in his keeping but in my own. And yes, Benaiah will hold to his word."

"You are sure enough of him to walk into that cage, to close that door upon your freedom?"

"No one can take that from me. My queen, Benaiah is an old man. I will give him whatever years he may take of me. If our Mother wills it, I will give him a son, and he will give me a daughter. And when Benaiah is gone from this life, so I will be gone from Jerusalem, I and my daughter."

"Nikaulis, why do you do this thing? Because Benaiah asked it of you?"

"Because he did not," Nikaulis said. "Let me go, my queen."

She is free to follow her heart; do not punish her because she may do what a queen cannot. Silent, Bilqis held out her hand; Nikaulis clasped the queen's hand and kissed it. Sheba laid her hand upon Nikaulis's cheek and smiled. "Go with the Lady's smile upon you. Go back to the man you love, and be happy."

Nikaulis nodded, and turned her horse, and rode away down the road that led back to Jerusalem's great gate. Sheba watched until the warrior-maid had ridden halfway up the hill, until a man who could only be Benaiah walked through the city gate and down the hill towards the rider. As they met in the road, Nikaulis pulled her horse to a halt and dismounted.

There was no passionate embrace, no clasp of hands. Benaiah and Nikaulis merely walked up the road, side by side, and through the city gate. When they could no longer be seen, Bilqis urged Shams forward. She did not look back again until she reached the crest of the first hill.

Once past the Hill of Olive Trees, she would no longer be able to see King Solomon's palace. Bilqis reined Shams to a halt and gazed back across the Kidron Valley. But she saw nothing—nothing save Jerusalem burning golden beneath the heavy sun. Already she was too far away ever to see Solomon again.

She stared until the sun-bright city filled her eyes even when she closed them against the glare. Then, blinded by the light, she turned away. The road south stretched before her, and at the end of it, Sheba waited. She touched her heels to Shams's sides, and began the long ride home.

Abishag

The smooth running of the women's palace was my task, and its peace my gift to my beloved. It was not easy for me to greet the king's new wives fondly, to smile upon them and call them "sister." At least Pharaoh's Daughter knew how to veil her feelings, as did those of Solomon's wives who were the daughters of kings. But as more women, and still more, entered the women's palace, each bringing her own servants and slaves, her own customs and beliefs, my task grew ever harder.

Those wives who clung to their status as good Daughters of the Law moved as a pious flock; set against their tight-woven virtue, the alien ways of the king's foreign wives flared like bright banners. At first there were clashes between the two sisterhoods, and I found myself powerless to force even a truce, let alone peace.

It would have been a simple thing for Queen Michal to intervene, but I understood why she did not. She waited to see if I owned the strength and skill to govern those in my care.

I thought, and watched, and listened, and then took the matter to Solomon. When he heard of the warfare in the women's palace, he summoned all his wives into the queens' court and commanded peace.

"No woman here stands higher in my sight than any other, and no woman here is to disparage any other. Within these walls you are all as sisters."

I waited until he had gone and then laid another decree beside the king's. "You have heard the king's wishes. Now hear mine. I will not have the king troubled. If I must, I will go to Queen Michal and ask her aid in teaching a queen's proper behavior to her king—and a wife's to her husband. Remember that, and act wisely."

Not one woman there wished to involve Queen Michal in their quarrels; invoking her was as chancy as rousing a quiet leopard. Queen Michal's only care was for King Solomon's peace, and she would stop at nothing to achieve that goal. So the women's squabbles remained hidden among themselves, low bitter whispers beneath the smooth hours of their days.

No one dared risk the summoning of Queen Michal to restore peace. To unwary eyes, the women's palace ran smoothly, placid as a tranquil pool.

The tranquillity was an illusion, and I knew it. And I dreaded the day Queen Michal would be gone, and I would stand alone, without her shadow to strengthen me.

Solomon

He had sworn he would not watch her ride away, and he had lied. Solomon stood upon the highest rooftop of his palace, and there, in the sky garden that had cherished their love, he watched as the Queen of Sheba paused where the road crested the Hill of Olive Trees. Distance and heat-shimmered air turned the queen into an illusion, unreal as a mirage.

One last look, queen of my heart. One last look.

And then, between one indrawn breath and the next, she was gone. *Gone forever. I could have kept you here. I should have kept you here. That is what a great king should have done.*

He stared hard at the empty road, but saw only the haze of dust that marked the passage of a great body of men and beasts. Soon that dust would settle back onto the road, and no sign would remain that the Queen of the South had ever passed that way.

A man would have kept her with him, no matter what he had to do to claim her forever. Just once, I wish I could act as a man rather than as a king.

But he knew he never would. Solomon the Wise could not afford such a luxury.

What would Great David have done, had it been King David who looked upon the Queen of Sheba with desire? Troubled though he was, Solomon smiled. The last and least son, he had been favored by the queen rather than by the king, had seen his glorious father only rarely. It had been the older princes—Amnon, Absalom, Adonijah—who had been granted their father's attention and love.

Always remember that your father is a king, Solomon. Kings do not love. That was what Queen Michal had said. *At least not as men and women know love. A king loves what he needs, and only for so long as he needs. Remember that, Solomon. Carve it upon your heart.*

A harsh judgment—but then, Queen Michal had hated King David. Even as a child, Solomon had known that. What he had never known was why she looked upon the king with cool unyielding eyes. Nor would she tell him, when he once dared to ask. *Past is past, Solomon; those years do not matter. What matters is the future you will build.*

And although when she looked upon David hate lay coiled like a dark serpent behind her eyes, Queen Michal had never once spoken a word against the king. *Not to me. To me, she always spoke in riddles when she spoke of him. Did she think I did not know what she truly felt?*

Past is past—Yet if the past did not matter, why did those forgotten years still poison Michal's heart?

As he grew, he gleaned knowledge of his father—or rather, knowledge of what others saw when they gazed upon King David in love or in hate. And that vision, bright or dark, changed with each man and each woman.

If King David has a fault, Solomon, it is that he is too softhearted. Even patience must have an end. He should never have forgiven Prince Absalom—of course I am only a woman and do not know all the king knows—but still, I would not have pardoned Absalom thrice over.

Those had been the harshest words Solomon had ever heard his blood-mother, Bathsheba, utter. For Bathsheba's nature was so sweet that the Lord might have formed her of honey fresh from the comb. Never did she see darkness, only light.

But there was no honey in his foster-mother, Michal, who saw neither light nor dark, but shadows.

She loved my mother, and she loved me. And—

And for all her cold hate, the night Great David died it was Queen Michal who wept long and would not be comforted. Her tears still fell, slow and hard, long after those whose grief flowed easily had dried their eyes. Solomon had not understood then, and still did not, what had lain between David and Michal. All that remained now of King David were his songs, and of Queen Michal—

All that remains of her is bounded by my crown. Solomon himself was Queen Michal's legacy. Sometimes he wondered if she had known what she had truly done when she raised him up to be king in her image.

For she had sought to create a paragon among men, a miracle of human fire and royal ice, of soft love and stern judgment. An impossible union and a heavy burden to place upon any man's heart. Solomon did not blame her; Queen Michal had sought only to summon a brilliant future.

But did it never occur to her that I saw what she did to make me king? Saw how she gathered up each incautious word, each unwary glance, as if they were threads for her loom? Just as King David carved the world to his desire, so Queen Michal wove it to her own pattern.

In the end, they were very much alike. King or Queen, all must bow to need. Love, honor, duty—even wisdom, in the end, must yield to that.

For what was wisdom, after all, but the grace to bow before the inevitable?

So this is the wisdom of Solomon. The wisest king in the world. So men called him; perhaps it was how history would remember him. *If I am remembered. Yet what profit will my kingdom have from my vaunted wisdom if an unwise king follows me? Perhaps it is time to have done with kings, to return to the ways of our fathers.*

At the wistful thought, Solomon found himself smiling; from the royal road there was no peaceful return. Long ago, before he became king, before Great David became king, before even Saul became king, a man had foretold what treasure a king would bring as gift to the Lord's people.

Taxation and conscription; regimentation and slavery. The worst slavery of all, its chains formed by men's own lusts for riches, for power, for peace.

Perhaps the price of kingship is too high.

He stared south; dust still hung rich and golden in the air, sign of the Queen of Sheba's passage. Her coming had shattered his hard-won serenity, tested his wisdom. And in the end, what was left?

Honor, Solomon. Honor and duty.

He knew Bilqis was right; for a king, those two virtues came before all others. Honor demanded he do what was best for his kingdom and its people. *That is a king's duty. But what is best?*

For all his life, he had thought peace the highest good. For all the years he had reigned as king, he had labored towards that goal. And he had sought to raise up a son who would follow the path he had laid out: the path to peace and tranquillity.

And he had been deliberately blind.

"My eldest son will be king after me." So he had sworn, to keep peace in the king's house and the crown passing easily from his head to his heir's. When he had made it, that vow had seemed wisdom.

But his eldest son was not fit to be king. At last Solomon faced that fact squarely. *Truth is truth.* The admission hurt; Rehoboam was his child, after all.

Rehoboam would be a bad king—*and would that be so ill a thing?* A startling thought, but kings were new to Israel and Judah; Solomon himself was only the third to be crowned and to sit on a golden throne. And none of those three had been eldest son of the king who came before him.

Watching the dust settle slowly in the south, Solomon silently set futures in the scales.

If Rehoboam becomes king, he will not sit long upon the throne. He will breed quarrels; quarrels will breed battles. Rehoboam will not speak soft when he must, tread gently when prudence demands it. He will sow resentment, and his harvest will be rebellion. King Rehoboam would shatter the kingdom.

So where did wisdom lie now? In a peace dearly bought and easy lost? *I cannot now declare another of my sons heir in Rehoboam's stead; he would not survive from new moon to full.* Naamah would see to that, even if her son did not.

So I will give the kingdom what I have already sworn to give: Prince Rehoboam as next king. I will do so knowing he will bring down the crown—and I will do so because I think it best for the land and the people that it be so. Because I wish it.

Why not? Was it not what his own foster-mother had done, after all? *I was the youngest, yet it was I who became king—because Queen Michal wished it.*

Michal had acted in the great tradition of the matriarchs; often in the past a woman had grasped the succession in her own hands, had spun a new future into being. Rebekah deceiving her husband Isaac to gain his blessing for Jacob, her favorite son; widowed Tamar tricking her father-in-law Judah into lying with her to conceive the child he had unlawfully denied her— they had lifted up sons *they* chose.

Solomon would do the same. The throne would not last; Rehoboam would shatter it.

We are not a people for kings. Royalty rots us. I will create a truth, and that truth will set the kingdom free— Ah, once again I grow pompous. Well, no matter. Like any other man, I strive to do the best I can. No man can do more, unless he be a hero.

A hero, like his father, King David. David the warrior, David the harper, David the golden king, the lodestone for all who would follow after. *David the hero.*

But this time, the bitterness that always followed that dazzling image of his father did not come. Solomon summoned up his father's memory, and felt only a wistful admiration for a man who could so easily win all hearts and minds save those of his own queen and the prince she raised up in Great David's shadow.

Now I know why Ahijah burns; what is the prophet Ahijah weighed against the great prophet Samuel? As I am shadowed by King David, so Ahijah is by Samuel.

He waited for the welling of the familiar resentment at the constant comparison between himself and his shining father, but that corrosive passion no longer burned. *He is dead and I alive. He is the past, I the present—and the future too. It is time to free my father's ghost.*

And it was time for other things as well. *If I am to summon any future at all, I must make amends to my wives.*

Bilqis had spread his own well-meant folly before him; Baalit had struck him in the face with that folly, a blow to— *To my pride.* To his pride, when it should have been a blow to his heart. And long ago, Abishag had tried to warn him.

"Solomon, you must promise me something." As another pain rippled through her, Abishag gripped his hand; he felt his bones press together.

"Anything, my dove. You have only to ask."

"Should I die—"

"You will not die, Abishag. All women think so, when their time comes—"

"And many are right. No, do not shake your head, and do not say again that I shall not." She gasped as another pain gripped her, then managed to smile. *"Were you king of all the world, Solomon, that you still could not promise me."*

"You must not think such things. Abishag, you are my rose, my lily, my only beloved. You

will live and our son also." He had spoken strongly, willing her belief; Abishag had only smiled.

"Perhaps, and perhaps not. And I must think such things, king of my heart, for you are only a man and close your eyes to darkness as well as light." Another gasp, and again, to his amazement, she smiled once more. "Ah, soon. And soon, king or no, my mother will order you from the room. And you will go, because you are only a man, and this is woman's work." She gazed at him with eyes dark as a shadowed well. "Promise me, Solomon, that should I die bearing our child, you will set another in my place. Either Nefret or Naamah—either, or another—your heart is not so weak you can love once and once only—"

She had spoken the last words in panting gasps, and then her mother came into the room and ordered Solomon out of it. "Go, fight some man's battle. This battle is Abishag's, and she must wage it without you."

Already Abishag seemed to forget he was there; she clung to her mother and cried out for her handmaiden Rivkah. Suddenly women crowded the room, and Solomon realized that in the face of this enemy, he was helpless. "But how can I help? What can I do? There must be something!"

"There is." Queen Michal's cool voice cut through the heat and fuss like a keen blade. Of course she had come; adept at midwifery, Queen Michal had aided many king's sons into the world—and long ago had delivered Solomon himself, claiming him from death by her skill.

"What may I do? Tell me."

"Go away and drink a great deal of wine," Queen Michal said, "and do not return to Abishag's door until I send for you."

And as Solomon gaped at her, Queen Michal and Abishag's mother Zhurleen exchanged glances of utter understanding. . . .

He had not drunk wine, but he had been sent for—suddenly and urgently, reaching Abishag only to hold her hand as her skin grew cold and she left him to journey alone into endless night. . . .

And as he stared into her lightless eyes, all he could think was that he had not sworn to do as she had asked, in those last moments that had been theirs to cherish—and that he was glad he had not bound himself to that promise. For he knew he could not do it. *No other woman can take your place, beloved. No one, no one but you, ever.*

It had taken the Queen of the South to show him he had been wrong. *And right, too, for it is true no other woman can supplant Abishag in my heart.* But another woman could hold her own place there. *"Hearts are not so small, Solomon, that they hold room for only one."*

Are all women wiser than men? I never promised Abishag what she asked—but it is not too late. While still we live, it is never too late.

He had laid Abishag to rest in a funeral cave smoothed by expert hands, its walls painted with swallows and roses; the stone that rolled before it carved with the image of a branching pomegranate tree by the finest stone-mason in the kingdom. A fine tribute to a beloved wife—so Abishag's tomb was called. Now Solomon knew it was time to do true honor to Abishag's memory.

It was time, at last, to keep his unsworn vow to his beloved wife.

Makeda

Prince David lay naked upon a new-washed sheepskin, kicking his legs and waving his arms fiercely, grabbing for the bright rattle his mother shook over him. The gilded walnut shells strung upon a leather thong clattered as Makeda dangled the toy before her child's sun-bright eyes; she held the rattle just far enough from his grasp that his seeking fingers could not quite touch it.

"That is right, little king, reach for what you want." She smiled, and David kicked harder, his face crumpling up as he began to wail. Makeda laid her hand over his mouth. "Hush, heart of my heart. Silence and strength, little lion, silence and strength."

Already he knew crying would gain him nothing; he bit at her hand, and she lifted it and laughed. "Yes, my son, yes. A fierce heart and a clever mind, my king of all the world. Yes."

She dipped the rattle low enough for him to seize in his small plump hands, and his chortle of delight warmed her blood like venom. "Little lion-heart." Makeda stroked her son's cheek. His skin was soft as a dove's breast, darker than ruddy amber; his hair curls of coals at midnight, shadow and fire.

"You are altogether beautiful, you are clear-skinned and ruddy; you are wiser than the serpent," she sang. "You are king of ten thousand thousand kings—"

She broke off, sensing another presence. One of her slaves stood in the doorway; she knelt as Makeda turned her gaze upon the girl.

"Speak." Makeda neither smiled nor frowned, waiting calmly to hear what would be said. Her servants knew better than to intrude upon her without reason.

"My lady, the king comes."

Of all the words she might have heard, these were the least expected. Makeda stared unblinking at the slave girl.

"The king? Here?" Makeda's thoughts darted, snake-swift, striking at possibilities. *It is not my night, so why does he come to me? Does he think to take David from me— No, he is still but a babe sucking at my breast—* Nothing tasted right; so great a change in the king's routine was unprecedented. *Wait,* the serpent coiled behind her mind commanded. *Wait, and listen, and trust in me to lead you safely home. . . .*

Wait and trust. About to rise, she hesitated, then settled back upon the leopard skin. Solomon knew well how she looked as an exotic mate. Let the king see her now as a mother. *As a queen, yes,* hissed Jangu-set, and Makeda smiled.

"Tell King Solomon he may enter," she said, and bent her head once more over her son.

Solomon

Coming upon his fierce dark Makeda curled on a leopard skin, cooing endearments over her infant son, Solomon stopped to gaze upon her. For on this visit he saw her unadorned, undefiant; soft with mother love. *Just like any woman. Is the exotic princess no more than a ruse, a ploy to arouse my interest?* Then Makeda glanced slantwise at him and smiled, her full lips framing teeth like ivory blades, and for an instant his midnight serpent flashed her fangs, untamed.

"My lord king. We are honored." Honored or not, Makeda made no effort to rise, merely inclining her head. "But unready to receive you. Has the Lady Chadara changed the order of our nights and our days? If so, she has forgotten to tell us. The fault is hers and mine."

"There is no fault." Although he heard the mockery beneath her humble words, Solomon refused to acknowledge its sting. Makeda had reason enough to upbraid him. *I have neglected my wives; slighted them—no, abandoned them for love of the Queen of the South.* That Makeda should rebuke him was no surprise. Solomon was glad that rebuke was no harsher.

Forcing himself to smile, he walked forward and looked down upon his son. Small David gazed up, eyes round, his body still for an instant. Then he flailed wildly, grasping at the golden fringes edging Solomon's sash. The nutshell rattle went flying, banging into Solomon's leg; he smiled again.

"So small and yet so fierce." Solomon knelt beside his son, allowing David to grasp his outstretched hand. "What shall you be, my son, I wonder, when you are a man grown?"

Smiling, he glanced sideways at Makeda and, as if he looked upon her for the first time, saw truly into her heart. *You have your own plans for your son's future; your own land and blood summon you. I know at last what you desire of me.*

Solomon looked down at his small son, at the tiny fingers so tightly gripping his own. "He is well named David. He will make a fine king, Makeda."

Silence; she stared slantwise at him. At last she said, "King of what, Lord of Wisdom? Prince Rehoboam will reign over Israel and Judah; so it is already written."

"Yes, the clay is long years dried upon that decree. But you have your own plans, Lady of Snakes, and your future does not lie within Jerusalem's walls. Nor does our son's."

She sat coiled, waiting, like the serpent he called her. Solomon smiled and lifted his small son into his arms. "I have been a great fool, Makeda, but not such a fool I cannot learn, and make amends for my folly. Stay as long as pleases you, as long as you require sanctuary." He stared into his son's bright eyes. "Stay until you may carry a king home with you."

"Truly Solomon is the wisest man in the world." Words that could mean anything, agreement or empty compliment.

"You need say nothing now; your king is too young still to embark upon great ventures." Solomon kissed David's cheek; the child's skin was warm as amber beneath his lips. "But when it is time, Makeda, you will go with all honor and with wealth that befits a queen—and enough armed men to ensure you retain both."

At last she smiled, and for once Solomon believed the light in her eyes that at least of fondness. "Truly, King Solomon is worthy of his crown," she said and held out her arms. Solomon handed their son back to her. "And he need not fear; I know how to wait."

"Yes." Solomon watched David clutch at his mother's breast. "Women are patient creatures."

"We have need to be," Makeda said and, smiling, kissed her son's soft cheek.

Nefret

So she is gone at last. Too late. The Lady Nefret stood beside the smooth pool at her garden's heart, staring at the sun-gilded water. Many of the king's wives had gone to the rooftop to watch the Queen of the South ride away forever. They had dressed in their finest gowns and jewels, as if this day were a festival; radiant with joy they made no attempt to veil.

They rejoice as if her departure washes away all sorrow. Nefret gazed unseeing into the untroubled pool. Did not the other women understand that, without the Spice Queen's presence, their alliances, their resentments, no longer owned a heart?

She is gone, and all will be as it was. A lie, and she knew it. Pharaoh's Daughter did not flinch from iron truth; she made herself face her cold future.

The Queen of the South had united King Solomon's wives, if only against her. *And with the king's daughter gone, there is no one to bind our small world together.* Suddenly weary, she sat down beside the garden pool, coiling her legs beneath her as she had done when she was a young girl and her body a supple, willing thing. *Nothing. That is what remains. The Sheban has taken the king's daughter and his heart, and left us nothing.*

One of her palace cats strolled into the sunny garden, wove itself against Nefret's legs. She bent to pick up the little animal and set it upon her lap. The cat tucked its silver-brown paws under itself and began to purr, softly, barely vibrating beneath Nefret's caressing hand.

How many years of this? How many years of tending lilies and cherishing kittens? Although she enjoyed gardening, and loved her sacred cats dearly, the thought that they would be all her life dimmed the day. She sighed and closed her eyes.

"My lady." Her slave's whisper barely disturbed the heavy air. "My lady, the king approaches."

Nefret opened her eyes and began to rise, but King Solomon already stood looking down at her. "No, stay. You look like a girl again, sitting there."

To her surprise, he sat on the pool's edge and laid his hand upon her little cat's head. "You are graceful as this cat, Nefret."

"The king is kind," she murmured. *No. Do not hope. Always he is kind.*

"No." Solomon stroked the cat's arching back; their fingers touched. "You are kind, Nefret. Kinder than I deserve."

She looked into his eyes; unlike his voice, they betrayed him. *Of course; he grieves. His heart's queen rides south, his best beloved child beside her. He is lonely now.* Enlightened, Nefret summoned the grace to do what she must. She smiled, and allowed her fingers to slide against his in a caress as soft as the cat's fur.

"My cook has a new dish he wishes to set before me; if the king has no objection to apricots, and to honey, perhaps he will honor me with his presence at tomorrow's evening meal."

"If Pharaoh's Daughter will so honor the King of Israel and Judah," he began, and then stopped and smiled. "Tomorrow, Nefret. Yes, tomorrow I would like very much to join you."

After he had gone, Nefret sat quiet for a time, the cat purring beneath her hand. Then she set the animal gently aside and rose to her feet. *The Queen of the South is gone—but I am still here. I am Pharaoh's Daughter, and King Solomon's wife—and I am not yet old or dead.*

She clapped her hands to summon her handmaidens, and when they bowed before her, she began to issue commands. "Air my new gown, then perfume it with lotus—yes, and with cinnamon. Prepare my bath. Tell my cook to come to me at once."

If Solomon were attending upon her tomorrow, she had a great deal of work to do today.

Solomon

He had spoken to Makeda, and to Nefret. One more task awaited him; he must speak also to Naamah. *I must reassure her that no other son will supplant Rehoboam. I must convince her that her son is not merely my eldest son, but my true choice as king to come after.*

Now—at last—that was the truth. Perhaps Naamah would be able to see that truth, although she would never know the reasons behind it. But Solomon hoped his words would carry enough conviction to ease Naamah's heart.

Yes, I must speak with Naamah. But not just yet. For he grew weary beyond endurance; already Bilqis's visit seemed to belong to the distant past, the palace to echo with Baalit's absence. Now he wished only to rest, to summon the courage to face all the tomorrows that awaited him.

Even a king sought sanctuary.

As if he were still a small boy, habit guided his feet unerringly to the Queen's Garden that had belonged in turn to three beloved women. *My mother Michal. My wife Abishag. My daughter Baalit.*

Solomon stared at the ebony gate. Then he set his hand upon the ivory laid within the dark wood like fangs and opened the gate into the Queen's Garden.

For a heartbeat he thought he had stepped back in time, for a woman sat beside the singing fountain. *Abishag. Beloved ghost.* Then the woman turned her head and slipped back her glittering veil, and Solomon looked into Zhurleen's night-dark eyes.

He stood silent as she rose and bowed low. "Greetings, Solomon the Wise. Live forever, O King."

"I am not wise, and I will not live forever, and you come too late, lady. Your granddaughter is already gone."

"I did not come for her."

"Why, then?"

Zhurleen looked steadily at him, then smiled and held out her hands; ink-dark serpents coiled from her elbows to her wrists, shadows beneath her skin. "I came for old love, and for new. I came because once I loved your mothers, and because I carried your wife beneath my heart for nine full moons."

"They are dead—and she whom my soul loves is gone also." Solomon walked forward into the garden until he stood beside Zhurleen. He stared into the fountain, saw only sun-dazzle and shadow. "Do not call me wise, Zhurleen, for I am the most foolish of men."

Beside him, Zhurleen laughed, a low, honeyed ripple of sound. "Only the truly wise know how foolish all men are—and all women, too. Yes, even the Queen of the Morning." A pause; falling water sang against alabaster. "Even Queen Michal."

Waning sunlight transmuted stone and water; the fountain glowed jewel-bright. "Why speak of her? She has lain long years in her grave—and she was the wisest woman I ever knew. Far wiser than I. Just as my father was a greater king than I."

My father would have known how to chain his beloved to his heart. If she had come to visit my father, the Spice Queen would never again have left this palace. Solomon turned to meet Zhurleen's quiet gaze. "In all things they won, and I have lost."

"If that is what you think, O King, then yes, you are foolish." Zhurleen reached out and took his hand; old she might be, but her hands remained strong and supple. "Solomon, I am both a priestess and an old woman; I knew Michal before you were born, before she knew your mother Bathsheba. Before power tarnished her."

Angered, Solomon tried to pull away; Zhurleen's fingers clasped his like chains. "No, Solomon," she said. "I have kept silent through three lifetimes—mine, my daughter's, my granddaughter's. Now it is time for me to speak, and for you to listen. It is time for you to learn truth, and to summon your own future."

She drew him to sit beside her on the fountain's rim. "You are no fool," she began, "and so you know as well as I how Michal hated David. Hated him so greatly her malice poisoned her. Hate that would have destroyed her had it not been for your mother—and for you." Slowly, Zhurleen began to relate the tale of Harper David and young Princess Michal—a princess won by a hero, love lost when Mad Saul sought the hero's death—

"This I already know. That song was sung before I could walk."

"Not all of it." Unperturbed, Zhurleen began reciting a different version of the song of King David and Queen Michal. "She dwelt in peace and love with Phaltiel for twice seven years; she cooked and spun and wove and warmed his bed and heart; her love grew as a thread grows upon a spindle.

"And then came the day of Gilboa, King Saul's final battle. Upon that day the hillsides and the valley ran red, and Mad Saul bravely died and his son Jonathan with him. And David-hero became David-king—in Judah only. But ambition ate David-king; its teeth gnawed his long bones. David would be king in Israel as well, but Mad Saul's son Ishbaal ruled Israel. So King David remembered Princess Michal, and sent for her. Why not? Was she not the last king's daughter? And she had loved David-hero hot and fierce.

"So he sent for Princess Michal, but Princess Michal no longer dwelt within Michal's skin. It was a farmer's good wife that David took, it was Phaltiel's wife whom King David claimed as his own."

Here Zhurleen slanted her long dark eyes at Solomon, as if gauging his temper before she spoke on. "It was Phaltiel's wife who doomed not only her husband but her own happiness. For she did not understand that David cared nothing for her, but everything for what she was: the crown incarnate. And by the time she learned that lesson, she had summoned demons that stalked her down long years. For Michal was a loving girl but not wise."

Solomon laughed, a bitter sound eaten by the falling water. "And I say again Queen Michal was the wisest of women. Did she not set me upon King David's throne?"

Zhurleen accepted the interruption placidly. "Young Michal was clever, not wise. I learned that when I tried to warn her, to open her eyes to the world as it is. But she refused to see through a queen's eyes until it was too late. She stood against King David in anger and in pride—and so condemned her husband Phaltiel, for King David must possess King Saul's daughter.

"Yet still she would not see what she must, and so left herself unshielded when she wove your mother Bathsheba into her life, and gave a weapon into King David's hand. For David's gift was to summon love—that was what Michal denied him, and that denial burned David's soul like acid. How could this woman refuse to surrender what all others granted him? She would not, and he must have—"

Zhurleen sighed, and shook her head; silvered curls shifted across her back, uneasy serpents. "And so King David summoned Bathsheba's love instead, and got her with child."

"Yes, I know. That tale is no secret, lady."

"But this part of it is, O King. What you do not know is that King David offered Queen Michal a choice. Bathsheba's life, or that of her husband, Uriah."

So that is it. The thought flashed through Solomon's mind, bright and deadly as lightning. "Uriah died in battle. Warriors often die so."

"Uriah died because King David ordered it—at Queen Michal's bidding. So." Zhurleen spread her hands, offering up truth. "The blood of three men stained her hands, their lives forfeit to her iron pride."

"Three men? You have named only two. Phaltiel and Uriah." Michal's husband, and Bathsheba's husband.

"And your half-brother Amnon." Zhurleen's voice was soft, her gaze upon him steady.

Amnon and Tamar, and their bright deadly love—

"No. Queen Michal wished Amnon king. She told me the tale and wept for Amnon and Tamar. She had promised them her aid."

"And dallied too long to give that aid. Solomon, you were both her heart's delight and her vengeance upon David. She could let no other usurp your place in the web she wove. She saw what she truly was too late. That is truth, O King."

"Why?" Solomon said, and she did not pretend to misunderstand.

"Because I swore always to be Queen Michal's friend, Solomon. And Michal wanted you to be—"

"King."

"Happy," Zhurleen said and rose to her feet. Even old, she moved supple as water. "You have done all asked of you and more, sacrificed desire upon duty's altar. Now you must take the happiness a king may have, when he strives to be a good man as well as a great king.

"Queen Michal battled ghosts all her life. King Solomon need not. Let them go." She reached out and took Solomon's face between her slender painted hands; bent and pressed her lips against his forehead. "Fare well, Solomon the Wise."

Solomon stood and watched her walk away. As she laid her hand upon the ebony gate, he called out her name, and she turned back to face him.

"And I suppose those ghosts haunted her until the day she died?"

"No," said Zhurleen. "What haunted her was that they didn't."

He let her words sink into his mind, weighing each against his memories of Michal, his second mother, King David's queen. "I understand," he said at last.

"I thought you would," Zhurleen said, and then she was gone, lost in the shadows of the women's palace.

Gone, as his daughter Baalit was gone; as the Queen of the South was gone. The Queen's Garden once again lay empty, tenantless. *My last love, gone—*

Even as the mourning words echoed silently, he found himself hearing other silent words, tart and bracing. *"Last love? And you with a good two score years left to you? Do not give yourself airs, young man!"*

Any of the women who had loved him might have so scolded him— *And now that they are gone, their memories act as their handmaidens. So the Queen's Garden lies empty? Well then—*

Well, then, I must fill that emptiness—or replace the garden with something else. I will ask Nefret what I should plant here. Yes, that is what I will do.

Nefret was good with flowers.

L'envoi: Morning Rising

Abishag

My only true sorrow was that I could not give Solomon a son. His other women quickened with child, and I did not; other women bore sons, and I remained unchanged, barren. In secret, I wept, for the loss of my hopes, and Solomon's. Our child would not wear a crown.

By the time I could go to my husband and say, "I am with child," half-a-dozen princes stood between any son I might bear and the throne. But we rejoiced nonetheless, for any child is a precious gift.

"Pray for a girl," my mother told me, and I smiled and laid my hands over my rounding body. "Yes," I said, "that would make all simple, would it not?"

"Simple—and safe. If you bear a son, Abishag, guard him as you would a casket of rubies, for you will be unable to trust a single one of the king's wives to so much as touch his cheek."

My mother cradled my hand in hers and closed my fingers over a small smooth object. "Pray to Her; She loves girls, as your husband's god does not."

Upon my palm lay an Asherah in ivory warm from my mother's skin; ivory old as love and dark as wild honey. And I did as my mother bade me. I prayed with all my heart and soul that my child be a girl. King Solomon already had too many sons.

My prayers were answered; I bore the king a daughter. But I would not live to see her grow, to raise her to be a queen in her turn. To cherish and to protect her—that task would fall upon my mother, and upon Solomon's. For I fought hard to bring my daughter into the world, and that bloody battle took all my strength. And as Solomon bent over me, I knew I looked upon him for the last time in this life.

"Beloved, we have a daughter," he said. "A girl almost as beautiful as you, my heart. Do you wish to see her now?"

Already he seemed far away, his image unclear, as if I saw him through rainwater, or through tears. And I knew that I must see my daughter now, or never. "Yes." The word seemed no more than a sigh; I hardly heard my own voice.

Solomon laid her in my arms; she curled there warm and small and perfect, her eyes seeming to seek mine. But that was illusion. My daughter would never know me; I could give her nothing. Nothing except a name I did not even know why I chose for her.

"Baalit," I said. "Her name is Baalit. Tell her I give her that, when she asks about me."

"You will tell her yourself," Solomon said.

"Solomon, my wise and foolish love, we both know I am dying." I thought I spoke the words, but Solomon did not seem to hear them. And I knew he would never hear my voice again.

Only one hope remained: that my daughter might someday hear me whisper in her dreams. Hear, and understand.

And—perhaps—remember.

Baalit Sings

This is how the harpers sing it, when they sing the end of the Song of Solomon and Sheba. It is, in its fashion, truth.

And when King Solomon the Wise and Mighty had proved himself a worthy match, the Queen of the South praised him, calling his land happy and his people blessed to own so great a king. And then she returned to her own land. . . .

And the king's daughter returned with her, gift of King Solomon to the Queen of Sheba. When we rode south, away from Jerusalem, she looked back. But Princess Baalit did not.

The visit of the Queen of Sheba to the court of Solomon the Wise had ended as all such formal visits ended: with treaties guaranteeing trade, with promises of eternal friendship, with gifts of treasure enough to ransom king or queen at need.

Other gifts had been given, and taken, and I knew why Queen Bilqis looked back, and why I did not. She in her wisdom had given my father back his heart—and he in his had gifted her with a past she could turn to for comfort in all her days to come.

But the gift he gave me was far greater: my father, who had always given me every precious thing I might desire, gave me a future. What I did with it would be my own affair.

If I had learned nothing else from my father's wisdom, I had at least learned that. I hoped it would be enough to help me live my life wisely and well. And if it were not—

If it were not, that too would be my own doing. The gods give us life for good or for ill. If we do not use their gift wisely—well, that is our own fault.

Not theirs.

Afterword

WISDOM'S DAUGHTER IS A NOVEL, A TALE SPUN FROM A BIBLICAL story, historical and folkloric sources, and the author's imagination. It is not history.

The story of King Solomon and the Queen of Sheba has been popular for three thousand years, inspiring poems, paintings, novels, and in the fullness of time, movies (including the truly unforgettable 1959 epic *Solomon and Sheba*, starring Yul Brynner as the king, Gina Lollobrigida as an extremely pagan queen, and for reasons passing understanding, the suave lounge lizard George Sanders as Prince Adonijah).

Sheba itself has been identified with a number of places, Yemen and Ethiopia being the strongest claimants to the title of home of the Queen of Sheba.

Although dogs are rarely mentioned favorably in the Bible, and cats are mentioned only once, both animals were well-established as pets and working animals in the ancient Middle East. The saluki is, of course, one of the oldest of all dog breeds. As is the Maltese; according to the Maltese breed club, the little white dogs have a history that dates back three thousand years.

Those who wish to read the official accounts of King Solomon's reign can find it in the Bible in I Kings 10:1–13, and in II Chronicles 9: 1–12. In the Qu'ran, the story of Solomon and Sheba can be found in chapter 27, *al-Naml* (The Ant). The Ethiopian sacred text the Kebra Nagast (The Glory of Kings) also chronicles the famous visit of the queen to the king's court, and its results. As for the king's children—

When Solomon died and Rehoboam ascended the throne, the people asked him to lighten the burdens King Solomon had placed upon them. The new king asked his father's expert and experienced advisers what he should do; the old men counseled patience, prudence, moderation, and soft words. Then Rehoboam asked his rowdy friends what he should do— resulting in a rousing speech to the people that led to instant civil war (I Kings 12:1–20; Rehoboam's people skills seem to have been staggeringly bad) and a divided kingdom. As Ahijah had prophesied, Jeroboam became king over Israel, while Rehoboam reigned in Judah.

And according to I Kings 4:11 and 4:15, King Solomon had at least two daughters, Taphath and Basemath, who were married to two of his governors. Obviously, they were born to his wives after Princess Baalit went south with the Queen of Sheba—Solomon was wise enough to take a woman's advice, even if that woman was his mother-in-law!